Bad Boys Need Love Too

Christa Tomlinson

Torlina Publishing

Thank you to everyone who has supported me in my writing adventures. Your messages, reviews, and emails mean so much to me. And they inspire me put fingers to keyboard every day.

Special thanks to Denise C and Cas A for helping out as beta readers. Thank you ladies!

CHAPTER 1

Joseph rode his motorcycle into the repair shop his co-worker's brother had referred him to. He killed the engine and set the kickstand, looking around as he dismounted. The place was clean and organized, bikes in different stages of repair parked in numbered squares painted on the ground. He noticed there were mostly standards and cruisers with very few racers. Joseph removed his helmet, brushing dust from the ride off his suit as he took in more details. The floor was polished and painted concrete, the walls decorated with framed posters of motorcycles. The typical curled-edge posters of bikini-clad chicks draped over bikes were nowhere to be seen. Nothing was out of place. The owner obviously took pride in his business. There was a service counter at one end of the shop, but there was no one behind it. He looked through a wide window that looked into a small waiting area. Someone was in there, but it was an older man flipping through a magazine. He looked like a customer so Joseph didn't bother to go in. As he walked around he finally noticed a man on the ground working on one of the bikes.

"Excuse me is the owner around? I'd like to have him take a look at my bike."

The man looked over at him for a moment before he went right back to what he was doing. "Why do you need the owner? You too good to talk to a lowly bike mechanic?"

Joseph's face flushed in anger at the man's rudeness. "No," he snapped back. "But my friend referred me here and told me to ask for the owner, Gage Mason. So get off your high horse and get him for me."

The man stood. "I'm Gage."

Joseph colored again, this time in embarrassment. "Oh." He went forward to shake the man's hand. "Joseph Naderi. And I'm sorry about my rudeness." Joseph assessed the shop owner as he wiped his hands on a towel and came forward. He looked like he belonged in this bike shop. He had thick, dark brown hair that lay in a careless sweep over his forehead. Eyes that were just as dark as his hair watched him with a steady, direct gaze. His jaw was hard and defined, shadowed by light stubble. His jeans were clean but ripped in a few places, giving Joseph glimpses of the hard thigh muscles beneath the denim. A close-fitting, dark t-shirt showed off his toned upper body. His arms were so nicely defined that the sleeves of the shirt were tight on his biceps. Scuffed but comfortable looking black work boots were on his feet. He looked tough and wild. The type of guy Joseph had always been attracted to, but never dared to approach. He got his mind back on the business at hand as Gage accepted his handshake and spoke.

"No problem. My fault for bustin' your balls. So what's going on with your bike?"

Joseph explained that he'd noticed his motorcycle, a Ducati Diavel, not getting as much power when he took it to high speeds. "I suspect it might just be spark plugs, but I'd rather have a professional look everything over to be sure."

Joseph watched as Gage ran his hand over the bike while he asked him more specific questions. Gage looked back up at him and Joseph found himself trapped by the oddly intimate power of his stare.

"It's a great bike. Fast and pretty." Gage stroked his hand over the bike seat. "Very pretty."

Unsure whether or not that was a come-on, and even more unsure how to handle it if it was, Joseph looked away. "So will you take a look at it for me?"

"Yeah, I'll get it going." He waved his hand in a wide arc, indicating the other bikes in the shop. But I got people in line before you so it'll take about a week."

"That's fine. Do I pay you now?"

Gage shook his head. "Nah. Let me see what I can do. I get it fixed I'll call you and you can take it for a run. When we get the ride as smooth as you want you pay." He headed over to the counter and picked up the parts and service brochure for his shop. "I don't bullshit around on labor hours or charge outrageous prices for parts." He handed the brochure over. "Here's a list of my prices. I'll call you to let you know what needs to be done before I get started so you can decide. That work for you?"

Joseph looked up from glancing at the reasonable prices. "That works for me." He held his hand out to shake the other man's again. This time a frisson of electricity ran up Joseph's arm as soon as their palms met. He looked into those dark eyes and saw them sparkling with what looked like amusement. Joseph found himself watching as a small smile quirked up the corners of the mechanic's sultry mouth.

"I'll see you soon, Joseph."

****

Gage watched as his new customer walked outside to the cab waiting for him. He was intrigued by Joseph Naderi. From the few minutes he'd spent in his company, Gage had already picked up on contradictions in the man. He'd come in wearing a sharp suit, with matching button down and a perfectly knotted tie. But he was riding that beast of a bike. And after a moment, Gage had noticed that Joseph's light brown hair wasn't just combed back, it was long and tucked into a neat ponytail. But those contradictions weren't the only thing that had Gage interested.

Joseph Naderi was beautiful. There was no other way to put it. He was tall, only a few inches below his own six foot two. His features were elegant and defined; high cheekbones, sharp nose and angular jaw. His mouth… pale pink and sweetly curved. Gage had found himself imagining everything he wanted to make those lips do as he watched Joseph talk. Thick brows and long eyelashes framed the most gorgeous eyes Gage had ever seen on a man or woman. They were sea green, lightened further by a ring of gold surrounding the pupil. It was those eyes that had held Gage's interest most. With the exception of that quick flash of temper, they were sweet and shy. And Gage had noticed the spark of attraction there in response to his flirting before Joseph had looked away.

Yeah, all of those contrasts, suit and motorcycle, shyness and temper, definitely had him intrigued. Gage looked forward to seeing Joseph again so that he could learn more about him. But he'd have to get his bike repaired before that happened.

Gage turned his attention to Joseph's bike. It was a Ducati Diavel, bright yellow with chrome and black accents. An expensive racer, heavy and substantial, unlike those flimsy crotch rockets he loathed. Gage smiled. He might do a little rearranging of his schedule so that he could get to work on the Diavel sooner, rather than later.

CHAPTER 2

Joseph sat in his small office in the major law firm where he worked. He was supposed to be working on a brief. Instead, he sat staring off into space thinking about Gage Mason. For three days, Joseph hadn't been able to get the bike mechanic off his mind. The way those dark eyes had watched him. So direct, like Gage had been studying him. And he'd gotten a vibe of what he was pretty sure was physical attraction off the other man. Was Gage attracted to him? He wasn't sure. Joseph had been surprised at the way Gage had spoken to him, accusing him of being too good to talk to a bike mechanic. That had both infuriated and intrigued him. Joseph wasn't a snob and he didn't appreciate anyone judging him to be so from one glance. But he also couldn't believe the man had the nerve to talk to a potential customer like that. Gage clearly wasn't one to be too concerned with making nice with clients. That was so unlike Joseph and the people he was used to that he couldn't even imagine what that was like.

Looking at the wall clock in his office, he realized he'd been thinking about that mechanic for a good ten minutes. He needed to get his mind on work. The title of partner wasn't going to fall into his lap while he was daydreaming. He'd just managed to push thoughts of Gage Mason aside when his cell phone rang. Checking the screen, Joseph saw the name he'd stored in his phone, Mason Bike Shop. Joseph's heart rate increased in nervous anticipation before he answered. "Hello?" Gage's voice came across the line low and throaty, not even bothering to ask who he was talking to.

"Hey, your bike is ready. Can you come check it out today?"

Joseph was surprised, but he answered quickly. "Yeah sure, no problem. But it will have to be after work. How late are you open?"

"I normally close at six o'clock but if you think you'll be later than that I can wait around for you."

Joseph was grateful for the offer. "Thanks, I appreciate that. I'll try to get there as close to six as I can."

"Good. I'll be here."

The phone clicked in his ear. Joseph set his cell down on his desk. His heart was definitely pounding now. He was going to see the man who'd been on his mind for days tonight.

****

Gage sat behind the counter and watched Joseph walk in. He'd finished the bike earlier than he anticipated solely because he wanted to see its owner again. Joseph looked very different tonight. Instead of a suit like before, he was in jeans that looked soft and well-worn as they hung off his narrow hips. A dark gray tee clung to his torso, just tight enough for him to see that his abs were smooth and hard. And his hair was down in a cloud of soft-looking brown curls around his shoulders. Gage's hand clenched into a fist. He wanted to grab up all that pretty hair and hold the man still so he could get his tongue deep into his mouth and find out what he tasted like. He hardened slightly imagining it. Joseph probably tasted like cherries. Sweet, with just a little bit of tart to keep him interested. Gage pushed the thought aside. Joseph was at the counter with an eager smile on his face.

"My bike is already finished? You work fast."

Gage let his lips curl in a slow smile. "Not always. I usually like to take my time." He watched as Joseph caught his meaning and quickly looked away. His smile grew. He loved that this pretty boy was slightly shy. That meant he'd get to corrupt him. He pulled the Diavel's keys from the drawer in front of him. "Take it out. See what you think." Instead of sliding the keys across the counter, he held them out in his open palm so that Joseph would have to touch his skin to get them. Joseph's eyes locked on his as he reached out and took the keys. His teeth briefly bit at his full bottom lip as his fingers brushed his palm. But once he had the keys in his hand he grinned, his excitement obvious.

"I'll be right back."

Joseph strode quickly over to his bike. In one motion, he swung his leg over to settle on the seat and pulled his helmet on. Once his face was covered he felt free to look over at Gage as he started the engine. That man had him tied up in knots. This time there was no doubt the mechanic was attracted to him. He just didn't know if it was something he wanted to pursue. The feeling he got when Gage looked at him, or whenever their skin touched was excitement laced with a little bit of fear. He could tell Gage wasn't like the men he usually dated. He was calm here in his shop, but Joseph sensed there was wildness lurking just beneath that façade. And Joseph figured he ought to keep his distance.

He wheeled the bike around and pulled up to the garage opening. After checking to be sure that the street was clear, he tore out of there. Bending low over the handlebars, he weaved in and out of the light traffic. The Diavel was performing beautifully, responding immediately to every twist of the gears. The roar of power beneath him was clear and throaty. Joseph grinned and gave a happy shout inside his helmet, pushing the bike even faster. He leaned far to the side as he rounded the street corners, but eventually he slowed. Joseph hated to end his ride, but he knew Gage was probably ready to close up shop. He turned and went back the way he'd come. He could go for a longer ride whenever he wanted. Joseph drove back into the garage, revving the engine unnecessarily out of pure joy as he rode almost right up to the counter. Joseph shut the bike down and took off his helmet. He ran a hand through his windblown hair and grinned at Gage.

"You do good work." He hopped off the bike and went up to the counter. "She rides like a dream."

Gage arched an eyebrow. "Your bike is a chick?"

Joseph laughed. "Yep. She's the only female I ride." Joseph's eyes widened and his laughter came to a choked halt. *Did he really just say that? That sounded like the cheesiest pick-up line ever.*

But Gage just shrugged unconcernedly. "Nothing wrong with that."

His face hot with embarrassment, Joseph waited while Gage charged him with the credit card he'd left before his ride. He waited there quietly as Gage took care of the transaction. Joseph considered asking Gage out. But he hesitated. Even though he was pretty sure the other man was attracted to him, that didn't mean that he was openly gay. Besides, something about Gage Mason intimidated him. One look at him and it was obvious he was a bad boy. Joseph didn't know if he could handle that. So he didn't say anything. He made small talk about the way the bike had performed and said thanks as he signed the receipt and paperwork. When he was finished, he held his hand out for Gage to shake. "Thanks, man. I really appreciate it." Gage's calloused, yet warm hand wrapped around his.

"You're welcome, Joseph."

Joseph had to suppress a shiver. The way those dark eyes watched him and the way Gage said his name in that low voice. It got to him more than the smooth pick-up lines of the guys he normally dated. He cleared his throat and pulled his hand back. "Thanks again." He mounted his bike and put his helmet back on without looking back, but he knew Gage was watching him. And as he rode out of the garage, the taste of regret was bitter on his tongue.

CHAPTER 3

"Hello?"

"Hey, little brother."

"Yousef! It's about time you called me back."

Joseph laughed and settled down on the couch to talk to his younger brother. It had only been a few hours since his brother left a voicemail asking him to call. But of course to a teen, a few hours waiting for the phone to ring was an eternity. "I'm sorry, Darius. What's going on?"

A loud sigh came across the line. "It's Dad."

Joseph sobered quickly and sat up straight. "Is everything okay? Is Father alright?"

"He's fine. He's just being a stubborn jerk again."

Joseph relaxed at his brother's words, frustrated though they were. He was all too familiar with his father's stubbornness. In fact, Joseph hadn't seen the man in nearly six years because of it. It hurt, but there was nothing he could do. He couldn't make Cyrus Naderi accept his son for who he was.

"What is Mr. Naderi putting his foot down on this time?"

"I want to go to school in Miami, but he wants me to go to Southeast Texas University *and* he wants me to live at home!"

That news didn't surprise Joseph. Southeast Texas University was an expensive, private university. It was a prestigious school, frequently named in lists for top schools in America. Cyrus Naderi considered it as the perfect place to get a degree in a respectable profession. But knowing his little brother, it wasn't the type of school he wanted to attend. Still, he tried to be the responsible big brother.

"Southeast Texas is an excellent school, Darius. You'll get an excellent education there. And I enjoyed my time there as well."

"I *know* that. But that doesn't mean that's where I want to be. I want to be on the beach and I want to study film, not medicine or law. Dad's just stuck in the fifties on what's an acceptable career. And he only wants me to live at home so he can keep an eye on me and make sure, well, you know."

Joseph did know. He'd dated a few girls in high school because that seemed like the thing to do. But once he was on his own at college, he'd finally worked up the nerve to date guys. Once he had, he'd realized that was who he was and never looked back. He'd waited until after he graduated with his undergrad degree to come out to his parents, thinking that their pride in his accomplishment and seeing him as a mature adult would make things go smoothly. They hadn't. Instead, his father had been furious and thrown him out of the house. He'd been cut off both financially and from his family.

"I'm sorry, Darius. I know my history is influencing Father's desire to keep you at home."

"It's not your fault, Yousef. Dad is just being ridiculous! How do I get out of this? I refuse to go to any school besides the one I pick. And if he tries to make me go to school here and live at home I'll say screw it and skip college altogether."

"You're not skipping college, little brother." He paused while Darius groaned. "You just need to be smart about this. Apply to the colleges you want and keep your grades up. That way if you have to pay for your own school and housing in order to go where you choose, you can try for scholarships. But don't give up on Father. Talk to him again, *calmly*. And get Mother on your side."

The sigh that came through the phone was filled with all the impatience and frustration of youth. "I shouldn't have to convince Dad to let me go to school wherever I want, but I'll try. And you're right, having Mom as backup should help."

"How is she?"

"Mom's alright. She misses you. You'll probably have to set up a not-so-secret, secret meeting soon so she can see you."

Joseph's laughter at his brother was tinged with just a bit of sadness. He hated that he was banned from the Naderi household, but at least his father turned a blind eye to his wife visiting her oldest son. And for the past two years, he'd allowed Darius to visit as well. "What else is going on? Are you still dating Yasmin?"

"No. We broke up. We both figured if we dated for too much longer our parents would be arranging a marriage. And neither of us is ready for that."

Darius laughed and so did Joseph. Their family might have assimilated almost completely into American culture, but there were some things from their Persian heritage they held on to. Preferring to arrange marriages for their sons was one of them. They clearly wouldn't have the opportunity to do so with him, but he was sure they still held out hope for Darius.

"So what's up with you? And don't just tell me about work. Hearing how much of your life revolves around that law firm makes me dread growing up."

Joseph shook his head. His brother was right, he didn't have too much else in his life besides work. He actually had to think before he came up with something to talk about. "I'm getting my bike tuned up at a new shop. The mechanic there is pretty cool."

"Cool, huh? Cool like you like him?" his brother asked in a sly voice.

"No Darius, not like I like him. He's too direct and rude and …" Joseph trailed off, trying to think of the right word to describe Gage Mason. Grungy wasn't right and sexy wasn't appropriate to say to his little brother. "He's just too rough," he finished.

"You mean he's not stuck up," Darius said with a smirk in his voice. "I don't know how you date those boring suits. I can't believe any of them can let loose enough to drop their pants for you. You should ask the bike guy out. I bet he's not a stick-in-the-mud in bed."

"Darius!" Joseph was glad Darius accepted his sexuality without question, but he was not going to discuss his sex life with his baby brother. "I'm hanging up. Keep me posted on what's going on with you and Father."

"Bye, Yousef. Good luck asking out your mechanic."

****

Joseph was out riding his bike around town. He didn't have any destination in mind, he was just enjoying himself. As always he loved the thrill the high speeds of his bike gave him. But there was something nagging at him. The feeling of regret from leaving without approaching that mechanic was still there. He'd expected it to fade. Gage wasn't the first guy he'd been attracted to, but not pursued. Usually, once the moment passed, he forgot about the guy and moved on. Not so with Gage. His interest in the man continued unabated, helped along by the conversation with his brother. At night when Joseph was alone or even sometimes when he was working, his mind would turn to Gage Mason. It was his voice that was most often on his mind. He heard it in his head, the rise and fall of its unique rhythm, the husky tone. He wanted to hear it again. Wanted to hear it not just as a memory in his head but coming from the man's lips.

Still, Joseph was hesitant to go for it. Gage had bad boy written all over him. In relationships, that normally spelled trouble. And he couldn't afford to get involved with anyone who might slow or possibly derail his progress at the firm. They didn't judge him for being gay, but they would judge Gage if things were to get serious and he started bringing him to company functions. That's just the way things worked. He'd seen a couple of people who were trying to climb the ladder dump someone they were dating because the partners didn't approve. The disapproval was expressed subtly, but it *was* expressed.

Rounding a corner he noticed a Sonic coming up on his right. Joseph checked to be sure he was clear and then got over to pull into the parking lot. He couldn't resist his favorite summer treat. Pulling into one of the berths, Joseph pushed the call button then took off his helmet to order. The voice that came through the speaker sounded young and excited to be at work. Joseph smiled to himself. He hadn't worked at that age, but he remembered what it was like to be excited at every teenage milestone.

A few minutes later Joseph sat there straddling his bike, slowly sipping a Slush. He'd made up his mind. He was going back to Mason's shop. If the other man still seemed interested, he'd ask him out. It wasn't fair for to judge him from two superficial meetings. Besides, one date didn't automatically mean they would ever have a relationship. Joseph decided to try to loosen up and just have fun.

Looking at his watch, he noted how close it was to six. He was tempted to hurry and drink, but he didn't want to get a brain freeze. Trying to ask someone out with a blinding headache probably wouldn't go over well. Forcing himself to drink slowly when he was eager to see the sexy mechanic again was hard, but he managed. When he was finally done, he threw the Styrofoam cup in the trash and pulled his helmet back on. His skin was hot with anticipation as he started his bike. Now that he'd made his decision, he really hoped the guy said yes.

****

Gage wiped his hands clean on a towel. It was six o'clock, which meant he was done working on the bikes

13

in his shop for the day. His assistant mechanic, Danny, had left an hour ago. Now he had an hour of paperwork to get through before he could go home. He hated that part of being a business owner, but it had to be done.

Gage settled down at the metal desk in his office to review invoices for parts orders. He'd only been at it for five minutes when he heard the sound of a motorcycle pulling up in front of his building. He could tell it was a racer by the sound of the engine. The shop was closed, but Gage still went to see who it was. If it was a friend, he'd let them in no matter the hour. But instead of seeing one of his buddies through the glass, he saw the distinct body of the Diavel he'd repaired last week and its owner, Joseph Naderi.

Gage smiled in pleased surprise and hit the button to raise the garage door. He hadn't expected to see Joseph again unless he went after him. He knew he did careful and thorough work so there was nothing wrong with that bike. Which meant that Joseph was here because he wanted to see him.

Joseph rode in and Gage walked over to him as he shut down the bike and pulled off his helmet. Gage didn't even try to keep the heat out of his expression as he looked at Joseph straddling his bike. Again he was dressed casually, and his long, curly hair was down, windblown from his ride. There was the faintest hint of a five o'clock shadow along the sharp line of his jaw and above the curve of his lip. And those gorgeous eyes of his were bright with excitement. This man was beautiful. Even in his jeans and tee, Joseph still looked fresh and neat and clean. Gage wanted to get him dirty. He wanted to see him sweaty with his hair even wilder and his clothes ripped and twisted half off his hard body. So many things he wanted to do, and now that Joseph was back it looked like he might get that chance.

"You're still here."

Gage quirked a brow. "Obviously. What are you doing here? Bike giving you trouble again?"

Joseph shook his head slowly. "No. I uh… wanted to say thank you for fixing her. The ride has been smooth just like you said it would be."

Gage smiled real slow and moved in closer. "You go around and personally thank everybody who does work for you? Your cable repair man? The guy who changes your oil?"

Again Joseph shook his head slowly. "Not usually."

Gage gripped the bike's throttle, watching as Joseph's gaze dropped to his hand. He squeezed the throttle once and saw Joseph's throat working as he swallowed. "Tell me why you're really here, Joseph." Sea green eyes rose to look into his. They were so expressive that Gage could easily read his nervousness. Gage smiled again. "I already know but I want to hear you say it."

"If you already know why do you need me to say anything?"

Gage released the bike and for the first time, touched that lean body. He put a hand on Joseph's thigh, feeling the heat of skin and firm muscle through the denim. He stroked lightly. "Because…" He drew the word out. "You made the effort to come here. I wouldn't want to deprive you of the chance to do what you came to do," Gage said as he squeezed the leg beneath his palm. Joseph's lips parted, surprise at his actions clear on his face. But he didn't try to stop him. That was good. "Go ahead, Joseph."

"Would you like to go out to dinner with me?"

"So formal. Are you also going to bring me a corsage? My favorite color is blue. That should help you pick out the ribbon."

Joseph's face tightened and his eyes quickly went from soft to snapping with anger. "Forget I asked."

He started to turn the key on the bike, but Gage closed his fingers over his hand before he could. Joseph had a temper. He shouldn't be surprised. He remembered how Joseph had snapped at him when they first met.

Gage liked that. It would take more than a pretty face and a tight body to hold his attention for more than one night. "Don't go. I was just fucking with you."

"Why are you so rude?"

Gage arched a brow. "Rude? How so?"

"You antagonize for no reason. It's frustrating. You could just be polite and say yes or no."

"Does it get under your skin, Joseph?" he asked while he tried to hold back a smile.

"Yes," Joseph snapped.

"Hmmm… I'll try to be more polite then." Joseph's fingers relaxed on the key so Gage let him go. "Yes, I'll go to dinner with you." Joseph smiled and Gage brushed a thumb over his lips. "Why is your mouth red?"

Joseph had to think for a moment. He was so flustered at the familiarity with which Gage was touching him that it took him a moment to remember why. "Oh. I had a Slush from Sonic."

"What flavor?"

"Cherry." A small smile touched the corners of Gage's mouth and his eyes sparkled with amusement. Joseph felt like Gage was laughing at a secret joke. But he didn't get it of course, and for some reason, Joseph felt like he needed to explain himself. He licked his lips, tasting a faint hint of the cherry flavoring.

"It's my favorite."

Before Joseph realized what was happening, Gage's hand slid into his hair gripping it tight. Joseph froze as he watched Gage's eyes drop to his mouth. His skin prickled with anticipation. Was he about to be kissed? He licked his lips again more out of nervousness rather than any attempt to entice. Gage's eyes tracked the movement before he looked back up at him. Joseph was taken aback by the intensity he saw in those eyes. They were bright with heat and sharp with hunger. He'd never had anyone look at him like that before. His heart pounded with an exhilarating mix of fear and desire. Maybe he was right before. Maybe Gage was too much for him.

Gage could feel his blood racing under his skin, thick and hot as it shot straight to his cock. He wanted to kiss Joseph, getting the taste of cherries on his tongue as he pulled this pretty boy off his bike so that he could fuck him right there on the garage floor. His fingers clenched on the silky strands of hair in his fist as he seriously considered doing exactly that. But although there was definitely desire in the wide eyes that stared back at him, there was also apprehension. Joseph wasn't ready for the furious passion he would unleash on him.

Normally with his partners Gage didn't give a fuck if they were nervous. He just did whatever was necessary until he got them to give him what he wanted. Oddly, for whatever reason with Joseph, he was willing to take his time and put him at ease. Closing his eyes to the sight of those pouty red-tinged lips, he ruthlessly pushed back his desire. Gage untangled his fingers from Joseph's hair, and opening his eyes, he took a step away from temptation.

"Friday at eight o'clock. Wilson's Steak House. You know it?" Joseph nodded. "Alright, I'll see you then." He took another step back, watching as Joseph started his bike and put his helmet on. He waved in response to the hand Joseph raised in goodbye before he rode off. After he was gone, Gage reassured himself he'd done the right thing. Good things came to those who waited, right? He wanted Joseph, wanted him eager and without any hesitation. So he would wait.

CHAPTER 4

I have to know. How did you wind up with that bike of yours?"

It was Friday night and Joseph was at Wilson's Steakhouse with Gage. They'd talked a little about Gage's life earlier, with him sharing that he'd wild when he was younger, before settling down enough to open up his shop. But for the past few minutes the conversation had centered on Joseph.

"I hate to stereotype, but I wouldn't normally think someone like you would ride a bike like that. He laughed. "Or any kind of motorcycle actually."

Joseph arched a brow. "Someone like me?"

Gage ran his eyes over him. "Well, you might not be in one tonight, but you're definitely the comfortable in a suit type. How is it you're just as comfortable on the back of a motorcycle?"

Joseph smiled and answered Gage's question. "I fell in love with amateur racing after I saw it on an ESPN special. My father indulged me when I was a teen so he bought me my first bike after I begged."

"Indulged, huh?"

"Yes. Not to stereotype myself, but I was a typical upper class Persian American kid. My parents got me whatever I wanted as long as I got the best education and chose a suitable profession."

"Sounds like a fair trade."

Joseph shrugged. "I held up my end of the deal. I graduated from Southeast Texas University with my undergrad and law degrees."

"And now you practice law here. Have you been anywhere else, Joseph? Anywhere fun?"

Joseph shrugged slightly. "Not really. Well, I went on my senior trip in high school and to South Padre for spring break in college once, but I've mostly just been focused on my education and then my career."

Gage shook his head, a teasing smile on his mouth. "Sounds like you've always been a good boy, Joseph." His gaze flicked up to Joseph's ponytail. "Do you ever let loose and let your hair down?"

"Metaphorically speaking?" he asked as he ran a hand over his hair. "Not really. I still race on weekends sometimes, but that's it. I don't know why I don't relax and have fun more often." Joseph looked down at the table for a moment before he looked back at Gage. "But I want to."

Gage leaned back in his chair, that smile still curling his lips. "I think I can help you with that."

Joseph started as Gage's leg brushed against his under the table. He thought for a second it was an accident. Until Gage's leg moved again, rubbing softly back and forth against his calf. Joseph didn't move. He sat there, allowing the touch, while he tried to describe what he did at his law firm. But the way the man across the table watched him made it clear he was thinking about things besides Business Law. As he talked, Gage's fingers found their way to his, distracting him further. Gage's thumb swept over the inside of his wrist, lightly, making goose bumps rise up on his skin. Joseph's breathing shallowed, his voice lowering. He cleared his throat in an effort to bring his tone back to one of polite conversation.

"We work with clients all over the south and I'm starting to work on higher profile accounts. I plan to make partner within the next three years."

"I don't doubt you'll make it. You seem smart and you're gorgeous. Not that you'd use your looks to get you what you wanted," Gage tacked on with a teasing wink.

Joseph shook his head. "Of course not. That wouldn't be appropriate."

"But there might be occasions where it'd be alright. Like with me."

Slight pressure from Gage's thumb had Joseph turning his hand over. A single finger danced over his palm as Gage traced indecipherable patterns on his skin. Joseph's fingers curled in reflexively, just enough to touch Gabe, but not enough to prevent him from continuing the delicate caress.

"I bet you could get me to do whatever you wanted with just a look from those pretty green eyes."

Joseph didn't know what to say to that. He'd never been the recipient to such upfront flirting. He glanced away and took a drink from his glass of water to cover his silence. Setting the glass down, he looked back at Gage. Again amusement was in his dark eyes. Joseph knew he was transparent right now, but he couldn't help it. He'd never been so affected from nothing more than conversation and innocent touches.

The server came by their table and Gage let him go to pay the check. Joseph belatedly realized he should have done it since he'd been the one to ask Gage out. He started to say something, but Gage spoke first.

"You ready to get out of here?"

Joseph swallowed hard and nodded. As they walked out of the restaurant Gage didn't touch him again. But he was so close Joseph could feel the warmth of his arm against his own. He swore he could feel an electric charge between them. Once they were outside, Joseph led them to his car. He'd driven instead of riding his bike tonight. Gage ran his hand over the hood of his black Nissan Z.

"Nice car." Gage leaned against it and crooked his finger at him. Joseph approached, irresistibly drawn to Gage. He looked good tonight. He'd dressed up for their date in black pants and a navy blue button down. But there were hints of the rough and tumble mechanic

Joseph had met in the garage. Gage's sleeves were rolled up, revealing thick forearms hard from the physical labor he did. His dark hair fell in a casually messy sweep across his forehead, curling at the nape of his neck. And nice clothes or not, there was no hiding his tall frame and broad chest. Leaning there, Gage looked like the bad boy who cleaned up just enough to seem respectable, but was still wild underneath. Joseph ended up standing in front of Gage, almost, but not quite touching him. Gage slowly brushed the back of his fingers across his cheek. His voice came out in a husky whisper that sent a shiver down Joseph's back.

"I need to see something."

"What?"

Gage brushed a thumb across his mouth. "If you still taste like cherries."

Joseph swayed forward, bracing a hand on Gage's chest. He ran his tongue over the spot Gage had just touched. "Go ahead." Joseph saw that flash of heat in Gage's eyes before he pulled him even closer. Firm lips settled on his. Joseph relaxed, following Gage's lead as they kissed. He was surprised at the slow pace Gage set. From the way he'd been watching him tonight he'd expected something a little more intense. But the man *had* said he liked to take his time.

Gage pulled back slightly. "Open for me, Joseph. Let me taste you." Joseph did as he asked immediately, a soft breath escaping from between those pouty lips. He leaned forward again, tracing his tongue lightly over Joseph's bottom lip before licking into his mouth. Joseph moaned and melted against him. Gage wrapped an arm around his waist, holding their bodies tight together as he deepened their kiss. He stroked his tongue along Joseph's, tasting him just like he'd wanted. Taking his time with slow, deep kisses, he sucked that full bottom lip into his mouth more than once it tasted so good. Desire pooled low in his stomach at the way Joseph was responding to him, kissing him back without any reserve. In no time at all Gage was stiff and hard in his pants. When Joseph pressed even closer to him, he felt that he was in the same condition. Gage definitely wanted to take things a little further. But he forced himself to remember they were in a public parking lot where anybody could be watching and ended the kiss.

Gage brushed his lips against Joseph's one more time before he pulled back. He tapped a finger against his bottom lip. "Sweet like cherries. Just like I thought." Joseph's long lashes rose to reveal green eyes soft and languid with arousal.

"I haven't had a Slush today."

Gage smiled. "It's got nothing to do with a drink." He put his hands on Joseph's lean hips and pushed him back a little. "We should get out of here. We've put on enough of a show for the fine patrons of Wilson's Steakhouse." He waited a beat to see if Joseph would say anything about them continuing the night somewhere else. When he didn't, Gage refrained from bringing it up himself. Instead, amazed at his uncharacteristic patience, he asked him out again. "I gotta take care of some things tomorrow night, but come out and shoot some pool with me on Sunday." Joseph agreed and they quickly made plans when and where to meet. Gage tugged Joseph close for one last kiss before he let him get in the car and drive off.

CHAPTER 5

Sunday evening, Joseph rode his bike to the local pool hall Gage had invited him to. Their date Friday night had gone so well that Joseph hadn't hesitated to say yes to a second date. Gage was definitely different from the men Joseph tended to go out with, but he was starting to think that wasn't such a bad thing. The scales were tipping more in favor of excitement over nervousness when it came to the sexy mechanic.

Joseph had just gotten off his bike and removed his helmet when Gage roared onto the lot. He was practically salivating as he watched, unsure if it was over the man, or the bike he was riding. He waited on the curb as Gage pulled into the space next to his bike. "Is this the Indian Chief Dark Horse?" he asked, trying to keep the awe out of his voice. Going by the cockily amused look on Gage's face, he didn't make it.

"Yep. You like what you see?"

Joseph looked at Gage sitting there on that sexy bike. He hadn't worn a helmet so his dark hair was tossed in windblown waves all over his head. Sunglasses hid his eyes, but that just meant that Joseph's gaze was drawn to that expressive mouth of his. A dark blue tee stretched across his chest, giving subtle outline to the pads of muscle beneath. His faded jeans molded to his thighs as he straddled the bike. Yeah, Joseph definitely liked what he saw.

Gage took off his sunglasses and crooked his finger at him. Joseph stepped off the curb to get a closer look. Nearly everything on the bike was a smooth black, from the wheel covers to the tail pipe. He ran his hand over the painted Indian headdress on the tank and looked at Gage. "This is a beautiful bike."

Gage pursed his lips, his chin coming up as he gave Joseph an arrogant stare. "You surprised I own something this nice?"

Joseph blinked. He wasn't sure what to make of that comment. "No, I just really like it." Gage smiled and the weird moment, if it even was one, passed.

"Hmm... maybe I'll let you ride it one day."

Joseph's eyes widened. "Seriously?"

Gage laughed and got off the bike. "We'll see."

****

Gage and Joseph walked into Red's Pool Hall. It was a typical setup. A long bar ran nearly the entire width of the building, with rows of green topped tables behind it. It was smoky and dim, the bar lit by neon drink signs and the pool tables lit by the stained glass lamps that hung above them. Multiple conversations created a low hum of constant sound, interspersed with an occasional shout from an enthusiastic player or spectator.

After they got a rack of balls and a couple of beers, they headed to a table towards the back. Joseph took his time choosing his cue, aware that Gage was watching him. Once they'd both chalked up, Gage gestured to the table.

"I invited you so you get to break."

Joseph grinned and stepped up to the table. He leaned over the green felt and set up his shot. Right before he struck the cue ball he looked over at Gage. "You're such a gentleman to let me go first." Then he struck the cue ball hard, scattering the bunch and sinking several into the pockets. He saw more stripes than solids fall, so he called those as his own as he straightened.

Gage looked at him with a rueful grin on his face. "Why do I feel like I'm about to be taken for a ride?"

The words were out of his mouth before he could stop them. "Don't worry. I'll make sure you like it."

Joseph was surprised at his boldness, but he didn't try to take back what he said. He liked Gage and he liked the way he made him feel. So when Gage gave him a look filled with heat, he just smiled and set up his next shot.

A few minutes later, Joseph had finally missed and Gage kneeled down to eye the table.

"So how'd you end up such a pool shark?"

Joseph took a sip of his beer. "Well, I told you I went to STU, but by the time I started on my law degree my circumstances had … changed. I relied on scholarships and financial aid for my tuition, housing, and books, but there wasn't much left over for anything else. I couldn't afford to go out every weekend so I hung out in the student center. They had a pool table there and I played. A lot. By the time I graduated I probably could have played pool professionally."

Gage finally took his shot, sinking two solids. "Why didn't you?"

Joseph shrugged. "Playing pool isn't what my family considers a respectable profession, and it's not what I went to school for. Besides, I didn't learn a bunch of trick shots and stuff like that."

Gage missed his next shot and stepped back. "But you learned enough to run the table?"

Joseph didn't answer at first. He knocked his last two stripes in then looked across the table at Gage. "Yep." He sauntered to the other end. Leaning over the felt, he pulled his cue stick slowly through his fingers several times while looking straight at Gage. "Eight ball, corner pocket." Then he struck the cue ball hard, sending the black eight ball streaking across the table to drop in the corner pocket. He straightened up and grinned. "I win."

Gage came over to him. "What do you want for your prize?"

"We didn't say we were wagering anything."

Gage's fingers brushed lightly over his stomach. "C'mon, Joseph. Winner always gets a prize. So what do you want?"

Joseph swallowed hard. "I guess a beer?"

Gage smiled real slow, before bringing his hand up and lightly touching his mouth. "You'd better hope I don't win the next one."

Joseph just barely restrained from licking his tongue out to taste the finger resting on his lips. Thankfully it was only there for a second before Gage headed over to the bar to get them another round. Even though he was the winner, he went ahead and racked the balls while he waited.

The next game Joseph wasn't as focused. Gage kept touching him every chance he got. A brush of his hand across the small of his back as he passed. His hand curving over his hip to gently move him out of the way so he could take his shot. And whenever they were on the same side of the table Gage didn't just talk to him, he leaned over and spoke softly right into his ear. Joseph was so distracted that he didn't realize he was losing until Gage only had one ball left before he was down to the eight ball.

As Gage lined up for his final shot, Joseph found himself hoping the eight ball would go in just so he could find out what Gage wanted for his prize. After spinning for what seemed like an inordinately long time the black ball finally fell into the pocket. Gage gave him a wicked look as he approached.

Gage watched Joseph as he went over to him after sinking the eight ball. He could see Joseph was nervous, wondering what he was going to claim for his prize. But to his credit he didn't back down. He just stood there and waited. When Gage was right in front of him, Joseph spoke.

"You don't play fair."

Gage smirked. "I play by whatever rules it takes to win the prize." He reached up to tug at a strand of the hair Joseph had left loose and curly tonight. "But don't worry I'll make sure you like it." Joseph's eyes widened as he turned his words back on him and he had to hold back a grin. Gage leaned in close until he could feel Joseph's breath on his lips. Then he pulled back. "On second thought, I think I'll collect my prize later."

Joseph cleared his throat. "Later?"

"Yep. Later." He stepped back out of Joseph's personal space. "Loser racks."

****

An hour later, they were on their fourth game. Joseph had won the third round quickly but when it came time to claim his prize he'd again asked for a beer. Now Gage had been quiet for some time, but he finally spoke right before Joseph took his shot.

"Let's get out of here."

Joseph stood up in surprise. "You don't want to finish the game? We've got the table for another thirty minutes."

"No, I don't want to finish this game." Gage canted his head low, looking at him with his dark steady gaze. "Do you?"

Joseph's lips parted. Tension crackled between them, making his skin prickle with awareness. He set his cue stick on the table. "No."

Gage's mouth twisted into a knowing smile. "I didn't think so."

Joseph stood still as Gage came close enough to whisper in his ear. His warm breath washed over his skin, sending shivers down his spine.

"Didn't they teach you any manners in that fancy law school, Joseph? Always return your cue stick to the rack."

Joseph narrowed his eyes at Gage. "I know that. But you…"

Gage raised an eyebrow when he didn't finish his sentence. "I what?"

Joseph didn't answer. He didn't want to admit out loud just how much Gage affected him. He put the balls back in the tray, ignoring the soft laughter he heard behind him. They finished the last of their beers on the way to returning the balls and settling their tab. Then they went outside into the cool night.

CHAPTER 6

As soon as they were outside, Gage pulled Joseph into the dark alley next to the building. He yanked him into his arms, kissing him roughly. Pushing Joseph back against the wall, he slid his hands into that cloud of curls and grabbed on tight. Gage ground his stiff cock hard against Joseph, who groaned and thrust right back. His fingers tightened even more when he felt how hard Joseph was. Gage circled his hips in a slow grind against Joseph over and over. He grew even more aggressive in his kiss, sucking hard on Joseph's bottom lip and licking at his tongue. And Joseph matched him kiss for kiss, his arms coming up to wrap around his back, pulling their bodies as close as possible.

"*Fuck.*" Gage breathed the curse into the hot mouth beneath his when Joseph brought his leg up, rubbing it against his thigh like a fucking cat in heat. Gage dropped a hand from Joseph's hair and reached down to grab onto that leg. He squeezed, wanting to rip off those jeans so he could feel Joseph's skin against his palm. Stroking his hand up his thigh until he cupped Joseph's ass in his hand, Gage squeezed again, this time drawing a moan from him in response. His cock hardened even further at the sound, making his jeans tight and uncomfortable. Gage pulled back and looked at Joseph. He was so damn turned on his voice came out even raspier than usual.

"I'm trying to be good here, but you have no idea how much you fucking tempt me. And I have no idea why I haven't coaxed you into my bed yet, or hell, talked you into letting me fuck you right here up against this wall." Joseph swallowed hard when he was done talking.

"It wouldn't take much," he said in a shaky voice.

Right then Gage realized what it was. He didn't want to *persuade* Joseph. He wanted this pretty boy to come to him. And until Joseph did he would wait. As long as he didn't take too long. He slowly released his leg, letting him drop it back to the ground. "I don't want it to take anything."

Joseph's heart was racing, his chest heaving as he struggled to bring his breathing back under control. He understood what Gage was saying. He was putting the ball squarely in his court, letting him decide when things between them went to the next level. He looked into Gage's eyes, black in the dim light of the alley. Physically Joseph was ready. More than ready. But something held him back. So he took a deep breath and slowly released it. "I have to go into the office early tomorrow morning."

Gage didn't say anything. He only nodded once and released the grip he still had on his hair to step back. Joseph immediately missed the solid warmth of Gage's body against his, but he didn't say anything either. He just straightened up and followed him out of the alley to go home. Alone.

CHAPTER 7

Gage lay back in his big bed, his fist wrapped around his cock, stroking slowly. He hadn't had sex since the morning before he'd agreed to go out with Joseph. Last night, when he'd said he was trying to be good, he hadn't been kidding. Normally when he saw someone he was attracted to he didn't play around with dates. For years now he'd had sex, lots of it, on a regular basis. He needed it as a substitute for … other things. But he was trying to resist that driving urge to thrust deep inside a willing body so that he could pursue Joseph. It wasn't something he usually did and he didn't know if he was going to be able to do it now.

He thought of Joseph as he pumped faster, his hand moving smoothly from the silky lube he'd used. He thought of those pouty lips and how soft they'd felt beneath his. Gage could just imagine how they would look, all pink and swollen as they slid up and down his cock. He groaned and pumped faster as the picture in his head switched to one of Joseph flat on his back in his bed, his hair a tangled mess across his pillow. And he would be on top of him, inside him, pushing deep and hard, driving them both towards climax. Gage knew without a doubt that Joseph would be tight and he groaned thinking about it. He squeezed his fist tighter around his shaft, but it was no substitute for what he really wanted. Still, he came quickly, which let him know just how desperate he was.

After his release, Gage lay there breathing hard. It hadn't really satisfied him. He looked to his phone on his nightstand. He was tempted to call one of his frequent flyers, see if he could get one of them over for a morning romp between the sheets. But then he thought again of Joseph. Pretty Joseph, with his gorgeous green eyes. He had a feeling Joseph wouldn't understand if he were to fuck someone else while they were dating. Gage wasn't sure why that mattered to him with this guy, but it did. So instead of making the call that would probably have someone knocking on his door within the hour, he went to shower and get ready for work.

****

Saturday afternoon, Joseph stared out the patio doors of his town home to the back lawn. The sprinklers were on, sending arcs of water over the thick green grass. He was restless. It was a feeling that had been growing in him lately. But instead of the usual thoughts of work and the partial estrangement from his family that plagued him, he was thinking about Gage.

He'd been surprised that Gage had let things play out the way they had last weekend outside the pool hall. But he appreciated it. As much as he wanted Gage, he was still a little hesitant about jumping into bed with him. He wasn't one to fuck around from guy to guy and Gage didn't exactly give him the feeling that he would be around for long. They'd talked on their two dates, but it had mostly been superficial stuff; favorite music, where they'd grown up, what their jobs were like. And even then it had been Joseph doing most of the talking. Gage hadn't shared much of himself. Joseph didn't expect to delve into life stories, but to him, that was normally a sign of a guy who wasn't looking for anything past a night or two.

Joseph sort of wanted to back away from Gage, to just let things end with the dates they'd already had. But he thought again of how Gage had left the decision up to him. That had to mean that he was at least a little interested in more than just sex. Besides, he liked Gage and was seriously attracted to him. Joseph admitted to himself that he really wanted to take things to the next level with the bike mechanic. Thinking of just how many nights he'd spent alone, Joseph decided to go for it.

Feeling like he'd just made another big decision concerning Gage, he picked up the phone to call him.

"Hey, Gage it's Joseph." Gage said hello, sounding distracted. Joseph could hear the sounds of motorcycles revving and people talking. "I know you're busy so I won't keep you. Just wanted to see if you have plans for after work tonight?" The background noise faded as if Gage had left the main garage area.

"Not really. Why, what's up?"

"I was thinking we could go out for a beer somewhere and watch the game." There was silence on the phone for a long time. Joseph would have thought he'd lost the connection if he didn't hear the slight noise of Gage's breathing. Finally, he answered.

"Joseph, I don't want to be with you surrounded by strangers. I want you to myself. I want you alone so that I can kiss you and lick you and get inside you. That's what *I'm* thinking I want to do tonight."

Joseph nearly dropped the phone. He hadn't expected Gage to be quite so blunt. But he wasn't going to be a hypocrite and pretend that wasn't on his mind too. Still, his mouth was dry just from picturing the images Gage's words put in his head. He had to swallow twice before he could answer. Joseph wasn't nearly as bold as Gage with his reply, but he was pretty sure he got his point across.

"We don't have to go out and watch the game. You could come over to my place and we could watch it here. Alone."

"You sure about that?"

Joseph's stomach gave a slight nervous jump, but he answered, "Yeah." He gave Gage his address and quick directions.

"Alright then. I'll see you at seven."

Joseph took a deep breath and put his phone down on the counter.

Tonight.

CHAPTER 8

A few minutes after seven o'clock, Gage rang the bell to Joseph's townhouse. He looked around the area as he waited for him to answer the door. The place was nice and well-kept, but bland. It fit in more with the suit side of Joseph rather than the ponytail and motorcycle side of him. He wasn't sure if he liked it or not. The door opened and an immediate wave of arousal washed over Gage. Joseph was dressed more casually than he'd ever seen him. His hair was in a sloppy ponytail with messy tendrils escaping randomly. He had on a t-shirt with the logo of a band he didn't recognize, and his frayed and washed out jeans sat low, really low, on his hips. The tattered hems of the jeans covered half of his bare feet. Gage decided he didn't care what the house looked like. If it let Joseph be this at ease, then he liked it.

Joseph smiled at Gage before stepping back to let him in. "Hey. You find the place okay?"

"Yeah. It was a pretty straight shot over here from the shop."

Joseph discreetly inhaled as Gage passed him. He'd obviously just gotten out of the shower. The clean scent of the ocean was on his skin and his hair was still wet and slicked back. Neatly trimmed stubble roughened his jaw. His body looked firm and hard in what Joseph had come to think of as his trademark outfit of plain dark tee and jeans. His palms tingled as he realized he'd get to fill those muscles soon. The man smelled good and looked even better. He noticed Gage watching him. Joseph cleared his throat, hoping he hadn't been too obvious checking him out. "The game's already on. I can grab us a couple of beers and then show you around if you want before we watch." Gage didn't say anything so Joseph took that as agreement and went into the kitchen.

Joseph grabbed two beers out of the fridge and took them over to the counter. He heard Gage's footsteps come into the kitchen as he set them down to look for a bottle opener. "I hope Shiner is okay. I like to drink local beers," he said without turning around. But again Gage didn't answer. His footsteps came closer and Joseph went still as he came up behind him. Gage brushed his ponytail aside and trailed his lips over the back of his neck before he whispered into his ear.

"I don't want to watch baseball." Gage's hand closed over his, moving it away from the bottle. "I don't want a fucking beer." That same hand drifted up his arm, raising goose bumps on his skin before it slid under his shirt to caress his stomach. "You already know it, but I'm telling you that I want you." Joseph's fingers clenched on the counter top as Gage's hand slid down to the waistband of his jeans, popping them open. The zipper went down, one slow metallic rasp at a time.

"So you tell me right now if you don't want this to happen."

Joseph could barely control his breathing as Gage's hand slipped inside his jeans to tease his growing erection.

"Otherwise, I'm gonna be deep inside you within the next fifteen minutes."

Gage squeezed his cock and Joseph moaned, pushing his ass back against the hardness he felt behind him. Gage groaned and licked his neck.

"Maybe sooner. What's it gonna be, Joseph?"

Joseph took a moment to answer. Not because he was unsure, but because Gage's fingers on his shaft, and his body heat against his skin, and *that voice* in his ear had his brain a little bit scrambled. "No baseball. I want you."

Gage spun him around so that his back was against the counter. And before he had his bearings Gage was kissing him wildly. Joseph was immediately into it. He opened up for Gage, accepting his tongue inside his mouth, fighting to keep it when he withdrew. Gage gripped his ponytail and yanked his head back.

"So eager. I like that." Gage leaned forward and lapped a long slow path up his neck, from collarbone to just beneath his jaw.

Joseph shivered as Gage sucked the skin over his pulse into his mouth. He settled his hands on Gage's back, sliding them under his t-shirt to the warm skin beneath. Gage released his hair and knocked his arms aside. Joseph was confused until Gage grabbed his shirt and roughly pushed it up his chest. Catching on quick, Joseph raised his arms to help him take it off. Gage threw it to the side somewhere. From the corner of his eye, it looked like it landed in the sink. He went to put his hands back where they were, but Gage grabbed his wrists and held his arms down. Joseph moaned as Gage's tongue came out, licking at his chest before his mouth closed tightly over his nipple, sucking hard. It felt good, but he didn't like that he couldn't feel Gage's body against his. He had to strain against Gage's strength, but he got his wrists free. When he did, he wrapped his arms around Gage, pulling his body back against his.

Gage straightened and looked at him, his dark eyes hot with passion. Joseph sucked his bottom lip into his mouth and pushed his hips forward, unashamedly rubbing his erection against Gage's. "Kiss me."

Gage smiled. "Not as shy as you seem. What a…" Gage licked the corner of his mouth " … lovely surprise."

Gage kissed him again even more fiercely than before. Their hips started moving, grinding their cocks together, Joseph's almost entirely out of his opened jeans. His heart was racing. Gage's kisses and hard body pressed against his had Joseph's skin tingling with pleasure. And it had been a while for him. Too much more of this and he was going to come right there in the kitchen. Thankfully, his chest heaving, Gage pulled back.

"Bedroom. Now."

CHAPTER 9

Joseph was on board with that plan, but he must not have moved fast enough. Because Gage cocked his head to the side and said, "Or kitchen table. Your choice." This time he got his feet moving and started to lead the way out of the kitchen. He stopped when Gage hooked a finger into the back of his jeans. Turning around, Joseph let Gage pull him back into his arms. Gage kissed him again and then started walking. They made their way to his bedroom that way, him walking backwards, with Gage's arms wrapped tight around his waist to hold him steady as they kissed. They bumped into a few walls but didn't knock anything down. Joseph wouldn't have cared if they did.

When they were in his room Gage finally released him. Joseph started to close the door, but Gage stopped him and pushed it all the way open.

"I want to see you."

Light from the hall streamed into the room. It was behind Gage, casting him into shadow. He looked big and dark and dangerous standing there like that, with his head canted low and arms flexed hard at his sides. A shiver of apprehension ran down Joseph's spine, but he still went over to him. Reaching out, he pulled Gage's shirt over his head. Joseph ran his hands over the pads of muscle on Gage's chest, across the broad width of his shoulders and down to the defined ridges of his abs.

Joseph looked up at Gage and saw him watching him with all the focus of a hawk. He got the feeling that Gage was allowing him to take the lead at the moment. He wasn't going to bank on that lasting for long. Joseph settled his fingers on Gage's waist, again walking backwards, pulling Gage with him until they reached the bed. He sat down on the edge and pulled Gage a few inches closer. Gage was still silently watching as he opened his jeans. Joseph wasn't surprised to see that he wasn't wearing anything beneath them. His shaft came into immediate view, big and thick.

Joseph swallowed hard and traced a finger along the thick vein that ran up the underside of his cock. The skin over the rigid column was soft, slightly darker than the rest of him. Silky, dark hair trailed a narrow path from bellow his navel to the sac below. He pushed Gage's jeans down just enough to be able to wrap his fingers around his cock. But just as he started to lean forward, Gage again grabbed his ponytail and yanked his head back. Joseph looked up at the man above him, his heart pounding as he waited to see what Gage would do.

Gage liked that Joseph had this hidden layer to him. The green eyes that stared up at him were so pretty and sweet. But his lips were parted, and his tongue darted out, obviously hungry for a taste of his cock. And Gage was throbbing, ready to let him have it. He roughly pulled the elastic from Joseph's hair, shoving his fingers through the loosened curls and wrapping them tightly around his fists. "You want to suck my cock? Go ahead." Joseph leaned forward, his eyes drifting closed. Gage pulled his hair just as his lips touched the head of his shaft. "No. Eyes open."

Joseph opened his eyes again and Gage stared down into them as he slid into his mouth. Gage wanted to see every expression in those eyes, wanted to see if Joseph's passion and hunger were as deep as his own. Joseph slowly moved his head back and forth, sucking and licking him with a hot mouth and wet tongue. The sight and feel of those pink lips moving on his cock had Gage's stomach clenching and his breath coming a little bit faster. It felt good, but he wasn't content to just stand there. Gage gripped Joseph's hair even tighter, holding him still. He began moving his hips, fucking into his mouth. He wasn't gentle, but Joseph didn't complain or try to get away. Instead, he moaned. And the faster Gage thrust forward, the tighter his grip on his hair grew, the more frequently the moans came. Joseph's hands came up, rubbing over Gage's stomach before one dipped down to cup his balls. Gage groaned and pushed forward hard. But he had to pull back out of Joseph's mouth as he started swallowing around his cock. That felt too fucking amazing, and he wasn't going to come like this his first time with Joseph.

His fingers still twisted in Joseph's hair, Gage cupped the back of his lover's head and pulled him back to his feet. He licked at Joseph's bottom lip. "I knew this pretty mouth would be perfect at sucking my cock." He kissed him, plunging his tongue in deep to tangle with Joseph's. Gage slid his hands into Joseph's jeans, pushing them down. Squeezing his ass, Gage pulled his lover's body tight against his. Their naked cocks touched for the first time and Joseph groaned into his mouth. Gage pulled back from their kiss and looked at his lover. His mouth was swollen, all the sweetness gone from his sea green eyes. Now they were heavy-lidded and sultry. Gage liked that look on him.

"Get up on the bed."

Joseph did as he was told, lying back against the pillows. Gage took a condom and lube from his jeans pocket and tossed them onto the bed next to him. Toeing off his tennis shoes, he pulled his jeans the rest of the way off before he joined Joseph on the bed. Gage came down over Joseph's long, hard body, drawing a gasp from him as their skin touched from chest to thigh. Gage didn't stay there long. He softly kissed his way down the soft skin of Joseph's neck and across his chest. When he reached a nipple, he roughly licked it before drawing it into his mouth. Gage sucked hard as he trailed his fingers down Joseph's flat stomach until he reached his cock. Joseph was already breathing hard, but when Gage gripped his shaft, he moaned loudly and thrust his hips up. Gage kept going, taking rough sucking kisses all over Joseph's body wherever he chose. And he kept pumping Joseph the whole time. He stroked fast until Joseph was writhing against him. Then Gage backed off, sliding his fist slowly up and down Joseph's shaft, pulling him back from the edge. He did it again and again, until Joseph was shaking on the bed, his fingers clawing at his hand. Gage bit his finger hard and Joseph pulled back with a surprised cry.

"Don't do that again. I set the pace. Not you. Understand?" Joseph didn't respond at first. Gage slowed the pace of his hand even more. "You'd better tell me you understand, Joseph. Or I'll keep you like this all fucking night. Right on the fucking edge. Is that what you want?"

Joseph somehow managed to shake his head no while whispering he understood. That was enough of an answer for Gage. He moved down and without another word, sucked Joseph's cock into his mouth. A curse exploded from Joseph and he arched his head back against the pillows. Gage watched him, saw him grab his own hair with one hand, the other rubbing over his stomach as Gage continued to suck. He lapped his tongue all along Joseph's cock, tonguing his slit to lick up the pre-cum spilling forth.

Reaching for the lube, he popped open the bottle to get his fingers slick. One touch of his hand to Joseph's thigh and his legs practically sprang open. Gage smiled around Joseph's cock at his eagerness as he slid a finger inside him. He sucked even faster, his own cock throbbing as he felt how hot and tight Joseph was around his finger. He worked him quickly, adding another finger almost immediately. Gage wanted to take a little more time. But he was so fucking hard and he'd wanted to be inside Joseph for days now. He couldn't wait.

Gage let Joseph fall from his mouth and pulled his fingers from his ass. He grabbed up the condom packet, tearing it open with his teeth. To his surprise, Joseph sat up and took the rubber from him, smoothing it onto his cock. Once he was sheathed Gage tangled his fingers in that long curly hair and pulled Joseph up while he leaned down until their lips met. He kissed him hard, falling on him with all his weight so that Joseph tumbled back against the bed. He reached down and grabbed his own cock, lining himself up against the heat of Joseph's entrance. They were still kissing as he pushed inside him. Joseph cried out, but he didn't stop. The sound had been one of pleasure not pain. He kept going until his balls came up against the smooth skin of Joseph's ass.

Gage stilled for only a second to let Joseph get used to his size. When he felt him relax around him, he started moving. He pulled back then pushed forward roughly, slamming into him. Joseph groaned and gripped his forearms. "Do you like that?" Gage asked.

Joseph looked at him. His eyes were definitely filled with the same hunger and passion that Gage felt. He licked his lips once. "Yes."

Gage pulled his hips back again. "Good. Because I've wanted to fuck you since you came into my shop in your prissy little suit." He pushed forward then leaned down. The kiss he gave Joseph was soft and sweet in contrast to the dirty words he whispered against his lips. "And now that I'm finally inside your tight, hot little ass I'm gonna fuck you until you can't breathe."

Gage licked across Joseph's mouth before he started fucking into him swift and hard. He ran his hands everywhere over Joseph's body, digging his nails into his waist as he thrust inside the hot channel gripping him so snugly. His cock was throbbing, his balls tight, slapping against Joseph's skin as he pumped into him. He sucked a bite onto Joseph's shoulder. "You feel so fucking good on my cock, Joseph." He kept going, his thrusts fast and rough, his stomach rubbing against Joseph's hard shaft with every movement. And he knew Joseph was loving it. He was moaning, fingers digging into his arms. The tension in his face drove Gage on until he was fucking into him so hard the room was filled with the sound of their bodies slapping together and the bed creaking rhythmically.

Joseph was close to losing it. Gage didn't stop with his touches and rough kisses once he was inside him. He continued until finally Joseph was writhing in pleasure, pushing his hips up hard to meet Gage's every thrust. His breath shot out of his lungs in sharp pants tinged with desperate moans. Joseph didn't know how much more he could take. Every inch of his skin was tingling and sensitive to Gage's touch. But that was nothing, nothing compared to the way Gage felt inside him. He was deliciously thick and hard as he forcefully rocked his body over his. Every stroke in hit that spot that sent shivers along his spine, making his stomach tremble. Joseph couldn't help it. He had his knees up to his chest and his legs spread wide like nothing more than an eager little slut. He'd never wanted to be as open for a lover as he was for Gage right now. And Gage took full advantage, grasping his legs and holding on tight so that he could push even deeper inside him. Joseph dug his fingers into Gage's back and he found himself begging.

"Gage, please. I can't … I need ..."

Gage laughed softly at Joseph's inability to finish a sentence. "What do you want, Joseph? You want to come?" Joseph nodded swiftly, his hair moving on the pillow. Gage kept pushing inside his lover. "And when you come, will this ass squeeze my cock even tighter? Because that's what I want, Joseph. I want you to squeeze me and milk me until I come. Will you do that for me?"

Joseph's eyes were closed tight, his lips parted as he panted. "Fuck! Yes. I'll do that! Just, *please.*"

Gage slipped his hand down to grasp Joseph's cock, feeling it throbbing and practically soaked with pre-cum. He pumped fast but steady, working Joseph into even more of a frenzy. Joseph's ass started to clench on his cock.

"Fuck! Gage! I'm coming!"

Gage smiled. He liked seeing Joseph wild and cursing, with his name a shout on his lips. Gage pulled back just enough to be able to see Joseph's stomach sucked in hard before his cock jerked and splashed his cum all over his stomach and chest. Joseph was still coming when Gage leaned down and kissed him, wanting to smile again as Joseph frantically sucked on his tongue. Instead, he groaned deeply as Joseph's ass clenched so tightly on his cock that it brought his own orgasm rushing up his shaft. His vision blurred and his breath hitched in his chest. Gage grabbed onto Joseph's hair, speaking in a harsh whisper into his mouth. "That's it Joseph. Squeeze me just like that. Make me come."

Joseph moaned his name, tightening his inner muscles even further around him. Gage thrust quick and deep several more times, cursing roughly as his balls drew up hard, that tight friction sending him over the edge. His release was an explosion of all the tension that had been riding him ever since he'd laid eyes on the man beneath him. And it felt fucking amazing.

****

Gage lay there for a moment on top of Joseph, their chests pushing against each other with their heavy breathing. Finally, he withdrew and rolled off him. He looked at the man next to him for a moment before he gave in to the urge to push the damp hair away from his face, twisting a strand of curls around his finger. "You okay?" he asked.

Joseph smiled, his eyes sleepy and low. "More than okay."

Gage surprised himself with the next words that came out of his mouth. "We can head back out to your living room and watch the end of the game if you want."

Joseph shook his head. "The TV in here works just fine."

Gage looked towards the foot of the bed. He hadn't even noticed the TV mounted on the far wall. His surprise must have shown on his face because Joseph laughed as he reached towards the nightstand for the remote. Gage had to grin as Joseph turned the TV to the right channel then excused himself to go to the bathroom and clean up. He took his turn after Joseph. When he came back, he slid between the sheets and sat with his back against the headboard. Joseph scooted up too, leaning against him. Without even thinking, Gage wrapped an arm around his waist. This definitely wasn't what Gage was used to after sex. But he kind of liked it.

CHAPTER 10

Now what? Gage had been asking himself that ever since he'd had Joseph the other night. The question was still in his head as he worked on a customer's big Boss Hoss. Finally, he'd had that pretty boy underneath him just like he'd wanted. But things after had been different from his usual sexual encounters. For starters, he hadn't left right afterwards. He'd surprised himself and stayed for a while, watching the end of the game with Joseph. When he *had* left he'd kissed Joseph gently again and again, first in the bed and then at his front door. That was so unlike him that he'd sat there on his bike for a moment, staring at Joseph's place and thinking before he finally started it up and drove off.

Now … now Joseph was still on his mind, and not in just a file him away for future sex kind of way. Shit, things with Joseph had been different from the beginning with the way he'd held off sleeping with him. And before they'd hooked up he hadn't given him the "let's keep things casual speech" that he'd perfected over the years. Now that they'd already slept together he'd be a supreme asshole if he said that. But it didn't matter, because he didn't want to only be fuck buddies with Joseph. He wanted to fuck him again, that was for damn sure. There were lots of things he wanted to explore with Joseph Naderi. Except for whatever reason, he also wanted to spend time with him. But he still had his other issue. How would that play out if he tried to date Joseph? When there was no answer immediately forthcoming from his brain, Gage shrugged to himself. He'd figure that out later. For now, he decided he wanted to see Joseph again.

He went into the office in the back of his shop and pulled out his cell make the call. He recognized Joseph's voice as soon as he answered. "I want to see you tonight."

Joseph sounded surprised. "See me tonight?"

"Yeah, for dinner."

"Oh. I thought you meant…"

Joseph trailed off, but Gage knew what he meant. That shyness drove him crazy. Especially now that he knew what was just beneath it. Gage smiled. "Don't worry. That's on the menu too."

Joseph laughed. "If I let you," he said in a flirtatious tone. "Where do you want to meet?"

A pulse of heat ran through him at Joseph's response. Which one was really Joseph? Flirt or shy? Ponytail or suit? Gage was intrigued and wanted to learn more about him. He gave the name and directions for his favorite burger joint. But before he hung up he had one more thing to say. "Oh and Joseph?"

"Yeah?"

"You're gonna let me."

****

Joseph looked around the restaurant as he finished the last of his fries. He liked this place Gage had picked. It was casual and laid back, but clean. And the food was amazing. Hot, greasy and full of flavor. He was considering getting one more refill of soda when Gage's hand landed on his leg. Joseph looked at him, noticing the wicked glint in his dark eyes. He raised an eyebrow. "Yes?"

Gage smiled, rubbing his hand up and down his thigh. "You gonna let me?"

Joseph pretended to ponder. "Hmmm … I don't know. I should probably get some laundry done tonight."

Gage's hand slid between his legs. His fingers just barely grazed his groin before squeezing his inner thigh. "Fuck laundry. Let me Joseph."

Joseph held back a smile. He liked this game. And he wasn't ready to give it up yet. He stood up and grabbed his keys. "We should get going." He saw the heat and excitement flash in Gage's eyes and smiled innocently. "I need to get a load of towels started."

Outside in the parking lot, Gage backed him up against the side of his car. Gage pressed in close, bracing his hands on the car on either side of him to cage him in. Joseph looked up the scant inches Gage had on him. "Did you need something? My laundry is waiting."

Gage shook his head, the corner of his mouth curled up into a half grin. "So snooty." Then he leaned forward and kissed him.

Joseph accepted his kiss, letting Gage's tongue slip into his mouth to curl against his own. Gage's hand slid under his shirt, softly caressing the small of his back.

"Let me, Joseph. You know you want to."

Joseph's body was waking up, getting hot, but still he managed to keep the game going. "Can't. I have to wash my hair."

Gage kissed him again, harder this time. Joseph ran his hands up Gage's arms to his biceps, feeling every hard muscle along the way. He shivered as Gage ended the kiss, trailing his lips along his cheek to whisper in his ear.

"C'mon, Joseph let me." Gage pressed his hips against him, rubbing their growing erections together. "Let me have you. Let me fuck you."

By the time he was done talking, Gage's hips were rolling smoothly against his. A moan slipped from Joseph's throat as he pressed back against him. He was fully hard now. And he was done teasing. Joseph pushed Gage back a little so he could get to his car door. He looked at Gage. "Follow me."

CHAPTER 11

Y ou have a beautiful body, Joseph. You know that?"

They'd made it back to Joseph's place. They'd gotten as far as the couch, with Joseph straddling his lap. Gage had his cock buried deep inside him, letting Joseph ride him at a smooth slow pace. He ran his hands up the bare torso in front of him, lightly tracing the sculpted abs. Joseph rose up on him again.

"Is that why I'm the only one naked?"

Gage laughed softly. "Yeah, that's it. It's got nothing to do with the fact that you jumped on my cock before I could get my pants off," he said, thrusting his hips up.

Joseph leaned forward to brace his hands on his chest. "That's not fair. You were all over me and had my clothes off the second we were in the door."

Gage twisted his fingers in the soft hair at the back of Joseph's neck. He pulled him down until their lips met. "I told you I don't play fair." He ran his tongue over Joseph's lips until they opened for him. "I just like to play." He kissed him hard, holding Joseph to him with a tight grip in his hair. He ran his other hand down his lover's back, brushing one fingertip along the ridge of his spine. Gage ended their kiss with one last lick to his bottom lip. He thrust up again, watching as Joseph's lips parted on a soft moan. Joseph started to increase the speed as he rose and fell on his cock, but that's not what Gage wanted. He gripped Joseph's hips and held him still.

"Ride me slow, Joseph. I want you sweaty and crying my name by the time you finally come."

Joseph moaned again. "At least take your shirt off."

Gage pulled his shirt over his head and threw it on the floor. Then he leaned back against the couch, slouching down so he had more room to move. He gripped Joseph's hips, his fingers wrapping around and digging into his ass. He pushed him up and pulled him back down along his cock agonizingly slow. The friction of those hot walls dragging along his shaft had him throbbing, a groan coming from deep in his throat. Joseph closed his eyes and tried to fall against him, but Gage wouldn't let him. "No. I want to watch you, Joseph." He pulled him down onto his cock again, pushing his hips up at the same time. "You're so fucking pretty."

Joseph opened his eyes to look down at him. "Thank you," he said in a polite voice.

Gage laughed. "So well-mannered," he mocked. "I can't even imagine calling you Joe or Joey." He ran his fingers down Joseph's stomach, following the soft trail of dark hair. "I like Joseph. It's proper, just like you." Gage moved his hand to grasp Joseph's cock. He stroked him slowly, at the same pace he was forcing him to keep. "You also have a beautiful cock, Joseph." He squeezed his hand around the slick head. "You gonna thank me for that compliment too?"

Joseph dug his fingers into Gage's chest. He was straining to stay slow like Gage wanted. But he wanted that fast friction that he knew would send him straight to orgasm. Not being allowed to have that movement had him shaking and craving it, especially with Gage's hand moving so slowly on his erection. His breath caught in his throat as he tried to answer. "Th-Thank you." Again Gage laughed. This time Joseph ignored Gage's order and pushed forward to kiss him. Gage growled but allowed the kiss. Joseph thought he would let it slide. He was wrong. Gage wrapped his arm around his back, holding him so tight that he couldn't even continue with the slow movements of before. Instead, Gage started circling his hips, grinding into him. Joseph groaned and pushed his hips as tight against Gage's as he could. That slow grind had Gage's cock pressing against the majorly sensitive bundle of nerves inside him. Sparks of pleasure tingled from there, to his stomach, right to his cock still in Gage's fist. "Gage … that feels…"

Gage circled his hips again. "Feels what?"

Joseph licked his lips, trying to breathe without whimpering. "Good, it feels good."

Gage's mouth twisted into an arrogant sneer. "Only good? What am I giving you, a damn foot rub?" Gage started to let go of his cock, his hips falling still. "Maybe I should stop."

Joseph practically panicked at the thought of Gage ending what he was doing to him without giving him a release. "No! It's fantastic, wonderful, fucking stupendous."

Gage laughed and started moving again. "Fucking college boy with your big words."

Joseph swore in surprise as Gage jerked him forward roughly. Their chests slammed together and Gage started pumping up into him hard. His movements were still slow, but at the crest of each thrust he circled his hips, continuing that amazing pressure against that spot deep inside him. Joseph was breathing hard, his cock stiff, his skin warm and sweaty everywhere he pressed against his lover. Gage released his arm from around his waist and Joseph started moving again, matching his rhythm immediately. It felt so good, but he needed more. He leaned down and pressed his lips to Gage's ear. "Gage … more," he whispered. "I want more."

Gage started to move faster, encouraging Joseph to keep pace with him. Joseph moaned and straightened up again, his head falling back. The long curve of his throat became exposed and vulnerable, his hair swinging in a dark mass behind him. Gage couldn't hold the slow pace any longer. He needed more too. Every inch of him was sheathed inside Joseph's tight heat, but his throbbing cock was demanding more. Demanding that he thrust hard and fast. He let go of Joseph's cock who cried out, "Don't!" Gage snatched up a fistful of that hair hanging down Joseph's back and yanked. "Shut up. You don't tell me what to do." When Joseph remained quiet, those big green eyes wide with surprise, Gage grabbed his hand and placed it on his shaft. "Show me how you like it."

Joseph tried to nod, but Gage kept hold of his hair, pulling his head back. Gage watched as Joseph started stroking himself, twisting his fist on the upstroke and squeezing the head. Letting go of Joseph's hair, Gage smoothed his hands up his back. The skin was warm and slick with sweat, just how he wanted it. He cupped his hands over Joseph's shoulders in a firm overhand grip, pumping into his lover a little faster. Joseph brought his head back up and looked down at him, the sultry look in those normally sweet eyes making his stomach clench tight with lust. Joseph rocked his hips back and forth, his lips parted in a perfect little *o*. Gage growled. "Give me that pretty mouth."

Joseph surged forward. Their lips came together in an open mouth kiss, tongues sliding and licking, lips sucking and being sucked. Gage increased the pace of his hips, fucking up harder and harder into the tight ass gripping his cock. Joseph's arm started moving faster, jerking himself off at the same speed as Gage fucked into him. "Is this how you want it, Joseph?" His lover was gasping, hot breaths flowing into his mouth.

"Yes. That's how I want it. Fuck me, Gage."

Gage licked Joseph's neck slowly, nipping at his skin. "Be careful what you ask for." Planting his feet wider on the floor, he used his grip on Joseph's shoulders to hold his body close against his. Gage slammed his hips up over and over, pushing his cock deep inside Joseph's ass. Joseph was moaning and panting against the side of his face, working his body so that his ass met his thighs at the same time that he thrust up. Their bodies coming together made a deliciously satisfying bump, adding to the dirty sounds of their groans, harsh breathing, and Joseph's hand sliding wet and fast on his cock. Gage was getting close. His balls were taut and the small of his back tingled with anticipation. But he wasn't ready to let go yet.

"Is this what you wanted Joseph, me pounding into your ass just like this?" Joseph nodded, his eyes heavy-lidded yet sparkling bright with passion. "I'm gonna leave you sore, Joseph. And every time you move around at work tomorrow in your pretty boy suit, you're gonna think of my cock stretching you and slamming into you." Joseph moaned and pressed closer, both of their chests slick with sweat now as they rubbed together from their rough movements.

"Oh god … Gage."

Gage kept moving, his skin flushed, and his shaft incredibly hard. "That's right. *Gage*. Later on, when you're by yourself, thinking of this while you jerk your cock off, make sure you say my name then too."

Joseph's breathing was all moans and whimpers, his hand moved even faster, his knuckles hitting Gage's stomach with each pump while he rode his cock. "Fuck, Gage. Harder! Fuck me. I'm coming!"

Gage licked his tongue out, feeling like he wanted to taste the air Joseph's dirty words floated on. "Such slutty moans and words coming from that sweet mouth." He licked from Joseph's chin to his top lip. "Wanna taste 'em, Joseph. Give me more." He worked his hand between their bodies to grasp Joseph's balls, feeling them swollen and hot in his palm. He squeezed, until with another string of moans and curses Joseph was pumping his cum out all over their stomachs, his body jerking in his lap. "Yeah … that's it," Gage whispered into Joseph's mouth. He stopped holding back his own orgasm, letting the rhythmic squeezing of Joseph's ass around his cock draw his cum up from his achingly tight sac. Gage threw his head back against the couch. "Fuck! Joseph! Goddamnit you feel good," he gritted out from between clenched teeth. His fingers cruelly dug into Joseph's shoulders as he held him still for his last stiff thrusts, his cock pulsing with each one, until finally he was spent.

****

Gage came back into the living room after cleaning up and disposing of the condom. Joseph was sprawled back against the couch wearing only his briefs. He pushed himself up and Gage couldn't help but admire the smooth way that long body moved.

"I'm still hot. You want some ice cream?"

Gage pulled his shirt back on. "Ice cream sounds great. But I gotta go." Joseph's face fell a little, but Gage didn't change his mind. "Maybe next time." Gage headed over to the door and Joseph followed, looking a little bewildered. Pulling it open, he gave Joseph a quick kiss on the cheek. "I'll call you." He closed the door behind him and left.

CHAPTER 12

Joseph sat at his desk at work. Every time he moved he felt a delicious soreness in his muscles. It made him think back to the amazing sex he'd had last night, just like Gage said he would. Joseph wanted to enjoy the reminder, but he couldn't. The way Gage had left had him confused this morning. *I'll call you.* He was no idiot. That normally meant that the guy had no intention of calling. He should know, he'd said the same himself a few times.

He didn't get it. The first time they'd had sex Gage had been very lover-like afterwards, giving him the sweetest kisses before he'd left. Last night he'd left abruptly. Joseph admitted to himself that he was kind of hurt at the change, especially if it meant what he thought it meant, that Gage was blowing him off. Taking a chance on a man he was attracted to but unsure of hadn't been easy for him. Joseph would be disappointed if things between them ended so soon. He didn't want to jump the gun though, so he decided to wait a few days to see if Gage did call before he assumed the worse.

****

"I'm assuming the worst." It was a few days later and Joseph was at lunch with a co-worker. Lila was a cute young paralegal with pale skin, long dark hair and retro cat-eye frame glasses. She'd tried to hit on him when he first joined the firm, but after he'd told her upfront that he was gay she'd immediately backed off. Now they were friends. She tried to set him up on dates, most of which he'd avoided. So she'd been really surprised when he told her that he was going out with the bike mechanic her brother recommended to him.

"Why don't you call him?"

"I don't want him to know I'm wondering if we're done."

"Why not? How else will you know if you guys *are* done?"

Joseph leaned back in the booth. She had a point. "He said he'd call me and he hasn't. I'll look like an idiot if I call him up and see what's up. I might as well ask your brother to give him a note that says, *Do you like me? Circle yes or no.*"

Lila laughed and pushed her long hair over her shoulder. "I wish we could do that. Dating would be so much simpler. Seriously, just call him, Joey. Don't agonize like a chic. Be upfront about it."

Joseph grinned. "I definitely don't want to act like a chic. If I agonized over stuff as much as you ladies do I'd never get anything done," he teased.

Lila took a slow sip of her drink. "How long have you been *agonizing* over whether or not you should call Gage?"

The grin dropped from his mouth. "Shut up."

Lila just laughed.

CHAPTER 13

Gage was irritated. It was strange to feel that way during his current activity. But it was true. The girl beneath him was too fucking loud. She sounded like a low-budget porn star. And her mouth was gooped with so much lip gloss that he couldn't kiss her even if he wanted to. Which he didn't. As he looked at that mouth, opened wide and shellacked in what looked like Dime Store Whore Red, his mind wandered to Joseph. Joseph and that pretty mouth of his, and the wonderful sounds that came from it. Curses and moans and soft little panting breaths. That's what he really wanted. Not this girl doing her best impression of an audition for Red Tube. He stopped moving. The girl beneath him kept up with her yowling until he went ahead and withdrew. She finally stopped and looked at him.

"What's the matter, baby? Was I not into it enough for you?"

"Oh no, you're definitely into it." He wasn't surprised when she didn't catch his sarcasm.

She smiled and reached for him. "Then let's keep going."

Gage avoided her grasping hands and lightly slapped her on the thigh before he got up from the bed. "Nah. I've got shit to do," he said as he headed into the bathroom. He heard her incredulous sounding voice behind him.

"What? You're just gonna leave me here like this?"

Gage snapped off the condom and dropped it in the trash can. He hadn't even been close to coming. He washed his hands before he came back out to pull on his clothes and boots. "Yep. But I'm sure you've got something in your nightstand that can pick up where I left off. I'll let myself out."

****

Two days later and Gage was still irritated. By now it was a constant burn beneath his skin. Everything pissed him off. He was trying real hard not to snap at everyone who came into his shop. Danny, the guy who worked there for him, had stepped in on more than one occasion to keep him from blowing up at a customer for asking a dumb question or the parts delivery guy for being late.

Gage needed to get this seething anger out of his system, but nothing was working. He'd smoked cigarette after cigarette. Nothing. He'd hit the gym. Nothing. Then he'd hit the streets for a run. Still nothing. He wanted to punch somebody in the face. That would help. Well, that or fuck somebody. But he'd tried that with the little blonde and it hadn't worked. Instead, he'd wound up thinking about Joseph. That had never happened to him before and it made him even more goddamn frustrated.

Joseph had no business being in his head like that. That was the whole reason he hadn't called him and had hooked up with that girl. He'd been trying to get Joseph out of his head, trying to prove that there was nothing special about him. Nothing to cause him to hang around after sex, kissing like he was some sorta chump. "He's just another warm body," he said beneath his breath.

He would find somebody and he would fuck them until they screamed. That would help. Maybe a redhead with big tits. That usually got him going. Or maybe he'd find a pretty boy. Like Joseph. Someone with dark hair and big green eyes. Like Joseph. Suddenly a picture bloomed in his head of Joseph in his lap with his head thrown back, that curly brown hair swinging behind him as he rode his cock. Gage was hard almost instantly. "Goddamnit!" His hand clenched into a fist as he tried to push that image away.

He looked intently at the screen, trying to focus on work. But then he saw that he'd fucked up. Majorly fucked up. He'd typed in the wrong column, erasing all the formulas necessary for balancing orders. That created a trickle-down effect, screwing up everything that was related to those equations. Gage slammed his fist onto the counter. "Motherfucker!" He smacked the cup full of logo pens off the counter, sending it flying across the garage. "Goddamnit!"

Danny, who was across the garage working on a bike, stopped what he was doing and looked up. "Hey man. Do I need to leave?"

Danny had permission to take off whenever Gage felt like he was losing it so that they didn't have any altercations. Gage took several deep breaths. "No. You're fine. Just ignore me." But he cursed again as his cell rang. He pulled it out of his pocket and saw Joseph's number on the screen. "On second thought, go ahead and take off." Gage unlocked his phone to answer. He had a feeling he wasn't going to be any calmer after this call.

****

Joseph hated that he was nervous. But he had to do this. He liked Gage and sensed that they could have fun together. But with the way Gage had left after their last time together, Joseph wasn't sure if Gage felt the same way. It had been over a week and he couldn't stand wondering anymore. He needed to know, so he picked up the phone and made the call. The connection was made after three rings. "Hey Gage, it's Joseph."

Gage's voice sounded different as he responded, almost like it was vibrating with anger. "Joseph. What's up?"

"Nothing. I was wrapping up my day at work and thought I'd call to see how you were."

"Yeah. Sorry 'bout that. Been busy at the shop and trying to take care of things."

"Really? What's going on?" he asked, trying to get Gage to elaborate.

"I'm trying to get this paperwork done and I've managed to both fall behind and fuck it up. Shop's always crazy at the start of summer when everyone starts taking their bikes out. Everybody wants their shit tuned up so they can ride and they all want it now."

Joseph felt a little bit of relief. Maybe it had just been work that kept Gage from calling. But even as he thought that he knew he was kidding himself. That didn't explain his abrupt departure that night. Plus, Gage had to have had at least five spare minutes to call him over the past week. He decided to give him a chance to either show he was still interested or blow him off for good. "I could swing by after work and help out if you want. I can't do anything with the bikes obviously, but maybe I can help with the paperwork side of things."

"I'd love to see you, Joseph. You can come over if you'd like. Keep me company while I take care of shit."

His relief growing, Joseph answered. "Okay. I'll be there soon."

CHAPTER 14

J oseph pulled up to Gage's shop. He hadn't gone home to change so he was still in his suit. But that didn't matter, like he'd said he wasn't there to work on any bikes so he should be fine. The door rolled up, closing behind him after he'd ridden inside. He took his helmet off and looked to see Gage leaning against the door frame of his office. He was the picture perfect image of the sexy mechanic. Messy dark hair and jaw rough with five o'clock shadow. His work shirt was open, showing the oil stained white t-shirt beneath. Jeans that looked faded and soft from numerous washings hugged his hips, clinging to his thighs. Joseph met Gage's dark eyes, watching as a slow smile curled his lips. Joseph quickly looked away. He didn't want this sexy bad boy to know how affected he was until they'd settled things between them.

"You came."

Joseph walked over to his office. Gage stepped out of the way to let him inside. "You sounded like you were having a pretty tough day. Like I said, I'm here to help if I can."

Gage looked at Joseph standing there in his light brown suit, the color a complement to the honey gold of his skin. His hair was slicked back into the neat ponytail he wore at work. He needed Joseph's help, but it wasn't with any fucking paperwork. He needed to get this furious energy out. And Joseph was here. In his shop where they were alone. And he was all prim and proper in his corporate world clothes. Maybe it was time to get him a little dirty.

"You can help me." He approached Joseph slowly. Deliberately. Joseph took one look at him before his eyes widened and he started to back up. But before he hit the wall behind him he stopped, his chin coming up.

"I hope you don't think I'm about to have sex with you after you pretty much blew me off."

Gage tilted his head to the side, a slow smile on his mouth. "Really? You're not gonna have sex with me. Then why are you here?"

"I told you, to help you with work."

Gage closed the last bit of free space between them, bringing their chests together. He kept going until he had Joseph backed up against the wall and brought his hand up to grasp the side of his neck. He hadn't had a chance to wash his hands yet and the grime from the bike he'd been working on was still on him. He didn't care. He rubbed it onto the smooth skin of Joseph's neck and smeared it across his cheek with his thumb.

"There's only one way you can help me, Joseph." He ground his swiftly hardening shaft against him. "I think you know that." Joseph started to shake his head, but Gage grabbed his ponytail and held him still. He pressed his lips to Joseph's, but he didn't open up and let him in. Again Gage didn't care. He just kept kissing him, smashing their lips together, until finally Joseph's lips parted. Whether it was from the pressure or the urge to take a deep breath, he didn't know. But he took full advantage of it, plunging his tongue in before Joseph could close his mouth again. Still, Joseph wouldn't kiss him back. He tried to turn his head away, but Gage held him tightly by his hair, licking into his mouth and sucking on his tongue. Gage pressed his hips against Joseph's. He heard a small moan come from him, so quiet and quickly hushed he almost missed it. Gage moved his hips on him again, thrusting hard. Another moan. Then he felt Joseph's fingertips land lightly on his waist. Almost. He almost had him. He pressed their groins together tight then circled his hips, knowing that Joseph liked that. It worked. Joseph gave a deep groan, his hands sliding up his back. And he was finally kissing him back. Gage indulged in several deep, long kisses before he pulled away.

Gage ran his hand up the lapel of Joseph's suit jacket, leaving a trail of black grime on the light fabric. "Huh… Look what I did. Got you all dirty."

Joseph looked down and saw the damage to his suit. "Gage what the hell? Do you know how much this jacket cost?"

Gage ran his hand up the other lapel getting that one dirty too. "I don't know. How much?"

Joseph narrowed his eyes. "Four hundred dollars. And you just ruined it."

Gage pushed the jacket off his shoulders, letting it drop to the dirty ground. "That seems like a lot to pay for one piece of clothing." He tugged at the knot of Joseph's tie, getting dirt on the paisley patterned material as he pulled it loose. "And how 'bout this tie?" he asked as he pulled it free of Joseph's neck. "How much did it cost?"

Joseph gave him a price with anger snapping in his eyes. But Gage could tell. He knew that Joseph was turned on. He might be mad about the jacket, but he hadn't tried to get away before he did any more damage. He was staying right there, his hips subtly pressing against his. Gage leaned in and kissed him. He gripped Joseph's crisp white shirt in his fists. Gage looked into those eyes, seeing fury first and passion hiding just behind. "Looks like I'm gonna owe you a lot of money." He ripped the shirt open. Fabric tore, buttons popped off, and Joseph cursed loudly.

"Goddamnit!"

Gage had his lips on Joseph's, his tongue in his mouth, before the sound of his shout faded from the garage. He reached his hand down between them and swiftly opened Joseph's belt and pants. Gage shoved his hand inside, wrapping it around his shaft. Joseph groaned, his hips curling up to meet him. Gage wasn't surprised to find him already hard, he'd felt his erection pressing against his thigh. But Joseph's cock head was already slick, and Gage loved that discovery. He swirled his thumb in the silky liquid, wondering just what exactly had gotten Joseph so turned on. He started pumping him, his hand moving tight and fast. There wasn't going to be anything slow with what was about to happen between them.

Gage lapped at the dirt he'd left on Joseph's neck. It tasted grimy, but beneath it he could taste the warm sweetness of Joseph's skin. "I got you dirty here too, Joseph. Do I have to buy you a fancy expensive soap so you can get clean again?" Joseph was panting, his face flushed as he arched up into his hand, but he wasn't cowed by Gage's goading.

"Fuck you."

Gage smiled. "Language, Counselor Naderi." He spun Joseph around so that his front was pressed to the wall. He sucked two fingers of one hand into his mouth while he squeezed and plumped Joseph's firm ass with the other. When his fingers were wet enough, he slipped one into his ass, Joseph groaning his name as he did. Gage pumped his finger in and out swiftly, his knuckles coming up against Joseph's smooth flesh each time.

"What Joseph? You wanna tell me the price of your designer underwear next?" Gage saw a muscle flex in Joseph's jaw before he answered.

"No. Add another finger."

"Fuck adding another finger. You're getting my cock." Gage stepped away from him for a moment to go to his desk drawer. He rummaged around for only a second before he came up with a condom and lube. When he turned back, Joseph was facing him instead of the wall as he'd left him. Gage opened his jeans as he walked back to him, pulling his cock out and stroking himself slowly as he went. "Turn back around," he ordered. Joseph did it. Slowly, but he did. When he was behind him again, he pushed Joseph's pants down his legs. He stroked a hand over his hip, knowing he'd have to prepare him. He planned to fuck him through that wall, but he didn't want to hurt him.

Gage dropped to his knees behind Joseph, and with a hand on each round cheek, spread his ass apart. He didn't play around with soft licks. He just shoved his tongue inside. Joseph grunted once, but he thrust his ass back against his face. Gage smoothed a hand from Joseph's ass, around his hip to grasp his cock. He started pumping him again, just as fast as before. In no time at all, Joseph was cursing and shaking, his muscles clenching as he thrust his hips forward to fuck into his fist, then back onto his tongue.

After working him good, Gage felt Joseph start to loosen up. He pulled back and let him go so he could put the condom on. Once he was sheathed and had lubed them both, he stood up and pushed into Joseph with one deep stroke. Gage didn't pause or let him adjust. He just started fucking into him hard and fast, his pelvis slapping and rubbing against Joseph's naked ass with each thrust. Joseph started to push back against him, but Gage rammed into him hard, pressing him up against the wall. He leaned against Joseph's back and rubbed his lips against his ear. "No, don't fucking move. Just take it, Joseph." He gripped his ponytail tightly. "Just let me fuck you. You wanted to help. This is what I need. Let me use you."

Joseph moaned in protest, wanting to move, but he did as Gage asked. He spread his legs but otherwise he held still and let Gage take him. He didn't understand what was driving him, but it had him incredibly turned on, so he went with it. Gage's fist kept working his cock, his rough grunts sounding in his ear as he slammed into him again and again. Gage still had a grip on his hair, pulling his head back. It was uncomfortable to have his neck held in this position for so long and the wall was hard against his front. But that didn't stop his orgasm from rising, especially once Gage changed the angle of his movements and started hitting his prostate with each thrust. It felt unbelievably good. Felt primal and raw to be trapped this way, with Gage using his body for his lust. Joseph was moaning with nearly every breath, his skin tight and hot over his muscles. Gage released his hair and grasped his chin.

"You and that slutty fucking mouth. Come here."

Gage twisted his head around just enough for them to be able to engage in the roughest, sloppiest kiss Joseph had ever had. And he loved it. Loved it so much that he kept moaning, right into Gage's mouth. That seemed to urge Gage on until he was fucking into him with brutal strength and speed, his hand sliding just as fast on his cock.

Joseph's body was coiling tighter and tighter until he felt like he was going to explode. He reached behind him with one hand and dug his nails into Gage's hips, trying to bring him even closer, as if that were possible. Gage hissed as he clawed at his skin. He rammed forward in what was definitely retaliation. But Joseph didn't care because he struck his sweet spot dead-on at the same time Gage squeezed his shaft. The electric tension that had him so wound up cracked loose, sending his orgasm rushing up his shaft to burst forth, splattering the wall. Joseph didn't care because the pleasure of his release had him trembling and shouting Gage's name. His hips pumped back forth, regardless of Gage's order to keep still. He couldn't help it. It felt so good and he kept going until every drop had been wrung from him.

When his body relaxed and his head cleared of that burst of sensation that blocked all rational thought, he became aware of Gage cursing and breathing even harder behind him. Gage's hand slapped onto the wall next to his head, bracing himself as his body went rigid and he shouted out with his own release. Joseph just stayed there against the wall, loose and floating in a haze of pleasure, his body pulsing with sweet aftershocks. He moaned one last time as, through the thin layer of the condom, he felt the heat of Gage's cum swelling forth inside him.

****

Gage withdrew from him slowly and his footsteps went across the room. After a moment, Joseph pulled his pants up and turned around to face him. Gage was leaning against his desk, his jeans open. He'd removed and tossed the condom, but his shaft was still partially hard and shiny wet from his release. Joseph was surprised when Gage lit up a cigarette and inhaled. He hadn't known that he smoked. "What was that?" he asked.

Gage looked at him for a long moment, his eyes narrowed against the haze of smoke in front of his face. It seemed as if he were contemplating something. When he spoke, it wasn't to answer his question.

"I like the way you look right now. Messy, ripped, and dirty." He blew out a long puff of smoke, his mouth twisted into a smug smile. "I did that to you."

Joseph shook his head. He wasn't going to be sidetracked on this. "Gage, what *was* that? And for that matter, why did you blow me off before?"

Gage inhaled once more before he braced his hand next to him on the desk, letting the cigarette burn. A cloud of gray smoke streamed from his mouth as he spoke. "Come home with me and I'll tell you."

Joseph's brow creased in confusion. "What do you mean come home with you? Don't you live in the apartment above this building?"

Gage took a hard drag off the cigarette before dropping it to the floor and crushing it beneath his boot. "What, you think I can't afford a fucking house?"

Joseph straightened up. That was the second time Gage had made a comment like that to him and he already didn't like it. "Just how big is this chip on your shoulder, Mason? I need to know so I don't keep accidentally bumping into it. I only asked that because you made it seem like you lived here with some of your comments. So don't give me that."

Gage looked Joseph over appreciatively as his temper made another appearance. He liked that. It didn't look like Joseph would be a pussy and put up with too much of his bullshit. He didn't apologize for his comment, but he did explain a little bit. "I don't live here. I rent it out but keep a few things for myself up there. I have a house not too far. Come home with me."

Joseph looked down at himself. "I can't get on my bike with my shirt ripped up like this."

Gage's lips twitched. "You can wear a Mason Bike Shop work shirt. It'll go great with your pants, which no doubt cost two hundred dollars."

Joseph's eyes narrowed. "You're replacing all of that."

Gage laughed. "I'll take you shopping, pretty boy."

CHAPTER 15

They'd arrived at Gage's place. It was a two story house. Joseph guessed it was nice. He didn't get to see much of it because Gage hustled him up the stairs to his bedroom. Once they were there, Gage started pulling his borrowed shirt over his head. Joseph allowed it, but he still wanted his answers. "Are you going to tell me now what prompted that madness in your garage?"

Gage threw his own shirt on the floor, then pulled off his boots and jeans. "Don't even try to pretend that you didn't like it."

"I didn't say that." Gage laid back on the bed on top of a rich black comforter. Joseph stood there waiting. He wasn't getting into bed with Gage until he got some answers. Gage finally got the hint because he sighed and started talking.

"I have an addiction." Gage laughed. "Actually I have an addictive personality. And I also have a *small* problem with anger."

Joseph could tell by the emphasis Gage put on the word small that he was being sarcastic. "What do you mean?"

"Sometimes I get so goddamn worked up that I can't calm down. The rage just stays there, constantly under my skin, burning and aggravating me unless I do something to fucking release it. Other times it just hits me out of nowhere and I fucking lose it. Just immediately lose it. When I was younger, I used to get into fights all the time. Someone would set me off and I'd be all over the son of a bitch."

Joseph had sensed a wildness in Gage from the moment they'd met, so this confession didn't surprise him too much. And he could picture a young Gage constantly getting into fights in school. He'd known a kid like that in middle school who had a hair trigger. His parents had taken him to see a counselor and had him enrolled in activities to learn to deal with his emotions. "Your parents didn't try to get you any help?"

Gage laughed. "My mom died when I was three. My dad didn't know anything about raising kids, so he passed me off to his parents and took off for parts unknown. But they were older. Grandpa Mason died and Grandma Mason ended up in assisted living. I was a ward of the state by the time I was nine. In the children's homes and fosters where I grew up, there wasn't time or inclination to care about one kid and his anger problems."

Joseph couldn't help but feel sympathy at the rough childhood he imagined Gage experiencing. Looking at the tense way Gage held himself, Joseph could tell he was uncomfortable with the subject. "I'm sorry, Gage. That sounds like an awful way to grow up."

"It is what it is," Gage said with a shrug. "Anyway, in eleventh grade I beat the holy hell out of this guy. He was bigger than me and a year older, but I kicked the crap out of him. His parents pressed charges. I was still a minor but narrowly avoided jail time by agreeing to go to anger management. It was just a bunch of bullshit about finding your inner chi or some shit and as soon as I was done with the court prescribed time, I didn't go back. But I knew I needed to find a way to handle my anger or I might not be lucky enough to avoid jail the next time. I turned to drugs. Anything to keep me calm and mellow. First it was weed. But that's a gateway drug, right?"

Joseph flinched as Gage laughed mockingly. He didn't know why, but it bothered him to hear Gage describing his life, which had clearly been a struggle, in such a nonchalant tone.

"After that it was Valium, Xanax, whatever. But I didn't always want to be brought down. Sometimes I wanted to be up. Way fucking up. I bypassed bush league shit and shot straight to cocaine to help with that. It wasn't until a good friend of mine died from a drug overdose that I realized I was killing myself. So I stopped. Cold turkey. It was hell and I wanted to kill everybody around me and a lot of times myself, but I finally made it. I got the drugs out of my system, but the anger was still there. It was my friend Max who suggested an alternative way to deal with it."

"What's that?"

"Sex. Lots of sex. With lots of different people. Whenever I start feeling like I want to rip somebody's head off, I put all that energy into sex. And when I come I let it all out. I keep going, keep fucking until I'm calm again." He shrugged. "It works for me. I don't have an expensive drug habit anymore and I'm able to get shit done, like own a small business."

Joseph was beyond shocked. He didn't bother asking how many people Gage had slept with. He didn't want to know. But he was a little pissed off. "You should have told me this before," he said with some anger in his voice.

Gage shrugged again. "I didn't plan on things going the way they have with you, Joseph. But I'm careful if that worries you. I don't have any diseases or babies."

That last word grabbed Joseph's attention. "Babies? You're bisexual?"

Gage snorted. "I like to fuck. Gender is irrelevant."

Joseph let it go. That was hardly the big issue here. "Why are you telling me this now?"

"Because I like you, Joseph. I want to spend time with you, not just call you up when I need to fuck somebody like I do with everyone else. And I thought you should know all this so you can decide if you want to hang around." He shrugged. "I've never told any of my partners this. They just know that I like to have sex and I like to keep things casual, no strings, and that they're not the only one. If they're down with it, great. We can both have a good time when we want. If they're not, it's no big deal, I move on."

Joseph stood there for a long moment, thinking over everything Gage had said. He'd need more time to process all of this later, but for right now he only had one question. "So you just told *me* all this. Does that mean … are you saying that you want *us* to be exclusive?"

Gage didn't say anything for a time. Then he lowered his head, looking up at him from beneath his lashes. Again Joseph thought that Gage looked dangerous. A chill chased across his skin as he imagined what Gage was like when he lost his temper. Gage finally spoke, but it was by no means a definitive answer.

"Let's just see how this goes." Gage held his hand up, gesturing for him to take it.

Joseph hesitated. Should he go with this? Maybe this is why he'd been hesitant about Gage, he'd sensed that he wasn't one to be in a relationship. It would probably be for the best if he went back down the stairs, hopped on his bike, and didn't look back. But as he looked at Gage lying there, with his hard muscles and messy, dark hair, he wanted to stay. Maybe … maybe this would go well if he took a chance and let it happen.

Gage crooked his finger at him. "C'mon, Joseph. Stop thinking and just be with me."

Gage hadn't really answered his question about being exclusive and that worried him. But he still raised his hand to meet Gage's, letting him pull him down onto the bed. And when Gage rolled him underneath him, his mouth on his in a deep kiss, Joseph let that worry go out of his head.

CHAPTER 16

S pecial delivery!"

Gage looked over his shoulder. Two men had just walked into the garage carrying pizza boxes and plastic bags. He stood up with a grin. "How many bozos does it take to deliver a pizza?"

The first of the two was a handsome, dark-skinned Black man. He was slightly shorter than Gage and was dressed in jeans and a dark ribbed tank. Intricate tattoos covered his muscular arms and chest. He laughed as they came his way.

"Be glad it's two of us. If it was just Nate you'd be eating a sauce-less, cheese-less veggie pizza."

The other, Nate, was a tall, blonde. His close fitting work-out shirt and pants revealed the hard muscles he'd developed in underground fighting clubs and in the gym. "C'mon now, boys. I'd let you keep the sauce. But the dough would have to go. Too many carbs."

Gages eyebrows shot up. "So I'd be eating broccoli sitting on top of a puddle of tomato goo?" He looked at Max. "You're right. I am glad it took two of you."

They all laughed as they set up the food and drinks in Gage's office. Pizza and soda for him and Max, grilled chicken and water for Nate. They might not all share the same eating habits, but they had a lot in common and had been friends for years. He and Max had both grown up in the system. They'd spent several years at the same boy's home, somehow striking up a friendship despite the fact that neither of them trusted easily. Nate wasn't an orphan, but he had been an outcast at their high school. Scrawny, friendless and gay, Nate had been an easy target for bullies. Gage and Max had come upon Nate being terrorized in the locker room one day. They'd jumped in and put a stop to it. After that, Nate had run with them and they'd made it clear that anyone who picked on Nate would have to deal with them. Now they were a decade out of high school, but they still all ran together.

Napkins were passed around and they started eating. As usual they jokingly discussed all the issues they had being business owners. Gage had his shop of course, while Max owned a tattoo studio and Nate, a fitness empire.

"This cuddly Grandma came in with her granddaughter, wanting a tattoo. I was congratulating her on getting her first ink when she whipped off her shirt and showed me this massive piece on her back." Max shook his head. "That's what I get for stereotyping."

Gage's lip twitched as he held back a smile. "Yeah, I'm learning that what's on the outside might be hiding something real interesting underneath." He saw Max and Nate exchange a glance right before Nate opened his mouth.

"Alright, Gage. What's up? You're looking pretty smug over there."

"Yeah, even more so than usual." Max rumbled in his deep voice.

Gage took another bite of pizza, making his friends wait while he chewed and swallowed. "I met somebody," he finally answered.

Max rolled his eyes and Nate leaned back in his chair. "Well shit. You always meet somebody. You meet several somebodies a week."

"Shut up, Nate." Gage glared at his friend. "This somebody is different."

"Different, huh? So is it serious?" Max asked.

"No. We're just hanging out."

"So then how is it different?"

"Damn, Max. I didn't know I was going to have to declare my intentions," Gage snapped. "I'm just mentioning it because he's fucking pretty. And I told him my background and he's cool with it, which means I get to have amazing sex with him whenever I want. That's all."

"Wow," Nate said, with his gray eyes wide. "You never tell any of your play toys that. You sure it's not something more?"

Gage looked at his friends, sorry he'd even brought Joseph up. "I'm sure. It's just physical."

CHAPTER 17

Later that night, Gage lay back on Joseph's bed. Joseph was in the living room taking a call from his office. After work, Gage had gone home for a quick shower and change of clothes and come straight over. He'd been eager to get here, to the point where he'd wanted to leave work early. He'd refused to do that. He had, however, decided to just go with the attraction he had to Joseph. From the moment Joseph had walked into the garage last night, Gage realized just how much he wanted him. He figured it was stupid to fight it. Like he'd told Max and Nate, it was only physical anyway. And if Joseph and his beautiful, deliciously tight body could give him what he needed, and Joseph was willing to go along with it, he might as well enjoy it. That's why he'd decided to come clean with him. Gage realized if Joseph were going to be around him he was going to need to understand the way he was with sex. When the time came where he felt like he needed someone else, well he'd cross that bridge when he got to it.

He looked up as Joseph came into the room, finished with his call. Gage took one look at his face and could see that he had something on his mind. He waited until Joseph sat on the bed before he asked. "What's up?"

"So, how does it work exactly?"

"What do you mean?"

"Using sex to control your anger. How does that work?"

Gage snorted. "What am I, a therapist?"

Joseph's voice sharpened. "I'm serious, Gage. If you're asking me to go along with this, I think I should know more."

Gage looked at Joseph and saw that he really was serious. He glanced away and thought for a moment, trying to put things together in a way that made sense. "When I get that anger, that fucking anger that streaks through me, clouding my head and making my fingers burn with the urge to destroy something, I have to have a release for it. It won't just go away on its own. I could let it explode in a fight with whoever sets me off. But that's careless and dangerous like I told you. So I find a sexual partner. And I take all that furious energy and focus it on them, on the things I'm doing to them." Gage looked up again to find Joseph watching him, worry in those amazing eyes of his. He could see that Joseph still wasn't sure about this, so he set out to put him at ease. Gage reached out to Joseph's thigh, stroking it lightly.

"You know how during sex you just blank out on everything besides the person you're tangled up with? All you can think about is how good everything feels." He teased his fingers up under Joseph's t-shirt caressing the smooth skin of his back, making him shiver. "You think about how hot your skin is." He gripped the neck of Joseph's t-shirt in his other hand and pulled him down until their lips met. "The way their tongue feels in your mouth," he whispered just before he kissed him slow and deep. Gage moved to pull Joseph further onto the bed while they kissed, turning him so that he was lying on his back. Gage eased back and looked into Joseph's eyes, now wide with anticipation. Pressing a finger to his lips, he felt Joseph's rapid breaths hot against his skin. "You get excited and start breathing just like this." He pushed Joseph's shirt up and off, tossing it to the side, and pressed his palm to his chest. "Your heart is pounding, pumping hot, thick blood straight down to your cock." Gage slid his hand into Joseph's sweats. "You're hard, and all you want is for your lover to take you in their hand and stroke you." He matched action to words, gripping Joseph's cock in his fist and stroking. Joseph's eyes drifted shut, his hips curling up to meet his pumping fist.

Gage slid down Joseph's body, pulling off his sweats as he went. "Maybe you want them to run their tongue along this vein." He licked his tongue along the thick pulsing vein running up the underside of Joseph's cock. "Or here across your cock head." Gage lapped at the broad head, getting the taste of his lover's pre-cum on his tongue. He continued on. "Maybe you want them to suck you into their mouth." The room grew quiet except for the sounds of Joseph's soft moans as Gage took him into his mouth, sucking him slowly. He kept going, moving his mouth up and down the thickness of Joseph's shaft, wrapping his lips tight around the head. When Joseph's fingers crept into his hair, Gage stopped and lightly shook him off. He pushed Joseph's legs open to cup his balls, squeezing and feeling how heavy they were in his palm.

"By now your balls are tight, full of cum. Isn't that right?" Joseph groaned a rough yes, his hips rising and falling in a smooth wave. "But here's where you and I differ." Gage grabbed the lube he'd placed on the nightstand earlier and coated two fingers with the warming liquid. He teased his finger against Joseph's entrance, pressing lightly. "You want my cock deep inside you." Joseph moaned as he slid one finger inside his tight channel. "Want me fucking you hard, making your body shake underneath mine." Gage worked another finger inside him, pumping them in and out gently.

"And I want to feel your tight ass squeezing my cock while I pound into you. Make you moan and squirm as you try to take the fucking I'm giving you." He scissored his fingers, then pressed in deep until Joseph's hips jerked up with a sharp cry. Gage smiled. There. He kept his fingers pressed against that spot, making Joseph writhe in pleasure beneath him. "But the end result is the same." He pulled his fingers out to reach for a condom, and continued talking as he rolled it on. "When we come, we won't be thinking about anything else. Nothing but that sweet release will be in your head as your body trembles beyond your control." Gage pushed into Joseph slowly. "And then, when you're finished, you're tired and you just want to rest and enjoy the last little tremors of pleasure.

And all that furious energy is just … gone." Gage pulled his hips back and pushed forward again. "Does that make sense?"

Joseph nodded. "Yes, but..."

"But what?"

Joseph licked his bottom lip and took a moment before he asked, "But why more than one person?"

Gage leaned down and kissed Joseph deeply, sucking on his lip before slowly letting go. He looked into Joseph's eyes and spoke the truth. "Because I don't ever want anyone to get too attached." A spark of hurt flashed in those sea-green depths, but Gage closed his eyes to it. And before Joseph could say anything else Gage kissed him again, hard and aggressively this time. He was done talking about it. Gage started moving his hips back and forth in shallow thrusts, trying to work his cock in further. Joseph was still really tight. The grip felt good on his cock, but he couldn't get as deep as he wanted. Gage ended their kiss, trailing his lips over Joseph's jaw until he reached his ear.

Gage coaxed his lover into doing what he wanted with hushed whispers in his ear. "Relax. Stop thinking about it. Just open up for me." A shiver ran through Joseph as Gage delicately licked the shell of his ear. "I want to go deeper. I need my cock all the way inside you. And I know you want me deeper so I can hit that spot that makes you moan. So relax." Joseph groaned and raised his legs, squeezing his knees against Gage's sides. Gage quickly changed position, hooking his arms under Joseph's knees and forcing his legs up even further. Gage returned to kissing him, sliding his tongue into his mouth slowly, again and again, until finally with a soft moan Joseph completely relaxed beneath him.

"*Fuck*." Gage cursed on a long exhale as his cock sank all the way into the snug heat of Joseph's ass. He held there for a moment, just enjoying the feel of his cock throbbing inside those tight walls. Joseph moaned when he started moving and Gage looked at him. That heavy-lidded look of desire was in his eyes, his lips parted slightly. "You look like you love this, Joseph. Do you?" Joseph nodded slowly and Gage smiled. "I know you do. I can tell by the way your pretty eyes turn hazy and lost, looking to me to make you feel good." Gage pushed into him hard, hard enough to move Joseph's body on the bed, making his hair slide on the pillow. Joseph's arms came up, wrapping around his shoulders in a tight embrace. Gage licked at his lover's mouth. "Yeah, you should hold on. Because I'm about to fuck you hard, pretty boy."

Joseph tightened his arms even more. "Good, because that's what I want," he said in a breathless whisper.

Gage grabbed onto Joseph's hair on either side of his head, wrapping the curly strands around his fists. And he gave it to him hard, fucking into him with swift tight strokes. Only his hips moved. He kept his torso pressed against Joseph's, pinning him down with his weight. And with his legs tangled up with Gage's arms and his hair in his fists, Joseph wasn't going anywhere. Still, he managed to roll his hips up, fucking himself onto his cock as much as he was able, moans falling from his lips with increasing frequency.

Gage felt a rush of pleasure that he had this beautiful man beneath him like this, so open and eager. He couldn't recall ever being as attracted to anyone as he was to Joseph. He moved his lips to Joseph's neck, sucking the soft skin into his mouth and pulling hard as he kept pounding into him. His cock slid in and out of Joseph so easily now, but he was still gripped tight, that sweet friction making his shaft tingle and his balls ache. Joseph pushed his hips up and squeezed his inner muscles around him. Gage shuddered and groaned against Joseph's neck. "Do that again."

Joseph dug his fingers into his back. "What, this?" he asked as he squeezed him again.

"Yes, *that*. Do it again." Gage cursed, his eyes nearly rolling back in his head at how good it felt as Joseph immediately obeyed him. "Again, Joseph." Gage kissed Joseph hungrily when he felt that sweet clench on his cock. "Again." His movements were rough as he thrust into Joseph's ass. Both their bodies grew slick with sweat, their breaths hot and heavy against their lips as they kissed. Joseph squeezed him once more, somehow even tighter. "Fuck!" Gage cursed into Joseph's mouth. "Again. *Again*."

Gage kept kissing Joseph deep and wild, sucking on his tongue. And Joseph gave it right back, biting at his lip and sucking it into his mouth. As their bodies slammed together, Joseph was squeezing him so damn tight it felt like he wouldn't be able to withdraw each time. But he did, pulling out and ramming back into him over and over until his lower back was tingling with the urge to come. Gage yanked on the hair he held as he surged up hard into his lover. Joseph cried out in pain, but immediately after he was kissing him even wilder than before. Gage took notice and kept pulling on the silky hair in his fists, their kiss growing even deeper and more frantic as he did. He felt Joseph's shaft stiff and wet against his stomach, but he purposely didn't reach down and stroke him off.

Gage barely had any control over his movements as he thrust faster and faster before he finally stiffened, his cock throbbing as his release streaked up from his sac in a hot rush. His fingers clenched tight in Joseph's hair as he threw back his head and exploded, Joseph's name a shout on his lips. He continued moving his hips, riding the waves of pleasure crashing through him and over him until he was completely spent. But he knew Joseph hadn't come yet, just like he'd planned.

He withdrew from Joseph carefully, ignoring his protests. Those protests dried up as Gage moved down and lapped his tongue across his lover's slick cock head. And when he started sucking him, nothing came out of Joseph's mouth except for moans.

CHAPTER 18

Joseph was trembling, just on the verge of orgasm. Gage had fucked him good and now he was sucking his cock in the most deliciously dirty way. Joseph watched as Gage licked his tongue out, swirling it in the liquid beaded on his cock head. When he pulled his tongue back, a long line of his pre-cum came with him, until Gage licked his lips and sucked it into his mouth. Joseph couldn't take his eyes off of Gage as that pink tongue darted forth again, making long lazy laps along his shaft. Gage rubbed his face on his cock as he licked down to his balls. The light stubble on his jaw tickled and made Joseph's stomach jump. Gage looked up and caught him watching.

"Yeah, that's it. Watch me Joseph. It'll make all this feel a hundred times better, I promise you." Gage licked him again. "So keep those eyes on me."

Joseph was happy to do as he was told, watching as Gage's lips closed over his cock, sucking him slowly. Gage pushed at his thighs and he parted them without protest, crying out with pleasure as two of Gage's fingers pushed inside him. Joseph lifted his legs, resting them on Gage's shoulders, pulling him even closer. Gage grabbed one of Joseph's hands from where he had it pressed onto the bed beside him. He guided to it to his cock, positioning his fingers so that only the forefinger and thumb supported him at the base, leaving room for that sinful mouth to suck along his entire shaft.

Now that Gage had both hands free, he reached down and cupped Joseph's balls, squeezing and rolling them in his palm. Joseph was more than trembling now. He was shaking from all the stimulation, his body tingling from head to toe. He pumped his hips up again and again, wanting all of it. He wanted Gage's fingers thrusting in his ass. Wanted his hand squeezing his aching balls that were so tight and full he thought he was going to burst. And that mouth. Fuck he wanted that mouth on him. Gage sucked him swiftly, his head bobbing up and down. His mouth was hot and wet on his cock, his lips making the most erotic sucking noises Joseph had ever heard. His orgasm was teasing at his cockhead when Gage pulled back. Joseph pushed his hips up, unashamedly moaning in protest.

Gage flicked his tongue over his sensitive slit. "I want you to come in my mouth Joseph. I bet you taste as slutty as you look right now with your legs tossed over my shoulders and your cock standing straight up, all shiny and wet."

Joseph groaned at Gage's words. He tried to hold back, tried to enjoy this amazing head just a little longer. But he couldn't. Gage was working him too damn good. His orgasm came rocketing up his shaft with his next breath. He wasn't even inside Gage's mouth when he started to come. But at his first spurt, Gage surged up, catching his cum with his tongue. Then he swallowed his cock back into his mouth. Joseph kept coming and Gage kept sucking him hard, still rolling his balls in his hand, his fingers still moving inside him. The feeling grew so intense that his head was blank to everything but that sweet buzzing pleasure. Pleasure that practically blinded him as his vision blurred. His breaths were so harsh they felt like they were being ripped from his throat until finally he lost all control and started shouting, "Gage! Oh god, suck me! Suck me!" Gage pushed his mouth even further down on his cock, pressing his finger hard against that bundle of nerves inside him. Joseph screamed a curse as his cock, his whole body, throbbed with one last deep pulse of pleasure.

****

Joseph lay there on the bed. He wasn't capable of moving. His arms, his legs, nothing moved. He couldn't even open his eyes. If breathing weren't automatic, his chest would have been still too. But he felt it rising and falling with his deep, shaky breaths. Every so often a whimper slipped from his throat as a shiver ran through him. Gage shifted next to him and Joseph lazily dragged his eyes open to look at him.

"Do you see what I mean now?"

Joseph breathed in deeply, then exhaled in a long drawn out sigh before answering. "Yes. But you could probably get the same release from playing sports or something."

Gage smirked. "Fuck sports. They only make me more aggressive." Gage looked down and trailed his fingers over his softened but still sensitive shaft. "And just so you know, sometimes I need that release more than once a night." Gage looked back at him. The messy hair falling into his eyes didn't conceal the wicked heat glinting in their chocolate brown depths. "Like tonight."

Joseph's eyebrows shot up. "Seriously?"

Gage smiled, the slowest, cockiest smile he'd ever seen in his life. "Seriously."

Gage's hand continued to tease along his cock, and surprisingly Joseph felt himself start to harden. However, he wasn't surprised when Gage's smile turned to one of knowing satisfaction. His voice came out in that low smoky tone that sent tingles down his spine.

"Turn over."

It took a moment for Joseph to get his muscles to cooperate. But eventually he turned over.

CHAPTER 19

Joseph was at a race track some twenty miles outside the city. It was early in the morning, early enough that the sky was still tinged with gray. He was there with his bike. His Diavel wasn't just for show. Like he'd mentioned to Gage, he entered races when he could, time and finances permitting. He'd been racing off and on ever since his father bought him his first bike. He'd been allowed to learn to ride and race as long as he kept up with his studies and entered STU pre-law. Joseph smiled slightly to himself. He'd chafed at the qualifier then, but now as an adult he realized it was to his benefit that his father had ensured he received the best education. Cyrus Naderi could be reasonable about some things. Joseph just wished he could be reasonable about who his son chose to love.

He looked around the track as he waited his turn. Even though it was early, there was still a good crowd of racers there. There was a race next weekend, which meant everyone, including him, was there to take advantage of the open track time for practice. Hearing someone calling his name, Joseph looked over his shoulder. It was his friend Nico, wheeling his bike over.

"Hey, Nico. What's up?"

"Not much." Nico pushed his white-blonde dreads over his shoulder. Just got back from a sky diving trip."

Joseph raised an eyebrow. "That's all? That's pretty tame for you. I thought you'd been off bareback riding Great Whites."

Nico grinned. "No, but that sounds like a great idea. I might try that. So what's been going on with you? Haven't seen you around the track these past few weeks."

Joseph shrugged. "I've been seeing somebody."

Nico looked surprised. "You've been seeing someone? Someone who's managed to get you off your bike? Must be serious."

Joseph wanted to laugh. He knew Nico was joking with him, but all he could think of was that 'must be serious' comment. He didn't think it was serious with Gage. Well, Gage wouldn't let it be. He did a very good job of keeping things between them very casual, even though they'd been seeing each other steadily in the two weeks since Gage had explained his anger management "technique". While somehow without realizing it, Joseph had already moved past the 'just wanting to have fun with a sexy bad boy' phase to wanting something a little more serious. He was silent for so long Nico noticed something was off.

"Woah, looks like I struck a nerve. You alright?"

"Yeah, just…" He trailed off not knowing what to say. Besides, his turn was almost up. "I'm fine, just overthinking things." He started to put his helmet on, but Nico stopped him.

"I'm going for a run this evening. Come with me. You look like you could use some air to clear your head. Then you can tell me what's going on."

Joseph thought about it. It would feel good to run later when it was cool out. Nico was a good friend, whether it was just listening or giving no nonsense advice.

"Alright, I'll join you for a run." He smiled, trying to lighten his heavy mood. "I just hope you'll be able to keep up."

****

The evening air was cool and breezy against his sweaty skin as he ran with Nico. They were on a trail in the park. An early rising full moon hung heavy and golden in the sky, lighting their path. Joseph was glad he'd taken Nico up on his invitation. It felt free and relaxing to run like this, enjoying the way his feet pounded the ground and his muscles burned. He would have been completely at peace, if it weren't for the conversation currently taking place.

"So let me see if I have this right." Nico's words came out slightly rushed as they ran. "You guys are sleeping together. A lot. And he may or may not be sleeping with other people. He doesn't ever stay the night with you and he refuses to have any conversation with you about being exclusive."

Joseph kept his breathing even as he answered. "C'mon, man. It's not that bad. We do hang out."

Nico managed to pull off a snort. "Oh yeah, in between all the fucking you guys go and get a beer. How romantic. What do you two even have in common?"

"Do we have to have something in common? Besides, maybe I'm not looking for anything romantic or serious." Joseph ran for a few more steps before he realized he couldn't hear Nico running just behind him anymore. He slowed and looked back. Nico was standing there with his hands on his hips and an incredulous look on his face. Joseph walked back over to him, stretching his arms over his head as he went.

"You're kidding me, right? You can tell yourself you're just looking to have fun all you want. But you know you want more than that. You haven't ditched that much of your background, Joseph. You want a relationship, but with the right guy. That's why you ended your last one. And somehow I doubt this Gage Mason is capable of giving you what you want."

Joseph frowned. "Just because we're not serious now, doesn't mean we can't become serious later. Relationships, and the people in them do change."

Nico shook his head. "I don't know, Joseph. It's always been my experience that people don't change. They just grow more like themselves."

CHAPTER 20

Joseph sat in his living room. The stereo was on, playing the latest release from one of his favorite bands, while the baseball game was on mute on the TV. Joseph wasn't paying much attention to either of them. His mind was on the conversation he'd had with Nico the other night. He didn't know what to do about Gage. They had fun together and of course the sex was great, fucking amazing. But Gage managed to keep his distance. Like he'd told Nico, Gage never stayed the night. Joseph took his cue from that on the rare occasions when they were at Gage's, leaving before he got too comfortable and fell asleep. And Gage never tried to stop him. He'd tried to ask Gage if he was seeing anyone else. His answers of, 'Not right now.' or, 'Don't worry about that,' weren't exactly reassuring. But still, he stayed tangled up with him.

Joseph was nearly confident that Gage wasn't sleeping with anyone else. They were together nearly every night for one. Besides, even when Joseph wasn't able to have sex, Gage hadn't left to find someone else, he'd just found another way to get what he wanted. He remembered how after what had turned into a marathon sex session, he'd been sore. The next night he'd told Gage no when he started kissing him. But Gage had kept up with his kisses, touching him everywhere, until Joseph was hard and wishing he didn't have to turn him down. But he did. Gage had only smiled and led him back to his bedroom. Joseph kept protesting as Gage stripped them both. Gage laughed and told him to shut up before pushing him down on the bed. He'd started to get mad, thinking Gage was ignoring him. But that wasn't the case. Gage had maneuvered them so they could pleasure each other with their mouths at the same time. Gage had sucked him slowly, softly squeezing his balls, taking him to the edge again and again before finally allowing him to come. It had taken all the concentration Joseph had to keep up with Gage and return the pleasure he was receiving. Gage's mouth was so fucking talented that he'd wanted to just lie there and enjoy it. But he also enjoyed the feel of Gage's cock in his mouth, his hips pushing forward so that Joseph took him even deeper. And he definitely enjoyed Gage's taste as he released onto his tongue, his rough groan as he came …

Joseph was starting to get hard, his breath coming a little faster just thinking about it. He was shifting on the couch when he saw his phone light up with an incoming call. Seeing on the caller ID it was Gage, he used the remote to turn off the stereo.

"Hello."

"Joseph. What are you doing?"

"Nothing. Just sitting here watching baseball." He tried to bring his breathing back to normal and get the thickness of arousal out of his voice. He must not have been successful because there was a pause before Gage spoke again.

"Hmmm… that's not what it sounds like. You sure you're not *busy*?"

"No, I was just thinking."

Gage laughed softly. "Thinking about what, exactly?"

Joseph cleared his throat and changed the subject. "You called me. What's up?"

Gage laughed again, but he allowed the subject change. "Come bowling with me."

Joseph looked at the clock. It was already a quarter to ten. "Now? It's kind of late and I have to be at work in the morning."

"We won't stay out that late. C'mon, Joseph. I want to see you."

Joseph still hesitated. It was late. And he'd already been dragging at work lately. "I don't think so, Gage." But

Gage wouldn't take no for an answer. Actually he never did.

"C'mon, Joseph. My friends are all going bowling and I want you to hang with us. You'll have fun I promise."

Joseph was surprised. He hadn't met any of Gage's friends yet. It had seemed to be yet another way Gage was keeping distance between them. But now he was inviting him to meet them. Joseph looked at the clock again. It wasn't really that late. He'd go just for a little while. "Alright, where's this place at?"

****

Joseph walked into the bowling alley. The place was smoky, dim, and loud with music, people talking and the clack of bowling balls knocking over pins. He looked around for a moment until he found a group of people heckling the bowler at the line. Gage stood there, dressed in faded jeans and a dark t-shirt, a beer in one hand and a cigarette in another, jeering and laughing right along with the others. Joseph headed that way. A pretty girl with short dark hair in a pixie cut and smooth brown skin noticed him before Gage did. She poked Gage, who was standing next to her. Joseph couldn't hear what she said, but Gage immediately looked his way. Gage set his cigarette down before he came over to meet him, throwing an arm around Joseph's shoulders as he led him to the group.

"Back up, Gia. This one's mine."

Gia arched a brow. "Since when are you not open to sharing?"

Gage laughed. "Be quiet, girl or you'll have him thinking I'm some kind of man-whore."

Joseph snorted. "I already think that."

Gia's eyes widened as she pursed her lips. "Oooh, Gage! Better watch out. I think this one's got your number." Then she laughed and held out her hand. "Hi, I'm Gia. Nice to meet you."

Joseph returned the greeting. He liked her and her playful attitude. She stepped back to allow him to meet more of Gage's friends: Danny, a younger guy who worked in Gage's shop, and his girlfriend Alyssa, Nate, a big blonde who was insanely ripped and a few others. Joseph noticed a good-looking black guy sitting off to the side by himself who didn't come over with everyone else. Gage had already gotten him a beer by the time he was finally introduced to the guy in the corner. He followed Gage over to his table.

"Hey, Max. Got somebody I want you to meet."

Max stood up and Joseph didn't know which he felt more towards the man, intimidation or attraction. Max was the same height as him, but his chest and arms looked hard with muscle. Numerous tattoos ran down the entire length of both of his thick arms and across his chest. His hair was shaved close to his head. The minimal style looked good on him, setting off his light brown eyes and high cheekbones. A goatee framed his full lips, and the entire package was wrapped up in smooth, dark brown skin. Of course, Joseph recognized the name as the friend who'd given Gage his anger management method. He stuck his hand out. "Hi, I'm Joseph."

Max's big palm closed around his and his voice came out smooth and low. "Joseph. Heard a lot about you."

Joseph looked at Gage out of the corner of his eye. "Really? I hope it's all been good, I don't want to get a bad reputation with his friends." He couldn't help but watch as Max's full lips curved into a smile before he responded.

"Don't worry, I'm sure there's nothing Gage could tell me that could top his bad reputation."

Gage's knocked his fist against their hands, ending their prolonged handshake. "Quit flirting. Joseph, try and fucking remember that you're here with me. And Max you're not even gay."

Both Joseph and Max laughed, but Max poked at Gage a little further. "You're right I'm not gay …" His gaze flicked back over to Joseph. "Yet."

Gage gave Max a dirty look and cursed his friend. "Fucking asshole." Max just gave another one of those deep chuckles while Gage twisted his fingers in Joseph's hair and led him over to the lanes. He got him all set up with a ball and shoes. Then he said he'd be right back. Joseph noticed he went back over to Max.

****

Gage leaned against the wall next to his friend. "So, what do you really think?"

"He's pretty like you said. I can see why you want to play with him." Max took a drink of his beer before he continued. "But I don't think you should."

"Why not?"

"Open your eyes, Gage. That boy is into you and not just in the way those hood rats you bang are. Besides, one look at him and it's obvious he's not one who's okay with just playing around. And if that's all you want to do, you need to let him go."

Gage straightened up from the wall. He was annoyed at his friend and it came through in his voice. "Joseph is a grown man and he knows what's up. I made that clear in the beginning."

Max looked over to where Joseph was talking to Nate. "You may have made things clear. But as time goes on, things like that tend to get murky."

Gage looked at Joseph too. He *had* made things clear and he wasn't ready to let Joseph go. He made *that* clear to Max. "Like I said, Joseph is a grown man. We hang out, we fuck and he's fine with it. You worry too much."

Max leaned back in his chair. "You asked what I thought and I said my piece."

****

Joseph had his bowling shoes on and rolled his wrists a few times to loosen up. He and Gage had been put on opposing teams and he was just about to take his turn when he heard Gage's voice behind him.

"I'm not about to watch you unleash some hidden bowling talent am I?"

Joseph turned around and smiled. "Not at all. I'm mediocre at bowling at best."

Gage looked at him with heat in his gaze, his mouth curled up in a sexy grin. "Trust me, Joseph. Nothing about you is mediocre."

"Don't even try it. You're not going to distract me like that this time."

Gage raised his eyebrows, his eyes wide like he didn't have a clue what Joseph was talking about. Joseph laughed and stepped up to the foul line. He cupped the ball in his hand, steadying himself before he swung it behind him and released it down the lane. He had the strength to give the ball speed, but as usual his aim was off. The pins in the middle fell, but he was left with a 4-pin split. As he waited for his ball to come back, he turned and gave Gage an, *I told you so*, look. Gage smiled and gave him a mocking salute with his beer. The guys Joseph was playing with all cheered him on as he tried to pick up his spare. He wasn't surprised when he only managed to get one pin, so he just laughed at the good natured ribbing that came from the other side.

The game went on, each player's turn dragging out due to all the shit talking from the crowd and the posing and bragging from everyone once they got up to the line. Joseph was having fun. Gage's friends included him in their joking around. Before he knew it, he was acting like a big shot before each turn, and cursing and blaming the ball each time he failed to knock all his pins down. Gage on the other hand, was in the lead. After his third strike, he turned around in a slow circle with his head back and his arms thrown out wide, shouting, "Worship me, bitches. I am a god!" Gage's team all fell to their knees bowing down and chanting his name. But Joseph's team threw popcorn at him, calling him a turkey.

Joseph was laughing as Gage strutted back to his table, his mouth twisted in an arrogant sneer. When Gage leaned against the table behind him and crooked his finger at him, Joseph crossed enemy lines to see what he wanted. When he reached him, Gage spread his legs and pulled him in between them.

"You suck at bowling. It's a good thing you're pretty or I might be too embarrassed to bring you around my friends again."

Joseph rolled his eyes. "I don't remember being this smug when I kicked your ass at pool. Ever heard of being a gracious winner?"

Gage snorted. "Gracious winner. That sounds like some vapid fucking beauty queen thanking all the other contestants." Gage reached up to tug on his ponytail. "You're not at work, why is your hair up?" When Joseph shrugged, Gage pulled the band from his hair, and from habit he closed his eyes and shook it out. When Joseph opened his eyes again, Gage slid a hand into his hair.

"You're so fucking gorgeous." Gage pulled him closer until their mouths met, kissing him lightly, just barely running his tongue over the curve of his lip before pulling back again.

Joseph looked at Gage with a slight smile. "I guess you don't have a problem with PDA."

Gage grinned. "Not at all."

Then he kissed Joseph again, this time much deeper. He slid his other hand underneath Joseph's shirt, stroking the skin of his lower back. Joseph moaned into their kiss.

Gage groaned in response, flattening his hand against Joseph's back to press him closer. But before he could deepen the kiss any further Joseph became aware of whistles and catcalls.

Gage ended the kiss and Joseph looked up just in time to see Gia sticking her finger through her open fist, while Nate shouted, "Get a room!" They broke apart, Joseph with a slight blush on his face, while Gage just gave them all the finger.

"Immature fuckers," he said

Gia laughed. "Come on, it's time to start another game."

Gage agreed, but Joseph shook his head. "I can't. It's late and I wasn't even planning to stay this long."

Gage hooked a finger into Joseph's belt loop. "Don't let these assholes run you off. Stay for another game. You can be on my team this time."

Joseph laughed, but he shook his head again. "No. Seriously, Gage, I really need to go. It's after midnight and I'm tired."

"Fine, I'll come with you. You might need help washing the cigarette smoke out of all this pretty hair."

Gage pulled him closer whispering in his ear, "Maybe after I help you with that I'll fuck you in the shower." Joseph shivered as Gage lightly traced his tongue over his ear. "And I'll definitely be fucking you in that big bed of yours. It's so nice, I have to work extra hard to make it creak. But that's okay, I like a challenge."

Joseph took a deep breath, trying to hold back his arousal as Gage stepped away from him to say goodbye to his friends. They all waved at Joseph too so he went over, exchanging handshakes and goodbyes. He liked them. They were a rowdy bunch, but they were cool. Max came up to Gage. Joseph wasn't trying to eavesdrop, but Max's voice was so deep it carried.

"Remember what I said, man."

Gage answered Max, but he was looking straight at Joseph when he did. "Don't worry about it. Everything is clear."

Joseph didn't know what they were talking about, but from the way, Gage was looking at him he knew it was about him. Gage came back over to him and slid his hand into the back of his hair. Joseph allowed it. He liked the way Gage seemed to be fascinated with his hair, always touching it, even in public, and pulling on it when they were in bed together. His stomach lifted lightly as he thought of how it felt when Gage yanked on his hair while thrusting inside him. As always, Gage must have read in his face some of what he was thinking because a slow smile curled up that expressive mouth of his.

"I'd love to know what that thought was. Let's go so you can tell me all about it."

Joseph walked out of the bowling alley with Gage. He had a feeling it was going to be awhile before he got to sleep.

CHAPTER 21

T he water was warm. Not so hot that it made them uncomfortable. Just warm enough to heat their skin and create a cloud of steam all around them. Gage had just finished rinsing the shampoo from his hair and his hand was sliding down Joseph's stomach towards his shaft. Joseph turned and looked at Gage over his shoulder.

"You forgot conditioner."

Gage looked confused for a moment. "What?"

Joseph held back a grin. "If you're going to help do it right. You have to put conditioner in next."

Gage grabbed the bottle off the shower shelf. "And here I thought your hair was just naturally soft."

Joseph laughed. "Sorry to disappoint you."

Gage smoothed the conditioner through his hair, his fingers gently sliding through the wet strands. Joseph sighed with pleasure, letting his head drop back to rest on Gage's shoulder. He opened up for Gage's kiss as his lips touched his. This time when Gage's hand slid down to his shaft, he didn't stop him. Gage stroked him, his hand still slick from the conditioner, and Joseph moaned. He felt Gage's cock hard against his hip and reached behind him to grasp him in his fist and do a little stroking of his own. In no time at all, their kiss went from soft to wild and hot, water splashing into their faces as they pumped each other tighter and faster. Suddenly, Gage knocked his hand away and Joseph felt his cockhead prodding at his ass. He pulled away.

"Don't! We didn't bring a condom in here."

Gage spun him around so that his back was against the shower wall. Water plastered his dark hair to his forehead. Droplets ran in rivulets down his face, catching in the stubble along his jawline before slowly slipping down his neck. That intensity was back in his eyes, that same look he'd had when they almost kissed after Joseph asked him out. It had intimidated him then. Now, it turned him on, made his breath come even faster. Gage roughly stroked his hands over his chest, then up his throat before he slipped a thumb into his mouth. Joseph sucked on the digit, swirling his tongue around it. The intensity flared even brighter in Gage's smoldering eyes.

"Goddamnit. The thought of fucking you bare, nothing between my cock and your hot little ass." Gage groaned and bit his shoulder. "I fucking want that."

Joseph swallowed hard. He wanted that too, and was pretty close to allowing it. He just managed to deny them both. He looked at Gage, his gaze steady. "You know what you have to do to have that."

A muscle ticked in Gage's jaw, but he didn't say anything. He just kissed Joseph hard, his hand coming up to squeeze around both their shafts and pumping them swiftly. Joseph wrapped his arms around Gage's waist, their hips moving in rhythm together. Gage backed him further up against the shower wall, his grip on their shafts tightening, the speed of his stroking increasing. Joseph's heart was racing, his body tingling in that way it did with an approaching orgasm. He dug his fingers into Gage's back, pulling him even closer.

"Gage, you'd better stop unless you want me to come right here in the shower."

Gage licked at his neck. "That is what I want. I want you to come right now so I can hear all those sweet moans and naughty curses. Give 'em to me Joseph."

Joseph pressed his head back against the shower wall. It felt so good to feel Gage's fist moving on him, their cocks pressed together that he couldn't help but moan like Gage asked. And when Gage's finger slipped into his ass he breathed out a curse. Gage's mouth crashed onto his, but he kept cursing in between kisses. His orgasm was pulsing in his cockhead and when Gage's finger pressed into him further, it burst forth, his hips jerking forward again and again. Gage groaned into his mouth, slamming against him hard as he came too. The release felt good, making his body throb. But Joseph knew this was only beginning of what was in store for them tonight.

Gage rested against him for a moment as they caught their breath. It wasn't long before they were kissing again. Joseph reached behind him to shut off the shower just as Gage pulled him out of the stall. They made their way out of the bathroom and over to his bed, water dripping from their bodies. Joseph didn't care that they were getting his bed wet as they fell onto it in a heated tangle of limbs, still kissing and caressing each other. Joseph ended up underneath Gage, but he rolled them until he was on top. He saw Gage's surprised expression just before he kissed him.

He slid his tongue into Gage's mouth, taking control of the kiss. Joseph moved down Gage's body, kissing his warm skin and using his tongue to lap up the drops of water. When he reached his shaft he licked it from base to tip, over and over, until Gage was hard again. Gage groaned, his hips pushing up. Joseph held his cock and took long slow licks over the head. Before long, pre-cum was beading on the tip and Joseph kept licking, savoring the taste on his tongue. Joseph looked up as Gage rasped out his name. He saw Gage's face tight with tension, his mouth pursed and eyes shut tight. He licked once more before he answered Gage's call. "Yes?"

"Stop teasing and fucking suck me."

"Like this?" he asked just before he sucked only the head of Gage's cock into his mouth. "Or like this?" he whispered before sliding his mouth all the way down Gage's shaft.

"Fuck!"

The curse exploded from Gage in a harsh shout. His hands came down, tangling in Joseph's hair, fingers pressing close against his scalp. His hips thrust up at the same time that he pushed Joseph's head down, forcing his shaft further into his mouth. Joseph moaned at the rough treatment and looked up to see Gage watching him.

"That's right, Joseph. Suck me."

Joseph moaned again as Gage started pumping into his mouth.

"Fuck, look at that pretty mouth sliding up and down on my cock." He continued pumping, his hips rolling up smoothly. "All that hair everywhere, your face flushed." Gage inhaled deeply before letting that breath out in a rough groan. "I can see from the look in your eyes how much you want my cock in your mouth." Gage pushed his hair back off his face. "So fucking gorgeous. And mine."

Joseph started to let his eyes drift closed. But when Gage claimed him as his, his eyes shot to Gage's face. The expression there, of both lust and possessiveness… Joseph was confused and turned on and he just wanted Gage so much. He pulled his mouth off Gage's cock and surged up his body to kiss him. Before the kiss got too deep, he sat up, straddled Gage's lap and reached to the nightstand for the lube. He poured some into his hand, then reached behind him for Gage's cock, sliding his fist over him slowly until he was covered. He used his slick fingers to prepare himself, as he leaned down to kiss Gage again. Pulling his fingers away, Joseph started moving his body so that Gage's shaft slid in between his ass, not penetrating, just giving them enough to want more. Giving them enough to know what it could feel like.

As he rocked his body over Gage's, his lover cupped his ass in his hands. Joseph moaned as Gage squeezed his flesh before spreading his ass wide. Joseph moved faster, Gage holding him open so that he could feel his cock even closer against his entrance. They were barely even kissing anymore, just their open mouths pressed together, hot rapid breaths flowing between them.

"Fuck, Joseph. Get a condom. Now."

Joseph shook his head, his heart racing, his cock hard and pressing into Gage's stomach. "Not yet. I just want to feel you a little longer." Gage's fingers dug deep into his ass and he started thrusting his hips up, matching his rhythm. But their movements were rough now, barely controlled. And whether by accident or because they both wanted it so much, Gage's cock head was suddenly pushing against his entrance. Gage's head pressed back into the pillow, his eyes closed and jaw clenched tight as he cursed.

"Goddamnit! Fuck! Goddamnit!"

Joseph watched as Gage's eyes flashed open. He could tell by the look in them that Gage was only a heartbeat away from taking what he wanted, from fucking him with nothing between them whether he said yes or not. He tried to raise up, both to put some distance between them and to get a condom. But Gage wouldn't let him. He wrapped one arm around his waist, keeping Joseph trapped where he was. Gage's other hand grasped the back of his neck to pull him down into a kiss. He gave a desperate cry as Gage inched inside him the barest amount. Joseph ended up blindly reaching out and searching for the condom on his nightstand. He knocked over his alarm clock and scattered loose change before his fingers finally closed over the foil packet. "Gage. Let me go. I have a condom."

Gage let him go, but the look he gave him had chills chasing down Joseph's spine. He scooted back to roll the condom onto Gage's shaft before covering the latex in lube. When he was finished, he lowered himself onto Gage's cock, going slowly to give himself time to adjust. After what seemed like an eternity of Gage's thick cock inching inside him with his harsh whispers urging him on, he was finally seated on him fully. Joseph moved slowly, each movement sending deep, drugging pleasure pulsing throughout his body. That didn't last long. Gage's hand closed around his cock pumping him swiftly.

"Stop fucking around, Joseph. You've already got me ready to fucking explode."

Joseph dug his fingers into the pads of muscle of Gage's chest. He fucked himself onto Gage's cock faster and faster, each thrust of his hips sending his cock through Gage's tight fist. He could feel sweat forming on his skin, see it beading on Gage's forehead as he rode his lover hard. "Is this what you meant?" He asked as he bounced on Gage's cock. "Is this fast enough for you?" He dropped down hard onto Gage, squeezing his inner muscles and grinding his hips in a slow circle. "Am I tight enough for you?"

Gage's eyes went wide with surprise, his hands clamping onto his hips to push him up. "Keep talking like that and I'll be coming before you know it," he said as he pulled him back down.

Joseph bit his lip to hold back a naughty grin, and peeked at Gage from beneath his lashes. "No, you won't. You know you want to fuck me a lot longer than this."

Gage groaned and dragged Joseph down to his chest, rolling them so that he was on top now. Gage immediately started fucking into him hard and fast. His hands locked onto Joseph's hips holding him still for his thrusts. Joseph was moaning, totally into the way Gage was holding him down while he fucked him so roughly, when Gage just stopped. Joseph gave a choked cry, his hands reaching for Gage's ass, digging his fingers into the muscled flesh to try and make him move again.

"What … why'd you stop?"

"You were about to come. So was I. And you're right. I'm not ready for that yet. So tell me, Joseph. What were you thinking of back at the bowling alley? What made these normally sweet eyes turn sultry right in front of all those people?"

Joseph licked his lips. "I was thinking … about how much I like it when you pull my hair, when … when you're inside me."

Gage smoothed his hand up his body to softly twine through the ends of his hair. "Is that right? I'm not exactly gentle when I pull on this hair when I'm fucking you, Joseph." Gage started moving again with slow shallow thrusts. "You don't mind?"

Joseph shook his head slowly, almost mesmerized by the low timbre of Gage's voice.

"Hmmm… so that means you don't mind if I get rough with you?"

Joseph swallowed hard, his throat thick with arousal before he answered. "No, I don't mind. I like it."

Gage pulled completely out of Joseph, ignoring his surprised protest. He grabbed his lean hips and roughly flipped him over onto his stomach. Then he dropped heavily down onto Joseph, making him grunt. Gage slid his hands into all those curls, wild from the rolling around they'd already done. He grabbed a huge handful of the silky strands in a tight fist, and slowly pulled Joseph's head back. "Spread your fucking legs for me. Now." Joseph did as he'd ordered, but he moved slowly. So Gage pulled on his hair, getting a yelp out of him, his legs spreading completely open beneath him. Gage pushed inside of him hard. Joseph sucked in a sharp breath, but Gage didn't stop, going deeper and deeper until his heavy sack was resting against the smooth skin of Joseph's ass.

"Right here is where I want to be. You underneath me. Me inside you. Fucking you hard. Forcing those shocked little gasps from your throat." Tightening his grip even more on Joseph's hair, Gage twisted Joseph's head to the side to expose his neck. He licked at that warm skin, sweaty even after their shower. Gage pumped into Joseph hard, tugging on the hair in his fist every time he jerked his body over the one lying under him so willingly.

"You taste so good Joseph. And you're so tight." Gage trailed his lips up to Joseph's ear. "So tight on my cock. Will you keep it tight for me, baby? Just for me?" He pressed the side of his face to Joseph's and felt him nod, heard him whimper close in his ear. "Yeah, that's right. You won't let anybody else have you. *I* won't let anybody else have you. I want you all to myself."

He surged up hard into his lover, enjoying the feel of his naked ass rubbing against his skin, while giving the pretty curls in his fist a swift yank. Joseph cried out in pain and reached back, his fingers clawing at his fist. Gage grabbed onto that hand, squeezing it and holding his arm bent back behind his head. "Sssh… You said you liked that. Remember, Joseph?" He didn't stop moving inside his lover as he spoke, his breath and his words coming out in harsh grunts. "Don't try to get away from me. I'll just pull harder and harder and fuck you deeper and deeper until you're screaming my name. Do you understand?" Joseph forced out a yes in a low whisper, but then he tried to pull away from him again. Gage laughed and followed through on his promise. He pulled on Joseph's hair until his head arched back from the pillow. Gage leaned down and sucked and bit and licked at the fragile curve of Joseph's neck as he thrust into his lover with all his strength, over and over, making the bed rock beneath them. Joseph started moaning his name, his voice getting louder and louder, rising over the sound of the headboard knocking into the wall.

The heat of Joseph's skin burned Gage where they rubbed against each other. The sweet clenching of Joseph's ass on his cock spurred on his need for release. Gage rolled onto his side, freeing Joseph's cock from where it was pressed against the mattress so he could stroke him off. Now he was ready for them both to come. His balls were tight and his cock was throbbing, and as he pumped Joseph he could tell he was just as ready as he was. Gage kept thrusting hard and fast into him, his hips pounding into Joseph's round little ass with a sweaty slap.

Joseph pumped his hips back and forth in rhythm with him, clenching even tighter around him and Gage was lost. His fucking fingers tingled and his ears buzzed and his vision went gray around the edges and he was coming. Coming hard enough that he stopped breathing for several seconds. He bit down on Joseph's ear, giving his hair one last pull. Then Joseph was coming too, his mouth tripping back and forth between moaning his name and cursing. They kept going, riding it out, their breathing hot and fast, their skin hot and slick. Finally, they both collapsed, sprawling against each other in a tangle of loose bones, satisfied muscles, and sweaty skin.

CHAPTER 22

Joseph lazed there in bed, drifting in that fuzzy place between sleep and awake. He heard Gage moving, but didn't look to see what he was doing until his hand brushed the hair back off his face. Joseph opened his eyes to see that Gage was stretched out on the bed next to him, but he was fully dressed.

"I hate to wake you and make you get up, but you need to come lock the door behind me."

Joseph reached out and wrapped his hand around Gage's wrist. "Stay. It's only a few hours until we have to get up for work anyway."

Gage pulled his hand away and leaned slightly back. "I can't. I need to get home."

"Why? It's not like you have a dog you have to let out." Joseph lightly pressed his fingers to Gage's chest. "Just stay with me, Gage."

Gage rolled off the bed and stood up. "Don't push me on this, Joseph."

Joseph, wide awake now, stood up too, dragging the sheet with him to wrap around his waist. "Why not? Why won't you stay and why can't I push you on it?"

Gage closed his eyes and rolled his head on his neck. "Because Joseph, I don't want to get into it. Just fucking leave it. We had fun tonight. Leave it at that."

"Fun." Joseph pronounced the word like it was foreign to him. "Fun is all we ever have."

Gage shrugged. "Why do we need anything more than that?"

Joseph didn't answer. He just headed towards the front door to let Gage out. When they reached it he stopped, but didn't open it. Joseph looked at Gage in confusion. "I don't understand you, Gage. You invite me out with your friends, say the things you said to me in bed tonight, but you won't sleep with me. I don't get it. What do you want from me?"

Gage's big body was tense, his face closed off as he answered. "I want us to have a good time and I want you to enjoy it. That's what I want."

Frustration rose in Joseph's chest. "I am enjoying it, but that doesn't mean you-." Gage cut him off by pulling him forward into a hard kiss. Joseph's frustration grew, but he realized it was pointless to continue. Gage clearly didn't want to talk about this. When Gage ended the kiss, he looked at him silently for a moment before he spoke. "One of these days you aren't going to be able to get me to shut up with just a kiss."

Gage rubbed his thumb over his mouth before he kissed him again. "But that day isn't today." Gage opened the door. "I'll see you later."

Joseph watched Gage head down the walk to his bike. His refusal to stay the night with him hurt. But apparently not enough for him to tell Gage not to come back. He stared off into the darkness even after the Indian's taillight had disappeared. He didn't want to continue on with Gage the way things were between them. But he didn't want to let him go either.

****

Gage didn't go straight home after leaving Joseph's. He drove around town, letting the wind rush over him as he thought about what he was doing with Joseph. Max had been right. The waters were murky. How ironic that he'd have that conversation with Joseph the very night he'd assured his friend everything was clear.

Gage came to a red light. He was tempted to blow through it since there was no one on the streets this late. But he eased to a stop and sat there idling. Why had he invited Joseph out with his friends tonight? Gage rolled his head on his neck. He knew why. He just wasn't sure he liked the reasons, either of them.

He'd wanted to show Joseph off to his friends. Wanted them to see that he was involved with someone like Joseph. Yeah, he'd had plenty of girls and guys before who were good looking. But there was just something about that pretty boy that made him stand out. And Gage wanted everyone to know Joseph was his. The light changed and he sped off. It was why he'd said what he said to Joseph about not letting anyone else have him. He'd meant that. He wanted Joseph for his own. Just the thought of someone else putting their hands on that golden skin, or kissing the sweet curve of his mouth, or fuck, touching even one strand of that pretty hair … It made him burn with anger. Made him imagine beating the shit out of anyone who would even think to touch Joseph.

But he didn't want to get too close to him. He didn't want to get too close to anyone. That's why he wouldn't stay the night. That type of intimacy would lead to an emotional attachment that Gage didn't want. And it was why he should have put the phone down as soon as he realized the other reason he was calling Joseph. Because he wanted to spend time with him, outside the bedroom and with people who were important to him. But he hadn't put down the phone. Now Joseph was hurt that he wouldn't stay the night with him. He was going to have to do something to fix that. Because even though he wouldn't give Joseph what he wanted, he wasn't ready to let him go. Not yet.

CHAPTER 23

J oseph, do you have a minute?"

Joseph looked up from the document he was reading to see Mr. Pruitt Sr., one of the senior partners, in his doorway. Mr. Pruitt was a tall, sharply dressed man. He kept in shape with golf and racquetball. He favored dark suits and pastel shirts with French cuffs. Typical high-powered lawyer look. It worked for him.

Joseph was tired from being up all night, his mind drifting to thoughts of Gage instead of focusing on the papers in front of him. But he made an effort to straighten up and look alert.

"Of course, sir. How can I help you?"

Mr. Pruitt smiled and came to sit in one of the chairs in front of his desk. "I don't need anything, Joseph. Just thought I'd stop in to check up on you. See how you were coming along with the Allen merger. I noticed you hadn't given any updates as fast as you normally do and you've been coming into the office a little later than usual."

Joseph colored slightly. Allen Brothers Beverages was a soft drink company that was looking to buy up three other soft drink plants in the region. Joseph was working to make sure the merger would be approved without any violations of anti-trust laws. And he'd been coming in later in the mornings because of his late nights with Gage. He was still there by nine, but he'd previously been coming in at eight. "My apologies, sir. I admit I've been a little off my game, but I'll be sure to have everything prepared by the end of the week."

Pruitt leaned back in his chair. "Off your game. I see."

His eyes dropped to Joseph's neck and he colored further when he realized he was looking at the visible passion mark Gage had left on his skin last night.

"Look, Joseph. I understand what it's like to be … off your game. I had my own times like that when I was young. But you have to keep in mind what's important. Rising to the top. You won't get there if you're letting the company you keep interfere with your progress."

Joseph nodded. He realized he was receiving a warning. It was phrased politely, like nothing more than a friendly, helpful chat from the man who'd recruited him to the firm. But it was definitely a warning. "Yes, sir. I understand."

Pruitt stood up. "Good. Just remember, everybody has to pay the price to get what they want. You just have to decide if you're willing to pay it."

****

Later that evening, Joseph was at home with papers spread out over his coffee table. The stereo was on. He'd stayed late at the office but finally just decided to come home and work. He needed the noise to block out his thoughts of Gage and making partner, and he couldn't get away with blasting the music he listened to at his firm. The soothing sounds of classical piano or Michael Bolton's voice were okay, but not the driving beats of the music he preferred. Joseph didn't really like to work at home, but he was determined to get back on track.

Of course at that moment someone knocked on his door just as his phone lit up with a call. He hit mute on the stereo remote and checked the caller ID. When he saw who it was, he cursed at the phone and slid his thumb over the ignore arrow. He had no desire to talk to that person. Joseph tossed the phone onto the couch before he went over to the door. When Joseph saw Gage through the peephole, he opened up in surprise. Gage had never come over without calling first.

"Gage, what's going on?"

"I brought you something." Gage pulled his hand from behind his back and held out a Sonic Slush.

Joseph didn't need to taste it to know it was cherry. Gage smiled at him and Joseph couldn't help smiling back. He just looked so boyish with his hair falling into his eyes as he held the cup out. Joseph stepped back and opened the door further to let Gage in. "What's this for?" He took the cup and sipped. It was cherry.

Gage shrugged. "I know it bothered you last night when I wouldn't stay over. And I just wanted to let you know I wasn't trying to hurt you by leaving."

Joseph took another big sip and licked his lips. "Oh." He wasn't quite sure what else to say to that. It wasn't an apology and it wasn't an explanation either.

Gage's gaze kept returning to Joseph's mouth as he drank the Slush he'd brought him. He watched his lips purse and close over the straw, his cheeks hollowing as he sucked the treat into his mouth. Already his lips were red. Gage looked Joseph in the eye so he could finish this conversation without getting turned on.

"Yeah, I wasn't trying to hurt you, but that's just not something that I'm ready for. Can you understand that?" Joseph took another sip. Licked his lips again. Gage found himself moving closer, brushing his thumb over those red lips. "Can you understand that, Joseph?" Joseph looked at him for a long moment and Gage could see in his eyes that he was trying to decide. Gage pushed a little more to get Joseph to let this go. "You know I like being with you and I've never even bothered to get this far with anyone else."

Joseph's expression immediately sharpened. "Why is that?"

Gage backed off. "Let's not talk about that right now." He looked and noticed all the papers on Joseph's coffee table. "Were you working?"

"Yes." Joseph went over and sat on the couch, setting the Sonic cup on the table. "One of the partners came in and gave me a little pep talk today. Basically told me to get my butt in gear."

Gage snorted and sat next to him. "I can't imagine that you're not busting your ass for that place."

"I do. But I've been a little distracted at work lately, not keeping the same hours I used to. They've noticed apparently."

Gage rubbed Joseph's thigh. "That's probably my fault. I've been keeping you up late at night. I know I should say I'm sorry, but I've enjoyed every minute of it."

Joseph grinned and shook his head. "No, it's not just you. I've been feeling off, sort of restless for a while. I've got a race this weekend and I'm looking forward to it. All that adrenaline should help get my head back on straight at work."

Gage thought for a second. "Have you considered that the reason you're restless is because you're doing something you don't want to do?"

Joseph looked at him with his forehead creased in confusion. "What are you talking about?"

"Shit, Joseph. You have a motorcycle you race on weekends. You wear suits but still have a ponytail. You're a fucking competition level pool player and you're feeling all itchy at work. Maybe that place isn't where you want to be, isn't who you really are."

Joseph frowned. "You're crazy. I can't make money with a bike and a cue stick. Those aren't respectable professions. Besides, I like practicing law."

Gage shrugged. "Who says those aren't respectable professions? Besides, you can still be a lawyer, it just doesn't have to be there." He shrugged again. "Look, sorry man. I wasn't trying to be your high school career guide. Just thought I'd mention things I've noticed about you since you said you were feeling restless. Food for thought or whatever the fuck."

Joseph looked at Gage. "Well, there is one thing that makes me restless."

"What?"

"Wondering if you're with anyone else."

Gage sighed and dropped his head back against the couch. "*Joseph*. Why are we talking about this? I'm here with you right now aren't I?"

"Yeah, right now. But I won't be one of many. Especially if you want to stop using condoms with me."

Gage thought of last night. That brief moment of inching into Joseph with nothing on him, feeling the tight heat of his ass on his naked cock … He was getting hard thinking of it, imagining what it would feel like to push all the way inside him just like that. Gage actually wasn't sleeping with anyone else. But that didn't mean he was willing to tie himself down to one person. And that's what Joseph wanted him to do. What he wanted him to say. He couldn't do that. That wasn't him. Gage turned on the couch to face Joseph. Sliding his hand into his hair, he guided Joseph to look at him.

"Listen to me, Joseph. Like I said earlier, I've never been this involved with anyone before." Gage paused for a moment. "I won't ask you to have sex with me without a condom." His fingers tightened in Joseph's hair as he said the words. He wanted to be deep inside him with nothing between them so fucking bad. Thanks to that little taste he'd had he couldn't stop thinking about it. He refused to analyze why any of this was important to him, but he knew he couldn't expect that if he wasn't willing to be exclusive. Gage forced himself to ease his grip and continued on.

"Just let that be enough. I don't think that's asking for too much." He brought them closer together, brushing his lips gently across Joseph's. He looked at him, reading the indecision easily in his expressive eyes. Still, he could tell from the way Joseph was relaxed in his hold that he wanted to give in to him. "For now, Joseph. Let that be enough." Joseph didn't pull away so he kissed him. His mouth was cold, but quickly heated up as their tongues softly rubbed together. And he tasted sweet. So sweet that Gage refused to let him go. He'd do whatever it took to convince Joseph to stay with him. Gage pulled on Joseph's hair until his head fell back. He kissed him even deeper, easing him to his back on the couch.

Joseph didn't know where his mind was. Or his willpower. But looking at Gage, his dark eyes so direct, that hypnotic voice falling from his lips, he was the sexy bad boy that Joseph couldn't stay away from. And he couldn't bring himself to say that wasn't enough for him. Maybe Gage just needed time. When Gage kissed him, he thought that he'd be willing to give him that. Time, just a little time. He let Gage lay him down on the couch, wrapping his arms around the solid width of his back.

Their kiss grew a little hotter, a little faster. Gage quickly worked his jeans open, pushing his hand inside. When Joseph felt that warm hand grasping his shaft, he moaned and rolled his hips up. Gage stroked him swiftly getting him hard in seconds. Closing his eyes, Joseph gave himself up to the pleasure of it. He dug his fingers into Gage's back, opening his legs so he could rest between them. The closer he got to orgasm, the slicker he grew in Gage's fist until he was sliding fast and easy in his grip. Gage kept kissing him and stroking him, pushing him even closer to the edge, making him moan and writhe beneath his lover. Then he pulled on his hair at the same time he squeezed him tight. Joseph gave a choked cry and arched up hard with his release. Gage kept pumping him as he came, but pulled back from their kiss. He opened his eyes to see Gage watching him.

"You're so beautiful like this, Joseph. I need this from you. Say it's enough."

Joseph managed to breathe out an answer in the middle of the exquisite tension of his orgasm. "*Yes.*" When he finally relaxed back against the couch, he closed his eyes again for a second before he looked back at Gage. "For now."

CHAPTER 24

Gage was irritated. He'd had nothing but stupid shit happen all week. Wrong parts being delivered. The power going out for several hours because the jackass next door didn't know how to cut down tree limbs without them falling on power lines. He was irritated and the idiot standing in front of him complaining wasn't helping. He held his temper as he explained that he didn't do illegal street mods to bikes. Finally, the guy gave up and left mumbling under his breath.

Gage closed his eyes and inhaled sharply. He wanted to pick up the wrench on the counter next to him and throw it at the back of that dumb fuck's head. Instead, he tried hard to swallow the irritation that was starting to shift into anger, pulsing out from his head straight down to his fingertips. His hands twitched and clenched into fists. Fucking illegal street racers. He wanted to bash them all over the head. He'd hated them ever since-

"You alright?" Danny came over with concern on his ruddy face, interrupting Gage's train of thought.

Gage cracked his neck. "Yeah, just some stupid prick who wanted me to modify his bike so he could pop wheelies on the fucking highway or some shit." Gage looked over as the door opened. When he saw who it was his anger spiked a little higher. "You have got to be fucking kidding me."

Danny looked towards the door too. "Christ. I don't know what to do. If I go, you might kill her. If I stay, I might be an accomplice to murder."

"Stay till her ass is out of here."

Danny nodded. "Alright."

He headed back over to the bike he'd been working on. Gage stayed right where he was, letting the woman come to him. She came tottering over in her trademark outfit of miniskirt, off the shoulder tee, and sky high heels.

"Gage! How are you? I've missed you!" She raised her arms like she was about to hug him but stopped at the look Gage gave her.

"Heather. What do you want?" He watched as she recovered quickly, her mouth forming into a pout. It wasn't nearly as enticing as it had been in years past. Mostly because of the lines around her mouth from years of sucking on a crack pipe and the brown burn marks on her lips that showed even through her lip gloss. Her voice came out soft like a little girl's.

"Gage, why do you always assume I want something? Maybe I just want to catch up with you."

Gage just stared at her. "Don't waste my fucking time with this, Heather. You only come around when you need some money or a place to crash. Well, you're shit out of luck. The apartment is rented out and I told you last time I'm not giving you any more money."

Heather came closer. "That's okay if the apartment upstairs is rented. I'd rather stay with you anyway. We could spend some time together, just like we used to." She trailed her fingers down his chest. "You know I know what you like, Gage. You know I'll let you do whatever you want to any part of me."

Gage stepped away from her in disgust. Her words weren't at all sexy to him. Instead she sounded like a fucking prostitute trying to pick up a John. After all this time of whoring herself out for drugs, that's pretty much what she was. Gage scoffed. "I wouldn't put my dick anywhere in you, Heather. No telling what flesh eating bacteria would attack me and make my shit fall off. So why don't you sashay your ass on out of here? I'm not interested."

Her expression changed from sultry come on to woebegone so fast that Gage knew it was fake. All of this was. It was nothing but a ploy to get what she wanted.

"Gage, I'm sorry. I don't have anywhere else to go and I don't know what to do. And you said…" she sniffed, running a finger under her eye to catch a tear. "You said you'd always take care of me."

Gage grit his teeth in anger. He had said that to her. Years ago back when they'd both been trying to kick their drug habits. Or so he thought. He'd learned to live without drugs. She'd learned to hide her habit. Before he'd quit using, they'd had many nights where they'd both been high out of their minds while they'd fucked. They'd snorted cocaine off each other, spilling whiskey in the bed as they'd drank straight from the bottle before passing out together. And she *had* let him do whatever he wanted to her. Both when he was high and didn't care what he was doing, and when he'd gotten sober and wanted to fuck until he couldn't think about drugs, or liquor, or rage. Seeing her now was dredging up all those bad memories and making him feel guilty that he hadn't done more to help her get clean. But they'd been doing this back and forth for years and Heather had never made any real attempts to sober up.

"Heather, when I told you that I meant I would help you get clean. Not support you so you could keep fucking around and shootin' up!"

The tears came a little faster now. "I'm trying Gage, I swear! I'm not as strong as you. I need help. That's all."

Gage clenched his fists in frustration. He had to help her if she really wanted to sober up. "Why don't you check into rehab? I'll foot the fucking bill."

Heather licked her lips, all signs of tears gone. "Gage I don't need rehab. I can do this on my own. But if you're willing to pay that much, just give me the money. I can get myself set up in a hotel and just wean myself off the drugs. That's how they do it anyway. They give you smaller and smaller hits until you don't need it anymore."

A hot pulse of anger beat in Gage's chest as he immediately saw through her ploy. She'd just said she needed help, now she was saying she could do it on her own. He'd been through this a dozen times with her. He took her in, offered to pay for rehab, but she never followed through. Gage was done playing this game. His lips barely moved as he spoke, trying to hold back from cursing her out. "Get out."

She blinked. "What?"

"I said get out. You think I'm some naïve little shit? You think I don't know you'll take that money and hole up in a hotel in a heroine induced stupor?" Gage sneered as he looked at her standing there with her mouth open. "You forget who you're talking to, honey. You can find somebody else because I'm not the idiot who's gonna fall for that shit. Now get out of my shop."

Heather gathered herself and smiled. "Gage you're right I'm-."

Gage slammed his fist down on the counter. "Shut up! Shut your lying, crack pipe-sucking mouth. Don't ever come back around me and don't fucking call me. You are on your own with that shit." He got up close in her face and she stumbled back a step. "Forget what I said to you back then. You had your shot to let me help you and you didn't. So as far as I'm concerned that debt is wiped clean. Now get the fuck out!"

Heather finally caught a fucking clue that he was serious and practically ran out of there. When she was gone, Gage slammed his fist on the counter again. "Stupid bitch!" He slammed his fist down again. "I don't need that shit!" He hit the glass again. "Fucking goddamn guilt-tripping, bitch!" He hit the glass hard and heard it crack. The glass cut his skin, but Gage had so much rage and adrenaline pumping through him that it didn't even hurt. He still cursed a blue streak, pissed off that now he'd have to replace the glass. He heard Danny behind him.

"Jesus, man. You're bleeding everywhere."

Gage looked down and saw the blood running down his hand and dripping on the floor. "Fuck! Just fuck."

Danny grabbed a clean towel and held it against his cut. "Gage, I don't mean to get up in your business. But you need to calm down." He paused for a moment. Danny had been around long enough to know how he handled things. "Where's Joseph?"

"Joseph is busy with work."

"Oh, well maybe you should call -."

"I'm not calling anybody else!" Gage snapped.

Danny took a step back. "Alright, man."

Gage took a deep breath, trying to get the heat of anger out of his face. "Go ahead and get out of here. Lock up behind you. I'm not in any kind of mood to deal with anybody else today." He took over holding the towel against his hand. "I'll clean up this fucking mess and go home."

Danny walked off to put his tools away and grab his stuff to leave. Gage used another towel to wipe up the blood on the floor, silently waving bye to Danny as he flicked off the Open sign and left. Once he was gone, Gage went to the bathroom and rinsed the blood off his hand.

Gage knew Danny was right; he did need to calm down. But he hadn't seen Joseph since the night he'd gotten him to agree what they had was enough for now. He'd left after giving Joseph his release so that he could finish the work he'd brought home, joking that he was capable of showing a little restraint. Joseph had been MIA since then, determined to get caught up at work. Gage hadn't tried to persuade him into coming over and he hadn't been with anyone else either. He couldn't believe it, but he was fucking trying to be monogamous for Joseph. Gage bandaged his hand as best he could. He was trying … but he really needed to calm down.

CHAPTER 25

J oseph went into his kitchen and poured himself a glass of soda. He was glad to be home. He'd been putting in long hours all week to get back on track with the Allen Brothers merger and show the partners he was serious about his career. Now it was finally Friday. He was excited for his race tomorrow. And after taking a long hot shower he felt relaxed. Joseph took a drink and pulled his phone out to call Gage. They hadn't seen each other for a few days and had only talked on the phone briefly. The phone rang several times before Gage answered.

"Joseph, what's up?"

Joseph immediately sensed something was off. Gage's voice was even lower than usual, and anger practically sparked right through the phone lines. "Are you alright?"

Gage laughed, but there was no humor in it. "Nope. I'm not alright. Having a pretty shit fucking day actually. How's your day? Everything going swell in lawyer-ville?"

Joseph sat his glass down. "Gage, what's going on? What happened?"

Gage was quiet for a long time.

Joseph stood there in his kitchen listening to the clock tick and the refrigerator hum. His skin prickled with anticipation, and his stomach clenched tight with the beginnings of desire. He knew what Gage was going to say before he said it.

"Joseph, I need you."

Joseph nodded even though he knew Gage couldn't see him. "I'll be right over." Joseph hung up and left his soda abandoned on the counter. He stuffed his feet into a pair of tennis shoes and grabbed his keys. He was in his car headed to Gage's within two minutes.

****

Joseph walked up to Gage's house. He went to knock, but something made him turn the knob. The door was unlocked and swung open when he pushed. He closed and locked the door behind him, then went into the dimly lit house looking for Gage. Joseph found him in the living room sitting on the couch. His chest and feet were bare, a pair of faded jeans the only thing he had on. His hair was more rumpled than ever, looking as though he'd run his hands through it more than once. Gage didn't say anything when he came into the room. He just sat there, rubbing a finger back and forth over his bottom lip, a muscle ticking in his jaw. His eyes were on Joseph with sharp concentration.

Joseph swallowed hard and walked forward. When he reached the couch, he dropped to his knees between Gage's legs. "You said you needed me." Joseph kept his gaze locked on Gage's as he smoothed his palms up his denim covered thighs. Gage was still, his body tense, his muscles tight. "I'm here for you." Gage eyes were bright with a furious mix of anger and passion. And they watched him closely. Very closely. Joseph had to look away for a moment before he could finish. "You can do … whatever you want to me."

Gage slowly took his hand away from his mouth. "Stand up."

His heart pounding, his mouth dry, Joseph followed Gage's order and stood. He couldn't believe he'd just said what he had to Gage, but he meant it. He took his shirt off when Gage ordered him to do so, and kicked off his shoes until he too only had on jeans. Gage curled his fingers over his waistband and jerked him forward. When he was closer, Gage opened his jeans, pushing them and his briefs down to mid-thigh. Then Gage leaned forward and sucked his cock into his mouth. Joseph inhaled sharply, his head falling back on his shoulders. His hands came up to Gage's head, sliding through the thick strands of hair before he finally gripped him tight. Gage sucked him furiously, only stopping to lick at the tip and tongue his balls. Joseph groaned deep in his throat. Gage's hands were everywhere, smoothing up his back, squeezing his ass, stroking his thighs. He was shaking, pumping his hips forward to keep up with that amazing mouth.

Joseph looked down at Gage when he slowly pulled his mouth off his cock, watching as he sucked a finger into his mouth. His tongue came out, swirling and playing around the digit, making Joseph throb with anticipation. He knew where that finger was going and he wanted it now. Not above begging, he pushed his hips forward again. "Gage, please."

Gage stopped licking his finger and his mouth, that wonderful mouth, curled up in a little grin before he slid his lips back over his shaft. Joseph moaned, then moaned again when that slick finger pushed inside him. Gage sucked him slowly now, his finger moving at the same speed, gradually opening him and going deeper. When he finally was all the way in, stroking against that spot deep inside, Joseph cried out. His hands dropped down to Gage's shoulders, fingernails digging into the hard muscles as Gage sucked him faster, pumping his finger in and out of his ass again and again, hitting that spot each time. Joseph was shuddering, his body curling closer to Gage as his balls drew up tight and hard until he exploded. He cried out as his release streaked through him. Gage grabbed his ass and pulled him even closer as he came, drinking him down swiftly, while Joseph kept moaning until he was spent.

****

Gage slowly let him go, licking at his cock as he eased back and taking his finger out of his ass. Joseph inhaled a shaky breath. "Gage-." He stopped as he finally noticed that Gage's hand was bandaged. "What happened to your hand?"

123

Gage glanced down at it as if he'd forgotten about the bandage. "Don't worry about it." He stood up. "It won't stop me from doing what I want to do to you tonight."

Joseph backed up some, letting Gage circle behind him. His arms wrapped around Joseph's waist, his good hand pushing his jeans down until Joseph was able to kick out of them. Gage kept him in a tight embrace, his hands touching him everywhere as he started walking forward out of the living room and towards the stairs. Joseph's skin tingled, from Gage's hands stroking over him and the rough fabric of his jeans brushing against his ass and the backs of his thighs as they walked. When they reached the top of the stairs Gage's hand slid down and grasped his shaft, stroking him back to hardness. Joseph moaned and thrust into his hand. They stood there for a quiet moment, Gage pumping his cock while Joseph leaned back against him, turning his head to kiss the soft skin of Gage's neck.

Eventually, they made it to the bedroom, Gage walking him over to the bed and shoving him down on it. He sprawled there without complaint, looking back over his shoulder to see Gage taking his jeans off. He went to his nightstand and took a condom and lube from the drawer, throwing them on the bed. Joseph's breathing quickened as Gage knelt on the bed behind him, thinking that he was about to fuck him. But he was wrong. Gage pushed him up further on the bed then slapped his ass hard. Joseph jerked in shock. Before he could ask what that was all about, Gage gave him another order.

"Spread your legs."

Joseph did it without hesitation. He was pretty sure he would do whatever Gage told him to do in that half sexy half scary voice of his. Gage came down on top of him and sucked a hard kiss onto his ass. Joseph moaned as Gage kept going, giving him those erotic kisses everywhere on his ass and down his thighs, every pull of Gage's mouth on his skin echoing in his cock. Gage bit him, making him jerk again before he licked over his skin to slide his tongue in between his ass. Joseph moaned louder, turning his face into the pillow as that nimble tongue flicked and teased at his entrance before finally pushing inside him.

Joseph squeezed the pillow in his fists, rolling his hips back towards Gage as he gave him the best tongue fucking of his life. He felt Gage's hot breath washing over his ass, felt his fingers digging into his hips, felt his hand sliding beneath him to grasp his shaft. Gage pulled at him sharply, popping his hips off the mattress. Now Gage's hand really moved on his cock, stroking and squeezing in a slow, steady rhythm. Joseph cursed, tearing at the pillow. That hot, wet tongue inside him and the warm hand pumping his cock had him already edging towards climax. "Gage, stop for a minute. Let me …" he trailed off on a groan as Gage squeezed his sac. "Let me touch you too."

Gage laughed softly. "You're crazy if you think I'm stopping. You said I could do what I wanted to you. Well, this is what I want. Want to make you shake, and scream, and come until you can't even move. I want to see you collapse in a boneless, sweaty heap when I'm done with you."

Joseph moaned. "Oh god…"

Gage went back to thrusting his tongue inside him again. His hand pulled back on his cock so hard that it moved his hips back to meet that thrusting tongue. Barely realizing what he was doing, Joseph started rolling up to Gage's mouth and down into his fist.

Gage groaned. "Yeah… you don't want me to stop. Not the way you're pressing this sweet ass against my face."

Joseph's fingers clenched on the pillow, surprised at the streak of arousal that went through him at Gage's words.

"You want to ride my tongue, don't you?"

Joseph didn't answer at first, his brain tripping between the pleasure of Gage's hand still stroking him and trying to respond to what he was saying. But Gage got his attention quick. He slapped him sharply on his thigh.

"Answer me."

"Fuck! Yes, please."

Gage slapped him again, harder this time so that his thigh stung. "Then do it. Show me how much you want it."

Joseph got up on his knees so he could move the way he wanted. Gage started licking him again and Joseph rocked his hips back to meet him. He moved faster and Gage stayed with his pace. Joseph shivered as Gage groaned, the sound vibrating against his skin. Gage's arm wrapped around his back holding him tight. Still Joseph moved, faster and faster, gasping for breath, his body hot and tingling. Gage's hand slid up and down his shaft, cupping and squeezing his balls, his tongue swirling and thrusting inside him. Joseph's orgasm was rising fast and he couldn't hold back. His cock pulsed and his body jerked and he was coming hard, shouting out loudly. "Gage! Fuck! I'm coming! Fuck, don't stop!" Gage groaned again and kept working him as he came in his fist, splashing the covers beneath him.

When he was done he wanted to collapse, not caring if he landed in the mess. But he didn't. Gage held him up and pushed inside him with one deep thrust. His voice came out in a dark whisper.

"I need to fuck you hard, Joseph. I need you to take it for me."

CHAPTER 26

Gage watched as Joseph looked back over his shoulder at him. He was still panting for breath as he answered. "I know. I remember." He lowered himself until he was on his elbows, thrusting his ass higher in the air. "Fuck me, Gage. However you want."

Gage groaned at how open, how generous Joseph was. He'd barely needed any lube as he'd pushed into Joseph, he was so wet and relaxed from the tongue fucking he'd given him. As he pulled out and slid back into him, he moved easily, the tight grip of Joseph's ass sliding over his sheathed cock. It felt amazing to be inside of him, feeling his ass still clenching slightly from the aftershocks of his orgasm. The only thing that could make this better would be if he were bare as he fucked his lover. Gage groaned and put that thought out of his head before he lost it and ripped the damn condom off.

He gripped Joseph's hips tight and started pounding into him. Each push of his hips into Joseph made him exhale hard until Joseph had the side of his face pressed into the mattress, his mouth open as he gasped for breath. Gage pulled Joseph back even higher and tighter against him, leaning back so he could thrust as hard as he wanted. All that rage that had been in him from his shit week and Heather's visit had morphed into a pulsing erotic heat that drove him on. Drove him to fuck Joseph until he was so hot sweat ran down his back. Made him keep pounding into Joseph hard and fast so that his aching balls slapped against Joseph's skin with every thrust. His thighs were trembling, but he wasn't ready to stop. He leaned over Joseph, grabbing the back of his neck in a tight grip. His chest and stomach rubbed against Joseph's back, their skin hot and slick as they came together. The change in position let him go deeper into Joseph, who didn't utter a single word of protest. He just took it and spread his legs even more, allowing him to support some of Gage's weight.

Gage kept fucking into Joseph. He couldn't stop. He needed this. He was so worked up that he needed to keep going until every fucking burning, ripping claw of anger was out of his head, out of his chest. He reached down with his good hand and grasped Joseph's cock finding him only semi-erect. Gage started stroking him, getting him hard yet again. Joseph groaned.

"Gage, don't. I can't come again."

"Yes you fucking can. You'll come for me, Joseph." Gage smoothed his hand down Joseph's neck to his shoulder blades. He raked his nails down his back once, then again. Joseph hissed, his back arching at the pain. But he didn't pull away, didn't ask him to stop. "C'mon, baby. I wanna feel this tight little ass squeeze me as you come." He worked his hand faster on Joseph, who was now moving with him, his cock hard and wet. "C'mon on, Joseph. Be a fucking slut and come for me again."

Gage thrust in deep, circling his hips and grinding his cock against that smooth spot inside Joseph that made him wild. Joseph cried out and pushed back hard against him. His ass started clenching on him again and again as he came in his hand. Gage threw his head back with a hoarse shout. "Aaah, fuck! Goddamnit you feel so good. So fucking tight."

He pulled his hand off Joseph's cock, rubbing his palm up his thigh and over his ass, smearing his cum into his skin. He ignored the pain in his cut hand and gripped Joseph's ass, plumping up those cheeks and spreading them wide. He looked down and watched himself stroking into Joseph. The sight was too much. His spine was tingling with his approaching orgasm. He squeezed Joseph's ass hard, thrusting into him even faster. "Fuck, Joseph, you're making me come." His breath rasped thick and heavy in his chest, his body tight with tension. The dirty sounding slap of their bodies coming together sent warm shivers from his ears down to his stomach. "God, I wanna spill inside you. You don't know how fucking much I want that. I want you Joseph, all of you."

He looked down at Joseph and saw those pale eyes on him. Joseph didn't say anything, but he could tell from the hungry yet giving expression in his eyes and the way he slowly sucked his bottom lip that Joseph wanted that too. He watched as Joseph slowly reached back and his heart stopped for a moment, thinking that he was about to remove the condom. But he didn't. Joseph set his nails into Gage's skin and deliberately raked them down his thigh. He lost it and shouted out Joseph's name as he frantically pounded into him. He slammed into Joseph one last time as his orgasm shot from his cock, holding him firmly in the grip of gasping, pulsing pleasure until he collapsed on top of his lover.

****

Gage rolled off of Joseph, still breathing hard. He maneuvered him around so he could get the wet comforter from beneath them. Throwing it on the floor, Gage laid back down, pulling the sheet over them both. He heard Joseph take a deep breath before he spoke.

"I'm going to need a minute."

Gage pushed Joseph's damp hair away from his forehead, looking at that beautiful face and thinking of everything this man had given him tonight. "Stay, Joseph. For tonight, just stay."

Surprise was clear on Joseph's face. He scooted closer, reaching for Gage, but his eyes were already closing and he stopped moving in the middle of the bed. Gage pulled Joseph the rest of the way into his arms and held him as he fell into a deep sleep. He lay there awake for a while, the violent storm gone out of his head, his blood no longer sparking with anger and racing in his veins. He was calm now thanks to Joseph. Gage took a deep breath and closed his eyes to go to sleep.

CHAPTER 27

Gage woke up slowly. As soon as he did he was immediately aware that he was in bed with Joseph. And not just lying next to him. He held Joseph tight against him, their arms and legs tangled together. Joseph was a little below him, his face tucked into Gage's neck. Gage had his face buried in Joseph's hair. He went still, not wanting to wake Joseph and have him see them like this. He eased back carefully, thankful that Joseph was apparently a heavy sleeper. After several tense moments, he was free and headed into the bathroom.

He turned on the shower and stepped in, letting the scalding water beat down on his head. Fuck. He didn't know what to think. Waking up with Joseph like that, wrapped around him, breathing in the clean scent of his hair, had felt … good. Felt really fucking good. Like Joseph was really his. And it shook him up, made him wonder what the fuck he was doing. He wanted to just give in and let their relationship play out without holding back. But what if he did? What if he committed solely to Joseph and he decided that he didn't want to help him when he needed it? Joseph had been amazing and generous last night. But that didn't mean that he would always be that way. Then where would he be? Furious and without an outlet for all that energy. Or even fucking someone else, which would put them right back where they started.

Gage laughed to himself and braced his forearms on the wet tile, the water streaming down his body. That wasn't quite true, if he fucked someone else after he'd told Joseph they were exclusive, he knew that would be the end to them. It was best to just let things stay as they were. Besides, he'd learned that for him, being in a relationship usually led to nothing but pain, and drugs, and death. And Joseph… Joseph didn't deserve any of that.

****

Joseph lay there in bed listening as Gage went into the shower. He'd woken up first and been surprised at how tight Gage was holding him in his sleep. He'd lain there quietly, enjoying being held against Gage's warmth and listening to his soft breathing. When he'd felt Gage shift as he'd come awake he still hadn't moved, waiting to see how he would react. His stealthy escape into the shower told him everything he needed to know. Joseph pushed himself up to sit against the headboard as the water shut off. He should have known everything that happened last night and his sleeping over hadn't really changed anything.

Gage came out of the bathroom, a towel around his narrow waist, his skin flushed and hair flat from the shower. When he saw Joseph sitting there awake, his eyes bounced away.

"Hey." He gestured towards the bathroom. "Shower's yours if you want it."

Joseph shifted. He was sore and a hot shower sounded great, but he'd rather take one at home instead of prolonging this awkwardness.

"No, that's alright."

Joseph waited a beat to see if Gage would say anything, encourage him to shower there, ask him if he was okay, offer him a bowl of cereal. Anything. He didn't. Joseph sighed and leaned over the bed looking for his jeans before he remembered they were downstairs. He stood up and wrapped the sheet around his waist. He started to go down to the living room when he saw that the pale blue towel around Gage's waist had blood on it.

"You're bleeding, Gage."

Gage looked down at his hand in surprise. His hand had been stinging like a bitch, but seemed like it was done bleeding. Apparently not. Joseph came up to him.

"Do you have first aid stuff in your bathroom?"

He nodded. "Yeah, I'll take care of it." Joseph gave him a look that for once he couldn't read and pulled him into the bathroom.

"I'll do it, just sit down."

Gage put the seat down on the toilet but before he could sit Joseph grabbed his arm to take a closer look at his hand. The cut was long, but not too deep, and right along the fleshy pad of his thumb.

"How did you do this?"

Gage cleared his throat, slightly embarrassed like he always was when he explained the dumb shit he did when he was mad. "Got into a fight with some glass. Glass fought back the only way it knew how." Joseph rolled his eyes and Gage sat. Joseph looked through his cabinets and pulled out bandages, peroxide, and tweezers. "What the fuck are the tweezers for?"

Joseph rolled his eyes again. "Because, idiot. I bet you didn't check to make sure you got all the glass out of the cut, did you?"

Gage kept his mouth shut because he hadn't. Joseph smirked and pulled his arm to rest on the counter, his hand over the sink. Despite calling him an idiot, Joseph's hands were gentle on his injured one as he turned it back and forth in the light, checking for glass. Apparently he found some because the tweezers came up. Joseph looked at him.

"This won't hurt. Much."

Gage sneered a little bit. "I'm not a pussy."

Joseph grinned. "Don't be so defensive, pussy cat."

Gage watched Joseph's curly haired head bend over his hand, his tongue between his teeth. "You're enjoying this too much." Joseph was quiet, getting a grip on the piece of glass in his cut and pulling it out. Gage winced just a little bit. When it was out Joseph laughed.

"I've had pieces of concrete and other stuff picked out of my skin from wiping out on my bike. It's kind of nice to be on the other side of the tweezers."

Gage felt a flash of jealousy run through him and his voice came out harder than he intended. "Who helped you with your cuts?"

Joseph looked at him and as he did his laughter faded. "No one special," he answered softly.

They stared at each other for a long moment. Gage wanted to reach out and touch Joseph, touch that golden skin warmed by the sunlight spilling into the room, and pull him down for a kiss. He had to clench the hand in his lap into a fist to keep from doing so. This … whatever it was between them had gone way past just physical. He needed to rein it in if he wanted to maintain their status quo. He cleared his throat. "I think I'm ready for the peroxide."

Joseph's lashes lowered, hiding whatever he was thinking. He picked up the bottle of peroxide and Gage grit his teeth as he poured some over his cut. The liquid bubbled and foamed for a few seconds before Joseph blotted him dry, put a bandage on it and wrapped his hand in gauze.

"That'll keep you from moving your thumb a lot so it won't hurt as much."

Gage held his hand out looking at the white strips around his hand and wrist. "You've got me looking like a boxer or something."

Joseph laughed and put everything away. "I'd better go," he said as he washed his hands. I need to go home and get ready for my race tonight."

"What time do the races start?"

"Seven o'clock but mine isn't until eight. Why, are you coming?"

Joseph looked at him again and now Gage could read him. Could easily see the hope in his eyes. Gage nodded. "I'll make sure to close up on time so I can make it out."

Joseph smiled, looking young and boyish in his happiness. "Right on. You'll have fun I promise."

Gage touched Joseph, just a little bit, just on his arm. "I don't doubt it."

CHAPTER 28

Dusk was approaching, the lights over the track showing brighter as the sun dropped over the horizon. There was a breeze cooling the air, but it was still warm enough for Joseph to feel a drop of sweat trickle down his back. His race suit did its job in protecting him, but it was hot. He looked at the clock hanging in the covered garage area where racers waited. 7:40. His race was up in twenty minutes.

Joseph put his earbuds in and turned up the volume on his phone. He hit play for his favorite song then closed his eyes. Drums and guitar blasted into his ears, pulsing into his brain and his blood stream, getting him hyped up for his race. He didn't care who was watching, just started banging his head and punching his fist in the air. Then he threw his head back and his arms up and roared to the sky. The scream didn't let the energy out, it magnified it, sent it bouncing around his cells until his hands tingled with the urge to grip his bike's handlebars. He bounced on the balls of his feet and punched the air one more time. Yeah. He was about to win this race. He felt it. He bounced one last time before taking his ear buds out. When he turned around, he jerked in surprise.

Gage stood and watched Joseph go through a wild, screaming ritual. Somehow he managed to look intense instead of crazy and as he threw his fist into the air Gage shook his head. He didn't see how Joseph managed to put this side of himself aside for so many hours each week. Regardless, the race hadn't even started yet and he was already glad he'd come. He liked seeing Joseph's wild side and when he turned around, he was even happier to be there. Joseph looked fucking ridiculously sexy in his bike suit. The black leather with bright green accents hugged his slender frame, tight on his thighs and abs. His hair was pulled into a sleek ponytail and his face was flushed with excitement. And of course Gage had checked out his perfect ass when Joseph's back had been to him.

Gage couldn't help but laugh as Joseph's eyes went wide when he turned and saw them standing there. He hadn't come by himself. He'd brought Gia, Nate, and a few others that Joseph had met at the bowling alley. He'd been determined that Joseph was going to have a loud ass cheering section up in the stands tonight. But he hadn't invited Max. He didn't want to hear his bullshit about leaving Joseph alone. Joseph came over laughing.

"You could have warned me, Gage! If I'd known you were bringing all these good people I would have worn my fancy suit." He shook hands with everyone and gave Gia a hug. Gia rubbed her palm over Joseph's leather covered abs.

"I think you look just fine in this one. Don't you think so Gage?"

Gage rolled his eyes and playfully grabbed the collar of her shirt. He tugged her away, ignoring her squeals. "The threesome isn't happening girlie. Let it go."

Joseph laughed again with a slight blush on his face. Gage wasn't sure what was cool on this track so he didn't kiss Joseph like he wanted to. He didn't give a shit, but he didn't want to cause any trouble for him. They looked over Joseph's bike for a few minutes with him explaining about the race before they had to go to their seats. Joseph grinned and waved at him one last time before he put on his helmet and wheeled his bike out to the track. Gage knew he'd made Joseph happy. Yeah, he was glad he'd come.

Joseph was even more hyped up as he sat on his bike at the start line. Gage had said he'd come, but turning around to see him standing there looking as good as ever in nothing more than jeans and a dark t-shirt had given him a deep feeling of happiness. And the fact that Gage had brought some of his friends with him to watch him race, that made him feel like things really were going somewhere between them. Joseph looked at the riders on either side of him and grinned to himself. They might as well head back to the garage. The way he was feeling he knew he was about to win this race. He focused himself as the starting light changed from red to yellow. When it turned green that emerald light seemed to echo in his head and his heart pulsed hard with a strong beat of adrenaline. He released the brake and took off, leaning tight over the handlebars. This win was his.

****

Joseph was surrounded by fans. It was always fun after a race, especially if you'd won, to interact with the people who came out. There were the kids who wanted to be racers, the people who enjoyed the sport, and the gals and a few guys who wanted to flirt with him. He signed some programs and took pictures, even letting a few kids sit on his bike for their photo. He looked farther out and saw Gage and his group making their way towards him, but before they could get there, the crowd parted to reveal one of his longtime supporters. He held his hand out to the handsome dark-haired man. "Mr. Montoya. Thanks for coming out tonight. I hope you enjoyed the races."

Montoya took his hand in both of his. "Joseph, how many times do I have to tell you? Mr. Montoya is so formal. Please, call me Rafael."

Joseph nodded. "Rafael." He felt a little funny calling this man, who was both older and very wealthy, by his first name. Montoya let his hand go, but his palm ran up his arm to his shoulder.

"You did great out there today, Joseph. A clear win. I arrived a little late, but I knew immediately which racer was you. He nodded towards his Diavel. Such a beautiful and distinctive bike." Montoya smiled, "And this ponytail flying behind you of course." Montoya reached up and lightly tugged on his hair. "You should let me sponsor you, Joseph. I can help get you into more and bigger races."

Joseph appreciated the offer. And he was tempted to take him up on it. But he knew it wasn't just sponsorship Montoya was interested in. He smiled and started to turn him down. But before he could Gage was there.

"Who is this?"

Joseph blinked. Gage didn't congratulate him on his win, he just asked about Montoya with clear hostility in his voice. He wasn't surprised when Gage read him this time, knowing his face had *what the hell* written all over it.

Gage closed his eyes for a moment. He was being an asshole. "Joseph, that was a great race. That was pretty fucking amazing to watch. I didn't know you could ride quite like that. But I guess I should have realized ..." He trailed off and didn't finish his sentence. Joseph grinned and he could tell by the sparkle in his eyes that he'd caught what he meant. But neither of them addressed it since they were surrounded by pretty little mommies and their big-eared kids. Joseph just said thank you and Gage turned his attention back to the slick motherfucker who'd touched Joseph so familiarly. "You the owner of this track?" The man smiled, adjusting the lapels of his white suit jacket.

"No. I'm just a fan of motorcycle races. And of our big winner of course." He held his hand out. "Rafael Montoya."

Gage stared hard for a moment. But then he realized he shouldn't be a dick to one of Joseph's supporters. He accepted the hand and shook it quickly before letting go. "Nice to meet you."

"Si, mucho gusto."

An arrogant smile crept onto Montoya's face as they held eye contact for a few seconds longer. Gage knew what that look meant, this Montoya wanted to be more than just a fan of Joseph's. His eyes narrowed and he was about to warn him off, eavesdropping kids be damned, when someone else joined the group.

"Damn, Joseph. I almost had you on the last lap, but then you just took off after the final curve."

Joseph laughed and reached out to shake the approaching man's hand. "That's because Gage got my bike tuned up right. Nico, this is Gage. Gage, Nico. He's my racing and sometimes running buddy."

Nico turned and looked at him. "So you're Gage Mason."

Gage raised an eyebrow and looked him over. He'd detected a judgmental tone in that greeting. He wondered what Joseph had told him and wasn't at his friendliest as he finally responded. "Yeah, last I checked."

Nico gave him an appraising look, but didn't say anything else. He turned back to Joseph.

"We're going to get something to eat, right man? I'm starving."

Joseph patted his flat stomach. "Yeah, me too. Winning always makes me hungry," he said with a cocky little grin, making Nico roll his eyes.

Gia spoke up. "We can go to my bar. It'll be busy, but I think I can make sure we get served quickly," she offered with a wink.

Everybody agreed, Joseph showing surprise that Gia owned her own bar. The people who weren't part of their group started to leave as Joseph started talking to Gia about her business. Gage's hackles went up when Nico invited Montoya, who was still standing there. He noticed Montoya's eyes went to Joseph, looking him up and down before he smiled and said yes. Gage knew he didn't have any right to be jealous of someone interested in Joseph since he wouldn't commit to being in a monogamous relationship with him. But he didn't give a fuck. He went up to Joseph and wrapped a hand around the back of his neck.

"Let's go then. Joseph, you ride with me."

Joseph shook his head. "I've got my bike. Give me a few minutes to hook my mirrors and brake light back up and I'll meet you there."

Gage squeezed Joseph's neck slightly. "I'm in my truck and I brought tie downs. Ride with me." Joseph looked like he wanted to say something, but after a brief pause he went ahead and nodded yes. Gage didn't bother to turn and look at Montoya. He knew the other man was watching.

CHAPTER 29

Joseph was as neat as possible, but he wolfed down his steak and fries. Their big group from the track had taken over several tables when they'd arrived at *Gia's Bar and Grill*, laughing and going over the races as they drank some amazing beers. But when the food had arrived Joseph let the conversations flow over him. He was hungry and the food was good. After the last bite, he raised his pint glass to Gia. "Tell your chef back there that was one of the best steaks I've ever had." He looked around, nodding his head to the beat of the live music playing. Big G's was decorated in a cool mix of Texas flags, multicultural cowboy art and vintage tin signs. "I like this place. It's actually close to my townhouse. I don't know why I've never come in here before, but I'll definitely be coming back."

Gia smiled with pride. "Thanks. I've owned it for a few years now. I took over from my father after he retired. I love it, but I'm running into a few problems with licensing some of my products and things like that. It's a headache."

Gage spoke up. "Joseph could help you there. He's a business law whiz when he's not winning motorcycle races."

Gia looked impressed and Joseph turned to Gage in surprised pleasure at the compliment. Gage looked back at him, relaxed and full of self-confidence. Joseph had just decided not to make a big deal of the remark when Gia laughed jokingly.

"Wow, Gage. You must be so proud of your boyfriend."

Joseph saw the immediate change that came over Gage. He stiffened, his dark eyes losing their easy going sparkle.

"What are we in junior high? He's not my damn boyfriend."

Gia kept teasing him, but Joseph picked up his beer and gulped it down. Gage had tried to make it seem like he was joking, but Joseph knew he was serious. The thought of him as his boyfriend made Gage uncomfortable. Gage's immediate reaction to Gia's kidding made him angry. Or hurt. He didn't know. And now Gage was refusing to look at him. Joseph felt like an idiot for again falling into the trap of thinking they were getting somewhere in their relationship. He needed to get away for a moment. He excused himself to go and get another drink, waving off Gia's offer to call over a server.

Montoya came up to Joseph where he waited at the bar. He'd been seated at a different table so they hadn't talked much. "I don't want to be intrusive, *mi amigo*. But this Gage, is he *su novio?*"

Joseph laughed ruefully before he looked at Rafael to answer. "I wouldn't say that he's my boyfriend. But we are lovers."

Montoya smiled slightly. "I see. I would try to entice you away from him, *pero* I can see it would be no use. You want him to be more to you."

Joseph stared down at the glossy bar top. "Yeah, I do. Too bad it will likely never happen." He took a drink of the beer the bartender put in front of him and looked back at Montoya. "I don't think I'll wait too much longer for something I'll probably never have."

"Well, if it doesn't happen, call me when you have that bad boy out of your system."

Joseph looked away, but Montoya lightly touched his jaw and turned him back. "You will call, *sí?*"

Joseph nodded. "Yes, I'll call you."

Montoya let him go and took several bills out of his wallet to pay for his meal. "I'm going. I can feel your lover's eyes burning a hole in the back of my neck. I don't think he likes me being so close to you."

Joseph looked and saw Gage was staring at them. He didn't even try to hide it by looking away when Joseph caught him. Joseph sighed and said good night to Montoya before rejoining their group. The adrenaline of the race had worn off and now he was tired. Tired of having his emotions jerked around by Gage. He'd been riding so high after the disappointment of that morning, but Gage's swift rejection of their relationship undid all of it, sending him crashing back down. Gage's conflicting nature was driving him crazy. Jealous. Aloof. Passionate. Unavailable. He decided he didn't want to deal with it anymore that night.

"I'm going to take off," he said to Gage.

Gage's eyes flicked to the door Montoya had disappeared through a few minutes ago before they settled back on him. "Why? Where are you going?"

"Home. I'm tired and I want to get some sleep."

Gage nodded and Joseph said goodbye to everyone, accepting a last round of congratulations on his win. It had been nice to hang out with his friends and Gage's, but he was definitely ready to be alone.

Out in the parking lot, Joseph was quiet as they walked to Gage's truck. When they were at his big Dodge Ram, Joseph reached for one of the cords that held his bike secure.

"Leave your bike there. I'll take you home."

Joseph started to say okay. But he knew if he let Gage drive him home, they would end up in bed together. And after that Joseph would probably be frustrated as he again stood in the doorway and watched Gage's tail lights disappear into the night. "No, that's okay. I'm fine to ride." Surprisingly, Gage didn't try to change his mind, he just helped him get the Diavel out of the back. But after Gage set the kickstand on the bike he pulled Joseph between his warm body and the truck.

Gage cupped his cheek, before sliding a hand into his hair. "You sure you don't want me to come with you? I thought you might want to celebrate your win tonight."

Joseph didn't say anything, his stomach jumping with anticipation as he thought of the things Gage would do to his body. Gage moved in close to kiss him and he almost allowed it. But just when he felt Gage's warm breath brush across his lips he turned his face away. "I'm not in the mood." Gage pulled back and Joseph looked at him. "I guess that means you'll probably find someone else to celebrate with, right?"

Gage stepped away, his expression hardening, and a muscle ticking in his jaw. "What's wrong with you tonight?"

Joseph pushed away from the truck and swung a leg over his bike. "What's wrong with me is that I wasn't fucking asleep this morning when you snuck out of bed. I don't get why you could call and ask for my help last night, but couldn't do it this morning for your hand. And it pisses me off that you have the nerve to be jealous of Montoya when in your head we're nothing more than fuck buddies."

He waited for Gage to say something, to give him a reason to think he saw more to their relationship. When he didn't, Joseph started his bike and crammed his helmet on his head. He looked at Gage one last time, but he just stood there with his arms crossed over his chest. Joseph was beyond frustrated and sick of dealing with the erratic ebb and flow of Gage's feelings for him. He flicked his visor down and sped out of the parking lot.

****

Gage took a deep breath of the warm night air after Joseph peeled out of the parking lot. He'd realized his comment earlier had probably hurt Joseph as soon as he'd said it. But he hadn't expected him to be that upset. Of course if he'd known Joseph was awake that morning he might have expected that.

Unlocking the truck door, Gage got in and started it up. Now that he knew Joseph hadn't been asleep it made sense why he'd been so pissed. That didn't mean he wasn't pissed too. Maybe he'd been an asshole with his comment, but he didn't like the way Joseph took off without discussing things with him first. And it made him wonder. If Joseph was going to cut out when things didn't go the way he liked, then why should he bother even trying to get serious with him?

After driving for a few minutes, Gage stopped at a light and pulled out his phone. Joseph had to be home by now. Gage didn't want to wait to find out if he and Joseph were done. He wanted his answers now. The phone rang twice before Joseph's still angry voice came over the line.

"Hello."

"Do you always take off like that when you've got a problem?"

"What?"

"You heard me."

"Don't give me that, Gage. You weren't exactly giving me a reason to stay."

"You didn't give me a chance." He heard Joseph give a harsh laugh.

"You weren't going to. I could tell by the stubborn look on your face."

"Four days, Joseph. Four fucking days. That's all it's been."

"What?" Joseph asked again, this time sounding exasperated.

"Four days ago you said this was enough for you for now. That ain't true anymore? Were you expecting me to change that fast?"

"No, but…"

"But what? If you've got me on some deadline, you should at least have given me the fucking courtesy of letting me know my expiration date."

"I don't have you on a timeline, Gage. It just hurt the way you left the bed this morning after … after the way things went last night. I tried to let it go because it was awesome the way you came to the track tonight and I appreciated that. But you just outright denying we're together one minute and then being jealous of Montoya the next … You've got me confused. If we're nothing more than friends who fuck, then why the hell are you jealous of Montoya?"

Gage had to pull over to continue this conversation. He sat there listening to the quiet but deep rumble of the engine before he asked a question of his own. "Joseph, did you ever stop to think this might be hard for me too?"

Now Joseph sounded more confused than mad. "What do you mean?"

"I don't know why things have been different with you than they have been from the way I normally go about being with other people. But they are and it's not something I've dealt with for a long time. I don't know what the fuck I'm doing. Or shit, even what the right thing to do is. Yeah, I was a fucking coward to sneak out of the bed this morning. And yeah, Gia's comment made me uncomfortable and I didn't handle it right. But you could have fucking talked to me about it instead of taking off like that. And I told you how I was, Joseph. You made the decision to stay with me. You can't expect me to go from that to boyfriend of the year overnight."

Joseph was quiet on the other end of the line. Gage cursed under his breath. He could sense that Joseph was still ticked off and realized he'd have to give a little more. "I was a jealous asshole with that Montoya guy. I admit it, because I don't just see us as fuck buddies." Gage stopped short of saying they were a couple. He still wasn't ready to make that commitment. But Joseph didn't let that slide.

"What *do* you see us as?"

Gage could have kicked himself. He really needed to start remembering he was dealing with a lawyer. He reminded him of their agreement. "It's only been four days, Joseph." Joseph was quiet again so Gage prodded him. "What's it gonna be, Joseph? Is my time up? Should I assume the way you rode off tonight means I won't see you again? Or will you give me a chance to figure out what the hell I'm doing with you?"

Joseph groaned. "Why do you have to be so convincing, Gage?" A deep sigh came over the line. "No, you're time isn't up you silver tongued devil."

Gage grinned and thumped his fist on the steering wheel. "So can I come over?"

"No, I really am tired and I know you'll have me up all night."

Gage rolled his eyes. "And maybe you're punishing me for being an asshole?"

Joseph laughed. "You said it, not me. Come get me tomorrow and we'll go get IHOP."

Gage snorted. "Great, we'll have make-up breakfast. Just what I was looking forward to," he said in a dry voice.

Joseph laughed again. "Count yourself lucky you're even getting that."

CHAPTER 30

Joseph stared at himself in the mirror. He wet his brush before he pulled the thick bristles through his hair, smoothing it back from his face. Then he pulled it into a tight ponytail at the base of his neck, looping the end back through the elastic and making sure there weren't any strands free. When he was done, he put the brush down and kept staring. But he didn't really see himself. His brain was focused on Gage. He knew he was probably crazy to stay with him. But he just felt like Gage was close to finally taking that next step.

He remembered back to what Gage had told him when he'd confessed about his addictions. *I like to have sex and I like to keep things casual, no strings, and they're not the only one. If they're down with it, great. If they're not, it's no big deal, I just move on.* That's how Gage operated. Except with him. For whatever reason, Gage didn't move on from him. Whenever they argued and Joseph tried to take a step back, Gage always found a way to make him stay. Yeah, he knew Gage was manipulating him. But the fact that he even bothered to do so told Joseph that Gage did feel for him, whether he knew it or not. It just didn't make sense that Gage would go through the trouble of persuading him to stay and do things like bring his friends to his race if he only wanted sex. And the possessive comments Gage let slip while they were in bed.

A shiver ran through him as he thought of Gage whispering in his ear, *I won't let anybody else have you. I want you all to myself.* Joseph suspected that was how Gage really felt, but something was holding him back. He'd told him that he didn't want anyone to get too attached and there had to be a reason for that. Joseph was determined to get Gage to open up so he could figure out what it was.

Joseph knew it wasn't going to be easy to get Gage to commit to him. And that he might end up getting hurt before he got what he wanted. But the advice Pruitt had given him at work applied here as well. He was willing to pay that price to have Gage. Joseph had fun with Gage. He felt like he was more himself with him than he had ever been with anyone else he'd ever dated. And of course the attraction between them was explosive, the sex amazing. It'd be outright stupid of him to give that up without making an effort to make things work. The doorbell rang, ending that whole thought process.

He headed out to the living room and when he opened the door, Gage was standing there. His hair was as neat as it ever was since he'd driven his truck instead of riding his bike without a helmet. "Good morning," he said as he stepped back to let him in.

Gage grunted, his voice rumbling out low and throaty. "I can't believe you want to go eat this early in the morning."

Joseph laughed and looked at his watch. "It's nine o'clock! That's not too early. Besides if we wait any longer the place will be packed with the church crowd." Gage took off his dark sunglasses and gave him a look that clearly said he wasn't buying that argument. Joseph shook his head at Gage's grumpiness and leaned forward, kissing him lightly. Gage kissed him back, his tongue coming out to tease his. His hand came up to the small of his back, pulling Joseph against his body. Joseph kept the kiss light, retreating and pulling back whenever Gage tried to deepen it. Gage's hand slid up his back and brushed against his bound hair. Joseph knew he was about to release his ponytail from the elastic and he stepped out of his arms before he could.

Gage looked confused. "Is everything okay?"

Joseph nodded, trying to look and sound calm, and not show how affected he was by their kiss. "Yeah, I'm just hungry that's all." He grabbed his keys and opened the door. "Let's go."

****

149

Two hours and several hundred calories later, they were back at his townhouse. Their breakfast had gone well, Gage perking up after coffee. They'd been relaxed throughout their meal, talking casually and doing a little early morning people watching. Joseph had enjoyed himself and he knew Gage had as well. Joseph knew it was just one meal, but their ease with each other was proof that they had something to build on. He wouldn't be putting forth the effort with Gage if he didn't truly believe that.

Joseph flopped back onto the couch. "I'm full."

Gage sat down beside him. "That's what happens when you stuff yourself full of ten pounds of pancakes."

Joseph laughed and raised his shirt to rub his stomach. "Shut up. You're the one that told the server to bring me an extra stack."

A smile curled up the corner of Gage's mouth. "That's because I saw you about to go for mine." Gage reached out and lightly ran his fingertips over his stomach. "Starting to realize I don't like to share," he said.

Joseph let Gage's hand wander a little lower, arching up slightly into his touch. "You're greedy."

Gage smiled again. "Yep." He moved over closer to him on the couch but Joseph stood up.

"I need to burn off all that syrup and fat. We should go workout." Gage looked at him suspiciously, but Joseph just gave him an innocent, wide-eyed look in return. "We can go to my gym, it's close."

Gage sat there for a moment looking at him before he sighed and stood up too. "Where do you work out?"

Joseph smiled and bounced on the balls of feet as he named the upscale fitness club he belonged to. "Titan Sculpt."

Gage's lip curled in disdain.

Joseph stopped bouncing and frowned. "What's wrong with Titan Sculpt?"

Gage shrugged. "Nothing, if you like working out in an overpriced *studio* with people who are more worried about their coordinated workout gear and how dark to go in the tanning bed than working out."

Joseph's mouth dropped open. "Are you serious? You're prejudiced against a fitness center? Then where do you work out?"

"At Nate's Gym. No pretentious assholes on site. He doesn't allow it."

Joseph rolled his eyes. "That's like reverse snobbification or something. Well, you and that chip on your shoulder can get over yourselves. We're going to Titan Sculpt. We can go to your gym next time." He looked at Gage's jeans. "You don't have to coordinate, but I'm sure you don't want to work out in pants. I'll get you some shorts."

Joseph headed back to his bedroom and grabbed a pair of shorts from his dresser. Gage was bigger than him, but the shorts were baggy and stretchy at the waist so it didn't matter. When he turned back around Gage was standing in the doorway. Joseph hesitated for a second before he went over to him. "Did you want to change in here?"

Gage blinked, then kicked off his shoes. "Yeah, I can change in here."

"Let me help you," Joseph said as he reached out to Gage's waist. He looked at Gage. Their gazes locked as Joseph unbuttoned Gage's jeans before slowly tugging the zipper down. His fingers grazed over the hardening shaft behind the cotton underwear as he pushed the jeans off his hips. A muscle flexed in Gage's jaw, but Joseph didn't say anything. He just dropped to his knees, pulling the jeans the rest of the way off. He held the shorts up for Gage to step into, pulling them up with him as he stood again. His fingers again brushed over Gage's cock, his erection obvious as it pressed against the soft cotton of his boxers. But this time he made it clear that it hadn't been an accident, his fingers curling over the thick shaft before the shorts blocked his access. When they were in place, he ran his fingers along the waistband. "Are you ready?" Joseph asked softly.

Gage moved so swiftly he didn't have time to react. His arms wrapped around Joseph, one hand at his waist, the other gripping the back of his neck. Gage pressed their bodies tight together and kissed him hard, his tongue deep in his mouth. Joseph didn't return the embrace. But he kissed him back, rubbing his body against Gage's, letting him feel that he was hard too. Gage groaned and nipped at his bottom lip before pulling away to look at him.

"Do you really want to go to the gym?"

Joseph licked his lips. What he wanted to do was fall back on the bed and let Gage fuck him till he couldn't move. Unfortunately, that didn't suit his plans for the day. "Yes, I need to go. I wasn't able to work out at all this week." Gage continued to hold him tightly for a long moment, that muscle flexing in his jaw, before he finally let him go.

"Okay, then. Let's go work out."

CHAPTER 31

Gage ran his forearm across his brow to wipe the sweat away, keeping Joseph in his line of vision. He wasn't sure what game Joseph was playing, but he was definitely playing at something. All day Joseph had been teasing him, egging him on. But every time he'd tried to get close he'd backed away. Was Joseph punishing him for yesterday? It didn't seem like it. Gage wasn't getting a spiteful vibe off him, so he didn't think it was anything like that. He moved to the high bar to do some chin ups. All he could do was wait to see what Joseph had going on in his head. He was on his fourth rep when Joseph came over and looked up at him.

"You're good at those. It doesn't look like you're straining at all."

Gage laughed and pulled himself up again. "I would show you that I can skin the cat, but I don't want to show off. There's enough of that going on in here." Gage nearly fell from the bar as Joseph reached up and traced his fingers over his stomach.

"I believe you can do it. You've got great definition here."

Gage hung there for a moment as Joseph smiled up at him, his green eyes sparkling and mischievous, before he walked away. He managed to get out one more rep. But then Joseph pulled the band from his hair and shook his head, setting his curly brown hair loose around his bare shoulders. Gage gave up and dropped to the ground as Joseph bent over and grabbed a pair of dumbbells. The thin material of his shorts molded to the round curves of his ass when Joseph squatted and started reps of triceps kickbacks. Gage just stood there and watched, not even realizing that someone had come up to his side until they spoke.

"Damn, man. I don't know whether to ask you if you're done with the bar or stand here with you and stare at that."

Gage looked to his left to see a muscle-bound, thick-necked freak staring at Joseph. His hackles immediately went up. "I suggest you move along to the bar," he said in a hard voice. The guy turned to him and after seeing that he wasn't playing around he put his hands up and backed off. Gage watched the man walk away, but he didn't look back. And when he got on the bar he faced away from Joseph.

Gage turned back to Joseph just in time to see him set the dumbbells back on the bottom of the rack, flinging his hair over his shoulders as he stood back up. Joseph stretched his arms high over his head, leaning back and pushing his hips forward. The lights caught the sweat on Joseph's bare torso, making his skin gleam golden. That was it. It was time for them to get out of there before he embarrassed himself with a very obvious erection. He went over to Joseph, getting close in his personal space.

"Are you done?"

Joseph ran his hand through his damp hair. "I was going to do a little more, but if you're ready to go we can leave."

Gage nodded. "I'm ready. Let's go."

****

They grabbed their water bottles and discarded shirts, turned in their towels and left. As they headed out to his truck, Joseph walked close to him, bumping his shoulder.

"That wasn't so bad was it?"

Gage went to his side and got in before he answered. "Guess not. Not as many posers as I expected. And they didn't have a juice bar, so that's a plus in their favor."

Joseph laughed. "Let me guess. Rather than a juice bar, you'd prefer it if they had rusty old water fountains with barely enough pressure to get the lukewarm water to come out."

Laughing, Gage got the truck started and drove off the gym's lot. "Not quite." He tensed as Joseph snapped off his seat belt and propped his elbow on the center console so he could lean closer to him.

"I liked working out with you Gage. You looked hot doing those chin ups."

"Is that why you thought it was a good idea to touch me like that in there?"

Joseph rubbed his hand over his stomach just like he had in the gym. Gage fought to keep his eyes on the road as Joseph's little finger slipped into his shorts, grazing his pelvis.

"You don't want me to touch you?"

Gage cleared his throat. "Yeah, I do. Just maybe not like that in front of people. I was about to pop a tent for everybody to camp under."

Joseph laughed and Gage clenched the steering wheel tight as his warm breath blew over his ear. "For a bad boy, you sure are modest."

"I never said I was a bad boy."

Gage was already semi-hard and he stiffened even further when Joseph's tongue traced over his ear and another finger inched inside his shorts.

"You don't have to say it. It's pretty obvious." His entire hand was in his shorts now, trailing up and down his cock. "What about now, Gage?" Joseph wrapped his hand around his shaft. "It's just us in here. Can I touch you now?"

Gage cursed as Joseph squeezed him. "*Fuck*. Joseph, I'm driving.

Joseph stroked him slowly. "So? We're almost to my place; just keep your eyes on the road."

Gage kept his grip tight on the steering wheel and pressed the pedal down a little further, edging past the speed limit. He cursed again and speed up even more as Joseph started stroking him faster, his lips trailing down to kiss his neck. He was forced to stop at a red light and Joseph raised his head to kiss him. Gage was breathing hard as he kissed him back, keeping his eyes on the light so he'd see when it changed to green. It seemed to stay red forever, which meant he got to enjoy Joseph's kiss longer, but he needed it to change so he could get him home and get inside him. The light finally flashed to green just as he started pumping his hips up into Joseph's fist. He ended up jamming his foot onto the gas too hard, sending the truck surging through the intersection. Joseph pulled back from their kiss and Gage got his speed under control.

"Almost there," Joseph said, still stroking him swiftly.

Gage grit his teeth. He knew Joseph was talking about getting to his house, but he might as well have been talking about him. *He* was almost there, ready to come in Joseph's fist, when he took his hand out of his shorts. "Christ, Joseph. What are you doing?"

"You're about to pass my house."

Gage stomped on the brakes. The tires squealed and Joseph braced his hand on the dash as he turned sharply into the driveway.

"Pull into my garage."

Gage gave a strained laugh, his cock still throbbing. "Is that some sort of porn star talk?"

Joseph snorted. "I didn't think of that." He reached into his drawstring backpack and took out a remote. He pushed the button and the garage attached to the side of his townhouse opened. "Pull into *this* garage."

Gage stepped on the gas and the big truck shot forward into the garage next to Joseph's bike, coming to an abrupt stop a hairsbreadth from the wall. He slammed the gear into park and turned to him. "You've been teasing me all fucking day. In the house. Now."

Joseph shook his head. "Not yet. Tell me one thing first."

"What?"

"Why are you so defensive about stuff like your bike and what gym you go to?"

Gage's eyes widened in surprise. "You're asking me that now?"

"Yes. I want you to open up to me, even if it's just a little bit." He tugged at Gage's shorts. "I'd be willing to show my appreciation."

Gage cleared his throat and stared out the windshield at the wall in front of him. He didn't really mind sharing this, especially if it got him what he wanted, which was Joseph naked underneath him. "I grew up in the system like I told you. I took off as soon as I was legal. Wild doesn't even come close to describing me back then. I didn't care about anything but hanging out with my boys, Max and later Nate. I didn't even graduate. And I came pretty close to being nothing more than a junkie. I uh… it seemed like I had nothing but people looking down on me; the judge who sentenced me after my assault charge, the counselor who wanted me to find my happy place, the banker who practically laughed when I walked in asking for a loan to start my shop."

He sneered a little bit as he thought back to that fat fuck telling him he was too much of a risk for a loan. "I fucking hate people like that." Gage shrugged. "I like the stuff I have and I know that I work my ass off in that shop to get it. But I know those assholes and everybody else like them are still fucking judging me. Always looking at me and assuming I'm nothing more than a loser."

Joseph had guessed it was something like that. Still, Gage was so confident, cocky even, that he was surprised to hear that he had those thoughts in his head after all this time. He lightly bumped his forehead against Gage's jaw to get him to look at him. When he did, Joseph smiled. "You know that's all bullshit, right? They're busy being judgey assholes to somebody else while you're out doing your thing on that sexy ass bike of yours."

Gage shook his head. He didn't laugh out loud, but it was dancing in his eyes. "Do I have to warn you again about language, Counselor Naderi?"

Joseph shrugged. "Fuck them."

This time Gage did laugh. "Yeah, fuck them."

Joseph grinned and went to hold up his end of their bargain. He tugged at Gage's shorts again, Gage lifting his hips so that he could pull them down to mid-thigh. His thick erection sprang free and without any hesitation, Joseph leaned over and sucked it into his mouth.

Gage groaned as Joseph took his cock deep into his throat again and again. Before he completely lost his mind, he remembered to turn the truck off and roll the windows down so they wouldn't pass out from carbon monoxide poisoning. Once that was done he leaned back against the bucket seat and gave himself up to the pleasure of Joseph sucking him off. Joseph worked him good, his head moving slowly up and down, his hot mouth sliding over his shaft. Gage's hips jerked forward as Joseph blew a warm breath over his cockhead, before he licked over the tip. Then he took him deep again, moaning, the sound vibrating up and down his shaft. Gage cursed softly, torn between wanting this to continue and wanting it to stop so he could fuck Joseph like he'd wanted to do since last night. Just then, Joseph sat back up and Gage looked at him, taking in his flushed face and swollen lips.

"Goddamn that pretty mouth. Come here." He tangled his fingers in Joseph's hair and pulled him forward, their lips meeting in a rough, hot kiss. He tried to ignore the streak of possessiveness that ran through him as he tasted himself in Joseph's mouth. But his fingers clenched tight on his lover, pulling him even closer. He wanted to yank Joseph over into his lap, but the steering wheel and center console didn't give them much room for that. Gage groaned in frustration. He was aching, feeling like he'd been aroused for hours.

Joseph broke away from him. "Now we can go." He scooted over to the passenger side door and got out of the truck.

CHAPTER 32

Gage stumbled out of his door, awkwardly pulling his shorts up over his erection as he followed Joseph out of the garage. Once they were in the kitchen Joseph stopped and turned to face him. "Goddamnit, you'd better not have another reason to put this off."

Joseph grinned before pulling his shirt over his head and throwing it to the floor. Then he reached into his shorts pocket and pulled something out. He held it up in front of his face and Gage saw that it was a condom. He stalked forward.

"You've had that on you all this time." Joseph nodded, his green eyes gleaming wickedly. "You got me all worked up on purpose." He nodded again. "So you're not surprised that I'm about to fuck you right here on this kitchen floor."

Joseph didn't say anything; he just put the condom packet up to his mouth and tore it open with his teeth.

Gage practically growled and took the condom from him. He yanked Joseph into his arms, kissing him hard. He roughly pushed his shorts down, immediately grasping his shaft and stroking him. Joseph moaned and wrapped his arms around his neck, pushing his hips forward. After a few moments of furious kissing and stroking, Gage knocked Joseph's arms aside. He quickly pulled his own shirt over his head then kicked his shoes off and pushed his shorts down. He stared at Joseph, saw his chest heaving as he stared back, watching him roll the condom on.

When he was covered Gage reached out for Joseph, kissing him once more before he pushed him down to his knees. Joseph looked up at him before he leaned forward and sucked him back into his mouth. Gage inhaled sharply, his body tense as he stared down at the beautiful man on his knees before him, his tongue coming out to lave his sheathed cock, getting him nice and wet. Barely a minute had passed when he pushed Joseph off him and went to the floor too. He spun Joseph around so that his back was to him and shoved him down hard. Joseph's hands flew out and he caught himself so that he was on all fours. Gage liked that position so he let him stay that way. He sucked two fingers into his mouth, ready to prepare Joseph for his entry. But Joseph started to crawl forward. Gage growled and grabbed him by the hips, yanking him back.

"Where the fuck do you think you're going?"

Joseph edged his fingers to his shorts. "Lube," he said taking a small packet of lubricant from his pocket.

Gage glared at him, but he took the stuff. He quickly dripped some over his fingers and on Joseph's entrance. Gage slid a finger inside him, biting his lip at the warmth that gripped him so tightly. Thinking that Joseph was trying to get away from him had made him angry, his blood pumping thick and hot. He'd felt like he would chase Joseph down if he had to just to get inside him. He wasn't waiting anymore. With no more preparation that that single lubed finger Gage fit his cock to Joseph's entrance and pushed inside. He went as slow as he was able, but Joseph still groaned in discomfort. He was calling himself an asshole even as he thought it, but right then he didn't care if it hurt. He moved his hips back and forth, working his cock in deeper.

"You'd better try and relax, Joseph. Because you've got me so goddamn worked up there's no way fucking way I'm stopping."

Joseph turned and looked at him over his shoulder, those golden green eyes as sultry as he'd ever seen them. He didn't tell him to stop. He just whispered one word. "Harder."

Gage cursed, digging his fingers deep into the hollows of Joseph's hips, pulling him back to meet every single one of his pounding thrusts. Joseph threw back his head, moaning and rocking his body back and forth in perfect rhythm with him. Gage groaned low in his chest, his skin tight, loving the way he fit so snugly inside Joseph's ass. His gaze landed on the curls sliding across Joseph's back. He was reaching for them, ready to tug on that long hair when suddenly Joseph pulled forward, out of his hold and separating their bodies. Again Gage was angry, angry that he wasn't inside Joseph. That he wasn't deep in him feeling that amazing friction on his shaft. "What the fuck?" he snapped.

Joseph rose up on his knees and turned to face Gage. He'd been priming Gage all day for the gamble he was about to take. He'd either get what he wanted, or push Gage away from him for good. Joseph set his hands on Gage's chest and gave a shove of his own. "Lie down."

Gage's eyes narrowed, but he followed his direction, lying down on his back on the kitchen floor. Joseph straddled his waist, rubbing their cocks together a few times before he rose up and slid down onto Gage's shaft. Gage blew out a harsh breath, his hands landing on his hips to push him up and pull him back down, controlling the pace. Joseph grabbed his hands, yanking them off his hips. Gage's mouth immediately opened, clearly ready to protest. Joseph leaned forward and kissed him, stopping whatever he was about to say. He brought Gage's hands up over his head, holding them down. Gage cursed and tried to pull away but Joseph used his own strength to slap his wrists back down to the floor. He looked down into the dark eyes watching him with a mix of anger and lust.

"How long are you going to wait, Gage?"

A frown creased Gage's brow. "What?"

"How long are you going to wait until you admit you don't want anybody but me?" Joseph squeezed his thighs against Gage's sides and moved slowly up and down on his cock. "When you finally do, you can have me the way you want me. You can fuck me with nothing on you, just your bare cock sliding deep, coming inside me." Gage's eyes closed and he thrust up hard into him, but Joseph maintained his slow pace. It wasn't easy to do so. His body was strung tight, he wanted to indulge in riding his lover until his stiff cock pulsed his release. And his heart was racing, both from his current activity and nervousness from what he was saying to Gage. He didn't know how he was going to react to it.

"I know how bad you want that. I bet you think about it all the time, don't you?"

Gage's jaw clenched tight, his lips barely moving as he answered. "Yes, goddamnit. You know I fucking think about that."

Joseph leaned down and whispered into his ear. "I've never let anyone come inside me before, Gage. You'll be the first. Unless you wait too long." Joseph increased his speed, his breath coming faster. He could feel the tension growing in Gage's body beneath him, his arms bulging as he strained to get free. "I won't wait for you forever. I'll fucking leave you and find someone brave enough to commit to me." Joseph moaned into Gage's ear as he pushed up hard into him once more. But he didn't get distracted from what he was saying. "Maybe it'll be Montoya who gets to fuck me and come inside me, Gage. Not you. Is that what you want?"

Gage finally snatched his hands free and rolled them so that he was on top. He grabbed tight handfuls of Joseph's hair, tight enough to make his eyes water. "Shut up," he hissed. "Stop fucking pushing me."

Joseph stared up into those intense, nearly black eyes. "I'm not pushing you. I'm just telling the truth." He closed his eyes and tilted his head back. "Now *you* shut up and make me come."

Gage groaned and leaned down, burying his face in Joseph's neck. He thrust into him hard and fast, so deep he was brushing against that sensitive spot inside him with each stroke. Joseph wrapped his legs around Gage's waist, ignoring the cold hard floor against his back. His orgasm was just there, teasing the head of his cock, his balls drawn up tight and hard, when Gage's hand slipped between them and grasped his shaft, pumping him in time to his thrusts. That pushed him right over the edge, his climax rising hot and fast. He dug his fingers into Gage's back. "Gage, I'm about to come!"

Gage moved even faster, his hand keeping pace. Gage mumbled his name into his neck, but Joseph couldn't hear what he said after that, just felt his warm breath soaking into his skin as he spoke. Gage lifted his head slightly and looked into his eyes. "Joseph…" He didn't say anything else. He just shook his head.

Joseph squeezed his inner muscles around the thick cock pushing inside him and pulled Gage back down against him. Gage kissed him roughly, his tongue sliding into his mouth to master his. His hand gripped Joseph's shoulder tightly, keeping him from sliding across the floor from the force of his thrusts. Joseph relaxed and let Gage have that power over him, let Gage ride him at a furious pace until their shouts echoed across the kitchen as they came.

****

Joseph pulled his shorts up, watching Gage, who was quietly dressing a few steps away. "You should probably go."

Gage's head whipped around to look at him, his expression half angry – half confused. "Joseph, what the fuck?"

Joseph shrugged. "I've got some stuff to do to get ready for work tomorrow. And you've got some thinking to do, am I right?"

"Goddamnit, Joseph-."

Joseph raised his hand, cutting him off. "You asked me last night if I was putting you on a deadline. Well, the answer is yes. Two weeks, Gage. I'm giving you two weeks to decide if you want to be with me and me only." He paused as Gage's eyes widened, his face flushing an angry red. "That's plenty of time for you to get your shit together and decide what you want." He shook his head. "I won't be one of many."

He forced himself to keep looking at Gage. All the confusion was gone from his face, now he looked furious. Joseph knew it was because he was backing him into a corner. Again he hoped his gamble would turn out the way he wanted. He caved a little from what he'd originally planned to say. "We can still hang out and be together like we have been up to this point. Nothing has to change there. But at the end of two weeks I want an answer. Either you're with me, or you're not."

CHAPTER 33

Gage wiped his hands on a rag and dropped it on his garage floor. He was at home working on restoring a classic Harley. He hadn't made much progress. He was still off kilter from his encounter with Joseph a few days ago. Joseph had caught him completely off guard that afternoon. He'd thought … he'd thought that from their phone discussion the night of the race that Joseph was fine. Having him fuck with his head like that during sex and then throwing down that ultimatum had been the last thing he expected to happen. Two weeks. Joseph was giving him two weeks to either commit or move on.

He should have known something like that was going to happen eventually. He was a complete fucking idiot to think that he could hang out with someone, having sex on a regular basis without them wanting something more. But that hadn't been on his mind the night he'd asked Joseph to stop thinking and just be with him. The only thing that had been on his mind was his eagerness to have frequent sex with someone he was unbelievably drawn to. It hadn't occurred to him that things between them would go past only physical no matter how hard he'd resisted it.

He'd wanted sex from Joseph that day and after hours of teasing he got it. But Joseph's game had him so crazy, so desperate that he'd been an easy mark for the images that he put in his head. Thinking of fucking Joseph bare was already becoming an obsession. Having Joseph taunt him with it while they were having sex … telling him that he could come inside him. *Christ.* Gage's fingers clenched so tight on the random tool he'd pulled from the drawer it dug into his skin. He'd never been bothered by the fact that having numerous sexual partners required that he always use a condom. But with

Joseph it was just one more thing that was different. Just like he'd said, he wanted to slide deep inside him with nothing between them. He didn't want to give that up to someone else. The threat of Joseph leaving him for Montoya or anybody else had made his heart beat hard with equal parts anger and fear. He'd been worked up enough that he'd whispered against Joseph's neck, asking him not to leave him. Thankfully, Joseph hadn't heard him and afterwards, Gage had calmed down and didn't mention it.

Gage didn't know what the fuck to do. Obviously he liked Joseph and for more than just sex. He wasn't so thick he didn't realize he wouldn't have gone this far with Joseph if he didn't want to be with him. But he was the way he was for a reason. He didn't trust easily. On top of that, he'd been to blame for the disastrous endings to his previous relationships. From that, Gage had learned that he did better on his own. Besides, he had to admit that he liked not being tied down to anyone. Was he willing to give up that lifestyle to be with Joseph? Could he even trust himself to be with him, or would he just ruin someone else's life?

Giving up on working, Gage went into the kitchen. As he got a drink from the fridge, he noticed how quiet the house was. He'd pretty much been alone with his thoughts of Joseph for days. The smile on his face when he'd turned and seen him at the race track. How amazing he'd been the night he'd lost his cool after Heather's visit. His wide-eyed look of hope and apprehension when he'd told him to stop thinking and just be with him.

Gage sighed. They'd grown close because he'd been the one to push for it from the beginning. And right now he missed being with Joseph. He took a long drink of his iced tea, finishing it off and putting the glass in the sink. Then he pulled his phone out of his jeans pocket. He unlocked it and opened up his contacts. He could call someone over to distract him from his thoughts. Or, he could call the person who was responsible for them.

****

Joseph was out for a run, solo this time. It had been almost a week since he'd told Gage to make up his mind. And he hadn't heard from him since. Joseph jogged in place at the curb, waiting for the light to change.

Gage had been pissed when he'd left, but Joseph hadn't thought he would be mad enough to blow him off entirely. It bothered him that Gage hadn't called him, but this time Joseph wasn't at all tempted to call. The little light up man gave him the go ahead to cross and he splashed down into the wet street.

He was going to let Gage do whatever thinking he needed to do without influencing him. And if that meant that Gage decided to move on then he'd just have to accept that. That wasn't what he wanted of course, but he couldn't make Gage be in a relationship with him. And he'd be damned if he was going to continue on the way they were, in this confusing non-relationship where he didn't know if Gage was off fucking someone else whenever he felt like it. He just really thought things could be good between them if Gage would open up and let go. So he wanted his phone to ring with Gage's call, but each day that passed without that number lighting up the screen made him less hopeful it was going to happen.

Blowing out a frustrated breath, he turned for home. His phone hadn't been completely silent. There'd been several calls from one number, all of which he'd ignored. That part of his life was over. Even if Gage never gave him the answer he wanted he wouldn't be going there again.

A car horn sounded, a long obnoxious honk at the car in front of it. When it stopped and both cars drove off, Joseph realized his phone was ringing. Pulling it out of his pocket, he checked the screen. It was Gage.

CHAPTER 34

Joseph followed Gage into Big G's Bar. They'd just come from watching a minor league baseball game, complete with fireworks for the coming Fourth of July holiday. It had been a long, hot day and he was looking forward to a cold beer. They waved at Gia, Joseph laughing when she blew him a kiss. The place was packed and she was working the bar so they didn't try to strike up a conversation. Gage tugged on his ponytail.

"Go get us a table. I'll grab us some beers."

Joseph nodded and walked off smiling. There were only three days left in his ultimatum to Gage. He hadn't given him an answer yet. But he was feeling pretty confident that when Gage did, it would be the one he wanted to hear. They'd been hanging together again, just like before, their sex life just as exciting. They hadn't discussed what would happen when time was up. Joseph didn't know if that was the right move or not.

He sat down at an empty booth and pulled out his phone to check the baseball scores while he waited. Joseph looked up from his phone with a smile as someone slid into the seat across from him. He assumed it was Gage. It wasn't. It was his ex, Ashton Andrews. Joseph was beyond surprised. "What are you doing here?" As usual, Ashton ignored him.

"Why haven't you been returning my calls?"

Joseph was immediately irritated. Same old Ashton. The man was good looking. His thick blonde hair was expensively styled, his clean-shaven jaw as sharp as a model's. And he managed not to look out of place in Big G's's laid back atmosphere even though he was dressed in a neat suit and silk tie. But this conversation had already started off just like nearly every other one they'd had before they broke up. Ashton was blowing off anything that he didn't want to hear, only concerned with what he wanted. Joseph answered him just to move the conversation along and hopefully get rid of him.

"Because I told you I don't have anything to say to you. We're done and have been for months. There's no need to keep hashing it out."

Ashton scoffed. "We're not hashing anything out, Joseph. I just want to discuss things with you, see if we can come to terms. We had a good partnership."

Joseph rolled his eyes. It sounded like Ashton was talking about a business partnership gone sour instead of a relationship. Before he could answer, however, a shadow fell across the table. It was Gage, back with their beers.

"Who is this?" he asked in a low voice.

Ashton glanced up at Gage, taking in his faded jeans and t-shirt. He immediately dismissed him. "Get lost we're talking."

Joseph froze. He saw Gage's hands clench on the glass bottles in his fists. Instinctively he took them from him and set them out of reach on the far side of the table. Gage's hand came up to his ponytail, stroking it lightly. Ashton's face tightened as he picked up on the implications of Gage touching him so familiarly.

"Joseph?"

Joseph cleared his throat. "This is Ashton. He's my ex-boyfriend."

"Is that right? And why is he here right now?"

"I don't know. I've told him I don't have anything to say to him."

Gage spoke to Ashton this time. "You want me to leave. Joseph wants you to leave. I'll give you one guess who's about to get their way."

Ashton's straightened up, anger clear in his face. "Listen here, buddy. Don't even think about threatening me. You might be tough in whatever *hood* you run around in but…" Ashton stood up revealing the fact that although he was dressed in a tailored suit, he was fit and hard with muscle. "You don't want to mess with me."

But that didn't deter Gage. Instead, he smiled and got up in Ashton's face. "You wanna see if might makes right? Well then let's go. Step on up to the plate and take this ass kickin' I'm about to hand you." He flicked Ashton's tie. "I'll try not to get blood on your fancy Brooks Brothers suit."

Ashton looked Gage up and down with a sneer. "Spoken just like trash." His blue eyes flicked to Joseph. "I can't believe you let this loser touch you with all the filth he must have under his nails. You need to come to your senses and come back to me where you belong."

Joseph's eyes shot to Gage's face. Ashton might not have moved, but he'd just squarely knocked that chip off Gage's shoulder. Gage's arm pulled back and Joseph flew out of his chair, grabbing his fist before it could snap forward into Ashton's smug face.

"Gage, don't! He's a lawyer. He'll press charges and probably sue you."

Gage held there for a moment, every muscle in his body tight as he glared at Ashton. Joseph brought his other hand up, resting it on Gage's shoulder. "Gage, don't do this."

Gage finally lowered his arm and turned to look at him. Anger was shining bright in his eyes, but when he spoke, Joseph knew that soon it would turn to something else.

"Let's go."

Joseph swallowed hard and nodded. He looked at Gia behind the bar and gave her a quick nod, letting her know everything was alright. Gage gripped his hand and started walking, Joseph following without question. But Ashton grabbed his arm.

"Wait a minute! I'm not letting you leave with this guy. He's clearly violent."

Gage spun around, immediately ready to go after Ashton again. Joseph managed to yank his arm away from Ashton and hold Gage back at the same time. "Listen to me, Ashton! We're done. I don't want you. Don't want to talk to you, see you, nothing! Now leave me the fuck alone."

Ashton finally looked like he caught a hint and didn't try to stop them from leaving this time. They left the bar and walked out into the warm night.

CHAPTER 35

It was quiet as they rode along in Gage's truck. The radio wasn't on. Neither of them talked. There was only the sound of the low growl of the engine and tires whooshing on the road. Joseph's nerves were stretched tight, wondering what would happen between them when they reached his house. But they didn't make it there. Gage pulled onto a small side street and stopped the truck. It was a cul-de sac, with only four houses. Each one had the warm glow of a porch light above its door, but they didn't do anything to penetrate the darkness that cloaked the rest of the street. Still, even though it was dark, Joseph recognized that he didn't know where they were. He looked at Gage in confusion. "Why did you st-?"

"Be quiet." Gage snapped. He got out and walked around to his side. When he opened the door, Joseph tried again.

"Gage, what's going on?"

"Get out of the truck, Joseph."

Joseph looked at Gage. His mouth was pursed and his jawline hard with tension. He was clearly still bothered about the incident with Ashton and Joseph figured they were about to talk about it. He stepped out onto the pavement. Gage pulled him out of the way to close the door behind him. Then without any warning Gage pushed Joseph up against it. His fingers slid into his hair to grip his head, pressing tightly as Gage started kissing him. Joseph was surprised, but he kissed him back, until Gage's hand left his hair and trailed down to his jeans. Joseph managed to break away from their kiss just as his zipper went down.

"Are you crazy? Someone could drive down this street at any minute." Joseph heard Gage's zipper go down next.

"Don't care. Either this happens now or I go back to Gia's and kick lawyer boyfriend's ass."

Joseph's mouth dropped open, but Gage didn't blink.

"Tick-tock, Joseph. Make your decision quick."

"Gage, just forget about what Ashton said, you know you're better than-."

Gage cut him off again. "Fuck that. I could give a rat's ass what he said about me." He pressed forward and kissed him hard. "But that motherfucker needed to learn to not even think about making a move on what's mine."

"I'm yours? Have you made your decision?"

That muscle flexed in Gage's jaw. "No," he answered shortly and without any explanation.

"Then you're not making any sense, Gage. Either you're with me or you're not. Why is that so hard?"

Gage's response was a low hiss in the night. "I don't have to make sense! You *are* mine, goddamnit. That lawyer and that oil tycoon or whatever the fuck he is, and everybody else thinking they can have you can go fuck themselves."

Joseph wanted to curse with frustration at them both. Gage was stalling, why he didn't know. And when it came right down to it, he was afraid to push him to find out why. But this mood Gage was in was different. Joseph could almost smell the aggression and need coming off of him. He could tell the incident with Ashton was driving Gage to stake his claim on him. Joseph didn't mind that, would be happy to be claimed by the other man. He just wanted Gage to commit to him as well.

Gage tilted Joseph's head back, staring into his eyes. "Tell me you're mine."

"Gage, don't. This isn't fair."

The wind rustled the leaves in the tree over their heads as Gage brushed his lips over his. He spoke in a husky whisper, his breath warm against his cheek. "Tell me, Joseph. You know you want to."

Joseph didn't say anything, but he sucked in a tight breath as Gage started moving against him.

"Just say it, baby."

Joseph felt himself giving in, but he tried one last time to resist. He put his hands on Gage's chest, not quite pushing him back, but keeping him from getting any closer. He shook his head as much as Gage's tight grip on him would allow. "Gage, you're asking too much from me and not giving me anything in return. No assurances, nothing. There's only three days left and you still can't tell me your decision. You just … you're just asking too much from me right now."

Gage kept moving on him. "I'm not. Two little words. That's all." He gave him another soft kiss. "Say it, Joseph. I need you to say it."

Gage kissed him again. Kissed him so deep and with so much passion that he couldn't think straight. And Joseph crumbled. Crumbled under the onslaught of that kiss. Crumbled under the pressure of their bodies moving together. Succumbed to the persuasion of that seductive voice in the warm night. When Gage put a breath of space between their lips, he looked up at him and gave him what he wanted. "I'm yours."

Gage smiled that sexy half-grin of his. "I know it."

Then Gage was kissing him yet again. Their hips started moving in unison, thrusting and grinding against each other. Their cocks were hard and soon both were flowing with pre-cum, giving them the slick slide they desired. Joseph forgot that he was outside in the open up against the side of a truck. All he cared about was the way Gage groaned into his mouth. All he wanted to feel were Gage's hands as they left his hair to travel down to his ass, squeezing him and pulling their bodies even closer together. All that mattered was how solid and warm Gage felt pressed so tight against him.

Suddenly, Gage spun Joseph around to face the side of the truck and tugged his jeans down to mid-thigh.

"Since you're mine, will you let me fuck you bare?"

Joseph shuddered at that request. He rocked back, pressing his ass against Gage's naked cock. The rigid heat of it against his skin made him moan.

Gage hissed his name. "Joseph?"

Joseph *wanted* to say yes. But he couldn't. He might have committed to Gage, but Gage hadn't committed to him in return. So even as he continued to press back against Gage, he whispered *no*, his breath fogging the window in front of him.

Gage cursed. "I feel like I'm in a fucking battle with you and those damn condoms." Gage kept grinding against him, his hand coming around to grasp his shaft. Brushing his lips up his neck, Gage whispered in his ear. "Why won't you just let me?"

Joseph exhaled on a shaky breath. "I can't, Gage. I need to trust that you're not with anyone else before I can…" Joseph dropped his forehead against the truck's window as Gage squeezed his cock hard. He struggled to finish his sentence while Gage kept squeezing and pumping him. "Before I can allow you … us … to have sex like that."

Gage pushed his shaft between his cheeks, sliding and rubbing between them just like the first night this had become an issue. Grabbing Joseph's hip, he pulled their bodies tight together. He almost, *almost* teased the tip of his cock inside him. "Are you sure, Joseph? I think you want it just as much as I do."

Joseph was shaking now. Gage was right, he did want to feel his lover bare inside him. But he wasn't going to give in to Gage on anything else tonight. He could resist that voice. Gage squeezed his balls, reminding him that he hadn't answered yet.

"Are you sure, Joseph?"

"Oh god… Yes, I'm sure."

"Sure about what, Joseph? Be clear so I know what you want."

Joseph's fingers curled into fists, his nails digging into his palms as he strained not to push back onto Gage. The way he kept saying his name was driving him crazy. "You know what I mean. The condoms stay." He found the strength to look at Gage over his shoulder and put some conviction in his voice. "Until you make up your goddamn mind."

With a low growl, Gage spun him back around. He gripped both their shafts, pumping them together, moving his hips against him as he initiated another kiss. Joseph brought a leg up to wrap around Gage's waist. Gage spoke right into his ear, his words quick and short, his breathing harsh.

"Don't you fucking threaten to leave me again, Joseph. I mean it, you're mine. Gage buried his face in Joseph's hair, biting his neck through the strands. "I have to have you."

Joseph turned his head, rubbing his face against Gage's. "Yes, you have me, Gage."

Gage groaned and pumped his hips even faster until Joseph felt his release against his skin, the hot liquid spilling onto their bellies and down both their shafts. Joseph dug his fingers into his lover's back, his name coming from him on a soft moan. "*Gage.*"

Gage's tongue curled around his ear, making him shiver. "Don't worry. You'll get to come too." Gage slipped his hand between them and Joseph felt it sliding and rubbing along their shafts. When he pulled his hand back, Joseph caught a glimpse of two fingers glistening in the moonlight before his hand went behind him. Joseph moaned, his head arching back against the truck window as a finger, slick with cum, pushed inside him. Gage started moving his hips again, his still hard shaft pressing against his.

"You see Joseph, if you weren't mine you wouldn't let me cum all over you in the middle of a fucking street." Gage's finger kept thrusting inside him, making him roll his hips back into his touch. "You wouldn't let me finger your ass where anybody could look out their windows and see if you weren't mine." Gage licked and bit at his neck, his next words whispered against the skin of his throat. "You wouldn't let me get even the smallest amount of my cum inside you…" He slid another finger into him. "… if you weren't mine."

He bit his lip, trying not to acknowledge to himself the truth of Gage's words. But Gage was Gage, and he knew how to work him. He circled his hips tight and hard against him and his fingers pushed in deep until they were rubbing against that spot that drove him crazy. And just when Joseph was right at the edge of his orgasm he whispered in his ear, "Tell me who you belong to, Joseph."

Joseph groaned, unable to stop himself from again giving Gage what he wanted, telling him that he was his. Gage licked his mouth. He kept stroking his fingers over that sensitive spot until he was coming in sweet pulsing waves, Gage's lips on his in a fierce kiss, keeping his moans and cries from ringing out into the night. Joseph collapsed back against the side of the truck as Gage pressed hard kisses to his face and neck.

"Fuck everything else. You're mine, Joseph."

CHAPTER 36

Joseph was relaxed from the release Gage had given him. That combined with the long day and confrontation with Ashton had him tired. So he was glad when Gage turned into his driveway. He was ready to go inside and be undisturbed with his lover.

Joseph got out of the truck once Gage turned the ignition off, waiting until Gage got out too and came around the hood before heading up the front walk. He slid the key into the lock. "Looking forward to that beer we didn't get to have at Gia's."

Gage's fingers landed on his hip and he kissed him behind his ear. "Gonna rain check on the beer. I'm just walking you to the door."

Joseph went still, the door unopened. He'd assumed Gage was going to stay the night with him. He could have let it go, but just like the condoms, Gage's refusal to stay the night with him had come to represent where they were in their relationship. Without meaning to, his voice came out angry and accusing. "You're not staying here?"

Gage immediately took a step back. "Joseph, don't make this a big deal."

Joseph turned to face him. "Believe me I'm about to make this a huge deal. Why won't you stay? After everything that's happened tonight, Gage. After what you had me admit in the street earlier, how can you not want to stay with me?"

Gage sighed but spoke calmly. "I still have three days."

But somehow Gage's calmness made him furious. Heat rushed into his face and he started shouting, uncaring that the neighbors would hear. "Fuck three days! There's no reason you can't make your decision right now. It shouldn't have even taken this long. You can't keep saying possessive shit like that to me when we're having sex and then go back to wanting it casual when we're done! Either you want me or you don't, Gage! Stop fucking stalling!"

"Joseph, calm down and listen to me. I'm not sleeping with anyone else. I'm only with you. I like what we have. Why do we have to put a goddamn label on it? We don't need to be official, whatever the hell that even means, for us to have fun and great sex. So what if we don't spend the night together? Let's just enjoy each other's company both in bed and out for as long as we want. That's all a relationship really is anyway, right?"

Joseph stared at Gage. The cold blue light from the porch lamp made his face appear even harder than usual – even more distant. Joseph felt like he was seeing the real Gage, who wouldn't ever want to move past where they were right now. "So basically you want to have a relationship without calling it a relationship. You want me to be your boyfriend, you want to fuck me like I'm your boyfriend, but you don't want to call me your boyfriend. Why is that, Gage? Why are you determined to keep that space between us?"

A muscle ticked in Gage's jaw. Without another word, he turned back towards his truck. But Joseph rushed after him and grabbed his arm. "Tell me why!"

Gage yanked his arm away and turned back to face him. His hands were balled up into fists, his arms tense as though he were holding himself back. "You want to know why, Joseph? Fine, I'll fucking tell you. I've had relationships with two people, Joseph. Two." Gage popped two fingers up in front of his face. "One of them is a fucking junkie because of me. The other one …"

Gage paused, his eyes bright before he looked away from him.

"The other one is dead. Because of me."

Gage looked at him again, nothing but anger in his face and eyes now. "So you'll have to fucking forgive me if I'm just a little leery about getting involved with someone else."

Joseph stood there, his eyes wide with shock. "Shit … Gage. I'm sorry. I didn't know…" He trailed off not knowing what else to say.

A cold sneer crossed Gage's face. "Well, now you do. So how 'bout it, Joseph? Still eager to be my boyfriend? Wanna go in the house and cuddle up with me to sleep so you can dream about how I'll fucking destroy your life?"

Joseph shook his head, about to say that he didn't think it would be that way. But Gage didn't let him get that far.

"Right. I didn't think so."

He turned and walked away. Joseph was still so thrown that he just stood there and watched as Gage stalked down the drive. He was still standing there as Gage drove off, once again watching his taillights disappear into the night.

CHAPTER 37

Joseph tried not to count the days. But he did anyway. One day passed. No word from Gage. Two days passed. No word from Gage. Halfway through the third day found Joseph sitting on his small deck, his phone by his side. Yet again the argument from the last time he'd seen Gage was in his head. He didn't know what to feel. Did he feel bad for pushing Gage the way he had? Sort of. Maybe if he'd kept his cool Gage would have told him his history and then stayed to talk about it instead of storming off. Or maybe not. Maybe Gage was stubborn enough to have kept that secret close to his chest instead of sharing it with him. And it was a heavy secret. Two lovers, both destroyed. According to Gage, it was his fault. Knowing some of Gage's history he could guess why he blamed himself for one of them being a drug addict. He'd probably been with someone while he'd been using and convinced them to try it too. But the other? He was afraid to guess. Had that person died from a drug overdose? Committed suicide? It couldn't have been natural causes or Gage wouldn't feel responsible.

Joseph admitted to himself he was freaked out by it all. He was aware of Gage's flaws. Gage was intense and dominant and manipulative. And now Joseph knew that he had some emotional issues they would have to work through if they were going to have any kind of real relationship. He knew all that. And he still wanted to be with him. Despite all that, or maybe even because of it, he was drawn to Gage. He might be freaked out, but he wasn't ready to give up on him. Joseph wanted to show Gage that he could be happy in a relationship and that it wouldn't end in disaster. It was time for Gage to let go of that pain and move on. He just wanted to make sure that Gage moved on with him.

His phone chimed with a text and his heart sped up as he looked to see who it was. He calmed quickly when he saw it was from Gia.

Are you coming to Nate's party tonight? I have something I want to ask you.

Joseph held the phone for a minute before responding. Nate had told them about his last minute Fourth of July party when they'd all been hanging out at Gage's earlier in the week. He hadn't forgotten about it. He just wasn't sure he should go. He'd been invited, but Nate was Gage's friend, not his. Joseph didn't know if he and Gage were still together, which meant he didn't know if he should still go around his friends. He started to text Gia that he wasn't going but that they could meet up some other time. Changing his mind, he tapped his thumb on the screen, erasing the message. If he went to the party tonight and Gage was there, maybe they could talk. He debated with himself for a while longer before he typed his response. *Yeah, I'll be there.* He hit send, hoping he'd made the right decision.

****

A couple hours later, Joseph pulled up to Nate's house on his bike. After responding to Gia's text, he'd showered and put on his favorite jeans and a snug-fitting t-shirt. He'd washed and blow dried his hair, leaving it down around his shoulders. He took off his helmet and ran a hand through his hair. He knew his primping was totally shameless, but he didn't care. Gage always called him pretty, and he knew it was his looks that had first drawn the man to him. He wasn't above using them to entice Gage tonight.

Joseph walked into Nate's house. The place was nice. Very open and spacious. The furniture was clean lines, with pale wood and creamy textured fabrics. He smiled when he saw Nate coming up to him and reached out to shake his hand.

"Very nice house, Nate. Owning a gym must be pretty profitable."

Nate grinned. "Yep. As long as people are willing to pay money to get fit, I'll be there with my gyms, videos, and shakes."

Joseph was impressed that another friend of Gage's was doing so well as an entrepreneur. "Are you sure you all didn't meet in the Wharton School of Business or something?" He heard Gage's distinctive voice behind him.

"Nah, we're just assholes who don't like anyone else telling us what to do. Having our own business was the only way to go."

Nate grinned in agreement before he walked away to greet someone else. Joseph turned and saw Gage standing there. He looked as good as always; his hair casually messy, a well-worn t-shirt and jeans resting easy on his muscular frame. His arm flexed slightly as he lifted his beer to his mouth.

"Hey."

Gage only nodded in response.

Joseph's heart was pounding, but he forced himself to move the conversation along. "Gia texted me, asked if I was coming."

"It's cool. I'm glad you're here. I wanted to talk to you." Gage led them over to a fairly quiet spot in the large living room. "This isn't the best place for any real sort of discussion."

Joseph nodded. He couldn't tell where Gage was going with this. Was he about to end things between them for good?

Gage sighed and ran a hand through his hair. "I shouldn't have dropped that bomb on you and then left like that. I'm sure you've got a shit ton of questions."

"Yeah, I've got a lot." He looked down for a moment before he met Gage's dark gaze. "I was wondering if you were going to call." He didn't mention the deadline he'd imposed, but it hung there in the air between them.

"I'm aware of the number of days, Joseph. And I did plan to call you tonight if you didn't show up here. I at least owe you that."

Joseph's heart dropped into his stomach. This was sounding more and more like Gage was about to say it was over. Gage reached out and wrapped a strand of his hair around his finger. Gage stared at the hair he played with instead of looking at him.

"You're so gorgeous, Joseph. And this soft, soft hair."

Joseph didn't say thank you. It didn't sound like Gage was complimenting him. He sounded angry, like he was blaming him for something.

"I can't stay away from you, even though I should. I should have just fucked you on my garage floor like I wanted to when you drove in to ask me out in that goddamn proper way of yours." He paused for a moment, still staring at the hair wrapped around his finger. "Maybe then this wouldn't have gone so far."

Joseph's face flushed hot, but he didn't look around to see if anyone had overheard Gage. He opened his mouth to protest, but he wasn't really sure where to start. He wanted to ask him what had happened in his previous relationships, but Gage was right. It wasn't really the place to have that talk. He was about to suggest that they leave or at least go to another room when Gia came up.

"Hey, lovebirds!"

They both turned to look at her, neither of them speaking right away. Joseph recovered first and tried to be polite. "Hey, Gia. How are you?" She belatedly realized from their expressions and the air of tension between them that they weren't just relaxing and enjoying the party. Her eyes went wide and she looked uncomfortable.

"Crap, I've interrupted at a bad time, haven't I?"

Gage dropped his hand from his hair. "No, it's fine. What's up?"

She looked between them again before she answered. "I wanted to talk to Joey but it can wait."

Joseph shook his head. "Now is alright." He figured he could see what Gia wanted, he and Gage could hang at the party a little longer, then they could get out of there to really talk. He looked at Gage. "I'll be back, okay?"

Gage took a swig of his beer. "Alright."

Joseph went off with Gia, saying hello to the people he'd already met as they went through the crowd.

"Let's go to the kitchen since you don't have a drink yet."

The kitchen was another big open room. Several large windows let in the late evening sunlight and Joseph saw that there was a pool in the back lawn. He helped himself to a soda from the open cooler by the counter. When he turned back to Gia she was looking at him with concern on her pretty face.

"Are you guys okay?"

He shrugged. "I'm not really sure."

Gia pursed her lips. "I almost feel as though I don't want to give you any encouragement, because I know Gage and I know how he is. But *because* I know him I know that he is actually a good guy." She paused for a second, looking like she was choosing her next words carefully. "I've never seen him with anyone the way he is with you, Joseph. He's stubborn. A little push and a lot of patience will be necessary with him. And I might be biased because he's my friend, but I think in the end it will be worth it." She shrugged, giving him a lopsided smile. "Just my two cents. For whatever they're worth."

Joseph smiled and gave her a one-armed hug. "Thanks, Gia." He appreciated her words. Hearing that she saw something in the relationship he had with Gage that she hadn't seen before gave him hope that this would work between them. "So what's up? What did you want to ask me?"

"How do you feel about doing some freelance work? I've got some legal issues that I need help with."

****

Gage migrated to Nate's study. Thankfully, the room was empty. He needed a minute to himself. He went and sat on the edge of the big glass and steel desk and finished off the rest of his beer. He'd come close, *that* close, to telling Joseph that they should stop seeing each other. But he didn't want to do it in the middle of a fucking party. Well, if he was honest with himself, he didn't want to do it at all. Goddamnit, he wanted to stay with Joseph. Just the thought of having him with him all the time, of finally having someone that he genuinely liked to get close to made him feel good. But it also terrified him. He would have to let go and have a lot of trust in both himself and Joseph. And he was fucking scared. Scared that the past would repeat itself and that he and Joseph would spiral into a mutually destructive storm of hate and regret and pain. And as a result, he would wind up alone. Again. He thought of Riley and the fights that they'd had. They'd made up each and every time. Except for their last fight.

The door opened and he looked up, thinking that Joseph had come looking for him. But it wasn't Joseph. It was Brianna. He had a history with her of late nights, beer drinking, and fucking. She was pretty, with long legs and dark brown skin. She was fun. They'd had some good times, but he wasn't interested in dealing with her right now.

"Brianna." His voice wasn't inviting. Because he wasn't inviting her in. But she either didn't pick up on it or chose to ignore it because she came into the room and shut the door behind her.

"Gage, how's it been?"

"Can't complain."

She tossed her long, black braids over her shoulders. "What's wrong? You act like you're not happy to see me. I remember at the last party Nate threw, you and me got a little bit sweaty in that chair right over there."

Brianna pointed at the chair from behind her hand, like it was a secret she didn't want anyone else to know. She smiled, knowing that he normally found her teasing amusing. Too bad he wasn't in the mood for her games. "I remember. But I don't think we'll have a repeat performance tonight."

"Really? Why is that?"

"I'm here with somebody."

She laughed and came to lean against him. "That tall guy who looks like an angel?"

Gage nodded.

"So? When has that ever stopped you? But he is gorgeous." She gave him a coy look. "Maybe we can all get together."

"Sorry, honey. Not interested."

Brianna's eyebrows shot up. "You're kidding me, right? *You're* only sleeping with one person?" The girl smirked. "I can't believe it. The great Gage Mason has been tamed by a pretty little fag boy."

Gage grabbed her braids in a tight fist and yanked her head back. "Watch it girlie. I haven't been tamed by anybody." She didn't complain; she just gave him a taunting smile.

"I see you still like to play rough. Or maybe this is just a front since you've been domesticated."

Gage snapped. He yanked her forward into a hard kiss, thrusting his tongue into her mouth deep enough to make her gag. She pressed closer to him, kissing him back. Running his hand down her body, he grabbed a tight handful of her ass in her obscenely short skirt. He squeezed hard, hard enough to make her wince. But he heard another noise over that. The sound of the door opening.

He broke their kiss and looked over Brianna's shoulder to see Joseph standing there. He didn't look shocked. But his eyes, those beautiful green eyes, were sad. Joseph spoke quietly.

"Someone told me you came in here. I brought you another beer."

Joseph carefully set the bottle of Shiner in his hand down and quietly left the room. Gage finally jumped into action and pushed Brianna aside. She squeaked and he heard her stumble, but he didn't bother to check if she was okay. He rushed out after Joseph. He was easy to spot in the crowd, his tall figure a head over most everyone else. Gage caught up with him outside just as he reached his bike. "Damnit, Joseph. Wait!"

Joseph turned around and looked at him. He still didn't look shocked or even angry. Just sad. So fucking sad.

"Wait for what, Gage? I told you I couldn't be with you if you still wanted to sleep with other people." He shrugged and looked down at the helmet in his hands.

Gage was relieved that he didn't have to see those wounded eyes anymore. Yet, he also had the sick urge to stare into them to determine just how deep Joseph's pain went. Was that pain real? Was Joseph really hurt at the thought of losing him?

"It looks like you made your choice so I'm out of here."

Gage expected Joseph to get angry and yell at him like he had the other night. But he didn't. His voice stayed quiet and calm. And small. His voice was small, as though he didn't want to disturb anyone. Gage tried to stay calm too, but he could feel himself getting angry, which was stupid because he was the one at fault. "I haven't made any fucking choice! I wasn't going to sleep with her."

Joseph looked at him again and Gage wanted to growl. Wanted to dig his fingers into Joseph's shoulders so he could hold him still. He needed to know what Joseph was thinking.

"That's not what it looked like to me."

Joseph put his helmet on and with the visor down Gage couldn't see anything of his expression. He didn't like that, but he couldn't rip the damn helmet back off his head. At least not without pissing him off. Gage continued to stare at the tinted visor as Joseph started the bike, but he didn't lift it or say anything else. He just backed the bike up and drove off around him. Gage stood there watching as Joseph left him behind.

CHAPTER 38

It had been a week since the party, and Joseph walking in on Gage kissing that woman. He'd spent the time morosely lounging on his couch. Joseph knew it was pathetic and pointless, but he did it anyway. Like now. The TV was on, but he wasn't really watching it. He was thinking about Gage. He guessed he shouldn't be surprised at what had happened. Gage had always ducked giving him a straight answer whenever he'd asked if he could be with just one person. It was stupid of him to think that Gage would give up his ways for him when he hadn't ever done so for anyone else. It was probably why he hadn't been angry when he'd walked in on him and that girl. He'd just been disappointed and sad that things were over between them. Gage hadn't tried to contact him since that day. That hurt. He'd expected to at the very least get a, *sorry things didn't work* out text.

Joseph heard the roar of a motorcycle approaching outside. He waited, his muscles tense, to see if the bike would stop in front of his house. It did. Joseph told himself that didn't mean it was Gage. He had several friends with motorcycles. A few moments after the bike was shut off whomever it was knocked on his door. Three slow heavy knocks. It was Gage. He knew it. Before he'd even decided if he wanted to see Gage, he was on his feet and crossing the room. Taking a deep breath, Joseph opened the door.

Gage was standing there in his usual uniform of faded jeans and snug dark tee. His dark hair was whipped and tumbled all over his head, letting him know that as usual, he hadn't worn a helmet. Joseph pushed back any hope he might feel that Gage was there to apologize. That wasn't Gage. He didn't want to drag out whatever Gage's reasons were for showing up so he got right to the point.

"Why are you here?"

"Can we talk?"

Joseph shrugged. "What's there for us to talk about? I told you I'm not willing to be one of many."

Gage braced his hand on the door frame, his stance making it clear he wasn't going anywhere. "We doing do this outside or will you let me in?"

Joseph sighed and stepped back to let Gage in. But he didn't go any further than a few steps into the living room, subtly letting Gage know he wasn't welcome to stay and get comfortable.

Gage closed the door behind him. "I didn't fuck her." He ran a hand through his hair. "I haven't fucked anybody since I was inside you last."

A shiver of arousal ran through him at Gage's words and the image they brought up, him gripping the headboard, with Gage taking him so fiercely from behind. Gage slowly walked over to him and he had to force himself to stand his ground. Joseph felt like he was being stalked and he knew he was going to succumb to whatever Gage wanted if he didn't think of something to keep him at bay.

Gage smiled as he came up against him, their chests brushing together. "Too late."

"What?" Joseph looked at Gage, saw his eyes focused on his mouth. Without meaning to, he licked his bottom lip. Then he swallowed hard, wishing he could take the movement back, as Gage glanced back at him with a look he recognized all too well.

"I can read you like a book, Joseph. You were trying to think of something to keep me off you." Gage gripped his ponytail and yanked his head back. He licked a long wet trail up his neck. "You couldn't do it. And now it's too late."

CHAPTER 39

Joseph was shaking with pleasure. He didn't know how it had happened. He was on his back on the living room floor. His shorts and boxers were off and thrown to the side. His shirt was twisted up under his armpits. His cock was deep in Gage's mouth, Gage sucking him with all the delicious skill he possessed. Joseph dug his fingers into Gage's strong shoulders as he moaned and thrust his hips up. It had been days since he'd gotten off and he was already close to exploding. Before he got there, however, Gage released him with a wet pop and his cock fell stiffly against his stomach.

Gage looked up at him, his gaze as intense as ever. He smoothed a hand up Joseph's leg and pushed slightly, spreading him open. Joseph didn't stop him. He couldn't even think why he should. He just watched, his breath coming fast and heavy as Gage bent his head and licked his way down to his entrance. Gage teased with light flicks of his tongue before he pushed it inside him. Joseph shuddered, his fingers digging deeper into Gage's shoulders at the feeling of that hot wet tongue moving inside him. Gage soon had Joseph writhing against his mouth as he alternated between teasing licks and strong thrusts. He sucked at the tender insides of his thighs and lapped at his cock head.

Joseph's heart raced as he lay there, letting Gage work his body like no one else ever had. Finally, Gage rose up and sucked a finger into his mouth. He lay down on top of him so that they touched from chest to thigh. Gage's hard erection pressed against him and Joseph shifted restlessly. A moan slipped from his throat as Gage worked his hand between them to ease that slick finger inside him. Gage groaned and buried his face in his neck. His breath was hot against his skin as he spoke in a rough whisper.

"Fuck, Joseph. Going a week without being inside you. I can barely hold off long enough to get you ready."

He pushed his finger in deep, pressing against that sensitive spot inside him. Joseph cried out as a spark of pleasure streaked up his cock. Gage kept touching him there, his mouth licking and sucking at his neck. Joseph was wild for it now. He needed to feel Gage inside him. And Gage knew it, because he pulled back to open his jeans and put on a condom. Gage looked down at him, those dark eyes sharp and glittering with arousal as he pressed the head of his cock to his entrance, sliding inside him slowly. Joseph pushed his hips up, forcing Gage inside him another inch. He wanted this. Until Gage spoke.

"I didn't fuck her."

The passionate fog started to clear from Joseph's mind at the reminder. "But you wanted to." Gage hesitated and Joseph saw the answer in his face. He froze for a moment then pushed at Gage's chest. "Get off of me."

"What?"

Joseph scooted backwards at the same time he pushed Gage again. "I said get off me."

Gage's eyes narrowed in clear anger. "Are you fucking kidding me?"

Joseph shook his head. "I can't do this."

Gage lunged for him, dragging him back underneath him. "I told you I didn't fucking fuck her!" he shouted down into his face.

"But you wanted to!" Joseph shouted back.

Gage's hand tangled in his hair, gripping it tightly. His jaw clenched so hard that when he spoke again it was obvious he was forcing himself not to yell. "That shouldn't matter."

"It matters to me."

Gage didn't answer. He just slammed his lips onto Joseph's, kissing him so hard he could hardly take in a breath. He ripped the condom off and his hips started moving, grinding their bare cocks together. Joseph groaned. God, he wanted this, wanted *Gage* bad. He wrapped his legs around Gage's hips, grinding back against him. The friction of their cocks sliding and rubbing against each other had him aching and ready for release. From the rough groans pouring from Gage's mouth as they kissed, he was close too. But he couldn't do this. He was not going to stay with Gage if he still needed to screw other people. He tore his mouth away from Gage's.

"Stop!"

Gage stopped. Although it was clear he wasn't happy to do so. He spoke in a voice tight with lust and frustration. "You're telling me to stop with your goddamn legs wrapped around me and both of us ready to burst?"

Embarrassed heat rose in Joseph's face and he lowered his legs back to the floor. "I'm sorry, Gage."

Gage saw that he was serious because he cursed loudly. "Fuck this!" He jumped to his feet, staring down at him as he jerked his jeans up and zipped them over his stiff erection.

Joseph felt vulnerable lying there naked on the floor, so he sat up and reached for his shorts. He might as well not have bothered. Because with one last angry look thrown his way, Gage strode over to the door and slammed out of the house.

****

Gage got on his bike and tore out of Joseph's neighborhood. He was furious with Joseph, letting things go so far and then stopping. He'd told him that he hadn't fucked Brianna! Gage couldn't even think he was so pissed, his face hot in spite of the cool wind rushing over him. He drove to Gia's bar, determined to sit in there and drink till Joseph was out of his goddamn head. Gia would drive him home or see that he got a cab.

195

Gia was behind the bar as he walked in. She took one look at him and got out a pint glass. He sat down, watching the dark amber liquid pour into the glass. She slid the beer across the glossy bar top to him while he lit up a cigarette. Gia teased him in a smarmy bartender's voice.

"Rough day? Wanna tell me about it?"

"I'm not in the mood, Gia."

"Things are still a mess with you and Joseph I take it?"

He took another drink. "Yeah," he answered without elaborating. He turned away from her to scan the bar. Anger was still coursing through him. He needed to get it out of his system and he no longer felt like drinking it away. He caught the eye of a good looking dark haired guy. When the man smiled and didn't look away, Gage crooked his finger at him. The guy hesitated for only a moment before he got up and came over. Gage got comfortable leaning against the bar top as he waited. When he sat down, Gage saw he wasn't nearly as good looking as Joseph. But he'd do just for one night.

"Hello."

"Hello to you. Saw you sitting over there by yourself with an almost empty glass. Can I buy you a drink?"

"I'm drinking Mother's Three Blind Mice if that's alright."

Gage laughed. "A fancy beer drinker. I'm impressed." He swiveled on his seat towards Gia and saw the disappointed look on her face.

"Gage, don't do this."

He met her stare, refusing to acknowledge her plea. "Get the man what he asked for."

Gia eventually looked away from him and served the beer. Then she stormed off to the other end of the bar. Gage knew he'd pissed her off. That was too bad. She could get over herself. He was the one who'd just been kicked out of his lover's, his *ex*-lover's house. He turned back to his new friend. "So, what's your name?"

"Ben. Ben Davis," he said as he held his hand out.

Gage shook his hand. "Hi, Ben. Nice to meet you."

CHAPTER 40

Joseph went to work. He did his job. He went home. He went to the gym. He worked out. He went home. He went to the grocery store. Shopped. Went home. For about a week. That was his life. He tried not to think of Gage too much. When he did, he was filled with confusion on how he'd managed to fall for him so hard and so fast. And anger at himself for letting Gage pull him into bed the night of his confession, stupidly thinking things with them would be different.

He could only imagine what Gage had done when he'd left his house the other night. He'd left pissed off and on the verge of orgasm. Knowing the way Gage handled his anger, Joseph figured he'd probably gone and indulged in an orgy. The thought tormented him, but he couldn't get it out of his head.

His doorbell rang and he looked towards the door with disinterest. He didn't feel like being bothered. But he heard Nico's voice.

"Joseph! I know you're home. Your car is parked out front and I can see you through the blinds."

He sighed and went to open the door. "Nico, what's up?"

"What's up with me? What's up with you?"

Joseph was confused. "What do you mean?"

"The mid-summer race festival is next weekend. And not only have you not been out to the track to practice, but I don't even see your name on the list of entrants! What the hell?"

Joseph ran a hand through his hair. He'd forgotten all about the race.

Nico brushed past him and came inside. "What's going on?"

"I uh… just been having a rough couple of weeks."

Nico looked at him for a long moment. "You're not with that Mason guy anymore?"

Joseph sat back on the couch. "Yeah. I caught him kissing some girl so I ended it."

"Oh. I'm sorry man. Look, I swear this isn't an, *I told you so*, but maybe that's for the best. From what you told me, that guy wasn't looking for anything serious anyway."

Joseph laughed bitterly. "I get that now. A little too late, but I got it."

"Come on, Joseph. I know break ups suck. But don't let it keep you away from what you love doing. Besides, maybe it'll make you feel better, take your mind off things. You know?"

Joseph sighed. Nico was right. Sitting here moping wasn't accomplishing anything. Tomorrow was Saturday, which meant the track was open in the morning for runs. "Alright. I'll enter the race. And I'll be at the track tomorrow at ten in the morning if you want to get some laps in with me."

****

By the time race day rolled around, Joseph was feeling more like himself. He'd taken Nico's advice and gotten back on his bike, going for late night rides. The offshoot freeway he picked was normally light on traffic, and late at night, he practically had it to himself. He'd pushed his Diavel carefully, testing both his and the bike's limits in preparation for today's race. Now he was ready, full of energy. He was so worked up from the situation with Gage, and stress from the Allen Brothers case that he didn't need to go through his screaming ritual. Instead, he stood next to his bike, bouncing slightly as he waited for his race to be up.

Suddenly, Joseph felt a tingle of awareness trickle down his spine. He turned around, not even surprised when he saw Gage standing a ways off, watching him.

Joseph stared back for a moment. Then he turned his back. He wasn't going to get tangled up with Gage again. He ignored both Gage and the feelings he got knowing he was watching him right up until it was time for his race. Then he didn't have to bother. Everything but the race faded to the back of his head once he was on the starting line.

****

Joseph kneeled on the ground to tend to his bike. He'd come in third. He'd stayed for the ceremonies to get his medal and hung out for a few minutes with the fans. Now he was ready to go home. Nico hadn't placed at all, so neither of them felt like going out for their traditional celebratory meal. A pair of expensive shoes came into his line of vision.

"Joseph, good race today."

He looked up to see Montoya standing in front of him. Standing, Joseph shook his hand. "Thank you, Rafael."

Montoya glanced around. "I see that *gringo* is gone from your side."

"Yes, he is."

Montoya smiled slightly. "Gone from your side, but not from here," he said touching his fingers to his chest.

Joseph didn't bother to deny it. "Maybe not now, but he will be."

"I see. Well, my offer of sponsorship is still open, Joseph. I do not like seeing you doing this work on your own. With my help, you could have a team to assist you."

For the first time, Joseph seriously considered Montoya's offer. "It would be nice to have some help."

"Why don't you think about it? Then we can get together and discuss."

A hard voice intruded on their conversation.

"Moving on already?"

Joseph spun around to see Gage standing there. He knew he didn't owe Gage any explanations, but he didn't want there to be a scene either. "I'm not. Rafael is a friend and he's offered to sponsor me. That's all." He planned to stay aloof, but his anger at the situation made him tack on a slight dig. "Besides, what do you care? I'm sure you've fucked about a dozen people by now, right?" He turned back to his bike, determined not to engage in any further discussion with Gage.

"No, I haven't. There's only one person I want."

Joseph's heart rate accelerated and his eyes flew back to Gage's face. He was watching him with that heavy-lidded direct gaze of his. Joseph's stomach jumped, but he quickly brought himself back under control. Words and manipulation. That's how Gage played the game, and it was how he'd gotten into this mess in the first place. He needed to remember that. He turned away again. "Save it, Gage. I'm not interested."

Gage stepped forward, "Goddamnit, Joseph! Do you think I'd be here if-."

Montoya stepped in front of him. "I think you should leave, *amigo*."

Gage sneered. "I'm not your fucking friend. Now get out of my way, this doesn't concern you."

"I don't think so, *amigo*. He said he's not interested. So you *will* leave."

Gage cocked his head to the side. "And who's gonna make me? You?" He scoffed. "You'd better take off that nice jacket first. I'd hate for it to get dirty. Or for me to fucking choke you out with it."

Joseph stood there dumbfounded as Montoya slowly took off his jacket. He held his arm out practically on autopilot and accepted it from him. Gage just stood there grinning, his arms loose, clearly spoiling for a fight. He got what he was looking for. Montoya's fist snapped forward, punching Gage dead in the mouth.

"Motherfucker!" He touched his hand to his mouth and his eyes went wide when he saw his blood. "You're gonna pay for that."

Montoya smirked. "I can afford it."

"I doubt it you rich piece of shit."

Gage launched himself at Montoya, his shoulder slamming into his stomach. Montoya grunted and went down. Gage was immediately on him with a hard punch to the jaw, before Montoya swiftly made it back to his feet. As the two fought, it was clear that Montoya had some sort of technical training in the way he moved with his attacks and his quick recovery when he couldn't avoid Gage's. On the other hand, Gage was a brawler. His punches were relentless and aggressive. The two battled back and forth, each of them landing hits over and over again. Montoya fell to the ground as Gage caught him with a knee to the face. He staggered back to his feet, diving right back into the fight.

Joseph jumped back out of the way as they came barreling towards him. He didn't even try to get involved or break it up. The rules of the track for racers were clear. Get in any sort of physical altercation and you were barred from the grounds. He was fine letting them fight it out, but someone noticed and screamed, *Fight!*

Three big security guys came rushing over, yelling at them to cut it out. Both men ignored them and kept throwing punches. Finally, two of the guys waded into the middle of it and pulled them apart. Gage and Montoya continued to stare each other down, clearly pissed that they'd been stopped.

"Do we need to call the police or can you two play nice until you're off our property?"

Montoya seemed to calm some. He dusted the dirt off of his clothes. "The police will not be necessary."

Gage swiped a hand across his bloody mouth then spit on the ground. "No police."

Joseph watched as the guard cautiously let Gage go. He stood there with his chest heaving, his dark hair a tangled mess all over his head. He looked wild; sweaty and bloody and dirty. But he didn't try to go after Montoya again. Gage looked over and caught him staring. Joseph jerked his gaze away. He handed Rafael his jacket while security waited. He felt like he should apologize. Gage wouldn't have confronted Montoya if it weren't for him. "I'm so sorry."

"It's not your fault," Montoya said as he shrugged into the jacket. "Besides, I don't mind getting into a scrap every now and then. It lets me express my *machismo*," he said with a grin.

Joseph shook his head and grinned back, staying behind as security escorted both men from the grounds. He told himself that he was irritated that Gage had come here today. However, as he watched them walk away, his eyes were drawn not to the sharply dressed Montoya, but to the rough and tumble figure of Gage.

CHAPTER 41

Gage slammed into his truck. He was so fucking furious he could barely see straight. That Montoya had some fucking nerve coming between him and Joseph! He'd taken quite a few punches from Montoya, and he was sore. But it was worth it for the blows he'd managed to land himself. Gage went roaring out of the parking lot, his back tires fishtailing on the gravel before the big Ram straightened out.

He wished he was on his bike so he could feel the wind on his face. But he'd driven the truck, because he'd hoped that he could persuade Joseph to leave with him, and knew he'd need the bed to transport his bike. His hand clenched on the steering wheel. But Joseph wouldn't even talk to him, barely looked at him. And that motherfucking Montoya was there! He cursed. The rage that went through him thinking that Joseph was off somewhere with that slick motherfucker was a giant, snarling, ugly ball in his chest and he felt like he was choking on it. He gripped the steering wheel and shouted at the air in front of him, trying to ease some of the tension from his bones.

He was angry with Montoya, with Joseph, with the whole goddamn situation. Mostly, he was angry with himself. He should never have kissed Brianna. That probably ranked up there with some of the dumbest shit he'd ever let his anger drive him to do. She'd been goading him and he knew it. He just had so much tumbling through his head with trying to make up his mind about Joseph and thinking about Heather and Riley. He'd started to feel like he wasn't in control and he hated that. When Brianna had taunted him, he'd kissed her not because he was turned on by her, but because he wanted to get a little of that control back. She might have thought she was getting what she wanted, but he'd been about to show her that you did not poke at him without paying for it. Besides, he didn't like anybody saying he was tamed.

When he'd seen Joseph standing there, the thought had run through his mind that he wouldn't have to figure out where to take things with Joseph after being caught with Brianna. It was done and over between them. He could return to his old life and not feel twisted and fucking conflicted anymore. Until Joseph had walked away. That was all it had taken for him to realize that he wanted to be with him.

He'd chased after Joseph to tell him that, but that hadn't been the time. Joseph was too closed off after what he'd seen. He'd tried again at Joseph's house, thinking if he could just get him soft and relaxed from sex, Joseph would listen to what he had to say. But thanks to his stupid impatience in bringing it up too soon, it hadn't worked that way. Now things were so fucked up, and all he was doing was making them worse. Approaching that Davis guy, not keeping his cool with Joseph when he'd seen him talking to Montoya, fighting Montoya. Christ, it was like he'd learned nothing over the years.

Gage took note of the sign for the next exit and realized where he was headed. He was tempted to keep on driving, but figured his subconscious wouldn't have taken him there if it wasn't where he needed to be. After exiting, he drove down quiet streets until he came to a familiar subdivision. Parking in the driveway, he got out and went up to the house that he knew almost as well as his own. Almost before he was done knocking the door swung open.

"Long time no see," Max said in his deep voice.

"Yeah, sorry I haven't been around."

"You never are when I tell you something you don't want to hear."

Gage didn't say anything to that because there was nothing to say. Max knew him better than just about anybody. He stepped inside and followed his friend back to the kitchen.

"Wash up. You've got blood all over your mouth and knuckles."

Gage headed over to the sink and turned the water on cold. He washed his hands and splashed icy water on his face. Knowing he was probably still bleeding, he dried off with a paper towel instead of one of Max's towels. Taking the beer Max handed him, he sat down at the table.

"I take it things got murky?"

Gage snorted and held the cold bottle to his busted lip. "Like a fucking swamp."

"You gonna tell me what happened or is this gonna be one of those nights where I have to pull it out of you?"

Gage looked at his friend, his brown eyes steady and calm as always. He took a drink before he started telling Max the whole story. When he was finished, Max leaned back in his chair.

"Fuck, man. I can't believe he stayed with you through all that."

Gage picked at the label on his beer bottle. "I know. I wasn't very good to him. But like I told you, I have tried to talk to him twice since the Brianna drama. But he won't-." Max cut him off.

"Did you say you're sorry?"

"What?"

"You didn't tell him you're sorry for all the shit you pulled, did you?"

Gage blinked. He hadn't told Joseph he was sorry. He never had. "No. I didn't even think …" He trailed off not having any reason for why he hadn't just apologized.

Max shook his head. "You went with your normal instincts, using manipulation and anger."

Gage cut his eyes at his friend. "You make me sound like a complete asshole."

Max smirked. "Well, you did try to fuck him on his living room floor and got into a fight with one of his friends as your way of winning him back."

Gage blew out a harsh breath. "I *am* an asshole."

Max laughed. "Yeah, but for whatever reason Joseph didn't mind it too much until you really fucked it up."

"Stop laughing at me and tell me what to do." Gage was frustrated. He just wanted to talk to Joseph, make him see that he wanted to be with him. But he didn't fucking know how to go about it. If he kept stumbling around like a fucking idiot, Joseph would be gone to Montoya or somebody else.

Max sobered. "Do you really want to be with him? No bullshit. Just you and Joseph in a real relationship. Be honest, Gage. Don't jerk that boy around anymore if you're just gonna cut out and chase tail when he gets too close."

Gage thought seriously for a long moment. He had fun with Joseph. He liked being around him, which was more than he'd experienced with anyone ever. He admired how smart Joseph was, even though he felt he was wasting his time at his current employment. Joseph's different sides intrigued him, sometimes quiet and reserved, sometimes wild and passionate. And he was pretty, so fucking pretty that he couldn't help but be drawn to him. He'd never had sex that was as hot and explosive as the sex he had with Joseph. Not only that, but when Gage was with Joseph he felt calm, felt like he was with the person he belonged with. Joseph just made him feel good. He wanted to sleep next to that long body and wake with that soft hair in his face again. He answered in a low voice, almost afraid to say it aloud. "I want him."

"Then talk to him. Tell him you're sorry. Don't try to fucking manipulate him again. Be honest and tell him everything."

Gage took a swig of his beer. "You make it sound so damn simple."

"It is simple. It might be hard to do, but it's simple. And Gage, all that old drama you're holding on to? You're gonna have to let that shit go."

CHAPTER 42

Gage was at Gia's bar. He hated to cook and he wasn't in the mood for any more fast food. A chicken strips and fries basket from Big G's had sounded good. He'd seen Gia when he walked in, and went over to say hi before he sat down and ordered. When he came up behind her, he noticed she was on her cell and overheard her conversation.

"Thank you so much for being willing to meet me at work Joseph. I've got a sick bartender so I have to stand in for her all week." She was quiet for a moment as Joseph said something on his end. "Okay, I'll see you then. Bye, cutie." She ended the call.

"Was that Joseph?"

Gia squeaked and spun around, her eyes wide with fright. She smacked him in the chest. "Gage! Don't scare me like that!"

Gage ignored her outburst, his mind focused on one thing. "Was that Joseph?"

She edged around him and walked over to the bar. He followed her.

"Why?"

"C'mon Gia. I know it was him. He's coming here? When?"

"Why do you want to know?"

"I want to talk to him."

"Then call him."

Gage clenched his jaw in frustration. "I have. He won't take my calls." He'd tried calling Joseph as soon as he'd left Max's Saturday night. He hadn't been surprised when he didn't get an answer, figuring Joseph was still pissed about the fight. He'd refused to think it was because he was busy with Montoya. But he'd called all day

Sunday too. And today before work he'd called, then again after he'd closed the shop. Every call went straight to voicemail.

Gia snorted and didn't say anything. She picked up a towel and started polishing the bar, ignoring him. Gage tried to stay calm. He didn't want to get mad at his friend, especially since she could tell him when he could see Joseph.

"Gia, help me out here."

Gia put down the towel and looked at him. "No. I won't help you. You're my friend and I love you. But Joseph has become my friend too and you hurt him. So other than saying yes that was Joseph and yes he'll be here one night this week, I'm staying out of it."

Gage kept his curse behind his teeth. He wanted to storm out of there, but for all he knew this was the night Joseph was coming to meet Gia. Pushing down his anger, he went to find an empty table and sat down to order his food.

****

Two days later, Gage still hadn't talked to Joseph. His calls continued to go to voice mail and he hadn't shown up at Gia's yet. He'd put on his stalker hat and driven past Joseph's townhome a time or ten. But the windows had always been dark and if Joseph was home, he had both the Z and his Ducati in the garage so Gage couldn't say for sure. The one place he knew Joseph would be he hesitated to go. He didn't want to get him in trouble at work so he'd avoided going to his firm. Which left him with no other option but to show up to Big G's every night after work.

Gage turned off the TV in frustration and tried to get comfortable enough on his pillows to fall asleep. His brain was so full of thinking about things with Joseph that he wasn't watching the TV anyway. He missed Joseph. He missed touching him. His body hardened as he thought

210

about feeling Joseph writhing and sweaty underneath him. He hadn't had sex for weeks now, the longest he'd gone in years. The thought of being with someone else didn't do anything for him. He hadn't even been able to go through with it with that guy he'd met at the bar. He'd been close to inviting him to take a ride somewhere. Instead, he'd abruptly made up an excuse about work and left without even attempting to close the deal. Now here he was, thinking about Joseph, his cock throbbing and his body desperate for release.

Sliding his hand under the covers, Gage reluctantly grasped his shaft. It felt wrong to get himself off to thoughts of Joseph, but he couldn't help it. His body didn't care what his mind thought, it just wanted release. He thought of what it was like to kiss Joseph, to slide his tongue into that mouth that always tasted so sweet to him. He thought about what it was like to pull on those light brown curls that were always so soft as they slid through his fingers. He thought about what it was like to have that pouty pink mouth sliding up and down his cock, Joseph on his knees as he sucked him. Gage groaned, stroking himself swiftly. He was turned on by the pictures in his head, but he wanted to get this over with quickly. He didn't want to linger since he wasn't getting the real thing, wouldn't be feeling the warm skin and muscle and bone of his lover. He pictured Joseph in his lap, working himself on his cock. His orgasm was coming quickly, his balls tight as he remembered what it was like to push deep into the snug heat of Joseph's ass.

But then the picture in his head changed. Joseph was in his darkened living room, on the couch. But it wasn't Gage he was riding. It was Montoya. His erection immediately retreated. He flung his hand away from himself, shouting out an angry curse.

Gage turned on his side, punching the pillow, trying futilely to get comfortable. He was aching now, but he knew he wouldn't be getting off. Not with that picture in his head. He squeezed his eyes shut tight, even though he knew he'd probably be up all fucking night. After about ten seconds they popped back open and he stared off into the darkness. "Goddamnit," he swore softly.

CHAPTER 43

Thursday night Joseph walked into Big G's, heading for the bar where Gia was. Before he made it there, he saw Gage sitting at a table facing the door. Their eyes met and Joseph came to a stop for a heartbeat before continuing on. Gage's presence had nothing to do with him.

"Hey, Gia." He leaned across the bar and kissed her on the cheek. She greeted him back before her eyes slid over to where Gage was sitting.

"He's been camped out here all week every night after work. If you want, you can go wait in my office and I'll be back there in just a few minutes."

"No, it's fine. I'm not worried about Gage."

Joseph got a basic idea of what Gia needed with her licensing and her federal obligations to her employees. He gave her a quick rundown, but he'd have to take a look at everything at home. She asked him what he charged per hour and his face heated.

"Don't worry about it, Gia. I'm just helping out a friend."

Gia winked at him. "That's what you think. I'm about to put you on retainer." She bounced a little bit. "Oh goody. Looks like I'm your first freelance client. Does this mean I get to help you pick your firm's name?" She pretended to think. "Hmmm… what's lawyerly and rhymes with hottie?"

Joseph laughed at Gia's teasing and gave her a fair price to help her out. When they were finished, Joseph took a deep breath. It was stupid of him to pretend like he didn't know Gage was there. He might as well be mature and say hello.

He turned around on his stool, ready to go over. He changed his mind when he saw Gage wasn't alone at his table. A young dark-haired man had just sat down. Joseph might have thought it was just a friend, except for the flirtatious look on the man's face. Joseph nodded to himself. Gage had obviously moved on, so there was no reason for him not to do the same. Ignoring the swirling disappointment in his chest, he left the bar.

CHAPTER 44

Gage sat up straight, every muscle tensing as Joseph walked in. Finally. After sitting here every night after work this week, Joseph was finally there. He wanted to go up to him immediately, but he held back. Joseph was there to talk to Gia. He didn't want to piss him off from jump by interrupting what he'd come there to do. So, impatient as he was, he waited at his table.

Gage didn't want to look like a total creeper sitting there staring so he got his phone out. He'd glance down every so often pretending to read the trending topics on Yahoo just to give himself something to look at. He kept glancing up to see Joseph and Gia engrossed, going over some papers. Eventually, it looked like they were wrapping things up and his adrenaline started pumping, thinking he'd get his chance soon. But the next time he glanced up someone was in front of him, blocking his view. It was that guy he'd almost made the giant mistake with. He looked at the man in annoyance when he gave him a flirtatious smile.

"I bet you don't remember my name do you?"

Gage shrugged. "Nope." The guy looked startled, like he hadn't expected him to be so blunt. Too bad.

"It's Ben," he said.

Gage nodded, not caring. Gage was glad when the guy sat, only because it reopened his line of sight to the bar. He looked and saw Joseph's back as he walked out of the bar. Gage jumped up out of his chair, ready to follow when he remembered he hadn't paid his tab. He pulled out his wallet, cursing when he saw he didn't have any cash. No way was he waiting for his server to go through the whole credit card payment process. Gage hurried over to Gia at the bar completely forgetting about the guy sitting at his table.

"Hey, I need to get out of here and I haven't paid my tab." He handed her his card. Put my bill on this and close it out for me will you?"

Gia looked down at the card but didn't take it. "Where are you off to in such a rush?"

"I'm going after Joseph."

"To do what?"

Gage was out of patience. "Fuck! To apologize Gia! To see if he'll give me another chance, which won't happen if you don't take this damn card."

She finally took the card from him, a sly smile tugging at her lips. "Alright then."

He spun away from the bar, ready to head out when he heard her call out to him.

"I might get myself some new shoes on here if you don't mind."

"Yeah whatever," he threw over his shoulder. Then he realized what she'd said. Still walking, he turned and pointed a finger at her. "Don't you dare." She laughed, and he finally got out of there.

Outside in the parking lot, Gage could hear the echo of Joseph's bike, which meant he wasn't too far away yet. And he was going in the direction of his house. Gage got on his own bike, starting it quickly to speed out of the parking lot after him. On the highway, Gage pushed his Indian as hard as he dared. He broke the speed limit, but he wasn't reckless. He wasn't going to catch Joseph, but on flat stretches of the highway he'd seen glimpses of his taillight far ahead of him. It looked like he was going straight home. Gage relaxed somewhat and settled in for the short ride. He'd be able to talk to Joseph soon.

Gage pulled up to Joseph's townhome just as he saw a light flick on, glowing from around the edges of the blinds. His heart was beating hard as he killed the motor. Joseph was here and it looked like he was alone. This was his chance. It felt odd to care so much about this, but he was determined not to let his hang-ups keep him from what he wanted. He took a deep breath, trying to calm himself. He was glad now that he hadn't caught Joseph at the bar. It was better to have this conversation in private. Gage went up the walk, running a hand through his hair both out of nervousness and to try and tame the windswept mess. Then he rang the doorbell.

Joseph hadn't been in the house for five minutes when someone rang the doorbell. Looking through the window, he saw it was Gage. He hesitated. He'd avoided Gage's calls all week, not wanting to fall for any more of his games. But Gage had seen him at Gia's, and it was obvious he was home. He might as well see what he wanted. After several weeks away from Gage, he trusted himself not to fall for his manipulations. Joseph opened the door. Gage stood there, looking uncharacteristically nervous.

"Can I come in?" He cleared his throat. "Please."

Joseph stepped back to let him in, shutting the door behind him. Gage didn't say anything. He just stood there staring at the floor, so Joseph prompted him. "Why'd you stop by?" Several more moments passed before Gage finally looked at him.

"I'm here to apologize."

Joseph went still. "What?"

"I wanted to tell you I'm sorry. I never once apologized to you. Not for snapping at you when you complimented me on my bike. Not for being a dick to you the night we went bowling when you asked me to stay. And *Christ* I didn't even apologize when you caught me kissing Brianna."

Joseph blinked. He couldn't believe what had just come out of Gage's mouth. It was true that Gage hadn't ever said he was sorry. He hadn't let it bother him then, always thinking that Gage just needed time to adjust to being in a relationship to learn how to say he was sorry. He'd given up on all that when he saw him kissing Brianna, but now Gage was here apologizing to him. Joseph wasn't sure what to say, so he said nothing. He just watched Gage to see what he would say next.

Gage ran a hand through his hair. "I'm sorry for all of it, Joseph. I had no right to make you wait two weeks while I decided what I wanted. I should have given you an answer immediately, whether it was yes or no. But I was a selfish fucking coward and kept looking for ways to keep you without committing to you."

Joseph was so surprised he still hadn't moved. And he was still quiet, but now it was because he wanted to see what else Gage was going to admit to him. He didn't want to say anything and stop Gage's flow.

"I swear to you I didn't kiss Brianna because I wanted to. I did it for dumb reasons that are nearly too fucked up to even put into words." He took a deep breath. "Basically I was scared. Scared of changing from the life I was used to, to one where I had to put myself out there in a way I hadn't for a long time. And I told you, the last time didn't end well. Then Brianna said I was tamed and it pissed me off. I reacted in the only way I know. Sex. It was dumb and I know it, but I swear I had no intention of sleeping with her."

Gage slowly walked up to him. Joseph's heart pounded as he came forward. He knew where this was going. Gage wanted him back. But so far he hadn't heard anything that would let him be with Gage again. Yet. He met Gage's gaze, saw him watching him closely. Joseph braced himself when Gage stopped just in front of him, ready to reject any physical advances if that was how Gage intended to play this. But Gage's next words shocked him.

"I almost don't want to approach you right now, because I don't want you to think I'm about to manipulate you again. Like I did every fucking time you tried to get close and I wouldn't let you." He shook his head like he was disgusted with himself. "I just … I just want to be close to you."

Gage touched his waist with his fingertips, running them down to his hip before he dropped his hand away. Joseph bit his lip to keep from asking for that hand back. Just that one touch and his body was already tuned to Gage's, wanting to be closer.

"I know the deadline you gave me is long past. But I'm hoping that you're still interested in my answer. Because it's yes. I want to be with you, Joseph. You and no one else. I just need you to give me another chance."

Now Joseph's heart was really racing. That's what he'd been waiting for. But he'd waited and waited and Gage hadn't come through. Was it too late for them? He looked at Gage, saw his jaw tight with tension.

"You haven't said anything."

Joseph shrugged. "I'm not really sure what to say. Last time I saw you, you were fighting my friend and glaring at me before you were kicked out of the park. And now you're here saying you want to be with me. I guess I just wasn't expecting this."

Gage stared back at him for a moment before pacing in front of him a few steps. "Fuck, I know I should have some sweet words or a present or something, right? And I'm probably saying all this in a way that doesn't make any damn sense." Gage cursed in clear frustration. "I feel stupid and hate that I'm fucking this up."

Joseph wanted to smile, but he didn't. He still wasn't sure about this. "You don't need a present."

Gage stopped in front of him again. His expression brightened, like he was taking his comment as encouragement. He closed the last breath of space between them and kissed him lightly. Joseph didn't kiss him back.

Gage closed his eyes, rested his forehead against his. "Please."

Joseph swallowed hard. He wanted to believe this but after Gage had fought so hard to keep things casual between them, it was difficult to trust that he'd changed. "Gage, I don't know…" Gage kissed him again, just as softly as before.

"Please, Joseph. If you only knew how desperate I feel right now…" He let the sentence trail away without finishing it. "Just please give me a chance."

That's all he'd wanted, for Gage to give the two of them a chance. And if Gage was honestly willing to try…This time when Gage's lips met his, Joseph kissed him back. They stood that way for several tense moments, their bodies barely touching, their lips coming together in a tentative kiss. Finally, Joseph wrapped his arms around Gage's neck pulling him close. Gage's arms went around his waist, slowly, like he was trying not to scare him off. But it had been too long since he'd been close to his lover. Joseph pressed his body against Gage's, until with a groan, Gage squeezed him tight. All the uncertainty fell away and Joseph parted his lips, allowing Gage to sweep inside. Their kiss grew in passion and intensity until Gage's hands were roaming up and down his back. He gripped Joseph's hips, pulling him up against his body. Joseph moaned, his stomach lifting with a swirl of desire as he felt Gage's erection pressing against him.

Gage pulled back, breathing hard. "Fuck. I'm sorry. I swear I didn't come here for that."

Joseph gave him that mischievous smile. "But you want to. If I let you."

Gage dug his fingers into Joseph's back. After nearly a month apart, thinking of Joseph, missing him, wanting to be inside him … Yeah, his body definitely wanted to. He cleared his throat, but his voice still came out thick with desire. "Yeah. If you let me. I swear I haven't been with anyone else."

Joseph looked at him with a steady gaze. "I believe you, Gage. And I want you too. I've wanted you every night for weeks."

Gage sucked in a breath thinking of Joseph alone in his bed at night, aching for him just as he had ached for Joseph. He brought them together again. He could take care of him right now, make him forget, make them both forget, all those nights alone. Gage brushed his lips across Joseph's, but before he could deepen the kiss, Joseph spoke.

"Just promise me one thing."

Gage pulled back and looked into his eyes, waiting to see what he wanted.

"After, you'll tell me all of it."

Gage nodded. "Yes, I promise. I swear, I'll be an open book, whatever you want to -." Joseph pressed forward and kissed him, cutting off the rest of his rambling.

CHAPTER 45

They made their way to Joseph's bedroom, still kissing, their hands all over each other, both of them naked by the time they reached the bed. Gage lowered Joseph gently down to the bed and stretched out on top of him. He kissed his lover everywhere, moving down his body slowly so his lips could touch all of that golden skin. He reached his shaft and rubbed his palm up the hard length. Joseph watched him, his pretty green eyes communicating what he wanted. Gage smiled and leaned down, running his tongue over the same path his hand had just taken. He reached the crown and licked at it, feeling it swell even further against his tongue. Joseph's hand came up to his head, pressing him down.

"Gage, I don't think I can take much teasing tonight."

Gage laughed softly, flicking his tongue over his cockhead a few more times before he sucked him in. When he took his lover into his mouth, Joseph arched up with a sharp cry. Gage took him deep, sucking him with long slow pulls. His own erection hung stiff and heavy, but he ignored it, focused solely on pleasuring Joseph. He slid a hand underneath him, cupping his ass and keeping him arched up against him. Joseph moaned, rolling his hips in rhythm with his sucking.

Gage looked up Joseph's body, needing to watch. He'd missed this, missed watching Joseph writhing in pleasure, the sweet curve of his mouth parted in that pretty little *o* as he dragged in heaving breaths. But he wanted a lot more from Joseph tonight. He took one last deep pull on the throbbing cock in his mouth, drawing another cry from Joseph, before he let him go.

Gage rose up over his lover. He felt like he wanted to spend hours making Joseph feel good in order to make up for lost time, but that would have to wait. He was about to reach for the nightstand when Joseph grasped his cock and started stroking him. Gage shuddered, choking on a harsh groan. He took Joseph's hand away from him, pressing it down to the bed. "I'm sorry. That felt great, but it's been awhile and I'm already close."

Joseph licked his lips and gripped him with his other hand. "It's been just as long for me. How do you think I felt while you were blowing me?"

Gage groaned again … and let Joseph do what he wanted. He held himself braced over Joseph as his warm hand pumped his cock slowly. Having Joseph touch him, working him until his cock was pulsing and slick felt beyond good. But it was torture. Torture that felt fucking amazing. Joseph squeezed him and he cursed. "Fuck, Joseph. Don't stop." He leaned down enough to take Joseph's mouth in a wild and frantic kiss, thrusting his cock into the tight grip of his fist again and again. His head was buzzing, sparks shooting throughout his body as he tried to hold back his orgasm. Joseph's hand trailed down to cup his tight balls. At that touch, he shot up straight and lunged for the nightstand, grabbing what he needed.

It took him only a second before he was back between Joseph's legs. He got his lover wet and stretched, both with his tongue and a lube-slick finger, teasing and pushing deep inside him until Joseph's legs were restlessly squeezing his head. Gage rose back up and rocked back on his heels. He'd grabbed a condom along with the lube out of habit. He picked it up from where he'd dropped it on the mattress. Gage hesitated. He looked at Joseph, not sure what to say. Joseph took the decision out of his hands. He sat up and kissed him, his fingers closing over his. Joseph took the condom from him and dropped it on the floor. Gage groaned and kissed him back with all the emotion that was churning within him. Emotion he wasn't ready to express just yet.

Joseph lay back down, watching him with wide eyes as he covered his bare cock with lube. When he was finished, he wiped his hand clean on the sheet and lowered himself over his lover. His eyes drifted shut in pleasure as he eased himself into Joseph, for the first time feeling how tight and hot he was with nothing between them. But he forced them back open so that he could meet his lover's eyes. "Only you, Joseph."

Joseph nodded, his lips parted as he panted softly. Gage pushed into him further, brushing a kiss across his mouth, up his cheek and to his ear. "I'm yours," he whispered. Joseph wrapped his arms around him tight, his legs coming up to squeeze him close as well. Gage groaned as he sank all the way inside him. He started to move, shivers of pleasure dancing over his skin at how good it felt to be connected to Joseph like this. He'd expected it to feel amazing physically. He hadn't expected to feel so close to him. He had to know, had to know if Joseph felt the same. Gage looked at him, but he didn't have to ask. It was there in his face, in his eyes, that the same feeling that was making his heart pound, was making Joseph's beat hard as well.

Gage stroked into his lover, slowly, dragging out the sensation of Joseph's channel gripping his bare cock. Their bodies slid against each other with every movement and it felt like they were touching everywhere. He could feel Joseph's erection pressing against his stomach, feel his chest pushing against his with each deep breath. Gage reached for Joseph's hand, watching as his eyes drifted shut when he laced their fingers together. Joseph breathed his name and Gage kissed him before burying his face in his neck. He stayed that way, breathing in the warm scent of Joseph's skin as he thrust inside him.

This sex was different than any he'd ever had and he made it last as long as he could. But eventually he couldn't hold back. His movements became more urgent, Joseph rocking his hips against him with the same passion. The heat between them rose, spiking higher until their bodies were slick with sweat. Gage thrust into Joseph hard, making him cry out in pleasure. He felt Joseph's cock jump against his stomach, felt his ass clench tight on his own cock. His spine tingled and he knew it was about to be over for him. He let go of Joseph's hand to reach for his shaft, Joseph moaning as he palmed him. He stroked him in rhythm with the movement of their bodies, pushing Joseph as close to the edge as he was. Joseph was giving him those throaty little moans that he loved and he kissed along his neck, feeling the vibration of each one against his lips. Suddenly, Joseph dug his fingers into his ass, gripping him hard and pulling his body even closer. Gage looked down at him, into eyes heavy-lidded with arousal.

"Come in me, Gage. I've been waiting to feel it. It's what we both want."

Gage groaned on a curse, leaning down and kissing his lover. He tried to hold out for just a little longer, but Joseph's ass was clenching on his cock and his balls were aching with the urge to come. He moved faster and faster, Joseph squeezing his thighs around his waist. His balls drew up even harder and he felt that tingling rush up his shaft, spurred on by the heat surrounding him. The feeling was even more intense than usual because there was nothing to block the sensation. Just his bare cock inside Joseph's ass. Joseph clenched on him again, this time drawing a string of curses from his mouth. "Fuck, Joseph, fuck!" He immediately felt bad for cursing in this moment. He was breathing hard as he tried to apologize. "Damnit, I'm sorry, Joseph. I probably shouldn't curse."

Joseph laughed softly. "I like it when you curse while you're inside me." Then he squeezed him again, even harder this time.

Gage cursed again and before he knew it they were kissing wildly. He pumped into Joseph with furious speed, stroking his cock just as fast. Joseph was shaking and cursing himself, before he pulsed in his hand with a sharp cry. He threw back his head, moaning out his release.

Gage followed him, stretching forward to steal that mouth again as he started to come too. This time he called out Joseph's name as his cock throbbed and he came inside his lover. Joseph hugged him close, his fingers digging into him once more. He slammed his hips against Joseph's, pushing hard, reaching as deep inside him as he could. It felt powerful and amazing to come like this, knowing Joseph could really feel him. He stayed pressed against him, his body shuddering, still kissing. Finally, Joseph trembled underneath him one last time and with one last deep groan he was drained too. They both drew in deep breaths, their bodies relaxing to savor the afterglow.

****

Gage reluctantly withdrew and rolled to Joseph's side. He looked at his lover, taking in how beautiful he was with his skin warm and gleaming with sweat, his hair a tangled dark cloud around his face. He'd come close to never seeing this again because of his bullshit. He reached out and twisted some of those curly strands of hair around his fingers. "Thank you for giving me another chance."

Joseph looked at him, his eyes still soft and languid. He smiled. "I knew you'd come around."

CHAPTER 46

Joseph rolled out of bed, headed for the bathroom. Before he could take a single step, Gage grabbed his hand.

"Where are you going?"

He looked back over his shoulder to see Gage watching him, his face half buried in the pillow, his hair tangled and falling into his eyes. "To shower. You can join me if –." He stiffened, his sentence coming to an abrupt halt.

Gage's brow furrowed in confusion. "What?"

A warm flush crawled up Joseph's neck to his face. He wasn't sure if it was embarrassment or not. "I just felt you … your cum … running out of me."

Gage's eyes dropped to his ass. Whatever he saw made those dark eyes brighten with a possessive gleam as they rose back to his. Gage reached out, teasing his fingers over the backs of his thighs. "Don't shower." He sat up and tugged at his hand. "Fuck, don't ever shower again."

Joseph laughed and let himself be pulled back into the bed. "I'd have to shower eventually. Can't go to work with your cum still inside me."

Gage groaned and kissed him. "Damnit, Joseph. Don't put the thought of you at work in one of your prissy suits with my cum still in your ass in my head."

Joseph grinned. "You like that idea?"

Gage nodded and kissed him again. "Fuck yeah, I like that. Turn over for me."

Joseph turned onto his stomach. Gage smoothed his palm over his ass, down his thighs and then back again. He looked at him, his eyes as solemn as Joseph had ever seen them.

"Being inside you like that, Joseph. It's been on my mind almost constantly. And not just because of how good I knew it would feel." Gage stretched out on top of him and whispered in his ear. "I knew it would mean you were mine." Joseph moaned as Gage slowly pushed inside him. "I wanted that so fucking bad, Joseph. Even though I wouldn't admit it, not even to myself. But now I have it. Now you're mine."

Joseph tried to stifle a moan, but he couldn't. Gage felt too good stroking into him with a smooth, unhurried pace. He drew in a deep breath, releasing it on a shuddering exhale before he answered. "I know. I wanted to be yours, wanted to feel you inside me." He pushed back against Gage as much as he could with his weight pinning him down. "No one else, Gage."

Gage cursed, his voice low and gravelly with desire. He kissed along Joseph's back, licking at his skin, biting at the sensitive spot where his neck and shoulder met. The feel of Gage's mouth on him was somehow both rough and gentle, making shivers run up and down his spine. Joseph moaned, his cock trapped underneath him, throbbing in time to his heartbeat. He called out his lover's name in desperate supplication, pushing his hips back. Gage knew what he wanted. He worked his hand underneath him, but didn't ease his weight off. Gage gripped his cock while it was still pressed tight to the mattress, stroking him in time with his slow thrusts.

They moved together, their breathing coming fast in nearly identical harsh pants, Joseph growing closer and closer to his orgasm. His stomach tingled and his shaft was pulsing in Gage's firm grip. He arched his spine, pushing his hips back, tightening his body around the thick shaft inside him. Gage groaned and buried his face in his hair.

"Fuck, gonna come inside you again, Joseph. Do you want that?"

His head was swimming in pleasure, but he managed to answer *yes*. Gage pushed into him faster and Joseph moved with him until everything was a sweaty, slippery blur of stroking and squeezing, groans and kisses and pounding deep thrusts. Joseph's fingers clenched in the sheets, his body humming with pleasure as he released into his lover's hand. He closed his eyes, listening as Gage claimed him. His words weren't pretty or sweet, but that was okay with him. He loved the way his bad boy talked to him.

"You're mine, Joseph. Just like I told you. Mine to fuck however I want. You belong to me, pretty boy." He emphasized his declaration with a strong thrust of his cock inside him, pulling on his hair.

Gage kissed him, rough and greedy, biting at his bottom lip. He pushed in hard one last time, stiffening with his own release. Joseph moaned at the feel of that heat flooding into him. He didn't disagree. He definitely belonged to Gage.

****

An hour later, Joseph still hadn't made it into the shower. He lay on his side, Gage's arms wrapped around him. Gage kept running his palm over his ass, his fingers slipping between his cheeks. He sucked a kiss onto Joseph's neck.

"I'll don't think I'll ever get tired of coming inside you."

Joseph laughed. "Easy for you to say, you're not the one wet and sticky."

A cocky grin appeared on Gage's face. He pushed Joseph to his back and slid on top of him. "I like you wet and sticky."

Joseph pushed at him half-heartedly. "Don't even think about it. It's already late and besides, if we do that again I'll be walking funny tomorrow."

One brow went up. "What, you don't want everybody to know you got laid?"

He snorted an embarrassed laugh. "No." Then he looked at Gage from beneath his lashes. "Besides, I think they'll already know from the way you always seem to leave a mark on my neck."

Gage smiled. "I'm not apologizing for that."

"I don't want you to."

Gage lowered his head and kissed him. Joseph kissed him back, opening his legs so Gage could rest between them. The kiss grew deeper and Gage started rubbing his renewed erection against him. Joseph tried to put up a protest between kisses.

"Gage, I'm serious. I'll be sore."

He shook his head. "I won't hurt you, Joseph. I promise."

Joseph relaxed and gave in. After so much time apart he found himself nearly desperate to feel Gage's body pressed against his. Gage kept kissing him, sliding his tongue into his mouth and sucking on his. He moved his hips against him so that their shafts rubbed together. Joseph wrapped his legs around Gage's waist at his whispered instruction, squeezing him tight and rocking his body underneath him. It took a while before he got there after already climaxing twice that night. But when he did it was a sweet, bone deep release that had him quietly groaning and shuddering beneath his lover. He could tell Gage's was the same. He didn't make a sound other than a shaky breath as he came on his stomach. His fingers dug deep into Joseph's thighs before he let go and fell limp against him. Gage rolled to his side, both of them lying there silently as they caught their breath.

This time Gage got up and went to the bathroom. He came back with a warm wet towel and cleaned off his stomach before returning it to the bathroom. Joseph bit his lip on a smile. Gage hadn't even made an attempt to wipe off the backs of his thighs and he knew it wasn't because he'd forgotten.

Gage came back into the bedroom and stopped next to the bed. Joseph watched him, wondering what he was going to do. If he didn't spend the night, he'd be okay with that. Things had already changed so much between them he couldn't expect to have everything at once. But Gage turned off the lamp and got back into the bed. He pulled him into his arms and Joseph returned the embrace.

"I'm glad you're staying."

Gage brushed his face over his hair, inhaling deeply. "I snore. You might not be glad when I wake you up in the middle of the night."

Joseph laughed. "I'll still be glad."

CHAPTER 47

The next day Joseph walked into the café where he was meeting Lila for lunch. When she saw him, her eyebrows shot up.

"You got laid."

Joseph's face burned hot. He slid into the booth quickly in case others were looking at the way he walked. "What? Why do you say that?"

Lila smirked. "It's all over your face. You've been moping around for weeks, but today you walk in here all smiles, with some pep in your step." She took a sip of her drink. "Only explanation is that you got you some. Am I right?"

Joseph opened his menu, the embarrassment fading a little. At least she hadn't said it was because he was walking funny. "Yeah … uh. Gage and I are back together."

"Really? Congratulations!"

Joseph grinned. "Thanks. We've still got some stuff to talk about, but it looks like we're together for real this time."

"So when do I get to meet this man you're so hung up on?"

"He's your brother's friend and you've never met him?"

Lila shrugged. "Maybe once a few years ago, but I wasn't paying much attention. You should bring him to the company picnic!"

Joseph thought about that for a moment. Their firm had a big picnic at the start of fall every year when the weather was cool enough to be outside. "I'll ask him, but his shop is open on Saturdays so I'm not sure if he'd be able to make it."

Lila tossed her hair over her shoulder. "Well, if not, you'd better find another way for me to meet him. I need to let him know not to hurt my Joey again."

Joseph groaned. "I thought I told you not to call me that?"

Lila smiled. "My bad … Joey."

****

This time it was Joseph's turn to be nervous as he walked to Gage's front door. They'd agreed to meet for dinner at his house tonight and then to talk. Joseph had a feeling Gage wanted to be on his home turf for this conversation. He understood that. He was nervous for what Gage was going to reveal so he knew the other man had to be even more so. He rang the bell and after a few moments Gage opened up. Joseph stepped inside, right into a kiss. Gage pulled back and grinned at him.

"Anybody comment on your walk today?"

"Yes, actually."

Gage's brows rose in surprise.

"Apparently I was walking with some pep in my step."

Gage grinned suggestively. "That's what happens when you get the D."

Joseph rolled his eyes. "You're so crass. Can you try to be a good host and feed me?"

Gage laughed and headed back into the kitchen. He'd made some steaks and vegetable skewers out on the grill. Joseph got drinks from the fridge while Gage brought everything to the table. After they'd eaten, Joseph leaned back in his chair.

"I have to say I'm surprised you can cook."

Gage snorted. "I can grill. There's a difference. That stove might as well be there as modern art."

"A Study in Bachelorhood: Brushed Steel?"

"Exactly." He took another sip of his iced tea. "So I guess you want to know some stuff."

Joseph was suddenly nervous again. "I guess."

"Let's go in the living room." Gage stood and held out his hand. Joseph took it and they went into the living room to settle on the couch. Gage ran a hand over his hair. "I might as well get the big stuff out of the way first, right?"

"However you want to do this."

Gage glanced at him, but didn't say anything for a long moment. He looked away from him before he finally started talking. "I told you how wild I was when I was younger quick to anger, quick to fight. And then how I got hooked on drugs. Well for a good part of that time I was with this girl, Heather. She was gorgeous but wild, just as wild as me. She partied, drank, smoked weed, did X, stole, you name it. We met at a party one night, did some X and fucked. From there, we just sorta started hanging out. There was never any 'will you be my girlfriend' type of conversation. We just hooked up at so many parties that people started assuming we were together. She stayed over at my place all the time and eventually she just didn't go home. That's how we started living together. Things with her were alright at first. We were both young and not looking for anything serious. We'd go out with our friends every night then come home and have sex. And uh… she was up for pretty much anything in bed."

Joseph was surprised to see a flush staining Gage's cheeks like he was embarrassed. He didn't say anything though. He wasn't there to judge. Gage continued.

"When I started using heavier shit than weed and X, I asked if she wanted to try it. She was a little nervous at first. But I talked her into it. Told her how good it would make her feel, how much better the sex would be. She tried whatever it was I offered her that night and soon we were both using pretty heavy. After my friend died, I decided to clean my shit up. I talked to her about it and she swore she would do the same. I believed her at first. But it's not easy to hide drug use from a former user. I noticed the glazed eyes, the sneaking off, the mood swings. When I confronted her, she said she was weaning herself off slowly. She wasn't strong enough to go cold turkey like I had.

I ignored it for a long time. Max had already suggested a new way for me to handle my anger and I was uh … using her for that purpose. But eventually I caught her snorting coke in the bathroom. I knew I had to get her out of there, knowing it was there so close might make me slip up. I kicked her out but told her I'd help her get clean whenever she was ready. It was my fucking fault that she'd gotten into the heavy shit. Over the years, I've helped her with a place to stay or money when she needed it. She's done rehab a couple of times, but it never sticks. And that's relationship number one."

Gage looked at him out of the corner of his eye like he was gauging his reaction. Joseph could see why he blamed himself for Heather's drug addiction. But he didn't see it as totally his fault. For one, people were responsible for their own life choices. And second from the way Gage described her, it sounded like she could well have become a drug addict with or without Gage's help. He didn't say any of that, however. He didn't want Gage to think he wasn't taking his confession seriously.

"That sounds like a crazy situation to be in. I admire the fact that you were able to pull yourself out of it and I'm sorry that she wasn't."

Gage shrugged. "Yeah, she's still a mess. She came into the shop awhile back. That's what set me off the night..." He cleared his throat. "The night that you helped me. Here."

Joseph flushed as he remembered Gage sitting on this couch, sucking him off until he came in a mind-blowing orgasm. "Oh." He'd wondered but never asked. "So she's still around then."

"Yeah. She's still in this city, but who the fuck knows where she's staying. I told her the apartment over my shop was occupied." He grew quiet.

Joseph waited for as long as he could, which was about ten seconds, before he prompted him. "And the other?"

"The other was Riley." He rubbed his hands over his thighs a few times before he went on. "Riley wasn't the first guy I was with. I'd already figured out by that time that I didn't discriminate sexually. But he was the first person I'd tried to have a relationship with since Heather. Riley was … Riley was great. Smart and good looking. And he was confident and cocky and outgoing."

Joseph felt a flash of jealousy. He immediately squashed it, feeling like the worst sort of scum for being jealous of his boyfriend's dead ex.

"We were a lot alike. Probably too much alike because we fought all the fucking time. We'd argue over big issues like whether or not we should move in together and dumb shit like where to eat dinner. We'd have these huge fights, shouting and cursing at each other. Then Riley would take off on his bike. He had one of those stupid crotch rockets that I hate. When he came back, we'd make up with half-angry sex. But we never actually solved any of our problems. One day we fought, he took off…" Gage took a deep breath "… and he didn't come back."

Joseph's chest was tight and uncomfortable. This was hard to hear. He knew what was coming but still stupidly asked, "Did he leave you?"

Gage huffed a humorless laugh. "He met up with some friends. They were all stunt riders. Riley was good, one of the best in his crew. But that time he lost control and wiped out. Fractured his skull." Gage paused for a moment, leaning his head back against the couch with his eyes closed. He took a deep breath. "He was already gone by the time I got the call."

Joseph swallowed hard. He was hurting for Gage, for the obvious pain he saw in his face. "Gage, that's awful. Both stories are, but especially Riley's. I'm so sorry he lost his life in that way and that you lost someone you cared about." He knew now wasn't the time to tell Gage the accident wasn't his fault. But one day he would. It wasn't fair for Gage to keep torturing himself for something he didn't directly cause. "I'm glad you shared this with me."

"It feels good to get it out."

"I can't even imagine. That's a lot to carry by yourself." He reached out and brushed his fingers along Gage's jaw. Gage turned his head and kissed his palm. He took his hand away from his face, but he didn't let his fingers go.

"So yeah. Clearly I have shit luck when it comes to trying to be with someone. I decided I was better off on my own. I found people to give me what I need. And I made damn sure I satisfied them and that we had fun. But I didn't want any more than that. I didn't want any attachments with anyone because I didn't want the guilt if I fucked it up. Or I guess I should say if I fucked them up."

"I can understand why you made that decision." Joseph took a deep breath of his own. "And I owe you an apology. I was selfish in wanting you to be in a relationship with me without stopping to consider why you might not want to be in one. I'm sorry, Gage."

Surprise crossed Gage's face. "Thank you for that. But I can't really blame you. I know I was sending you all kinds of crazy mixed signals. I wanted to be with you, knew I felt something different towards you from the moment you asked me out. I just couldn't let go of the fear that I would somehow ruin you."

"Well, you won't have to worry about that with me. I think I'm strong enough to make my own decisions and not let you influence me." He grinned, trying to lighten the mood. "I did manage to hold out when you were trying to have your cake and eat it too. I made you put up or shut up."

Gage looked at him, a smile teasing at his mouth. "They teach you those clichés in lawyer school?"

"No, they were too high brow for that."

"Well, you did. Not gonna lie, Joseph. That was one of the scariest fucking things I've ever done, putting myself out there like that. Especially since you weren't saying anything."

"Sorry about that. You surprised me. Plus, I needed to be sure you were serious."

"It's okay. It was worth it."

Joseph poked at him. "So does this mean you're going to be a sweet, good boyfriend now?"

"I don't think so. If you want, I could bend you over the arm of this couch to show you I'm the same old Gage." He smiled, a naughty grin that made a dimple appear in one cheek. "Just maybe not as much of an asshole."

CHAPTER 48

Sunday morning, Joseph woke to sunlight warming his face. He was lying on his front, his head turned towards the window. Gage lay next to him, on his front as well, his arm a heavy weight draped over Joseph's back. He was tempted to lay there and fall back asleep to the sound of Gage's soft snores, but his stomach was growling. He turned over, dislodging Gage's arm. When he was free, he sat up. His movements woke Gage, who groaned and tried to pull him back down.

"Why are you awake? It's Sunday. Go back to sleep."

Joseph laughed. "You are definitely not a morning person."

Gage opened one eye to look at him. "After two weeks of sleeping together, you're just now figuring that out?"

Joseph smiled. He and Gage had indeed been back together for two weeks now. They'd spent nearly every night together, splitting their time between each other's homes. This morning they were in Gage's large bedroom. And as usual Gage was reluctant to be dragged out of sleep.

"I'm hungry."

Gage raised his hand to rub across his stomach. "You're always hungry. Where do you put it all?"

Joseph got out of the bed. "Shut up. I want donuts." He bent over to grab his jeans from the floor. Gage whistled.

"Oh yeah, that's where you put it all."

Joseph turned back around to see Gage grinning at him wickedly. He arched a brow. "You complaining?"

Gage shook his head. "Hell no."

Joseph continued getting dressed and pulled his hair back into a sloppy ponytail. "I didn't think so." Then he cursed. "Shit, I forgot you drove me over here last night. Any chance I can convince you to get out of bed and take me to get some donuts?"

Gage stretched and pulled the covers up his bare chest. "I'm not getting up. Take the Indian."

Joseph's eyes popped wide. "Are you serious?"

Gage shrugged. "Yeah. I trust you. Keys are on the rack next to the garage door in the kitchen."

Joseph grinned with excitement and started out of the room. Gage called him back.

"Hey. There's a helmet for you on the shelf out there."

Joseph looked at Gage in surprise. "Thank you." Gage waved him off and he went bounding down the stairs.

Down in the garage Joseph saw Gage's three motorcycles. But he ignored two of them and went for the Indian Chief Dark Horse. He couldn't believe Gage had said he could ride his motorcycle. Joseph ran a palm over the muted colors of the headdress logo. The rest of the bike was a rich black. It looked strong and solid as it sat there, a perfect match to its owner. Joseph swung his leg over and mounted the bike. He'd found the key and a shiny black retro-looking helmet just where Gage had said they'd be. The helmet was obviously new and fit his head perfectly. He started the bike and it came roaring to life. Wheeling it over to the garage door, he hit the button to open it, drove through, and put in the code to close it again. Joseph didn't even try to hold back his grin as the big bike rumbled beneath him. He just revved it up and drove off.

****

Gage looked towards the door as he heard Joseph coming up the stairs. He breezed into the room, bringing the scent of fresh air, motorcycle exhaust and sugar in with him. Joseph jumped on the bed, straddling his waist.

"I love that bike. The ride is so smooth and easy. And it just rumbles, deep and throaty. The power in it was awesome as I was cruising along. And the bike is just cool, especially all dressed in black like that. I swore I could hear Foghat's *Slow Ride* playing somewhere in the atmosphere."

"I would say you've never had anything that powerful between your thighs, but you've had me," Gage teased. He liked that Joseph enjoyed his bike so much.

Joseph rolled his eyes and dug into the white paper bag for a donut. He bit into the pastry and moaned. "Chocolate icing." He licked his lips. "Yummy."

Gage folded his arms behind his head and watched Joseph, still on top of him, eating that donut.

"Are you going to offer me any?" he asked when there was only one bite left.

Joseph looked at the piece of donut in his hand and then down at him. "Nope. You should have gotten up and come with me." Then he popped it in his mouth.

Gage smacked him on the ass, making him jump. "If I'd gone with you, you wouldn't have gotten to ride my bike."

Joseph grinned as he pulled out another donut, this one glazed. "Oh yeah. Forgot about that." He held the sugary treat up to his mouth for Gage to take a bite.

They shared the next two donuts, Gage laying there and letting Joseph feed him. When the last crumb was gone, Gage reached for his hand. Pulling it up to his mouth, he slowly licked the sugared icing from his fingers. Joseph watched him with those gorgeous green eyes so he made a show of it, darting his tongue out in teasing little laps. His eyes slid shut as Gage sucked a finger into his mouth, swirling his tongue around it before he bit down on the fleshy pad. Joseph made a soft little sound of surprise, his hips jerking in his lap. Gage smoothed a palm up Joseph's denim clad thigh, feeling the warm skin and hard muscle beneath the material. He curved his hand around to cup Joseph's ass, Joseph subtly grinding against him as he did. He called his lover's name.

"Joseph."

When he opened his eyes and looked down at him, Gage told him what he wanted him to do.

"Take your shirt off."

Joseph obeyed him, pulling his t-shirt over his head and dropping it to the floor. Gage traced his fingers over his well-defined abs, smoothing his palms up to the pads of muscle on his chest. Gage smiled to himself. He might hate that fancy gym Joseph went to, but he loved what it did for his body.

Gage wrapped a hand around the back of Joseph's neck, tugging him down until their lips met. They kissed, their tongues slowly and softly playing together. Gage stroked Joseph's ponytail, winding the curls around his fingers as he lightly sucked at his bottom lip. He pulled the band free from his lover's hair and the silky strands fell in a dark curtain around them. The kiss went on, sunlight filtering through the cloak of Joseph's hair, Joseph sighing into his mouth. Gage pulled back and looked up into his lover's eyes. His pretty, gold and green eyes. He would be careful with Joseph, and never hurt him. He promised himself that. Gage stroked his thumb over Joseph's mouth.

"I didn't think you could taste any sweeter."

Joseph smiled. "Now are you glad I woke you up for donuts?"

Gage made a noise that was a non-answer and pushed Joseph up until he was sitting upright again. Looking down, he saw Joseph's erection pressing against the front of his jeans. He rubbed his palm there, feeling how hard he was. Joseph bit his lip, his hips moving forward slightly. Gage watched him as he slowly popped the button loose and pulled the zipper down. Joseph hadn't put his underwear back on before he'd gotten dressed to leave, so his bare cock peeked out from his opened jeans. Gage teased his hard shaft with one finger. Joseph pushed his hips forward more insistently this time, forcing his cock to come out of his jeans a little more.

Gage pushed Joseph up off his lap and pulled his jeans down hard to get the tight fitting material just low enough to bare his ass. He was naked, so all he had to do was shove the sheet covering him out of the way. Gage reached over to the nightstand for the bottle of lube. He covered himself in the liquid, then worked a slick finger up into Joseph to get him ready. Joseph was squirming in his lap, constricted by the jeans around the tops of his thighs.

"Gage. I can't move like this."

Gage grabbed Joseph by his narrow hips and started easing him down his shaft. "That's what you get for wearing these tight ass jeans."

"You like them."

"I like the way your ass looks in 'em."

Joseph closed his eyes and exhaled hard as Gage brought him firmly down onto his cock. "Same thing."

Gage laughed and smoothed his hands up Joseph's back. He was all the way inside his lover, but he didn't start moving yet. He picked the bottle of lube up and taking Joseph's hand, squeezed some into his palm. Joseph immediately grasped his shaft and started stroking himself. Gage watched while he kept a grip on Joseph's hips with both hands, pushing him up then slamming him back down onto his cock, thrusting his own hips up to meet him each time. Joseph couldn't move restrained by his jeans the way he was, but Gage was still enjoying feeling him clench around his shaft.

Joseph's eyes were closed, his head thrown back. A particularly long moan came from him when he squeezed his cock hard. Gage stopped moving. Joseph was still moaning and stroking himself when Gage pushed him off and tossed him to the side. He landed facing away from him.

Joseph looked over his shoulder. "Hey! What was that?"

Gage smirked. "You weren't paying enough attention to me."

Joseph's eyes narrowed. "You're the one started this with my pants on me so that I could hardly move."

"That's no excuse. Show me you like what I'm doing to you. Not what you're doing to yourself."

"You're kidding me, right? You're jealous of my hand?" he asked, disbelieving laughter in his voice.

Gage grinned. "Yep." He yanked Joseph close against him until they were pressed together, his front to Joseph's back. Now he pushed Joseph's pants all the way down, Joseph toeing off his shoes so he could take them completely off. "If your hand is making you feel that good, what do you need me and my dick for?"

Joseph laughed. "You know I want it."

"Yeah, yeah." He grabbed Joseph's hands, holding them up over his head, and pushed back inside him. Before he even started moving Joseph let out the loudest moan he'd ever heard.

"Ooooh, Gage! That's the stuff right there!"

Gage buried his face in the crook of Joseph's neck, laughing into his hair. He pulled his hips back and slid back into him slowly. Joseph kept up with his obviously fake moans.

"Yeah, baby! I was so wrong to want my hand on my dick. Bad hand! Bad me!"

Gage was nearly howling with laughter now. He'd never laughed like this during sex. "You obnoxious little fucker."

Joseph looked back over his shoulder. "I believe you're the one doing all the fucking."

"That's right," he said with a grin. He kissed Joseph, pushing his tongue into his mouth. He thrust into his ass hard and Joseph cursed for real that time.

"*Fuck.*"

Gage's laughter was smug now as he fucked Joseph, listening to his moans change from ultra-fake to genuinely passionate. He glided into him again and again, still holding Joseph's arms up over his head. He pressed their mouths back together, sucking and biting at his soft tongue and pouty bottom lip. Joseph was breathing hard, writhing against him. He twisted his body, throwing his leg over Gage's. Gage pushed his thigh between Joseph's legs, lightly pressing it up against his balls. They were hot and swollen against his skin and Joseph groaned into his mouth as he rubbed his thigh back and forth against them.

Gage finally released his grip on Joseph's wrists, bringing his hand down so that together they grasped his cock. They both stroked him, Joseph's hand on top, his on the bottom, their fingers knocking together as they pumped.

"I'm about to come," Joseph breathed out.

"Of course you are, now that you're touching yourself."

Joseph half laughed – half groaned. Gage doubled the force of his thrusts, fucking him hard and fast, his hips slapping against Joseph's ass. His spine was tingling, his balls as tight as Joseph's felt against his leg. "If you make me come first I'll let you ride the Indian again."

He'd barely finished speaking when Joseph started pushing his ass back and forth in rhythm with his thrusts. He laughed at that quick response, but it quickly changed to a groan as Joseph pressed his ass tight against him, grinding and clenching hard on his cock. He could have held on a little longer, but he didn't. Gage let go, relishing the feel of his orgasm tingling and racing up his shaft until he released deep into his lover. His cock was still throbbing with delicious aftershocks, but he gave his attention to Joseph, jerking him off swiftly, making him moan and come in a hot rush over their hands.

****

Joseph took a deep breath and let it out in a loud sigh. "Donuts, riding that bike, and sex with you. Three great ways to start the day."

Gage lightly ran his fingers over Joseph's hip, making him shiver. "Which was your favorite part?"

Joseph was quiet for a moment before he answered. "I'm gonna have to go with riding the Indian."

Gage laughed and smacked him on the ass.

CHAPTER 49

The next weekend, Joseph was at home, checking out racing suits on the internet. He didn't need a new one, but he liked having different designs. His phone rang and he grabbed it from where it sat on the desk. Joseph winced when he saw who it was on the caller ID.

"Mr. Montoya, I mean Rafael. How are you?"

"I'm well, *gracias*. I am calling because we never finished our talk about me sponsoring you."

Joseph cursed under his breath. He'd totally forgotten that he'd finally made the call to Montoya to accept his offer of sponsorship while he and Gage had been apart. "Rafael, I'm so sorry. But actually … ummm… Gage and I are back together."

"I see. Well, I will not lie, I'm disappointed to hear that Joseph. But that doesn't mean that I can't still sponsor you."

Joseph was surprised. "Oh. I didn't think the offer would be open any longer if…" he trailed off, realizing he was drifting into territory that would embarrass them both. But Montoya laughed.

"You thought I would only sponsor you if you were a part of the package."

"Yeah, I guess so."

"I would love to have you as my own, Joseph. And to hear that won't happen… *Sí*, it makes me sad. But I still admire your abilities on the track and I'm still interested in working with you."

Joseph was surprised but decided not to turn down the help. "That's great then. When do you have time to go over everything?"

"I have some free time today. Would you like to meet for lunch?"

Joseph looked at the clock. Gage was coming over that evening, but that was several hours away. And he'd already started baking some chicken for himself. "Why don't you come over here? We can have lunch while we talk."

"That sounds good. I will see you soon, Joseph."

****

Gage pulled up to Joseph's townhouse. He'd parked on the street because there was an expensive car in his driveway. A really expensive car – a silver Porsche Spyder. Gage frowned as he passed the car on the way up the walk, wondering who it belonged to. Maybe one of the partners at Joseph's firm had stopped by. Joseph opened up after he rang the doorbell. He stepped inside and came to an immediate halt. That slick motherfucker Rafael Montoya was sitting on Joseph's couch, the couch that *he'd* fucked Joseph on. He looked comfortable, like he'd been there for hours and planned to stay for several more. Gage's eyes narrowed at Montoya's smarmy smile.

"What the fuck is he doing here?"

Joseph put a hand on his chest. "Calm down. He's here to talk about sponsoring my races. That's all."

Gage continued to glare at Montoya, whose oily smile widened. Until Joseph turned around that was. Then he looked concerned and friendly.

"*Sí.* I have offered to sponsor Joseph and he has accepted." He stood up and walked over to them. "And we are both mature men. We can put our differences aside for this business relationship."

Gage looked at Joseph. "Are you kidding me? He wouldn't have bothered to fight me before if he was only interested in a business relationship with you, Joseph."

"I know that. But I told him that we're together and he still offered. Rafael is heavily involved in racing and has lots of great connections. He said he's willing to let what happened stay in the past and knows we won't be more than friends. He's sponsored lots of other racers before, it won't be a problem."

Gage wasn't buying it. He clenched his jaw, holding back from outright calling Montoya a liar. He didn't want to upset Joseph. Montoya spoke up.

"I don't want to cause any trouble in your fragile new relationship. I'll go and let you explain what I can do for you, Joseph. Call me when things are settled between you two." He shook Joseph's hand and offered Gage a slick smile before he let himself out.

Gage moved Joseph's hand off his chest. "I'll be back. I need to talk to this guy."

Joseph frowned. "I'd better come with you."

"No. Stay here. I mean it, Joseph."

Joseph crossed his arms over his chest. "Do not fight on my front lawn. I mean that."

He pulled the door open. "I won't. I promise."

Gage went outside, closing the door behind him. Montoya knew he would be following him out there, he stood in front of his car waiting.

"You're not here to start another brawl are you, *amigo*? You heard Joseph. I'm just here to help him with his sponsorship. You'll just have to accept our friendship."

Gage walked right up to him. "Cut the bullshit, asshole. You and I both know you're only offering to help Joseph because you're hoping in the end you'll wind up with him. Well, I'm telling you now, it ain't gonna happen. You lost. I won. Joseph is mine."

Montoya smiled. "For now. You won't keep him. Joseph is playing at being with a bad boy. But I know that he is too refined to stay with someone like you for long."

Gage clenched his jaw. That lawyer ex of Joseph's had said something similar and he didn't like it.

"Keep thinking that. Joseph isn't going anywhere. So you can take your goddamn offer of sponsorship and shove it up your ass."

Montoya's eyes flicked towards the house where he knew Joseph was probably watching from the window. Gage stepped in front of him, blocking his view. "Get lost and don't come around Joseph again. You won't be sponsoring him. You see him at the track you wave and move the fuck on. You understand, amigo?"

Montoya stared back at him, but Gage didn't back down, he didn't even blink. He tilted his head to the side and took a step closer. Finally, he noticed a subtle retreat in the other man. A second later his eyes dropped and he took a step back. Neither of them said another word. Montoya walked away, got in his car and drove off.

Gage took out a cigarette and lit up as he watched the car drive away. He stayed outside until he'd smoked the entire thing, thinking about what Montoya and that other guy had said. That Joseph belonged with someone classier. He wouldn't believe that. He knew who Joseph really was. When the cigarette was finished, he dropped it to the ground, grinding it under his boot. Then he headed back inside.

"Did you two get that pissing contest taken care of?"

"Yep. It's all settled. I'll be sponsoring you."

Joseph's mouth dropped open. "What?"

Gage shrugged. "It'll be good publicity for Mason Bike Shop. That is how it works right? I give you money and you wear my brand and talk about how awesome my shop is in return?"

Joseph's mouth was still hanging open. "Yeah, but…"

"But what? You need a sponsor and Montoya isn't an option. And I could always use new ways to bring in more customers."

Joseph finally closed his mouth. "I guess I should be happy you didn't pee on me to mark your damn territory."

He snorted. "Don't be silly Joseph. I'm not into water sports."

Joseph wrinkled his nose. "You're disgusting. So what are we doing tonight?"

"Let's go shopping. I owe you a suit, remember?"

Joseph's face lit up. "I can't believe I forgot about that. You do owe me a new suit. Let's go."

CHAPTER 50

Gage walked through the mall with Joseph. He didn't know where any of the stores were in here. He hated shopping, and when he did go it wasn't to a mall if he could help it. Joseph knew exactly where he was going. Gage stayed with him, occasionally rubbing his hand over the small of Joseph's back. Every time he did he caught people giving them looks. Admiring ones from several women and a few guys. Judgmental ones from jerk-offs who clearly had an issue with a gay couple. Well, that was too bad for them. It was 2014 and he wasn't hiding who he was to satisfy their narrow-minded views of who should be in a relationship. Those folks he glared at until they either looked away or passed by. He smiled back at the people who looked at them with friendly envy. He knew the man he was with looked good.

Joseph finally slowed and Gage looked up to see what store they were at. Even he recognized the stark chrome lettering on the black background. EXPRESS. "I should have known."

Joseph grinned. "Yep."

Gage followed him in. "Everything in here is so skinny."

Laughing, Joseph headed back towards the suits. He was browsing through the racks when a salesman came up to him.

"Hello. What can I help you find today?"

Joseph looked at the salesman. He was about his age with short dark hair and gray eyes. "I need a suit. I had an unfortunate run-in with motor oil and ruined one." He looked at Gage with wide eyes, a slight pout on his mouth. "It was my favorite too." He looked back at the salesman. "But Gage here has kindly offered to replace it."

The salesman glanced over at Gage, who was shaking his head at him. He looked back at Joseph and smiled. "I see. This is our sales rack. Let's get you over to our new arrivals. I'm sure you want the best to make up for losing your favorite suit."

Joseph grinned at Gage and followed the salesman. "You're right about that."

They went through a couple of suits before he pulled out one in caramel colored twill. It was slim cut, the lapels narrow. The fabric gleamed with a soft sheen.

"What do you think of this one?"

Joseph looked at his name tag. "Evan, I think that you've got great taste. I love it."

Evan pulled out the jacket, vest, and pants in his size. "Will you also need a shirt?"

Joseph nodded with mock sadness. "Yes. Somehow the buttons got ripped off the one I always wore with my favorite suit."

Gage groaned and Joseph held back a laugh. Evan the salesmen coughed, clearly trying not to laugh as well. They picked out several shirts and ties to go with the caramel suit and Evan got him set up in a dressing room. Joseph looked behind him, expecting to see Gage, but he wasn't there. He shrugged and stepped into the space, pulling the heavy dark curtain closed behind him when Evan left. He'd undressed down to his underwear when the curtain was jerked back. Gage was standing there.

"You can't come in here."

"I brought you something else to try on."

Joseph looked at what he held. A handful of black briefs with different colored piping on each pair. "You're not allowed to try on underwear!"

Gage grinned and yanked the curtain closed. "But I ruined the pair you had on that night. How can I replace them if I don't know if they fit?"

Joseph didn't say anything, he just let Gage come close to his nearly naked body. Gage pushed his hands into the briefs he was wearing, cupping his ass then pushing them off him until he *was* naked. He swallowed hard.

Gage smiled then looked over his shoulder at the mirror behind him. He smoothed a hand down his back and smacked him on the ass, catching him right underneath his left cheek. His eyes gleamed at whatever he saw.

"Jiggle, jiggle." Gage whispered in his ear.

Joseph blushed, but Gage had already moved on to helping him step into the underwear he'd brought in. He tugged them into place then turned him to face the mirror. Gage slid his hand down his stomach, teasing at the bright green trimming on the waistband.

"I like the color. Matches that print you have on your bike suit."

Joseph licked his dry lips. "Yeah, it does." He was about to say something intelligent, he knew he was. But Gage cupped his balls through the tight black underwear. He squeezed, his middle finger sliding between his legs and rubbing over the sensitive skin there. Joseph moaned softly. "Gage, don't. Not in here."

Gage kissed his neck, their eyes meeting in the mirror. "I'm not doing anything. Just making sure these fit." He slid a hand into the underwear. "Do they feel comfortable, Joseph? They're so tight." He stroked a hand over his growing erection. "Do you have enough room if this happens?"

Joseph cleared his throat. "I … they're fine. They fit."

Gage pulled away from him. "Hmmm… better make sure the other colors fit too." Gage hooked his fingers in the waistband of the underwear and pulled them down his legs. The next pair he held up for Joseph to try on were black trimmed in hot pink.

He arched a brow. "Really? Pink?"

"What? I might have a secret fondness for the color."

"Is this some sort of kink I don't know about?"

"You'll find out."

Joseph didn't know what to make of that. But that fell out of his head as Gage dropped to his knees before him. He stepped into the black and pink briefs. Gage drew them up his legs, his fingers teasing and playing between his thighs as he did. He clenched his fist at his sides while Gage touched him everywhere as he tugged the underwear into place.

"I don't know Joseph. I think these might be smaller than the other pair." He stared up at him and cupped his shaft through the soft cotton. "Or maybe it's just because this is bigger. What do you think?"

"I think … I think they're the same," he breathed out as Gage stroked him.

"If you say so."

Joseph stood absolutely still, almost frozen, as Gage gently tugged the briefs down just enough to free his stiff length. Gage licked his tongue out, curling it up just out of reach of his cock. Joseph's heart was racing. He didn't care they were in a dressing room in the middle of a busy mall. He wanted to feel Gage's mouth on him. He reached out and twisted his fingers in the thick strands of Gage's hair. Gage leaned forward with deliberate slowness. The tip of his tongue had just touched his aching shaft when they heard the salesman's voice.

"Sir? There's only one person allowed per dressing room."

Gage pulled back. "He needed help with his zipper. It should only take me about three minutes to help him."

It was silent for a moment.

"Okay then. I'll be back to check on you. In *five* minutes."

Gage grinned up at him, then leaned forward to suck him into his mouth. Joseph bit his lip, trying to stay quiet. Gage moved his mouth on him quickly but not rushing. He cupped and squeezed his ass and Joseph brought his own hands up to hold the back of Gage's head. He pumped his hips forward, staring down and watching Gage's lips sliding back and forth on his cock. Gage flicked his tongue over the sensitive underside of his cockhead and Joseph moaned quietly. His thighs clenched as he fought to stay upright.

Gage sucked him amazingly fast now, slipping a finger into his ass and teasing against that bundle of nerves. His hips jerked forward hard. "Fuck." He whispered the curse as he started to come. Gage kept brushing his finger over that spot and hummed softly, the sound vibrating up and down his shaft. Joseph bit the inside of his cheeks, but a little cry still slipped out as his climax rushed through him.

Gage surged back to his feet, pulling his body up against his. He kissed him hard, thrusting his tongue into Joseph's mouth. Joseph wrapped his arms around Gage's neck as he kissed him back, tasting himself on his tongue.

Joseph looked at Gage when he pulled back from their kiss. His hair was a mess from his fingers running through it and his eyes had that intense look that caused delicate tremors to dance up and down his spine.

"Hurry up and try on that damn suit. I'll wait outside."

****

Fifteen minutes later, Joseph walked out of the store with Gage. Evan had rang up the suit, two shirts, three ties, and the briefs in each color. His face had been hot with embarrassment when Gage shoved the two he'd already tried on into the bag and told the guy to just ring the tag five times on the pair he handed him. But the salesman hadn't batted an eyelash. He had however, grinned as Gage slipped him a twenty dollar tip. Joseph had thanked him for his generosity, he hadn't expected him to go above and beyond what he'd said he'd replace.

Now he moved closer to Gage who with the ease of familiarity, rested his hand on the back of his neck, toying with his ponytail as they walked. Joseph smiled. He liked this. Really liked it. Not because of what Gage had bought him, but because Gage was Gage.

CHAPTER 51

S o you've got some contracts to write up."

Joseph looked over at Gage, who was lounging in one of his kitchen table chairs. "Huh?"

"Contracts. You can't just expect people to give you money without some sort of agreement."

Joseph finished pouring the chocolate syrup over the warm brownies and vanilla ice cream he'd just dished up. "What people are you talking about?" he asked as he brought the bowls over to the table. He sat down and pushed Gage's bowl across to him.

Gage took a bite. "I got a few more people to sponsor you. Gia, Max, and my buddy Owen, who owns a barbershop. I would have asked Nate, but he's out of town. I'll ask him when he gets back." He took another bite of brownie and ice cream. "This is good."

Joseph just stared at Gage as he nonchalantly ate his dessert. "You went out and got me more sponsors? Why would you do that?"

"I know how expensive racing is. You need new tires every race, entry fees, constant adjustments on your bike. And if you're going to have people help you on race day you'll have to pay them. Am I right?"

Joseph was dumbfounded. "Yeah, but I wasn't expecting you to do that for me."

Gage shrugged. "Like I said, I hang with a bunch of assholes who do better working for themselves. And the crowds who'll see your sponsors are a great target audience for their businesses."

Joseph dropped his spoon and jumped up out of his chair. Stepping over Gage's long legs sprawled in front of the table he yanked him up from his chair. "Thank you, Gage! Holy shit this is amazing!" Joseph threw himself at his boyfriend, wrapping his arms around his neck in a tight hug. "I can't believe you did this for me."

Gage laughed as Joseph jerked him back him back and forth in a wildly exuberant hug. Then he pushed him away slightly, smiling at the shocked happiness on Joseph's face. "It's not that big of a deal. Come on and sit down. Our ice cream is melting." Joseph squeezed him once more before he went back to his side of the table. Gage sat again and listened to Joseph rattle on about all the races he'd be able to enter now while he ate his dessert.

****

Joseph sat in the conference room at work. They were having a meeting on a new case they'd taken on. A big corporate giant was suing a mom and pop over similarities in logos. But his mind was barely there. He was still surprised at what Gage had done for him. He'd be able to enter a lot more races now. And of course if he won, he'd bring home bigger purses. He was going to have to think of a way to thank Gage. Maybe he could cook him dinner. No, he wasn't that good of a cook. He could get him a really nice bottle of whiskey. Gage had mentioned wanting to try a bottle of Macallan once. Joseph grinned. Or he could detail his truck and somehow manage to get himself soaking wet while doing it. They'd watched Wild Things the other day and Gage had commented on how hot Denise Richards looked in the car wash scene. He'd rolled his eyes and acknowledged that she had an obvious appeal. Joseph imagined Gage peeling off his wet, soapy shirt and fucking him up against the side of his truck. Of course, it might be too cool outside to get drenched by a water hose. Then shrinkage would be a prob-.

"Joseph!"

Joseph snapped to attention. "Yes, sir?"

Mr. Pruitt looked at him sternly. "I asked if you were up to the challenge of being one of the leads on this."

Joseph cleared his throat. "Yes, sir. I apologize for wool-gathering but I'm definitely up to the challenge. Thank you for the opportunity."

Pruitt kept his eyes on him for a long moment. He finally looked away and Joseph let out a soft breath of relief. He looked down the table at Lila, who was there taking notes. She gave him a, *what the hell?* Look, to which he shrugged in response. Joseph got focused and stayed tuned in during the rest of the meeting.

****

A few days later, Joseph came out of Gage's bathroom already in his underwear, his hair slicked back into a ponytail. "I don't want to go to work."

Gage lay on his side in the bed, watching him get dressed. "Then don't go."

"I have to. Especially after I got caught day dreaming the other day in a meeting. They'll have my ass if I take an unscheduled day off right when they assign me as lead on a case."

"What were you fantasizing about?"

Joseph's face warmed slightly. "I didn't say fantasizing. I said daydreaming. There's a difference."

"My mistake. So what were you daydreaming?"

"Like I'm telling you. Your head is big enough as it is."

Gage laughed. "You don't have to tell me, Joseph. You pretty much just admitted you were thinking about me. That's enough to boost my ego right there."

Joseph shook his head at Gage's cockiness and went to kiss him goodbye. Gage grabbed his hand and tried to tug him down.

"Don't you dare. I'm not letting you wrinkle my new suit."

Gage ran his eyes over Joseph standing there in the suit that he'd bought him. "We wouldn't want that." He'd teased Joseph for everything in EXPRESS being skinny, but that slim fit looked great on him. "What time do you normally go to lunch?"

"Twelve thirty. Why?" Joseph asked as he clasped on his watch.

Gage shrugged. "No reason. Maybe one day we can meet for lunch."

Joseph grabbed his wallet, keys, and phone. "That would be nice. We'll have to plan that. I'll see you later."

Gage stared through the doorway Joseph had just disappeared through. He smiled as he thought how good Joseph had looked in that suit. He didn't see the point in waiting for one day when there was something he wanted right then.

CHAPTER 52

Joseph looked at the clock. Ten more minutes before he could break for lunch. He forced himself to look back at the papers in front of them. Before the ten minutes had passed, someone knocked at his door. He looked up to see Gage leaning against the door frame, a takeout bag dangling carelessly from one hand.

"Gage. What are you doing here?"

Gage came into the office and closed the door behind him. He held up the bag. "It's twelve thirty. Time for you to have lunch." He shrugged out of his jacket and threw it over the back of the chair in front of his desk.

Joseph laughed and cleared his workspace off for the food. "When you said we could meet for lunch I thought we'd go out to a restaurant."

"This suits my plans better."

****

Joseph balled up the wrappers and threw everything in the trash. The sub sandwiches that Gage brought had been really good. They'd talked about Joseph's current project and the bikes Gage and Danny were working on while they made their way through sandwiches, chips and cookies. Joseph wiped his fingers off and dropped the last napkin in the trash.

"How much time did you say you got for lunch?"

"An hour. Why?"

"It's only twelve fifty. You've got forty minutes before your lunch break is over. How should we pass the time?" Gage stared at him as he took a long sip of his soda.

As he looked into Gage's teasing eyes, it dawned on Joseph what he meant. "I don't think so. We are not having sex in my office at work."

Gage grinned. "Why not? Who's not a fan of a little afternoon delight?"

Joseph sputtered. He actually sputtered. He couldn't think of what to say. Gage was so bad … and he really wanted to be bad with him. He bit his lip in a mix of nervousness and enticement.

Gage crooked a finger at him. "Come here, Joseph."

Joseph slowly rose out of his chair, feeling like there was a cartoon bubble with the word *Gulp!* floating over his head. He went around his desk and started to go to his office door.

Gage grabbed his wrist. "Where are you going?"

"To lock the door. We can't get caught."

"Already locked it when I first came in." Gage stood and pulled him up against him. "You look really good in this suit."

"Is that why you came up here? To molest me at work because you like my new suit?"

Gage smiled without saying anything. He just pulled him closer for a slow deep kiss, his hands drifting down to open his pants. Joseph moaned into Gage's mouth as his warm hand wrapped around his cock, pumping gently. Joseph's hands drifted down to do some touching of their own. He ran his palms over Gage's denim covered ass and squeezed. Gage bit him on the lip.

"Turn around for me."

Joseph followed the quiet order. His heart was racing as he turned around to face the desk and braced his hands on the edge. He couldn't believe they were about to do this. Looking back over his shoulder, he saw Gage go in his pocket and pull out a small bottle of lube. Gage opened his jeans and pulled his cock out. He squirted the lube into his palm generously and stroked his hand over his shaft. Gage watched him as he pumped himself, that teasing glint still in his eyes. Joseph loved the sight, but he'd rather he was the one taking pleasure in that thick cock.

"How much of this forty minutes are you going to spend playing with yourself?"

Gage smirked and walked back over to him. He pushed his pants down until they fell around his ankles, slipping a finger under the edge of his briefs.

"Your ass in these tight black underwear. Makes me wanna spank it." He swatted him lightly once then gripped him firmly. "Would you let me spank you one day, Joseph?"

"Yeah." Joseph cleared his throat, turned on by the thought. "If that's what you wanted."

Gage swatted him again, a little bit harder. "You'd let me do anything I wanted to you, wouldn't you?"

Joseph arched his back. "Yes," he answered in a drawn out whisper.

Gage tugged his briefs down and slowly eased into him. Joseph moaned softly, his eyes drifting closed as Gage worked his entire length inside him. He expected Gage to take him quickly, but he didn't. He stroked into him slowly, running his hands up and down his back beneath his shirt. Joseph managed to stay quiet until Gage reached up and tightly gripped his ponytail. He pulled on it hard and Joseph couldn't help but cry out, pushing back to meet Gage's thrusts.

Gage laughed. "You want me to be rough with you, don't you pretty boy?"

Joseph nodded as best as he could with his hair still held in Gage's fist.

"Well, I won't. Not until I have you home in my bed. I'll throw you down and keep you trapped underneath me. You won't be able to move unless I let you. And I'll pound this tight little ass until you scream." Gage yanked on his hair hard. "You'll scream for me, won't you Joseph?"

"Oh, fuck yes," he groaned.

Gage pulled him up until they were pressed together, back to chest. His hand slipped down his stomach to grasp his cock, stroking Joseph off as he whispered in his ear. He told him how he would spank him till his ass was red. How he would fuck his mouth then hold him down and fuck his ass fast and hard until he begged to be able to come. The entire time he talked he stroked into him slow and easy, the thickness of his shaft stretching him and brushing over all the nerve endings inside him. Gage's long fingers skimmed up and down his side, dancing across his stomach, pinching at his nipples. Joseph reached back and wrapped an arm around Gage's neck, rubbing his ass against him. The contrast of the slow, quiet sex and the rough images Gage was creating in his brain was driving him crazy.

He turned his head and Gage's lips found his, kissing him with deliciously teasing licks of his tongue. Gage kept pumping him gently, fucking him softly, until with a shuddering gasp Joseph was climaxing, spilling into Gage's warm hand. Gage whispered a curse and pushed deep into him one last time. He bit at his neck to muffle his groan, his orgasm making Gage squeeze him tight as he pumped his hot release inside him.

****

Joseph braced his hands on the desk again. "Damnit. I don't have any Kleenex in here." He eyed the trash, thinking about the napkins he'd used and tossed from lunch. He looked over his shoulder at Gage. "I don't suppose you brought some wet naps?"

Gage smirked and pulled his t-shirt over his head using it to wipe off his hand.

"Classy."

"Do you want me to be?" Gage asked with an eyebrow raised in question.

"Hell no," Joseph laughed.

"I didn't think so."

Gage turned him around and used the tail of his shirt to clean him up. Then he put it back on and pulled his jacket on over it. He helped Joseph put his clothes back together and zipped up his jeans. "I'll see you tonight."

Joseph shook his head at his dirty boyfriend and followed him over to the door. They exchanged a quick kiss before Gage unlocked the door and left. Joseph stepped out to watch him stroll down the hallway, the cocky swagger in his walk making him smile. Gage looked back and winked at him before he rounded the corner out of sight.

"Damn. No wonder you look like you're in a daze half the time."

Joseph looked to see Lila standing there. She'd obviously just watched Gage walk off too.

"I'd look like that too if I had a man as fine as that."

Joseph laughed. "Be quiet, Lila. I don't look like I'm in a daze."

She snorted. "That's what you think." She coughed lightly. "And ummm… Joey? You'd better fix your hair."

CHAPTER 53

Joseph stood on the crushed seashell at the Regal Pines Country Club. They were at the company picnic. He'd asked Gage to come, but as he'd expected Gage had turned him down. He knew it was unlikely he would have said yes. Saturday was the busiest day of the week for his shop. He looked around at the scene in front of him. The tall trees were bright with fall color, but if any of their leaves had fallen, they'd been ruthlessly raked off the still green lawn. Tables were set up with chafing dishes of finger foods while people strolled around with mugs of hot cider. Most of the men were dressed as he was, in richly colored sweaters and slacks, the ladies in feminine versions of the look. This picnic wasn't just for members of the firm and their families. Their clients were invited as well and Joseph had been introduced to many that he hadn't worked with yet. This event was more net-working than get together. There was lots of schmoozing taking place in between the lawn games being played.

Right now he was having a schmooze free moment with Lila. She was pouting that Gage hadn't made it, ignoring the fact that her own boyfriend was absent as well. Joseph heard a rumble in the distance as they talked. As it grew steadily louder, the hairs on the back of his neck stood up. By the time the sound became the distinct rumble of an approaching motorcycle Joseph knew that Gage had come. He turned and sure enough, Gage was riding up to the gate on a big Harley. He'd seen the custom painted bike in Gage's garage, but he'd never seen him ride it. He started to excuse himself from Lila to go and meet Gage, but she protested.

"I don't think so. I'm coming over to meet this boy."

Joseph rolled his eyes at Lila calling Gage a boy, but walked with her to greet Gage. He took in his appearance as he approached. His hair was smoothly slicked back and for once he'd ditched his tee and ripped jeans. They were replaced with a flannel button-down patterned in light blue, white, and yellow. The shirt was tucked into neat jeans and a thick brown leather belt circled his waist, matching the brown boots on his feet. He wore a pair of mirrored sunglasses but pulled them off as he came up to them. Joseph had to smile at how desirable he found his boyfriend. Gage reached them and Joseph gave him a quick kiss. "You made it."

Gage kissed him back, wrapping an arm around his waist. "Yep. Conned Danny's big brother into coming over and helping out so I could get away."

Joseph smiled. "I'm glad you did."

Lila cleared her throat loudly.

"Gage, I've got someone I want you to meet. This is Lila. She used to try to set me up on boring dates with boring dudes, but now she just pesters me for news about you."

Lila smacked him on the arm. "Joseph! That is not how you introduce people." She flipped her hair over her shoulder and held her hand out. "Hi, I'm Lila. It's nice to finally meet you Gage."

Gage smiled and shook her hand. "Nice to meet you, beautiful. Thanks for trying to set Joseph up with losers. That made him ripe for the picking when I came along."

Lila giggled. "Joseph, you didn't tell me he had dimples."

Gage's smile turned roguish. "I bet there's a lot he didn't tell you about me."

Lila giggled again then quieted as Mr. Pruitt came up to them. Joseph caught her mouth *'lucky'* at him before she slipped away.

"Joseph! Who do we have here?"

Joseph stood up straighter, but he didn't step out of Gage's loose embrace. "This is my boyfriend Gage

Mason, sir. Gage, this is the great mind who recruited me to Pruitt, Locke and Rosenfeld. Mr. Ted Pruitt, Sr."

Mr. Pruitt smiled and extended a hand. "Welcome to our picnic, Gage. I saw the bike you rode up on. Is it yours?"

Gage shook the partner's hand, but his jaw tightened at that question. Who the fuck did he think the bike belonged to? He was the one riding it. "Yeah, it's mine. I restored it myself. I have my own bike shop. It's how Joseph and I met."

Joseph spoke up. "He does amazing work. And he also has this great Indian. It's beautiful and he finally broke down and let me ride it last week."

"Yeah, Joseph has quite the hard-on for that bike." Joseph laughed at his remark. But Gage noticed Pruitt's lips press together tightly before his jovial smile returned.

"Joseph we've been rude. Your guest doesn't have anything to drink. I'll keep him company if you want to go and get him something."

Joseph looked at him and asked what he wanted. Gage just asked for a soda then immediately looked back at Pruitt as Joseph went off to get it.

"You know, Joseph is a real up and comer at Pruitt, Locke and Rosenfeld."

"I'm not surprised. He's smart and likes being a lawyer."

"That's true. And we've never had a problem with him being gay."

"How magnanimous of you," he replied in a dry as dust voice.

Pruitt gave him a tight smile. "Yes. Of course right now he's having a rough time, but I'm sure he'll get through it with no trouble and get back on track."

Gage knew he was being baited, but he went ahead and bit at the hook. "Really? How's that?"

"He's taking on more responsibility at the firm, so he's no doubt figuring out how to balance his work and social life." Pruitt laughed, but it was increasingly clear his joviality was fake. "He reminds me of my son Charlie a few years ago actually. Joseph is sowing some wild oats." Another laugh. "Is it appropriate to say a gay man is sowing wild oats? Regardless, he'll settle down soon."

Gage lost his patience for their little game. "I might be dating a lawyer but I ain't one myself. So why don't you cut the side talk and say whatever the fuck you want to say."

Pruitt's face hardened, his eyes instantly going cold. "Fine. Joseph needs someone who is on his level. Someone he can bring to important functions like this one without the risk of embarrassment. Someone who knows what fork to use, which wine to pair with the right cheese, and who doesn't need a plastic bib to eat lobster."

"Wow. You sure are preoccupied with this mythical boyfriend's eating habits." Gage's tone was as blasé as could be, but inside he could feel his rage starting to build. Who the fuck did this guy think he was?

Another tight smile. "Clever. Don't make Joseph damage his reputation by sticking with you for much longer. If you have any integrity and you care about Joseph, you'll end things with him so that he can advance."

Gage couldn't believe this asshole. No, that wasn't true. He could believe that this snobby prick had just told him that he wasn't good enough to date Joseph. But he damn sure didn't like it. Gage took a step back. He figured he'd better get away from Pruitt before the growing rage in his chest made him say something to Joseph's boss that could cause trouble for him. But Joseph came back over to them just then, holding two plastic cups of soda. Pruitt, with a hearty smile on his face, made his excuses and left. Gage took his soda and drank it down in one go. He handed the cup back to Joseph.

"I'm taking off."

Joseph's brows shot up in surprise. "What? You just got here."

"True. But I think I'd rather be somewhere else." He headed back over to his bike, Joseph trailing behind him after he tossed the cups in the trash.

"Are you serious? Why'd you come then?"

"I came for you," he answered simply.

Joseph just stood there, confusion clear in his face.

Gage put his sunglasses back on and mounted the Harley. He put the key in the ignition, but he didn't turn it. "Get on."

"What?"

"C'mon. You look like a bored Ken doll standing around in that country club with your preppy sweater and slacks. You're done with this shindig. So let's go."

Joseph crossed his arms over his chest. "Ken is blonde. And you're crazy. I'm not getting on that bike with you." He frowned. "Why are you on this big Harley anyway?"

"Because there's not enough room on the Indian for you to ride bitch. C'mon Joseph. Do you want to stay here and play fucking badminton or do you want to come with me and have some fun?"

Joseph took a step towards him. "This is like something out of a Brat Pack movie."

"Did John Hughes do any gay flicks?"

Joseph snorted a laugh. "Not that I'm aware of."

He took a few more steps forward then went to look behind him. Gage stopped him. "No. Don't look back. Just get on." He watched Joseph take a deep breath then swing his leg over the bike behind him. Joseph settled his hands on his waist and Gage grinned. He started the Harley and they roared out of the parking lot, leaving the pretentious assholes of Pruitt, Locke and Rosenfeld behind.

CHAPTER 54

The crisp fall wind rushed over Joseph as he rode bitch behind Gage. He had to laugh at Gage calling it that. He'd never ridden a bike with another man before. He knew they were getting stares, but he didn't care. He was having fun with Gage and that was all that mattered. They'd joined Nate, who might or might not have been on a date with a guy named Kevin, and a few others at a skeet shooting range. He'd watched in awe as Gage shot down disk after disk. It was Kevin who'd come closest to beating Gage's score. He'd laughed it off as beginners luck, but when no one else was around he'd admitted to Joseph that he'd done skeet shooting in college. Joseph liked him. The group had followed it up with a meal at Gia's. Now he and Gage were riding across town as the sun set. They cruised to a halt at a stoplight.

Joseph casually looked at the gold Mercedes next to them. It was nearly dark, but he could still see the lady in the passenger seat and her disgusted expression. Joseph laughed and stuck his tongue out at her.

Gage turned his head slightly. "What's so funny?" he asked over the rumble of the bike. Joseph pointed at the judgmental priss. She was still glaring at them. Gage snorted when he saw her expression and turned even further around. Joseph knew immediately what he wanted. He leaned forward and kissed Gage, licking into his mouth and sliding his hand under his shirt to caress the warm skin over his hard abs. The light changed to green and the Mercedes' tires squealed it took off so fast. Joseph pulled back from their kiss, laughing. Gage turned back around and got the bike moving. He assumed they were going to head back to the country club so he could get his car, but Gage turned east towards the park. Once he turned into the lot, he killed the engine and put the kickstand out. Joseph got up from the bike, pushing his hair back from his face. It was a mess from the wind.

"What are we doing here? The park closes at dusk you know."

Gage laughed and opened one of the saddlebags on the side of the bike. "Joseph. Don't tell me you've never made out in a park at night?" He pulled out a blanket. "If you haven't, I'm about to pop your late night - tryst in the park - cherry."

Joseph grinned. "What if I say I have, are we going to leave?"

"Nope. I'll just have to find some other cherry of yours to pop."

A warm flush of arousal spread over Joseph's skin, the cool night air doing nothing to stop it. He walked with Gage to the top of the hill in front of them. Gage spread the thick blanket out over the grass and pulled him down on top of it. Gage stretched out on his back, his arms folded behind his head while Joseph lay propped on an elbow.

"Did you have fun today?"

"I did. Although I can't believe I left the picnic with you."

"What does it matter? Were you required to stay there until the end or something?"

"No … just. I don't know. They can be funny about some stuff."

"That's for damn sure." Gage said under his breath.

Joseph looked down at Gage. He couldn't quite make out his expression in the growing dusk. "What's that supposed to mean?"

Gage looked at him for a long time before he spoke. "Why do you work there?"

"I've told you this before. I like being a lawyer."

"Yeah, but why do you work there? Do you see yourself having a life like the partners there one day?"

Joseph thought about it. "I don't know. I guess. That's what most people strive for, right? To be the tops in their career field and have all the prestige and material shit that goes with it." He shrugged. "I don't think too much about it. I'm too busy slogging through day by day. Why?"

"Where does racing and pool fit into your life if you get to that level, Joseph? Where do I fit?"

A frown creased Joseph's forehead. *Where was Gage going with this?* "I'd hate it, but I guess eventually racing would have to take a back seat. And I barely have time to play pool anyway. But you'd fit in just like you do now."

"Do I fit in, Joseph? I'm hardly the type of guy who'll put on a tux and clap politely at the opera."

Joseph grinned. "That's too bad because I think you'd look great in a tux. But I hate the opera so it doesn't matter." He got serious. "What's up, Gage? Where are you going with this?"

"Joseph, I … like you. You know that. But if you think you'd be better off with a classier guy so that you can reach the top at that firm, don't be afraid to let me know."

Joseph barked a laugh. "Do you think I put up with all of the drama to get you just so I could say thanks for the good time but now I have to go find an opera aficionado?" Joseph leaned down over Gage and brushed their lips together. "You made me work to get you and now I want to keep you."

Gage's fingers slid into his hair, keeping their faces close together. "Is that right?"

"That's right."

"Well then I guess you can keep me. Especially since you let me do dirty things like fuck you in your office while you're wearing one of your pretty boy suits."

Joseph shook his head, a smile tugging at his mouth. "You really liked that, huh?"

Gage's voice was husky in the night. "Damn right I did. I thought about it all fucking day. Thought about you sitting in some boring meeting with some of my cum still in your ass." He slipped a hand underneath his sweater, his fingertips ghosting along his spine. "Did you think about it too, Joseph? Tell me the truth."

Joseph nodded, brushing their lips together in another kiss. "I did. I could barely concentrate the rest of the day." He trailed his lips up to whisper in Gage's ear. "I couldn't think about anything except for the way you felt so thick and hard inside me."

Gage groaned lightly, his hand sliding into Joseph's pants and gripping his ass. "Would you like to feel that again?"

"Here?"

"Hell yeah, here." Gage pushed him to his back, rolling on top of him. "It's dark and we have a blanket. What else do we need?"

Joseph stared up at Gage, only able to see the outline of his face. "Maybe privacy?"

"There ain't nobody here but us." He slipped the button on his slacks open, his fingers easing inside to tease along the sensitive skin of his pelvis. "C'mon Joseph, let me have you."

Shivers danced down Joseph's spine. He figured he'd probably never be able to say no to Gage when he asked him that question. He answered by undoing Gage's belt buckle.

Gage made a noise of appreciation. But it turned to one of frustration as he roughly pushed his sweater up his chest only for it to fall right back down. His fingers tightened in the material. "Goddamn these prissy clothes."

"Don't you even think about ripping anything off of me tonight. I am not riding home on that Harley without any clothes."

Gage grinned. "Why not? You could give old Lady Godiva a run for her money."

Joseph laughed. "No way. Besides it wouldn't be a true competition. My hair isn't long enough. And I'm not blonde."

Gage laughed and kissed him. "That can be fixed."

Joseph shivered as Gage got his clothes out of the way to his satisfaction. He moaned, his eyes drifting shut and his head arching back as Gage eased inside him. When he opened them again, he was staring up at the sky, watching the stars twinkle above them. Joseph wrapped his arms and legs around Gage, holding on tight, letting the solid warmth of his body protect him against the cool night air. His view of the stars was blocked when Gage leaned down over him to steal a kiss. But he didn't care. This night with Gage hadn't gone as he'd imagined it would when he'd invited him to the picnic. It was better. Definitely better.

CHAPTER 55

Joseph had had a grueling two weeks at work. He didn't mind the work. He did mind the attitude he'd been on the receiving end of from Pruitt. He'd been overly critical of his work, ridiculously demanding of deadlines. He wanted to ask the partner what his problem was, but he wasn't exactly in a position to do so. There was a quick knock at his office door before it opened. Speak of the fucking devil, it was Pruitt. He came in with his mouth pursed in a disapproving frown, the same way he'd looked at Joseph for the last two weeks.

"Joseph, I'm going to get right to the point," he said as he sat in front of his desk. "I'm pulling you off the Berkeley trademark case. You're not ready to be lead on something that big yet."

Joseph was surprised. "What? I've done great so far. They even commented on it at our last meeting."

Pruitt sighed and steepled his fingers. "I didn't want to say this, but they're a company with some pretty rigorous family values. I'm afraid we can't have you working with them with the lifestyle you lead."

Joseph's face flushed hot in angry embarrassment. "Excuse me? My lifestyle?"

"They are too good of people to say so, but I'm sure they were uncomfortable when they saw you embracing that boyfriend of yours at the picnic. So I'm saying it for them." He politely coughed behind his hand. "Maybe if you hadn't been so obvious about things. And if your choice in date was a little more presentable."

"What do you mean presentable? It's not like Gage showed up drunk and in work overalls."

"I think you know what I mean. We talked about this before Joseph. If you want to get to the top of this firm, you have to work hard and take care of your reputation. It's clear that someone like that isn't one we want to see a future partner bringing to company functions. You're on a slippery slope, especially with the way you rode off with him at the picnic. You need to get back on track. I'm sure as soon as you stop seeing that Mason fellow that you will. Until then, you're off the Berkeley case. I'm reassigning you to work with some start-up companies." Pruitt rose and made to leave the room. "I'll send Lila by to collect the files from you later."

Joseph sat there in shock. He'd just been knocked down the ladder to work with start-ups. That was first-year level work. All because Pruitt didn't like his choice of boyfriend. The hard work he'd done on the case didn't matter to him, not more than who he chose to date apparently. The shock quickly faded, replaced by anger burning through his veins. It burst out of him before he even realized he was going to speak. "No. Fuck that."

Pruitt turned back around. "Excuse me?"

"Fuck you reassigning me. Fuck you telling me who I can and can't date. Fuck you!" Joseph shot up out of his chair, his heart pounding, his hands shaking. "I don't need this shit from you or this law firm." He yanked open the desk drawer to grab his keys and cell phone. "Consider this my resignation letter. I don't need to work for a stuffy prick like you. I quit." Joseph snatched his framed degrees off the wall and shoved them under his arm, Pruitt watching with a comical expression of shock frozen on his face.

"What?"

Joseph strode over to his office door and yanked it open. The area outside was filled with people as always, but Joseph didn't let that stop him. "You don't understand? Maybe you want me to put it in a brief for you? I quit!" He stormed off, leaving Pruitt standing there with his mouth still hanging open.

****

279

Joseph flew down the highway on his Ducati. He was half in shock at what he'd done. Half glad that he'd done it. He didn't want to work for anyone who tried to push their narrow views of what was presentable onto him. He hadn't taken that from his father and he wasn't going to take it from his boss. But holy shit he was out of a job! He hadn't thought of that in the middle of his righteous walk out. He'd simply shoved his diplomas at Lila to hold onto for him and continued on his furious way. He'd figure work out later. Right now there was something else he wanted to do.

CHAPTER 56

Gage looked up as a bike pulled into the garage. When he saw who it was, he did a double take. It was Joseph on the back of his Ducati. That didn't surprise him. Joseph often rode his bike to the office. But it was two o'clock in the afternoon. Too early for him to be off work. Gage noted that he looked wild as he ripped his helmet off. His hair was a mess, the sleek ponytail he'd left the house with that morning a memory in the wind. His suit jacket was missing, the white dress shirt un-tucked.

Gage stood up from the cruiser he was working on, watching as Joseph cut off his bike and dismounted. Joseph walked straight up to him, his gaze focused on his, and pulled him into a kiss. Gage didn't know what was going on, but he wasn't about to turn down what Joseph was offering. He shoved his hands in that wild mane and held Joseph steady as he took control of the kiss. Gage was covered in grime but apparently Joseph didn't care that he was getting his clothes dirty. He wrapped his arms around him tight, pressing their bodies together. Joseph rubbed against him and Gage's erection made itself known, straining against the unyielding fabric of his jeans. Gage groaned. He didn't want to stop, but he was aware they had an audience. Danny was there and so was a customer. He pulled back.

"Joseph. You know I'm glad to see you, but what the fuck is going on?"

"I just quit my job."

"What? Holy shit! Why? How?"

"Why? Because Pruitt of Pruitt, Locke and Rosenfeld is an asshole. How? By telling him I don't need his shit or his law firm."

Gage was amazed. "Are you serious?"

"As a heart attack. I don't want to work anywhere that tries to dictate what I do outside of work. I am who I am and if they can't accept that, I'm glad to be rid of them."

Gage looked at Joseph, seeing the strong, sure confidence in his expression. He'd been careful not to mention to his conversation with Pruitt to Joseph, not wanting to put him in an uncomfortable position. He figured he'd pushed the guy's buttons when he'd rode up to the country club's gates on his loud Harley. But it looked like Pruitt hadn't been able to leave well enough alone. And even though he knew Joseph's decision to quit his job wasn't just about him, he couldn't help but inwardly crow over the fact that Joseph had picked him.

"Well let's go celebrate then." He turned to Danny, who was unashamedly watching them. "You hear that, Danny?"

He nodded. "Yep. Congrats Joseph." He looked back at Gage with a rueful grin. "Does this mean I'm on my own here for the rest of the day?"

Gage laughed. "That's right. Lock up when you're done." He pulled Joseph along to his truck. "I'm gonna take you somewhere nice. This occasion deserves it."

****

Twenty minutes later, they sat in the Sonic parking lot sipping Slush's. It was a little cool for them, but when Gage had pulled the truck into the lot Joseph had laughed and ordered his favorite treat.

"You and that cherry. You should branch out and try something new." He took a sip of his own Banana Taffy Slush.

Joseph laughed. "Nope. I prefer to stick with the classics."

"Too bad. This is good."

"You know what else is good?"

"What?"

"When you let me be on top."

Gage took a slow sip of his drink. "Be *on* top? Or *top*?"

Joseph's face heated. "You've never let … you know what I mean."

Gage grinned. "When you're ready for that you can have it. But in the meantime..." He started the truck. "I'll let you bounce on my cock all afternoon if you want."

****

"You sure about this?"

"Hell yeah. Pull over there." Joseph directed Gage where to go in the covered parking garage. He looked up to make sure they were in a visible spot. They were. A quick glance at the clock told him this was a good time. The workaholics in the building attached to the garage wouldn't be leaving for a few more hours yet.

Gage laughed and turned the truck off. "You're a wild man today. I like it." He slid his fingers into his hair. "Come here."

Joseph leaned over, meeting Gage's lips in a kiss. But the kiss Gage gave him wasn't what he wanted. It was too gentle. With the adrenaline, and fury, and fear pumping through him he needed more than that. He bit Gage on the lip hard, making him curse. Gage dug his fingers into the side of his neck and yanked him up closer against him. Now he kissed Joseph the way he wanted to be kissed, pressing their lips together roughly, sucking and biting at his lips and tongue. Joseph returned the kiss with equal fervor, leaning into Gage so hard he forced him back against the bucket seat.

Joseph started trying to open his shirt, but with Gage kissing him so fiercely he couldn't focus. The tiny buttons kept slipping out of his fingers. Gage knocked his hand out of the way before he grabbed a fistful of the shirt.

Giving a swift yank, he ripped it open. Joseph heard the buttons ping off the dashboard, but he didn't give a damn. He shoved the ruined material off of him, still kissing Gage. He bit him again, then trailed his lips down to his neck as he frantically worked Gage's jeans open. He bit Gage behind his ear as his fingers tugged at buttons and zippers. Joseph pushed Gage's t-shirt up, trailing his lips over the firm muscles of his torso. He roughly licked at him, tonguing his nipples, taking small nips at his skin as he made his way down to his lap. His jeans were unzipped, his rigid length stretching up to his stomach. Just when Joseph opened his mouth over his slick cockhead, Gage pulled at his hair.

"You'd better not fucking bite my cock, Joseph."

Joseph laughed. Leaning over, he took Gage into his mouth. He sucked him fast and sloppy, not even attempting to use any finesse. Apparently Gage didn't care, because he was still groaning, pushing his hips up so that his cock slid even further into his mouth. Joseph held him steady for his licks and sucking with one hand while he used the other to open his pants. He got them open and rose out of the seat slightly to push them down. His movements caused him to lose even more control over what he was doing and his teeth scraped Gage's cock. Gage drew in a sharp breath. Joseph decided that couldn't have bothered him that much so he did it again, raking his teeth over him with a little more force. This time Gage had more of a reaction.

"Fuck!" Gage pulled him off him. He glared down at him, his eyes narrowed but still bright with lust. "I don't know if I want to make you do that again or spank your ass like I've been threatening to do."

Joseph licked his lips. "Since when are you indecisive during sex?"

Gage arched a brow. "You're right. I can have whatever I want. Hurry up and get those pants off and suck me some more."

Joseph grinned and obeyed. He moved his mouth up and down on Gage's thick cock, getting him slick and wet all over. Each time he scraped his teeth over his shaft Gage cursed, his fingers clenching in his hair, pushing his head down hard. Just when his mouth started to get tired, Gage tugged him up again. He pushed the driver's seat back and reclined it as far as it would go. Then Gage engaged the lever to raise the steering wheel out of the way. It was still cramped, but it would have to do.

Joseph took a moment to prepare Gage with the lube they'd stopped to get then climbed onto his lap. Once he was straddling him he reached behind him and grasped Gage's shaft, working it inside him. He went slow, Gage groaning, his fingers gripping his ass tight. Once Joseph had taken all of him in he leaned down to give him another wild kiss. He started to move, rising up on Gage's shaft and slamming back down. He rode him fast, a crazy mix of passion and anger driving him. He was breathing hard, moaning into Gage's mouth when out of nowhere his ass stung. Gage had slapped him there, hard. Joseph paused for a moment in surprise. Gage spanked him again.

"Don't fucking stop, Joseph. Keep riding me." Another slap. "Keep fucking me."

Again Joseph obeyed, fucking himself onto Gage's cock. Each time Gage's palm crashed onto his ass a surge of furious lust rushed through him, swirling in his stomach and making his cock throb. Joseph dug his fingers into the upholstery next to Gage's head, pushing his aching shaft against his stomach. "Gage," he whispered in a needy tone.

"Not today. This is all you, Joseph."

Joseph groaned. But he reached down and grasped his own shaft. He pumped his fist up and down, getting himself off while Gage rubbed his stinging ass.

"Let me know when you're about to come," Gage whispered.

Joseph nodded, burying his face in Gage's neck as he worked them both. When he felt his orgasm rising, his back tingling and stomach clenching tight, he let him know. "I'm coming, Gage." He yelped as Gage grabbed his hair and yanked him up into a fierce kiss. Gage smacked his ass one last time, harder than before, making Joseph jump and curse into his mouth. "Fuck!" His cock pulsed in his grip and his release burst out of him. He pumped his hand faster, determined to squeeze out every little bit of pleasure from this encounter that he could. Finally, Joseph slowed to a halt, his chest heaving as he dragged in gulps of air. But Gage hadn't come yet. And he let Joseph know it.

"You're not finished yet. Make me come, pretty boy."

Joseph renewed his movements. He shoved a hand into Gage's hair, this time holding him steady while he became the aggressive one in their kiss. Gage cupped his ass, but he didn't help him move. He made him do all the work. And that was fine with Joseph. He worked his body over Gage's, pushing him into a groaning orgasm, savoring the way he shuddered beneath him. When Gage was done Joseph collapsed against him. Gage's hand tangled in his hair again, pulling him up into a deep and passionate kiss.

****

In comparison to the frantic way they'd just had sex they were downright slow and lazy as they put their clothes back to rights. Gage put his hand on the key but didn't turn it.

"You ready to go?"

"Almost." Joseph rolled down the window and looked at the camera above them. He stared for a moment then mouthed three words. *Fuck you, Pruitt.*

CHAPTER 57

So what are you going to do today, Brain?"

Joseph rolled over and watched Gage pulling on his clothes.

"Well, I was planning to take over the world, but I guess I should figure out what I want to be when I grow up first."

Gage laughed and sat on the edge of the bed. "You don't have to figure everything out in one day. Take your time." Gage pulled him in for a kiss. "Maybe you could come and stay at my house for a while and take a break."

Joseph was surprised, they spent nights at each other's places all the time, but never for extended periods. "You'd want that?"

Gage kissed him again. "I wouldn't hate it." He got up from the bed. "Think about it."

He left for work, leaving Joseph surprised at how much he'd changed. Eventually, Joseph got up. He went to his closet and pulled on sweats and running shoes. He'd be able to think better about his situation if he were moving.

Outside, Joseph jogged through his neighborhood. He still couldn't believe he'd up and quit his job like that. He knew it was unprofessional of him, but Pruitt had pissed him off beyond belief by practically holding his career over a barrel until he dumped Gage. And he'd picked up on Pruitt not being as okay with his sexuality as he pretended. So overall he was glad to be out of there.

Joseph ran through the park. He had it almost to himself since the rest of the world was at work or school. He wasn't completely stupid. He had six months living expenses saved up for emergencies. This definitely qualified as one. So even though he'd quit his job without another one lined up, he'd be alright. He knew there was no way in hell he was going to get a reference from Pruitt and that could be a mark against his resume. But there were others at that firm that he could probably count on. And he'd worked in other places. He had two options. He could get his resume out to firms in the area. Maybe pick some that weren't as high-brow as the one he'd just quit. Or he could work for himself.

He remembered Gia saying that she was putting him on retainer. She hadn't been joking. She'd approached him about taking over all of her needs in that area. He hadn't given her an answer yet because he wasn't sure he had the time. But now he did. He could put his shingle out and take her on along with other clients. It wouldn't be easy, but it was possible. He thought of Gage and his friends. Just about all of them were entrepreneurs. There was no reason he couldn't wrangle that same spirit and get his own practice going. And he couldn't deny there was a big plus in favor of working for himself. Joseph turned and headed back towards the house.

If he worked for himself, he'd be able to set his own hours, which meant he'd be able to race a lot more. Maybe he could even start playing pool competitively. He smiled at the thought. He could have everything he wanted. Gage, his career and his passions. He just had to be willing to pay the price for it. Just like Pruitt had said.

****

Gage opened the door for Joseph. He wasn't surprised to see the two duffel bags slung over his arm. Joseph had called him earlier that day and taken him up on his offer to come stay with him for a while. Gage liked the idea of Joseph staying with him. He'd get to fall asleep with Joseph beside him every night. And Joseph would be here in his house waiting for him while he was at work. He really liked that. Gage took Joseph's bags. "Did you bring any of your fancy suits?"

Joseph laughed. "No. Just regular clothes, workout clothes, and my laptop. I've seen that decrepit computer you have. I know I'm going to need mine for research."

"I don't really use that computer for anything but spreadsheets for work." He shrugged. "And looking at porn. So what are you researching?"

"Before I tell you I want to give you a present."

Joseph took one of the bags back from him and pulled something out. Gage's eyes widened when he saw what it was. "Woah. Macallan. That's a nice Scotch. What'd I do to deserve that?"

"I really appreciate you sponsoring me and getting some of your friends to sponsor me as well. Now more than ever that's gonna be helpful so that I can race. And also for not saying anything about Pruitt."

"What do you mean?"

"C'mon, Gage. I thought about it, especially after what he said to me yesterday, and I know why you wanted to leave the picnic right after you got there. Pruitt said something to you, didn't he?"

Gage headed into the living room. "He expressed some opinions."

Joseph followed after him, shaking his head. "I bet. So he said something rude to you but you were man enough not to bring it up. You knew that would have put me in a tough spot with him. And even though I ended up quitting anyway, I appreciate you not trying to push me into it."

Gage mumbled a quick you're welcome. It would have been a real dick move for him to mention it so he didn't feel like Joseph needed to thank him. He changed the subject. "So what are you researching?"

Joseph ducked his head sheepishly. "I'm going into business for myself." But then he forced his chin up. "I'm starting my own practice."

"That's fucking great! I mean that, Joseph." He flopped down on the couch, spreading his arms across the seat back behind him. "Nothing better than being your own boss."

Joseph grinned and sat next to him. "Thanks. I'm pretty excited about it."

"I'd be glad to help with whatever you need. Seed money, drumming up business, whatever."

"You don't have to do that. I mean, I'd be glad to take any advice you have and definitely some referrals. But you're already sponsoring me. I can't accept anything else."

Gage blinked at the rejection, but he didn't mention it. He hefted the bottle of scotch. "Let's crack this open and celebrate."

"I don't really drink hard stuff. But for everything that's happened in the past twenty-four hours, I think I can make an exception."

CHAPTER 58

A week later, Gage walked into his house after work. It had been a long day so he went into the kitchen and poured himself two fingers of the scotch Joseph had bought him. The stuff was too fancy to guzzle, but he didn't believe in saving it for fancy occasions. Gage put the bottle away and took a sip. He was surprised at how quiet the house was. He knew Joseph was there because his bike and his car were outside. But he was nowhere to be seen. Gage headed out to the hallway and called out for him. Joseph's voice floated down from upstairs.

"I'm in your room."

Gage went upstairs with his whiskey.

"What are you doing, hiding or something?" he asked as he pushed the door open.

"Not quite."

Gage came to a stop, his glass halfway to his mouth.

"What do you think?"

Gage could tell Joseph was nervous but he didn't see why. He looked so fucking good. Joseph stood there in one of his tight pairs of jeans. He was shirtless, showing off the naturally tan skin and taut muscles of his torso. It was his hair that had Gage speechless. It fell in soft waves around his shoulders as usual. But he'd had subtle blonde highlights put in. The golden streaks sparkled in the late afternoon sun pouring into the room. Gage went over to him, lifting those lightened locks. "I like it." He looked at Joseph. "It's pretty. Pretty and very … slutty." He brought Joseph's hair to his face, inhaling the scent of coconut shampoo. "It even smells slutty. Makes me want to treat you like a slut. Is that what you want, Joseph?"

Joseph's lips parted in surprise, and he blinked those big green eyes. "You already do."

Gage smiled. Slow. Wicked. "Do I?" He took a sip of his drink. "Get on your knees." Joseph stared at him for a moment before he did as he said. Gage kept his hand tangled in Joseph's hair as he dropped to his knees in front of him. He didn't say anything, just arched an eyebrow and waited. Joseph opened his jeans, freeing his cock. He leaned forward, his mouth open and ready to suck him. But Gage shook his head. Still clutching Joseph's hair, he stroked his cock himself, the strands soft as they slid up and down his cock. Joseph's eyes went wide as he watched him and he smiled again. He rubbed that pretty hair over the head of his cock. Feeling the wetness there, he knew he'd gotten some of his pre-cum in Joseph's hair. Gage pulled his hand and the hair tangled in his fingers back far enough for Joseph's mouth. "Now you can suck me."

Gage took another sip of his whiskey, hips lazily thrusting forward as Joseph sucked him. He kept pumping his cock, his fingers bumping Joseph's lips as they met in the middle of his shaft. Joseph was working him good, running his tongue up and down his shaft and over his cock head. But Gage wanted to look into those pretty green eyes while Joseph was on his knees. He whistled once, low and quick. Joseph looked up at him. "You know I like to watch, Joseph." A look of annoyance flashed across Joseph's face. Gage knew it was because of the rude way he'd just gotten his attention, but he didn't care. He smirked down at Joseph who kept sucking him off, looking up at him like he wanted. After a few more moments, he pushed Joseph's head back.

"Get up and take off those slutty jeans."

Joseph stood, taking off his pants as he'd ordered. "You're an asshole."

Gage pulled Joseph close and kissed him. He shoved his tongue in his mouth, tasting himself there. He loved the sense of ownership over Joseph that gave him. "Yeah, I am. But you like it."

Joseph's lashes dropped for a second. "Yeah. I do."

Gage kissed him, walking him backwards to the bed. When the mattress stopped them from going any further Gage gave Joseph a small shove, so that he sprawled on the bed on his back. Gage stood there looking down at him.

"Make yourself come for me, baby."

Gage watched, admiring the picture Joseph made as he started stroking himself. One smooth leg raised, stomach tight as his hand slipped up and down his cock. And that hair, a gorgeous mix of chestnut and gold tossed all over his pillow. He wasn't content to simply watch for long. Still with all his clothes on, Gage crawled onto the bed, his eyes locked with his lover's. He poured a bit of his Macallan onto him, the amber liquid spilling over Joseph's cock and fingers. Gage leaned down and licked, getting the flavors of both Joseph and whiskey on his tongue. He closed his lips over the tip of Joseph's cock, sipping at him to draw forth his pre-cum. Joseph moaned and pushed his hips up.

"Fuck, Gage."

"What? I want to see which one tastes better. Come for me baby, give me a real taste."

Joseph groaned, his head arching back into the pillows as he stroked himself faster. Gage kept licking him, darting his tongue in between his fingers. With another groan Joseph came, splashing onto his stomach. Gage tipped the glass over him again, tossing it aside when it was empty. Joseph's writhing made some of the alcohol spill down his sides. Gage chased the trickles with his tongue, lapping it up. He kissed his way back to his lover's stomach, licking at both the scotch and Joseph's cum. He looked up Joseph's body, into eyes soft and low from his orgasm. "They both taste good, but you're definitely sweeter." He swirled a finger in the cocktail of Macallan and Joseph's creamy release and brought it to Joseph's mouth. "Taste it."

Joseph parted his lips and Gage slipped his finger between them. He reached down to open his pants and grasped his cock, pushing inside Joseph as he was sucking on his finger. He set a slow pace, sliding into Joseph leisurely, lingering to enjoy being so deep inside him before he withdrew. Gage took his hand away from Joseph's mouth so that he could kiss him, licking at his lips then over his cheek. Joseph moaned, raising his legs and curling his hips up to meet his thrusts. Gage skimmed a hand along his sides to his arm, feeling the muscles twitch under his touch. He grasped his wrists and held them down over his head.

He kept stroking deep into Joseph, his fingers squeezing his wrists. "You feel so fucking good, Joseph. It's killing me to go so slow." He buried his face in the newly blonde hair. "But I want to savor it, savor you. Just like that scotch."

Joseph moaned, arching up, rubbing his legs against him. "Gage, faster. Please."

"Shut up."

Gage stayed at his pace, fucking deep into Joseph with slow rolls of his hips. He raised his face from his hair and looked down at him. "You're so slutty Joseph, laying under me with your legs open, begging for more. The hair just tops it off, lets the world see what I already know." Gage pulled out, flipping Joseph over onto his stomach. Yanking him up onto his knees, he pushed back inside him. He gripped a handful of hair and pulled hard, making Joseph's head arch back. Gage smacked a hand against the round ass in front of him, watching as the smooth flesh jiggled for a heart-stopping second. He liked the sight so much that he did it again, drawing a groan from Joseph.

"Pretty ass. Pretty legs, pretty hair, pretty mouth. Is it any wonder that I think about you all the time? That I get hard at work when I'm thinking about getting home and getting inside you?" Gage pulled Joseph up against him so he could whisper in his ear. "Did you know that I had to go to the bathroom and jerk off I got so fucking turned on from thinking about how you look sucking my cock? And how good it feels to make you come when I'm inside you?" He laughed, still gliding into Joseph's tight ass. "It's probably not healthy how much I think about you, Joseph. But I don't fucking care. You don't mind do you?"

Joseph shook his head, his voice low and husky as he answered. "I don't mind. You can think about me all you want as long as you make me feel like this."

Gage's own voice was husky as he laughed at Joseph. Slipping his hand down, he grasped his cock. He stroked Joseph hard and tight and slow, refusing to go faster no matter how much his lover begged or writhed against him. When his orgasm started to rise, he had to fight both Joseph and himself to keep from speeding up. He wanted to pound the ass gripping him so tightly, but he fought it. He wrapped an arm around Joseph, his fingers digging into his chest as he held himself back. Gage was breathing hard, his heart racing, every muscle in his body tight, but he stayed with his slow strokes. He shoved his face against Joseph's neck, cursing loudly as his cock pulsed hard. He worked to get Joseph off and when he felt that sweet clenching on his shaft, he finally lost it. He pushed Joseph forward, falling on top of him. Joseph begged him to fuck him faster, pushing his ass back against him. Gage gave into his body and to Joseph, slamming into him over and over, Joseph's desperate moans driving him on until he was spent.

Gage rolled off of him, drawing in a deep breath. He'd had a lot of sex in his life. But somehow the releases he had with Joseph were always more powerful than any he'd ever had.

Joseph turned over. He was sweaty, strands of hair sticking to his face. "So you like my hair?"

Gage ran his fingers through it. "I fucking love it."

CHAPTER 59

L et's go shoot some pool tonight."

Joseph came out of the bathroom with a towel wrapped around his waist. He'd just taken a shower to get the sticky alcohol off of him. Gage was sitting on the bed holding a scrap of what looked like pink lace. "What is that?"

"Something I got for you."

Full of curiosity, Joseph went over to him. "For me? What is it?"

Gage held the material up and Joseph saw what it was. His eyes widened. "No way. I am not wearing those."

"Why not? I told you I have a secret fondness for the color."

"Fine, Then I'll get some *men's* briefs in pink."

Gage stood up and walked over to him. "That's not the same, Joseph." He twirled the panties around on one finger. "See, I told you gender is irrelevant to me. Boy, girl; doesn't matter. But there is one thing about women that I really like." He twirled the lace around again. "Sexy little pink panties." Joseph stood still and let Gage pull the towel off his hips. "And just because I'm with a guy shouldn't mean that I don't get to enjoy them anymore, right?"

Joseph swallowed hard. Licked his lips. Cleared his throat. "I guess not."

Gage gave him that wicked smile again, a dimple creasing his cheek. "So then you'll wear these for me?"

Joseph looked into the dark eyes watching him so closely and found himself nodding. "Okay."

That smile grew as Gage handed him the underwear. Joseph was surprised. He'd expected Gage to put them on him like he had the briefs in Express.

Gage watched as Joseph awkwardly stepped into the panties, drawing them up his long legs. He tugged a little too hard, nearly ripping the fragile material as he settled them into place. Gage held back a smile. "Careful."

Joseph looked down at himself and frowned. "They barely fit."

Gage went over to him and smoothed a palm along Joseph's hip and over his ass. With his hard, sculpted body and overall attitude, Joseph was definitely a man. But his skin was smooth and his features elegantly refined. Joseph was a fascinating combination of masculine and feminine beauty, of strength and vulnerability. The delicate underwear enhanced both sides of him in a way that Gage found immensely appealing. The panties were made of hot pink mesh, with pale pink lace around the waist and legs openings. They were tight on his narrow hips and Joseph's thick cock was clearly visible behind the mesh, straining the material. Gage was sure there was something perverse about liking the way a man looked in ladies underwear, but he didn't care. Joseph looked amazing.

"That's because your ass is so round," he finally answered.

"Or maybe because of my dick. I don't think the designers at Vicky's planned for that."

Gage grinned and cupped his balls. "Don't forget these. They're taking up a lot of room too." He ran his hand over Joseph's cock. "I'm gonna be hard all night thinking about what you have on underneath those tight jeans of yours." He felt Joseph hardening under his palm. "Looks like I won't be the only one."

"That's only because you're touching me."

Gage arched a brow. He dipped a finger under the edge of the leg opening, running his finger along the lace. "Really?"

Joseph blushed, but he didn't say anything. Gage stepped back and looked him over. "Blonde hair and pink panties. And I thought they stopped making Twinkies."

Joseph cast him the dirtiest look ever. "Ha-fucking-ha. And just so you know, they are making them again."

"Damn, that's too bad. I was just gonna fill you up with cream and put you on the shelf."

Joseph threw up his hands with a frustrated groan and turned away from him to get his clothes. Gage tried not to laugh as he watched his hissy-fit. The panties rode high on his ass, leaving two tantalizing slices of bare cheek free to jiggle as Joseph stomped around. Gage smiled and shook his head. Prettiest ass he'd ever seen.

****

"This place is packed tonight."

Gage swung into a parking space at Red's. "Yup. It's always packed when they're having a tournament."

Joseph opened his door and got out. "Tournament? Well then we probably won't even get a table. Let's just go somewhere else."

"Nope. I entered you yesterday. So you're playing."

Joseph looked at him in surprise. "Why would you do that?"

"Because you want to play."

"Yeah, but I don't have my cue and I haven't practiced."

"Don't worry about all that. Just play. And if you want to play more, then you should. You don't have to rush to get back behind a desk Joseph. There's nothing wrong with taking a little time to race, play pool and just relax."

Joseph looked towards the pool hall. "I don't want to take too long to get things rolling. But I guess there's no harm in entering a few tournaments in the meantime."

Joseph walked into the smoky building with Gage. He checked in at the table, flushing slightly with embarrassment when the registrar commented on him not having his own cue. But he let that roll off his shoulders and went to find one that would work for tonight. He didn't need fancy equipment to play. Or to win.

Gage settled on a stool with a beer to watch Joseph play. He was serious, focused on nothing but the game. He'd tied his hair back so it wouldn't get in his way. His t-shirt clung to the muscles of his torso, his jeans tight and low on his hips. Gage couldn't help hoping he'd catch a glimpse of pink lace every time he bent over the table. Joseph was just so fucking pretty and he loved knowing that the man was his.

Gage moved to a new chair twice to follow Joseph as he won his first two rounds and advanced. The second guy Joseph beat wasn't happy. He cursed and threw his cue stick on the table. Gage glared at the crew cut sporting idiot having the temper tantrum until he walked off. Joseph came over to him smiling after his win. He took a quick sip of the soda Gage had gotten for him.

"This is fun. Thank you for signing me up." He leaned in close and whispered in his ear. "Maybe these will be my lucky panties."

Gage groaned and reached his fingers out to Joseph's hip. But he'd already stepped away from him, giving him a naughty grin before he went to get set up for the next game.

Joseph won the next one and then lost just before the final round. He put his borrowed cue stick away and stood next to him as they watched the last two competitors battle it out. The winner turned out to be a short, stocky guy who looked ecstatic at the two hundred dollar check and small trophy he received.

Joseph and Gage finished their drinks and headed outside after the celebration. Gage wrapped his arm around Joseph's neck, telling him how well he did. Just ahead of them was the cue stick tossing bro who'd lost to Joseph, and his friend. The crew cut guy looked back over his shoulder and saw them.

"I fucking knew it. Can't believe I lost to a fucking fag."

Gage tensed. "What'd you say asshole?"

The two stopped and turned around. "I said, I can't believe I lost to a fucking fag."

Gage dropped his arm from around Joseph and walked up to the guy. "Maybe you ought to spend time bettering your game instead of talking shit in parking lots. Then you could be a gracious winner instead of a shitty loser."

"Who the fuck do you think you are?"

"I think I'm the man who's about to teach you that it's not nice to use the word fag."

The guy laughed, pushing his chest out. He wasn't taller than Gage, but he was bigger, a lot bigger. "Is that right, faggot?"

Gage smiled, showing teeth. "Yep." Before the other guy could blink Gage clocked him in the jaw, making him stagger back in surprise. Then the guy lowered his head and charged straight at Gage.

Joseph watched the fight. Gage took it to the homophobic shit head, landing several face and body shots. He danced back out of the way of the big guy's slow punch then ran forward to jam his knee into his gut.

Joseph caught movement out of the corner of his eye and saw the man's friend trying to sneak up on Gage. He jumped forward and grabbed him. Spinning him around, he caught him under the chin with a hard uppercut. The guy cried out in pain and Gage looked over in surprise. Joseph shrugged then gave his attention back to the man swinging at him. Ducking under his arm, Joseph came up with a roundhouse to the jaw. This time the guy stumbled back and fell. His friend ran over and kneeled down to help him.

"Fuck these assholes. Let's get out of here, man."

But Gage stopped him. He crouched down and grabbed a fistful of crew cut's shirt. "I don't think so. You're not going anywhere until you apologize for calling my boyfriend a nasty name. And you're going to very politely congratulate him on his win."

Joseph stood there, trying hard not to laugh as the guy swiped a hand over his bloody mouth and apologized in a frustrated voice. He accepted his congratulations and Gage let them both go. Joseph looked at Gage, kneeling on the concrete, his chest pumping and his hair a tangled mess all over his head. He looked good, just as tough and wild as Joseph had thought when he first met him.

Gage jumped to his feet and came over to him. He tucked his fingers in the front of Joseph's jeans and yanked him forward into a hard kiss. "I've never popped a boner during a fight before, but I did tonight. That was hot watching you throw some punches."

Joseph raised his chin. "Pretty boys can fight too you know."

"Apparently. That guy's face is gonna be sore as hell tomorrow thanks to you."

Gage slung his arm back around his shoulders and they headed for his truck. As they walked Joseph started to laugh.

"What's so funny?"

"Just thinking about you defending my manly honor, while I'm wearing pink lace panties."

Gage barked a surprised laugh of his own. He slid a hand down into Joseph's jeans, his fingers teasing along the waistband of the panties. "No one has to know about that but us."

CHAPTER 60

J oseph sat with Gage in a booth at Big G's, Gia across from them. They'd stopped by to have dinner. Gage hated to cook and while he didn't mind it, he hadn't felt like bothering that evening. They were finished with their meal and Gia was hanging out with them for a few minutes before they left.

"I like your hair, Joseph. You look good as an almost blonde."

Joseph smiled. "Thanks. Gage compared me to some famous blondes twice in one night so I figured he must want me to be one."

Gage laughed and tugged on his ponytail. "I never said that. But I do like it."

Gia smiled at them both. "Who did he compare you to?"

Joseph's face heated a little bit. "The Ken doll and Lady Godiva."

She started laughing. "A Barbie doll? And a naked lady on the back of a horse?" Gia laughed so hard she leaned over and laid her head on the table top, her shoulders shaking from the hilarity. When she was finished, she sat up, wiping her eyes. "Well, Joseph you have to admit. You *are* pretty."

Joseph rolled his eyes. "Now that I'm not working at Pretentious, Manipulative, and Stick-Up-Their-Asses anymore, I can get away with hair like this."

"Oh, that's right you're flying solo now. Does that mean that you'll take me up on my offer?"

"Yes, if you'll still have me. I've been working on getting things going during the day while Gage is at the shop."

"Of course I still want you as my lawyer!"

Joseph was pleased that Gia had been serious about wanting him to work with her. She was his first client, which gave him a sense of confidence that he'd be able to find more. "We'll have to sit down and go through exactly what you need."

Gage slapped his hand on the table. "You'll have to do that some other time. We need to get going Joseph."

Gia looked up at Gage as he slid out of the booth and stood. "Where are you boys off to?"

Joseph followed Gage. "We're going to look at some new tires for my bike. Have I thanked you yet for sponsoring me?"

Gia laughed again and stood. "Only about a dozen times. I'm glad to do it. You brought in a really big crowd with you after your race before. I'd love to get some more of that traffic."

"Well, thanks again. It's really helpful and I'll be able to do so much more now," Joseph said as he gave his friend a hug.

Gia squeezed him back. "Good. Get some wins. That'll make me look even better since I'll be sponsoring the best."

Gage threw his arm around his shoulders. "Don't worry he will. I've got an incentive plan all set up for him."

Joseph looked at Gage in question, but his boyfriend just winked at him and led him out of the bar.

****

"Hello, welcome to Low-Town Specialty Tire Shop. Anything you need help finding, just let us know."

Joseph and Gage both nodded their thanks at the friendly greeting. Thankfully the place was low-key so they were able to wander around on their own. They were looking at some Pirelli's when Gage asked Joseph a question out of the blue.

"Is your family coming to this race? I noticed they didn't make it out to the last one."

Surprised, Joseph looked up from the tires he was checking out. "Uh… no. My mother doesn't come to my races often because they make her nervous. My little brother might come, it depends on what he's got going on with his social life."

"And your dad?" Gage prompted.

Joseph a hand through his hair and sighed. "My father and I don't exactly see eye to eye on certain things."

"He doesn't accept that you're gay."

Looking at Gage, Joseph noted the hard expression on his face, like it angered him that his father had rejected him. "No, he doesn't. In fact, when I told him I was gay, he kicked me out of the house and called me *bacheh mozalaf*, which basically means faggot." Joseph tried to laugh and make light of the situation. "It was almost funny, him calling me that. It's so rare that we speak Persian I almost didn't know what he'd said. Anyway, that's why I played so much pool while I was in law school. I went from having my parents' financial support to being completely on my own."

Gage came over to him. "I want to call him a prick, but I won't because he's your father. I hope for both your sakes you reestablish your relationship one day."

Joseph shrugged. He remembered all too well the disgust that had been on Cyrus Naderi's face as he'd kicked his eldest son out of the house. He wasn't counting on there being a reconciliation any time soon, despite what his mother often said. The past couple of years, every time they talked or visited she said he was "coming around." Joseph didn't believe that for an instant. He pushed those memories out of his head when Gage tugged him close and kissed him on the temple, as usual not caring what anyone might think.

"C'mon, let's get you the best set of tires in this place."

****

A couple hours later they were in Gage's garage. The door was down to block out the cool wind and rain of a fall storm. Joseph sat on the couch made from the back seat of a classic Dodge Challenger, watching Gage put the new tires on his bike. They'd bought a set of Continental Trail Attacks, very nice, expensive tires. He was going to go for a run on them and if he liked the way they felt he'd get another set to have fresh for race day. With his sponsors, he'd be able to afford to swap out tires more than he had before.

He'd offered to help, but Gage had laughed and said he'd be done much faster if he worked on his own. So he watched. Watched Gage. Watched his lips form a curse around the cigarette dangling from his mouth as he fit the wheel on the tire stand. Watched the smoke curl up over his head. Watched the way his long fingers gripped the tire iron as he worked the front tire off the wheel. Watched the way his jeans hugged his firm thighs and ass as he bent and rolled the old front tire off to the side.

Joseph knew he was close to being obsessed with his boyfriend, but he didn't give a damn. Gage was so different from all the other men he'd ever dated and he loved it. Loved his attitude and the way he carried himself, like he didn't give a damn what anybody thought of him. Loved the way he looked with his hair tumbling over his forehead, the muscles in his shoulders and back bunching up with his movements. His dark, short-sleeved workmen's shirt he wore over a white t-shirt was frayed, his jeans torn and stained with grease. Joseph loved how gritty Gage was. He couldn't imagine Ashton getting dirty like this. No, Joseph didn't care that he was so into his boyfriend. Besides, Gage had admitted how much he thought of him. Joseph bit his lip, his cock hardening as he thought of Gage getting himself off at work because he thought of him so much. Gage looked up just then and caught him staring.

"What are you looking at?"

"You."

Gage took a deep drag on the cigarette then exhaled and stubbed it out on the bottom of his boot. "Got something on your mind?"

"You."

Gage grinned. "Is that right? What are you thinking about little old me?"

"Thinking how I like watching you get your hands dirty."

Gage crooked a grimy finger at him. "Come get dirty with me."

Joseph stood and walked over. "I thought you worked faster alone."

"Sometimes it's not all about speed. Didn't I tell you that I liked to take my time?"

Joseph remembered back to that night, when Gage had returned his bike. "That's true, you did say that." He tskd. "Flirting with your customer. Isn't that a violation of ethics?"

Gage laughed and pulled him in between his hard body and the tire stand. "Nah. Not fucking the client is only for doctor and lawyer types like you." Gage took the band from his hair. "I don't know why you tie your hair up around me. You know I'm going to take it down." He fluffed his hair out around his shoulders. "I've wanted to run my hands through it ever since you came in with it loose and wind-blown all over your head."

"I wore it down that night on purpose. So you would know that I was more than just a suit."

Gage brushed his hair over his shoulders, baring his neck. "Oh, I knew. Even though you were shy and you left, I knew that you wanted to get dirty with me and that you'd be back." Gage kissed him behind his ear. "And I was right."

Joseph started to turn around, but Gage stopped him.

"We need to get this tire off." He picked up the rubber material that went between the tire iron and the wheel rim so it didn't get scratched. "Gotta use protection."

Joseph looked back over his shoulder at Gage. "I thought these were called *protectors*."

"Oh yeah, that's right. Using protection is what you held over my head until you got your way."

Joseph laughed as he popped the tire off the rim. "You should be thanking me. It was time for you to stop whoring around."

Gage kissed him behind his ear again, whispering against his skin. "Thank you, Joseph." Joseph shivered as Gage slipped his hand under his t-shirt to stroke across his stomach. "Go ahead and grab the new tire."

Joseph did, but Gage didn't move back, so when he bent over his thick erection pressed against his ass. Joseph bit his lip to hold back a little moan. He was determined to do this and be as nonchalant about the arousal building between them as Gage was. He set the tire on the stand, spraying it with a soap and water mix before he started pushing it down onto the rim. Gage stayed behind him, his fingers resting on his hips as Joseph worked around the entire tire. Gage whispered in his ear.

"Harder, Joseph. Push harder."

Joseph groaned a laugh. "Only you could make changing tires sound raunchy."

"Raunchy, huh?" Gage laughed too, his warm breath blowing over his cheek. "I know it's tight, but just keep pushing, baby. You'll get it in. I mean *on*." Gage grabbed his hips and ground his cock against him. "Push hard."

Joseph did moan that time, thrusting back to meet Gage's hardness pressing against his ass. Finally, the tire was on, but Joseph didn't move. He looked down to see Gage's dirty hands glide down his forearms, rubbing grease onto his skin before he twined their fingers together. For once, his hands were just as dirty as Gage's. His voice sounded in Joseph's ear, low and seductive as ever.

"What do you want, Joseph?"

CHAPTER 61

J oseph looked over his shoulder at his lover. "I want to suck you off, right here. I want to be on my knees for you, on the ground, getting dirty … for you."

Gage took his time answering, lighting another cigarette first. Smoke streamed from his nose when he finally gave his response. "I'm not going to say no to that."

Joseph shook his head. "You and those cigarettes."

Gage took another drag. "You're not going to tell me how I'm slowly killing myself are you?"

Joseph pushed Gage back, walking him to where he wanted him to go. "Nope. I'm more concerned with what you can do in the immediate future. You should wear a helmet when you ride."

Gage looked at him, his eyes big with surprise. They widened even further when Joseph gave him a quick shove, sending him toppling back onto the bench seat. "But I won't look as cool."

Joseph laughed and sank to his knees. "Trust me, you'll look just as cool with a helmet on as you do without."

One dark brow arched. "Because safety is sexy?"

Joseph pushed Gage's legs apart and crawled in between them. "That's right." Joseph let the matter drop. He didn't want to push Gage, but he really did want him to start wearing a helmet. He was surprised he didn't after what had happened to his previous boyfriend. He figured planting the seed was a good start to making that happen.

Joseph opened Gage's jeans, tugging them down a little so he could get to all of him. He latched onto Gage's thighs, digging his fingers in hard as he licked up and down his shaft. When he reached the base of his cock, he kept going, laving over Gage's balls, feeling the hair there soft under his tongue. He sucked one into his mouth, pulling on it hard. Gage cursed and Joseph released him with a pop, moving back up to flick his tongue at that spot just underneath his cockhead.

Gage spread his legs further and Joseph lost his balance for a moment. He braced a hand on the ground to steady himself and felt it slip in a spot of oil. Once he was settled again he sucked Gage's shaft into his mouth, moaning softly at the feel and taste of him. The rain continued to come down, the steady sound of it serving as a backdrop for their quiet moans.

He glanced up to see Gage relaxed against the Challenger's seat back, looking up at the ceiling, clearly enjoying himself as he thrust up into his mouth. Gage put the cigarette to his lips and breathed in, smoke billowing around his head when he exhaled. Again Joseph thought of how different Gage was from all of his previous lovers. And he preferred Gage over all of them.

Joseph stroked his hand up Gage's torso, leaving a trail of grease and grime on his white t-shirt. He bunched the material in his fist, yanking on it so that Gage looked down at him. He took his mouth from him for a moment. "I thought you liked to watch."

"Mmmm… you know I do." He put the cigarette between his lips again, the tip glowing bright red as he inhaled. He blew out a long breath, the gray cloud of smoke momentarily obscuring his face. "Give me a show, baby."

Joseph kept his eyes on Gage as he licked all over the tip of his cock before he sucked him back down. He moved his mouth on Gage slowly, his lips sliding over the silky skin of his shaft. Gage watched him, still smoking, his eyes narrowed behind the haze. Joseph stopped again for a moment. "Put it out."

Gage puffed out a smoke ring. "No."

Joseph didn't say anything. He just started sucking again, going fast this time. He leaned his head forward so that his hair fell into his face, blocking Gage's view. Gage gripped his hair, trying to push it back. But he couldn't do so with one hand.

"Goddamnit, Joseph," Gage cursed before he put the cigarette out on the metal arm of the couch. Now he tangled both hands in his hair, holding on to his head and thrusting up roughly into his mouth. Joseph moaned, letting Gage fuck his mouth, swallowing him down as far as he could go. He kept his grip on the t-shirt, reaching up further to tug the collar down. He scratched at Gage's chest and he groaned, his fingers tightening in his hair.

"Fuck, I'm about to come."

Joseph immediately pulled back and stroked Gage with his fist. Gage glared down at him.

"What the fuck, Joseph? Keep going."

Joseph shook his head. "No. I don't want you to come in my mouth this time." Gage continued to stare down at him, his eyes narrowed in annoyance now, instead of from the smoke. "And you can get that glare off your face or I'll stop altogether." Gage shut his eyes and Joseph kept pumping, Gage's hips rolling up to his fist, until with a harsh curse he was coming. Joseph watched, his gaze flicking back and forth between the creamy release spilling from Gage's cockhead, to his face tight with tension as he rocked through his orgasm.

Gage finally relaxed and looked down at him. "Now who's the asshole?" he asked as he lit yet another cigarette.

Joseph raised a brow. "I think I've got a long ways to go before I catch up with you."

Gage twisted his fingers in his hair and pulled him up. Joseph crawled onto Gage, straddling his lap. Gage kept pulling and Joseph leaned down so that his hair shut them in, their faces close together. Gage exhaled, smoke streaming from his mouth just as their lips met. Joseph cursed, but he opened up for Gage, their tongues licking and battling in a deep kiss flavored with the tastes of sex and smoke. Gage eased back and looked up at him, finally responding to his earlier statement.

"You're right about that, pretty boy."

CHAPTER 62

By the time Saturday rolled around, the sky was clear. The temperature was warm and breezy, typical of Houston in late September. Joseph realized he'd let the entire summer pass without seeing his mother. He decided to see if she could meet him for lunch. He wasn't sure she'd be able to make it since it was last minute, but she'd said yes when he called. And to his happy surprise, his brother had blown off hanging with his friends so he could come too.

Now the three of them sat in a big red booth at a local retro diner, sipping on milkshakes. His mother had wanted one and demanded her sons get one too so she didn't feel guilty for indulging. They'd agreed, although Joseph didn't see any reason why she should feel guilty. She was still petite, her long hair thick and dark with only a few glittering streaks of gray. Darius took after their mother in his coloring while Joseph had received his lighter hair and green eyes from their father.

"So how are things for you, Yousef? Is work going alright?"

Joseph hesitated. He didn't want to lie to his mother, but he didn't want to ruin a rare happy lunch with her and Darius by telling her he'd quit his job. He decided to tell her later. "Work is fine. Stressful and trying new things," he hedged.

"You'll figure it out. You're such a good son, Yousef." She turned to Darius. "Now if I could just get this one to behave."

Darius rolled his eyes. "You mean fall in line with Dad's orders."

Joseph gave his brother a sympathetic smile at the look of pleading he sent him. He clearly still needed help getting their mother on his side. "So Father wants Darius to go to school here?"

"Yes. There is nothing wrong that school."

"But you know that's not what he wants. You always said you just wanted your sons to be happy. Shouldn't that apply in this case?"

His mother glanced between him and Darius. "He would be so far from home."

"That's part of growing up. There's phone calls and visits to keep in touch. And did you know that lots of universities have online programs where you can check a student's grades?"

Darius opened his mouth, a look of protest on his face. Joseph raised his hand slightly to shush him. He sensed their mother about to give in. "I'm sure if you set up some ground rules, everything would be alright. Darius is a good kid. You can trust him away from home."

Mrs. Naderi pushed the empty milk shake glass away and crossed her arms over her chest. "There will be rules, Darius Naderi. Keeping your grades up, no drugs, and no getting any girls pregnant."

Darius's young face turned scarlet with embarrassment. He looked around the diner to see if anyone had overheard. "Mom! Don't talk about that."

"Why not? I gave your brother the same talk about sex with girls." A smile curled her lips and she looked at Joseph out of the corner of her eye. "Although it turns out he didn't need it."

Now it was Joseph's turn to burn with embarrassment at his mother, while Darius laughed so hard, he choked on his milkshakes.

"You just got burned by Mom, big bro!"

Joseph shook his head, laughing himself. He didn't mind his mother's teasing. It felt good, like when he'd been a real part of the family. And he'd convinced her to help Darius attend the school he chose, so that was all that mattered.

His mother reached across the booth top and squeezed his hand. "I don't know if you know how I feel, Yousef, so I'm telling you now. Who you love doesn't matter to me. I love you as my son and that is all there is to it. So I will tease you and ask who you are seeing as a mother should."

Joseph returned the squeeze. "Thank you, Mother." He sobered a little. "I wish Father felt the same way."

"Give it just a little more time, sweetheart. I know this is hard on you. It's hard on all of us. Your father and I have been talking. He'll come around soon. Now don't dodge my question. Who are you seeing?"

"His name is Gage Mason," Joseph said with a smile.

"And what does Gage Mason do?"

Joseph finished the last of his shake. "He owns a motorcycle repair shop. He fixed my bike, and that's how we met."

Darius slapped his hands on the table. "You asked out that bike mechanic? I knew you liked him!"

Joseph lightly punched his brother on the arm. "Yeah, you were right for once," he teased.

"Tell me more about Gage Mason. I want to know all about him."

Joseph settled back in the booth, knowing he'd be there for a while. When it came to her sons and who they were dating, Amira Naderi wasn't satisfied until she had every last detail.

****

Later on that evening, Joseph was at Max's house. After his lunch with his mother and brother, he'd received a text from Gage. The weather had been nice all day, the sun drying up that week's rain. Max was having an impromptu barbeque and wanted them to come. Joseph thought it sounded like fun, so he'd agreed to meet Gage there, who was coming straight from work.

It was still a little early, so Joseph, Max and a few people who were there so far were sitting on the wraparound porch of Max's big house.

"This is a great house, Max. But big for one man. Do you plan to have a family and kids?"

"Yep. I'm actually looking forward to it. Just haven't found the right person yet."

Gage had told Joseph some of Max's history. He'd grown up in a boy's home because his mother was heavy into drugs and unable to care for him. She hadn't told the rest of her family she was pregnant, so his grandmother wasn't known of his existence until Max was twenty. Joseph figured because of his upbringing that having a family was important to him. Reaching out, Joseph tapped his beer bottle to Max's. "I'm sure it'll happen for you soon."

Max laughed. "Here's hoping. My grandmother keeps bitching she wants great grandkids before she dies."

Joseph laughed with him until a rumble echoed down the street, drowning them out. Joseph looked up, recognizing the sound of Gage's bike. When he came into view Joseph was surprised. Gage had on a helmet, solid black like his Indian. He hadn't thought Gage would take his advice so soon, but he was glad he had. Max interrupted his thoughts.

"So has he told you yet?"

"Told me what?"

"That he loves you."

Joseph was taken aback. He hadn't expected Max to say that. "No he hasn't —wait, what makes you think that he does?"

"I've known Gage for a long time. And I've never seen him wearing a helmet. Five bucks says he's wearing it because of you. I bet if you think about it you'll come up with plenty more examples to prove that he does." Max took a pull of his beer. "He's got a few things he's going to have to get straightened out in his head before he says it. But pay attention Joseph. He's telling you."

Joseph was still surprised both at the helmet and Max's revelation, but he got that expression off his face and stood up as Gage walked up to the porch. The first thing Gage did was grip his ponytail and kiss him, greeting him with *Hey, baby* in his low voice. Then he greeted his friend. Max grinned at him, his eyebrows raised as if to say, *See? I told you so.* Joseph just shook his head as he looked at Gage talking to his friend. Maybe … maybe Gage did love him.

****

Joseph was in the kitchen getting drinks for him and Gage. The party had moved outside where the meat was ready on Max's big, brick grill. He heard a pair of heels clicking on the tile and turned to see who it was. He recognized the woman. Even though they'd never been introduced he knew her name. Brianna. There was no way he could forget her. She had a big smile plastered across her face as she approached him. Joseph didn't trust it for an instant.

"Hi! It's Joseph right?"

Joseph nodded. "That's right."

She held her hand out. "It's nice to meet you under less embarrassing circumstances."

Joseph shook her hand, but raised an eyebrow. "Is that what they were?"

Brianna shrugged. "You know how it is. You can't trust Gage alone for more than a second. Take your eyes off him and he's got his hand up somebody's skirt."

"That might have been the case before, but those days are over for him."

"Really?"

"That's right. Gage is with me. Exclusively." He didn't have a problem warning her off approaching Gage again.

Brianna gave him a little smile. "Oh honey. Gage couldn't be exclusive if his life depended on it. Not with all the wild shit he likes to get up to."

"He doesn't need to seek anybody else out for anything," he said in a hard voice.

Brianna cocked her head to the side, that snide smile still on her face. "Really? I wouldn't have pegged you as somebody down for threesomes and kinky sex while high on X."

Joseph let the part about threesomes go. And as far as he was concerned Gage was welcome to get as kinky with him as he liked. But he had to address the last part. "Gage doesn't do drugs anymore."

"Is that what he told you?" she asked with a laugh.

"Yes. And I believe him."

Another voice sounded behind him before Brianna could say anything else.

"Brianna what are you doing? Stirring up trouble as usual?"

They both turned to see Gia walking into the kitchen.

"Not at all. Just discussing our mutual love for Gage with Joseph here."

"Somehow I doubt that. You've never loved anyone but yourself. Now why don't you run along and stop with whatever lies you were putting in Joseph's head."

Joseph slung an arm around Gia's shoulders when she stopped next to him. "Yeah Brianna, run along. Gage doesn't need or want anything you have to offer. And if you get in my face again with that bullshit, I'll sic Gia on you."

Brianna flounced off, leaving Joseph and Gia to laugh and head outside to the backyard. When Joseph's feet hit the grass, he stopped for a moment. Gage was there, but he wasn't alone. He stood close to a young Hispanic man. He looked hard, his head shaved and tattoos running from his wrists all the way up his neck. But he looked at ease standing there with Gage's arm thrown over his shoulder. Joseph didn't want to jump to the conclusion that Gage was doing anything untoward, especially since the two men were surrounded by people. But when Gage playfully pretended to punch the guy in the stomach, then appeared to *tickle* him Joseph frowned. Tonight, two people who knew Gage very well had expressed their opinions on who Gage was and where he was in their relationship. And Joseph wondered who was right. Max? Or Brianna?

****

Joseph crossed the yard to reach his boyfriend. Gage looked up from where he had the guy in a headlock. A big grin split Gage's face when he saw him.

"Joseph! Come meet this asshole."

Joseph relaxed a little. If Gage was this enthusiastic about introducing them, there was probably nothing there. As he headed over he decided to put all the doubt raised by Brianna out of his head. Brianna was pretty, but clearly spiteful. If he was going to believe anyone about the way Gage might feel, he'd choose Max over her any day. By the time he shook the man's hand Joseph was completely at ease. "Hi, I'm Joseph." The handshake he got in return was firm and confident.

"I'm Luis. Nice to meet you."

Gage leaned over Luis's shoulder and spoke in a loud stage whisper. "Joseph is my *boyfriend*."

Luis's eyes widened. "Get out of here!"

Gage's mouth curled in that arrogant sneer that Joseph loved. "What? You think I can't pull somebody this hot?"

Luis rolled his eyes. "No I can't believe your wild ass settled down enough to learn what the word boyfriend means, let alone actually get one."

Gage knocked his knee into the back of Luis's, making his leg buckle. "Shut up, asshole."

Joseph watched the playful shoving match that started up between the two for a moment before he spoke up. "So how do you two know each other?"

Luis straightened first. "I kicked his ass a couple of times. Then once he was subdued enough I offered him my friendship."

Joseph laughed, but his eyes shot over to Gage as he protested loudly.

"Like hell you kicked my ass! Besides, who ended up with the prize? Me. So clearly I won."

Joseph arched a brow. "You two fought over a girl?"

Gage scoffed, his hands tucked into his front jeans pockets. "C'mon now. I'm not fighting over a piece of ass. It was this sweet leather jacket that a friend was throwing out."

Joseph laughed. "Are you kidding me?" Both of them laughed and shook their heads. Joseph looked at his boyfriend. "You're an idiot." He looked over at Luis. "You both are. So what do you do?"

"I do custom airbrush jobs for bikes and cars. Gage here has been trying to get me to come work in his little rinky dink shop for a while now."

Gage raised his brow, holding up a finger to stop Luis. "Okay, first of all, my shop? Not rinky dink. Second. You're here in town that must mean you're ready to do business."

Luis shrugged. "We'll see. You know I don't like being tied down in one spot."

Gage rolled his eyes and the three of them started talking about some of the paint jobs Luis had done.

****

The party eventually started to wind down. Gage tangled his fingers in Joseph's hair. As usual, he'd pulled off the band holding it back earlier that evening.

"You ready to go home?"

"Yeah, I'm tired." They headed over to say bye and thanks to Max, then walked around to the street. Gage straddled his bike, pulling his new helmet on. Joseph grinned and tapped it.

"Nice. But it wouldn't hurt to doll it up a little bit. Maybe get Luis to airbrush something on it."

Gage snorted. "I'll leave the fancy bike gear to you."

Joseph leaned in and kissed Gage lightly. "Thank you for wearing it. And you still look cool."

Gage grinned. "Thanks. I guess I can sacrifice my sexy windswept hair in order to keep from smashing my brains out all over the highway."

As soon as the words were out of his mouth Gage's grin faded. Joseph knew he was thinking of his boyfriend Riley who had died in a motorcycle accident. He immediately sought to put Gage at ease from his gaffe. "So that jacket you won from Luis. You still got it?"

Gage looked up at him. "Yeah, why?"

"Maybe you could model it for me later?" He waggled his eyebrows, doing his best impression of Groucho Marx. "And maybe nothing else?"

The pain left Gage's face, his smile returning. "I might. As long as you prance around in those pink panties for me again."

Joseph laughed. "Good lord. What kind of night am I in for?"

Gage did his own eyebrow waggling. "Guess you'll find out." Gage tugged him down for a kiss. "I'll see you at home."

Joseph stepped back, trying to hold back a stupid, sappy smile as Gage started his bike and rode off. Home. Gage had said home instead of his house.

CHAPTER 63

Gage looked at the clock in his shop. It was half past four. He wanted to go home. Joseph was there waiting for him. He smiled a little at the thought. He liked knowing that Joseph was there in his space. Liked knowing that Joseph was under his roof. They'd grown close and Joseph was his like no one else had ever been before. He was thinking about asking Joseph to make it permanent, to give up his townhome and move in with him. Then Gage could take care of him, support him while he went after his dreams of racing. He could do it, he had more than enough money to support them both. And Joseph would be his.

Gage smiled again as he thought back to that morning when he'd left the house. Joseph had still been in bed. He'd offered to get up and make Gage some breakfast before he left, but he'd passed. He wanted the image he took in to work to be Joseph in his bed, his hair tossed across his pillows. He'd given his lover one last kiss, then forced himself to leave and come into work. And now he couldn't get that image out of his head. Not that he wanted to. Those sweet green eyes heavy lidded with sleep. The softness of the beard that Joseph had let get scruffy on his jaw since he didn't have to be neat for the office anymore. Smooth, tan skin and hard muscles. Flat stomach leading to places just barely covered by the blanket. Gage swore Joseph had strategically placed it to keep him from seeing what he really wanted. Gage looked at the clock again. Maybe he could leave early just once…

"Hey man, I hate to interrupt whatever thoughts are bringing that smile to your face, but I figure now is a good time to ask for a favor."

Gage looked at Danny. "Yeah, what's up?"

"I need to take some time off."

"How much time you thinking?"

"About a week. I want to take my lady on a vacation."

Gage shrugged. "Sounds good to me." He didn't have a formal policy on applying for time off. If Danny needed to go, he let him know and went. He'd never abused the courtesy and Gage didn't think he ever would.

"Alright, thanks, Gage. You want me to call around and get some temporary help? Or maybe see if I can get my brother in again?"

Gage started to say yes. Then he changed his mind. "No, that's alright. I'll get Joseph to come in and help me out."

Danny raised a brow. "Joseph? Does he know anything about bikes other than how to make 'em go fast?"

"No. But he can hold a wrench for me."

Danny rolled his eyes. "Just make sure that's the only thing he's holding. This is a place of business, not a pleasure palace."

Gage laughed. "No promises."

****

A couple hours later, Gage was finally home. He headed back to his study after Joseph called out to him from there. Gage rested his hip against the desk Joseph had taken over. He didn't mind, he preferred to do his work in the shop's office. "Hey, how was your day?"

Joseph pushed the papers in front of him aside. "Good. Got lots done. Found somebody to do my website and a few places to look at to lease an office."

"Nice. You make any progress on the race that's coming up?"

"Yes. Got my entry fee paid today."

"You should have spent your day out practicing then."

"There'll be time for that. I can't neglect getting my firm off the ground."

Gage shoved his fingers into the soft hair on the side of Joseph's head. He tugged, tilting Joseph's face up to him. "I'm ready to see you on the back of a bike again." Gage leaned down to kiss his boyfriend, but at the last second changed his mind and ran his tongue over his lips instead. "I want to see your ass in that tight bike suit."

Joseph smiled. "You want to see my ass in anything."

Gage smiled too. "True." This time when he leaned into Joseph he did kiss him. "I have a favor to ask you," he said after he pulled back.

"Of course."

"Danny is going out of town for a week and I need some help in the shop. Do you think you could come in for him?"

"Are you sure you want me? I don't know how to fix bikes."

"Don't worry about that. I might get a little behind, but I can handle all of the labor. I just need you to take care of everything else for me and free up my time. Answering the phone, taking payments, accepting deliveries, shit like that. And the pay is good."

Joseph laughed and pushed himself out of the chair. "Payment is not necessary. I'm glad to help out."

CHAPTER 64

Joseph sat behind the counter in Gage's shop. He'd been there helping out for three days and so far things had gone well. Gage had showed him all the processes for taking appointments, ordering parts and everything else that went into running the shop. There were a few things Joseph thought might be helpful to tweak, and it would be an extra boost for business if he could get Luis or someone like him in to do custom paint jobs. But overall he was impressed with Gage's business.

They were about fifteen minutes away from closing when a group of sports bikes rode through the open garage door. Joseph went over to greet them, but Gage stood up from the bike he was working on and got to them first. The guy in the front had barely taken off his helmet when Gage barked his question at him.

"What do you guys need?"

Joseph's eyebrows shot up at the note of clear hostility in Gage's voice. The rider looked taken aback too, his young face showing his hesitance as he explained what he needed done.

Gage flicked his eyes over the bike. "We're a man down so it'll be awhile before I can get to it. You might want to check out another shop."

The young man ran his hand over his curly red hair. "Oh, that sucks. I heard you were one of the best in town."

Joseph stepped in when Gage just shrugged. "Hi, I'm Joseph." He stuck his hand out. "Nice to meet you."

The young man accepted his handshake. "I'm Dave."

"I like your bike. We can get that taken care of for you. Like Gage said, it might be a small wait." The work Dave needed done wouldn't keep him from safely riding his bike. "Why don't you bring your bike back in three days so it's not just sitting here in the shop?" He went over everything with the guy and then checked with Gage for verification of everything he'd said.

Gage had removed himself from the conversation and was back to working on the bike. He didn't bother to look up when Joseph addressed him. All he got in response was a surly "*Yeah.*" Dave was again looking uncomfortable so Joseph made a joke.

"Somebody didn't get their morning coffee. Makes him cranky all day." The guy laughed a little and pulled his brightly colored helmet back on. When they were gone, Joseph went over to close the garage door and turn off the open sign. He walked back to Gage, who was still on his knees in front of the bike.

"What was that?"

Gage still didn't look up. "What do you mean?"

"C'mon man. You were a complete dick to that guy. I haven't seen you talk to any other customers like that."

Gage kept refusing to look at him, continuing to turn the wrench in his hand. "Just didn't like him."

"Why not? You don't even know him."

"I just don't like the guys who come in here on those stupid fucking crotch rockets. That's why."

"Are you kidding me? You dislike an entire subset of motorcycle culture?"

"Yep. You got a problem with that?"

Joseph was taken aback that Gage's hostility seemed to be moving to him when it clicked in his head what the problem was. His former boyfriend Riley had been into trick riding. And sports bikes, or crotch rockets as Gage called them, were the types of bikes trick riders favored. Joseph started to back off. He knew how Riley's death had affected Gage. But then he remembered what Max had said. Gage was going to have to get stuff straightened out in his head before he could really move on. His guilt over Riley's death was undoubtedly one of them. So

Joseph decided to push. "Was Riley wearing a helmet when he died?"

Gage went still, the wrench ceasing to turn. "No. Why?"

Joseph shrugged. "Just wondering. Seems stupid to ride a motorcycle without a helmet, especially while doing stunts."

The wrench clattered to the floor, the metallic clang loud and echoing in the large space. Joseph pushed on. "Even more stupid for you to hate an entire group of people for his mistake when they had nothing to do with it."

Gage shot to his feet, a hard glare on his face. "What the fuck did you just say to me?"

Joseph crossed his arms over his chest. "You heard me. Riley made a dumb decision and he died for it. He still might have died even if he were wearing a helmet. But not wearing one didn't help. And you being an asshole to potential customers because of it is crazy." Gage took three quick strides forward, getting right up in his face. Joseph unfolded his arms. He forced himself to stand his ground and look into the hard eyes snapping with vicious anger.

"It's my fucking business. I'll be an asshole to whoever I fucking want to," Gage snarled.

Joseph kept his voice calm. He wasn't attacking Gage, he just wanted him to see how he was still letting Riley's death affect him. "It's ridiculous letting personal stuff make you lose customers. Because I bet you if I hadn't stepped in that guy would have ridden off, costing you money. He still might not come back after the attitude you served him."

"I don't give a shit if he comes back or not. I don't need him or any of the other idiots I've run out of here."

"You can't blame every trick rider for his mistake."

Gage's fingers flexed once, his nostrils flaring. He was clearly trying to keep from blowing up. "I don't."

"You do. Instead of accepting Riley's death as a stupid, horrible accident, you take all the blame for him running off half-cocked that night. But then you refuse to acknowledge that guilt, so you shove it off onto other trick riders because hate is an easier emotion for you to deal with."

Gage sneered. "You're about two hundred pounds, a stupid Texas accent and a cheap suit away from becoming Dr. Phil."

Joseph let the insult roll over him. "You're pissed. Because you know I'm right. Will you hold on to that anger or get it out of your system?" Gage took a step back, his chest pumping. But Joseph followed him. "No drugs to calm you, Gage. You and I both know how you get that anger from underneath your skin." He put a hand on Gage's chest, feeling the warm pad of muscle and the rapid heartbeat just beneath. "Will you use me to get it out?"

Joseph leaned forward and gave Gage a soft kiss. Gage's lips remained closed, the kiss unreturned. Joseph didn't give up. "Use me," he whispered against Gage's mouth. Gage grabbed a tight fistful of Joseph's loose hair and yanked his head back. He didn't say anything, just continued to glare, a muscle jumping in his clenched jaw. Joseph's neck was stretched past the point of being comfortable, but he kept his eyes on Gage's, ignoring the sharp pain prickling his scalp. "Use me," he repeated.

As soon as the words left his mouth, Gage's lips crashed onto his. Gage kissed him hard in a fury of lips and teeth and tongue. Joseph felt his lip split, but he didn't protest. Instead, he wrapped his arms around Gage, pulling him closer. He felt Gage's foot behind his ankle, but before he realized what was happening, Gage had tripped him and pushed him down to the floor. Gage dropped to his knees, immediately climbing on top of him.

"You don't know what you're talking about." Gage ripped his shirt off, his muscles tense as he reached for

Joseph's and tore his away too. "But I'll use you if that's what you want."

Joseph raised up to aid in getting the shirt off. "I *do* want you to use me. And I *do* know what I'm talking about."

Gage didn't answer. He just shoved Joseph back down and took off his shoes and jeans. Gage paused when Joseph lay on the bare concrete, naked except for a pair of black briefs. His eyes locked on Gage's, Joseph raised his hips. Gage's lip curled in anger as he stared down at him. And even though Gage was rough as he yanked his briefs off, Joseph was pretty sure it was anger at himself. When he was naked, Gage pushed Joseph's legs apart and practically fell on him. He immediately thrust his tongue into his ass and Joseph groaned. He slid one hand into Gage's hair while he stroked himself off with the other. Gage's fingers dug into his ass, pulling him closer against his mouth. Joseph raised his legs and locked them around Gage's shoulders. He felt the hot breath of Gage's words brushing over his skin, but couldn't tell what he was saying. From the tone and the way Gage's fingers kept pressing hard into his skin, Joseph assumed it wasn't anything nice. Joseph dropped his legs and reached for Gage. He ignored the curse that shot from Gage's mouth and yanked him up until they were face to face.

"You know I'm right," he whispered again. Before Gage could respond Joseph pulled him down into a kiss. They tongued each other fiercely, Gage's anger and Joseph's determination cycling between them as they rolled around on the dirty floor, fighting for dominance. Joseph felt Gage's fury under his skin everywhere Gage licked, or gripped, or bit him. He shoved his own emotions right back onto Gage, refusing to give up control and let Gage do nothing but take. Joseph would give him what he needed.

Joseph's cock was stiff, rubbing against Gage's jeans when he got the upper hand in their struggle to be on top. Twisting their legs together, Joseph used his lower body strength to keep Gage subdued as long as he could. He kissed him, while his hands went straight to the waistband of Gage's jeans. Swiftly opening them, Joseph pulled them down just far enough to get at Gage's cock. Gage hissed as Joseph wrapped his hand around it and he squeezed hard, loving the thick heat of Gage's shaft against his palm.

He'd barely had the chance to pump Gage off when his boyfriend grabbed his shoulders and threw him back to the ground. Gage reared up over him. This time Joseph lay compliant, letting Gage win control. He watched as Gage spit into his hand and smeared it along his cock.

"You wanted it like this. So don't expect me to get up and get the goddamn lube."

"I don't expect you to do anything except fuck me." Joseph ran his tongue over his bottom lip. "And realize that I'm right."

Gage's eyes narrowed as he gripped his cock and started to push into him. He reached up and wrapped a hand around Joseph's neck. Joseph placed his hand over Gage's, digging his fingernails into his wrist. He didn't try to pull Gage away, he just wanted him to feel the pain. Gage continued to glare down at him as he slowly pushed inside. Joseph's eyes nearly crossed at the delicious pressure of Gage sliding into him, raising his hips to speed the process along. Gage got the hint and slammed fully into him, making both of them grunt in a mix of pain and pleasure. Gage kept himself braced on the floor with one hand, the other still wrapped around Joseph's neck. He squeezed, not enough to cut off Joseph's air, but enough for him to feel the control that Gage wanted over him. Joseph gave into it, tilting his head back and letting Gage fuck him harder than he ever had before.

In the back of his mind, Joseph was aware that the hard floor was hurting his back. He was aware that he was sliding slightly in a spill of oil on the ground. But he wasn't focused on that. He was focused on Gage. He ran his fingers up the arm Gage was holding him down with, feeling the soft hair and hard, bunched muscles. "That's right, Gage. Take it out on me." Gage lowered his head as he pumped into him, his hair falling into his eyes. Still, Joseph saw the wild storm of emotion in those eyes. He saw it in the bitter curl to Gage's lip and the angry flush on his face. Joseph smiled and decided to push again. He reached down and slapped his hands onto Gage's ass, digging his fingers in just as deep as Gage had done to him. "This is nothing. I said use me, Gage."

Gage's eyes opened wide in angry surprise before they narrowed again. Gage's fingers clenched even tighter on his throat, his lips parting to release what might as well have been a growl. "I'll fucking use you." He lowered himself until they were pressed together, chest to chest, lips to lips. "Use you so goddamn hard you won't be able to feel anything but me. I'll fucking take you over."

Joseph stared up at Gage. "You already have."

Gage blinked. He paused in his movements so briefly that Joseph almost missed it. Then he was moving again, kissing Joseph as he pumped into him with rough and frantic thrusts. Joseph wrapped his legs and arms around Gage. He relished the heat and the sweat, the pain and the pleasure, the hardness of Gage's body on top of him, the stiffness of Gage's cock inside him. He moaned shamelessly, wanting to just lay there and take it all in, to let it soak into his pores. But he remembered that he'd started this for a reason.

Joseph pushed at Gage's shoulders forcing him to roll over onto his back. He grabbed Gage by the back of the neck and yanked him up to a sitting position. Joseph held on tight, digging his fingers in deep to the thick muscles of Gage's neck. Now it was his knees that were pressed against the cold, dirty concrete but he still ignored it as he slid up and down on Gage's cock, riding him furiously. Gage's hands settled on his hips, helping him move. Joseph pulled him even closer, staring into eyes still bright with fury.

"Forgive yourself, Gage. It wasn't your fault."

Gage raked his nails down his back so hard Joseph felt the skin break in several places. He hissed, arching his back, making his cock rub stiffly against Gage's stomach.

Gage spoke from between clenched teeth. "You don't know shit."

"I know you can't keep pushing your anger and guilt about it onto everybody who rides the same type of bike." He moved his fingers from Gage's neck up to his hair, grabbing a handful of the short strands. "Fucking let it go." Joseph kissed him hard, shoving his tongue into Gage's mouth, taking complete control of the kiss. Gage fought him for that control, but Joseph refused to relinquish it. He bit at Gage's lip, tugging at it before kissing him deeply again. Gage raked the nails of one hand down his back again, the fingers of the other hand tangled in his hair. They held on to each other tight as Joseph kept fucking himself onto Gage's cock, still thrusting his tongue into his mouth. Finally, he felt Gage give a little. Felt his lips and tongue soften. Gage's grip on his hips eased, his hands guiding instead of demanding.

Joseph brought both hands up to cradle Gage's head, gentling the power of his kiss. He pulled back and looked at Gage. Saw that he'd calmed. Some. Just a little bit. His eyes were still bright and full of emotion. But they were no longer wild. Joseph brushed his lips over the stubble along Gage's jaw up to his ear. "Let it go, Gage." He heard Gage curse softly. Then his arms went around Joseph's waist in a tight hug, holding him close against his body.

Joseph slowed his movements just enough to be able to whisper in Gage's ear. "I'm here, Gage. And I want to feel you come inside me." Gage moaned his name, the muscles of his arms and thighs going rigid as he buried his face in Joseph's neck. Gage groaned and cursed his way through a body shuddering orgasm. Joseph groaned too, pumping himself off as he felt Gage swelling thick and hot inside him. He followed with his own climax immediately after. The intensity of their coupling magnified the power of his release, making his stomach clench tight and his breath hitch in his throat. They'd raised a crazy powerful storm between them. Joseph hoped when it calmed, Gage's conscious would finally be clear.

The tension eased from his body, Joseph relaxed against Gage, who took his weight. But he stayed sitting up, his face still shoved against his neck. Gage turned his head slightly and Joseph felt the roughness of his light beard. And the dampness of tears. But he didn't remark on it. Gage didn't say anything either.

Eventually, Gage eased to his back on the floor and Joseph rolled off of him to his side. But he didn't go far. Gage's arms stayed wrapped tight around him. Joseph winced as he pressed against one of his scratches. Gage's eyes went wide and he rolled Joseph to his front so that he could look at his back.

"Jesus…"

Joseph turned back around and looked at Gage. His eyes were red and his fingers shook as he reached up to stroke them along Joseph's jaw.

"Fuck. Joseph, don't push me like that. Don't do that again."

Joseph reached up and grabbed his fingers, squeezing them tight. "Shut up. Fuck those scratches. Whatever you need, I'll give it to you, Gage."

CHAPTER 65

Gage carefully rubbed ointment onto the smooth back in front of him. They'd both just come from the shower, cleaning up after what went down at his shop. Joseph's skin was flushed from the hot water. Certain areas of his back were even redder. The places where he'd set his nails into Joseph's skin and gouged him like he was a fucking animal. Gage's face burned with embarrassed disgust at himself. He'd promised himself that he'd be careful with Joseph, that he'd never hurt him. Already he'd failed. "I'm sorry," he said in a hoarse voice.

Joseph looked over his shoulder at him. "It's okay. It'll be worth it if it makes you open up to me."

Gage sighed. He closed the tube and wiped his fingers on the towel he'd brought out with him. "I honestly thought I had. I told you the story of what happened and it felt good to get it off my chest. I figured that was enough."

Joseph turned around fully to face him. "Did you know that you were taking your anger out on sports bike guys?"

"Yeah, I knew it. But it made sense, you know? I just had so much rage at the way Riley lost his life. And in my fucked up head, blaming the machine and everyone involved with them made so much sense, you know?"

Joseph nodded, his face showing concern. "I get it. But it's not healthy to hold that inside. How long has it been since Riley died? You never told me."

"Five years."

"Five years. Five years you've been blaming yourself for Riley's death. Why?"

Gage looked down, running a hand through his still damp hair. "Why wouldn't I? It was my fucking fault."

Joseph's fingers dug into his thigh, making him jerk in pained surprise. He looked up to find Joseph's green eyes practically glowing as they burned into his.

"Did you force him out of the house?"

"No."

"Did you make him ride without a helmet?"

"No."

"Did you make him fall off his bike?"

Gage clenched his jaw. The logical part of him understood what Joseph was getting at. But the guilt was a big heavy thing. He'd pushed it to the back of his mind for years, now that it was out in the open it weighed him down. Made him remember what a bastard he'd been. It clawed at his skin, making him burn with shame.

"Tell me, Gage. If you didn't do any of those things, how is Riley's death your fault?"

Gage set his hands on the mattress and shoved himself back, away from Joseph, until he was resting against the headboard. "Because I was the asshole always pushing and trying to get what I wanted. I didn't know how to handle being told no. I'd push and push until Riley would lose his shit and come right back at me. And whenever our fights got out of control Riley would take off. I knew that, but I couldn't ever just let shit go."

Joseph crawled forward on the bed. When Joseph tapped him on the thigh, Gage opened his legs so he could kneel between them. Apparently Joseph didn't want them separated. As Gage felt the warmth of Joseph's skin easing onto his, he realized he didn't want them separated either.

"You both handled your fights badly. But you guys weren't the only couple in the world that doesn't know how to argue without blowing shit out of proportion. Yes, you could have stopped antagonizing him and yes he could have found another outlet for his anger other than getting on the back of a dangerous machine when his head wasn't in the game. But that's not what happened."

Gage scoffed. "What's that saying about hindsight again?" He saw Joseph's lips press together in what was clearly frustration and felt like an ass. Joseph was trying to help him, but he just couldn't let that guilt go. It had been a part of him for so long.

"Was Riley a petty person?"

"What?"

"Was he a jerk, a douchebag, a shit head?"

"No! What the fuck, Joseph? Riley was a good guy."

"I believe you. So if Riley was a good guy do you think he'd be holding a grudge against you for an accident? A shitty unfortunate accident? Do you think he'd want you to keep blaming yourself for this to the point where you can't fully move on and … grow close to anyone else?"

Gage looked at Joseph kneeling in front of him. He hadn't missed Joseph's hesitation. He knew he'd been about to say something else. A four letter word. A small word. A big word. That word wasn't in his vocabulary. Not even when he'd been with Riley. They'd never said that word to each other. He thought of Riley, his sunny disposition only broken by the quick flashes of temper that always blew over after a ride on his bike. As always Gage felt regret that his life had ended so soon. "I loved Riley. I never told him, but I did." He huffed out a short breath. "Just one more thing I did wrong."

Joseph reached for his hand, lacing their fingers together. "You might not have told him, but he knew. People have a way of realizing someone loves them even though the words might not be said."

Looking at Joseph, Gage thought of the two helmets he'd bought. One for Joseph so he could ride his Indian. The one bike that he'd *never* let anyone else ride. The other helmet he'd bought for himself to put Joseph's mind at ease. Gage wasn't an idiot. He knew what that signified. And apparently Joseph did too. But he wasn't ready to go there yet. There was something else he needed to say first.

"Four little words Gage. Say them and let it go."

Gage looked at Joseph, who knelt there patiently watching him. He looked like he was prepared to stay in that spot until Gage said what he wanted to hear. His nostrils flared and he had to force himself to open his mouth. He spoke, his voice low and hoarse, the words barely audible. But he got them out. "It wasn't my fault."

Joseph smiled and Gage reached up to tangle his fingers in Joseph's hair. It was so thick and curly, unlike the silky straight blonde that had graced Riley's head. He tugged, bringing Joseph down closer to him. "Kiss me," he said.

The smile still on his face, Joseph came close enough to softly press their lips together. They kissed lightly, Joseph's warm breath heating his mouth, his palm coming up to rest against Gage's chest. Joseph eased back.

"Say it one more time for me, Gage. I promise it'll be easier."

"It wasn't my fault." This time when Gage said the words, he didn't feel he was choking on them. He realized it wasn't a betrayal to Riley to say them. Muscles he didn't realize were tense eased. Gage said it again, this time looking Joseph directly in the eye as he did. "It wasn't my fault."

Joseph leaned in for another soft kiss, whispering against his mouth, "It wasn't your fault."

CHAPTER 66

So if you switched to an accounting program it'd be much easier for you. You wouldn't have to dick around with Excel anymore."

Gage looked over at Joseph sitting behind his customer service counter. Today was the last day he'd be helping him out in the shop. Danny returned tomorrow. Gage decided to bring up something that had been on his mind in one form or another for a while now. "You know what would really make things easier for me?"

"What's that?"

"If you came to work for me."

Joseph's head snapped up from behind the computer monitor. "What?"

Gage stood, nervously wiping his grimy hands on his jeans. "Come work for me. You can do all those upgrades you've been harping on about. And you can take over the paperwork side of things. Plenty to keep you busy." He decided to bite the bullet and go for it all. He approached the counter. "And move in with me. You haven't been back to your place in weeks."

Joseph just stared at him, his eyes wide. "Wow, man."

Gage took a step back. That wow hadn't sounded like Joseph was impressed with his ideas. More like he thought Gage was crazy. Gage flexed his fingers, fighting the urge to let them ball up in a fist of frustration. "Forget it," he said as he turned to go back to the bike he'd been working on.

"No, I won't forget it. You wouldn't have asked if it wasn't something you've been thinking about. But this is the first time I'm hearing about it, so give me a minute to catch up."

Gage rolled his head on his shoulders and turned back around to face Joseph. He tried to make light of the situation. "All you need is a minute?" he teased with a light leer.

Joseph grinned but didn't pick up that ball. "I'll move in with you."

Gage grinned too. That had gone much easier than he expected. He started to head over to his lover, but his next words made him slow in his approach.

"But … I can't come work for you, Gage. I need to focus on getting my practice off the ground. That's going to take a lot of time and energy if I want to do it right."

Gage came to a stop. He didn't know why, but for some reason, Joseph's plans to start his own firm made him feel … twitchy. Whenever Joseph brought them up, Gage wanted to tell him to just forget about it. He'd rather Joseph concentrated on racing, pool and being with him. But he didn't say that. He was getting one thing he wanted, Joseph permanently under his roof. He'd be happy with that for now.

Gage went up to the counter. Instead of going around it, he planted his palms on the thick glass and vaulted over it. Landing next to Joseph, he leaned in and planted a big, smacking kiss on his mouth. Joseph groaned, making like he was disgusted. But Gage could tell from his smile that he liked it. "Let's get out of here and celebrate."

Joseph shut the computer down. "What are we going to do, celebrate our cohabitation by picking out a new dinette set? Or maybe new sheets?" he joked.

"That's not a bad idea. I wouldn't mind seeing you spread out on red silk sheets. Or maybe gold to match that gorgeous skin of yours."

"Are you sure it's alright if we leave early?" Joseph asked as he flicked off the *Open* sign. "I don't want you to fall behind."

Gage tossed an arm over Joseph's shoulders, herding him out of the shop. "It's cool. I know the owner."

****

It was finally race day. Joseph stood a few steps away from his bike. He was nervous. Other than his practice runs, he'd never raced on this track. It was bigger and there were a lot more competitors than what he was used to. The crowd was huge too, adding a little more pressure. But Joseph was prepared. He'd gotten lots of track time in, getting used to the Continental Trail Attacks he'd switched to. They were slick and light. He had to take serious care to keep control of the bike on them. But they were superfast so he was okay with the tradeoff. Joseph popped his knuckles and bounced on his feet a few times. He could do this. He didn't even have to place. It was his first time here, he just needed to get the lay of the land so to speak and put in a good showing.

"You ready?"

Joseph swung around at Gage's voice. He'd been over at his bike with the guys he'd brought on board to be his pit crew. He liked them all. There was Danny of course and two others, Fred and Tony. Joseph had gotten to know them pretty well being around Gage's shop and now having them on his crew. They were all helpful and it felt good to know he had back up for this race. They'd be there to keep him tuned up for anything that needed adjusting tonight. He finally answered Gage.

"Yes, I'm ready."

Gage's eyes narrowed and he tilted his head as he looked at him. "No, you're not. You got a bunch of other shit in your head. Get it out."

Joseph's eyebrows shot up. "What?"

"I said get it out. You can't win if you're not focused on winning. So do that screaming banshee routine you do before your races and get that bullshit out of your head."

Joseph stared at Gage who only looked back at him in dead seriousness. He hadn't planned on doing that tonight, thinking that with the bigger race on a bigger stage that he should have a little more decorum. Apparently Gage didn't agree. "I don't have my-." Gage cut him off before he could finish.

"Got 'em right here." He reached into his back pocket and pulled out Joseph's phone, his earbuds wrapped around it.

Joseph took the technology out of Gage's hand. He put one of the ear buds in, slightly self-conscious. Gage spoke up again.

"Fuck everybody else, Joseph. It's just you, your bike and that track. Do what you have to do to get to that place."

Joseph couldn't hold back his grin at Gage's encouragement. He popped the other ear bud in and scrolled through his phone until he got to the song he wanted. Closing his eyes he listened as the wild beat and rough voice of his favorite band filled his ears. He threw his head back, letting the drums and guitar fill him up. Joseph blocked everything out. The other racers, the noise of the crowd, even Gage. He felt the cool wind brush over him, drying the sweat on his forehead. Felt the asphalt vibrating from the current race under his motorcycle boots. Joseph pictured himself winning. Pictured himself laying damn near on his side as he took the curves of the track. He pumped his fist, jumping around in a circle as he saw his bike shoot past everyone else to edge over the finish line first. The song built to a crescendo and Joseph built with it until he screamed at the end, his mind finally clear.

He took the ear buds out, still hyped, his blood pumping. Joseph grinned at Gage. "Thanks, man."

Gage grinned back. "No problem. I know what your crazy ass needs."

Joseph went over to his bike, full of confidence now. That inner monologue about he didn't even have to place *had* been bullshit. He was here to win. Not just make a good showing. Joseph swung his leg over his bike. He was just about to put his helmet on when Gage stopped him.

"So remember that incentive program I told you about?"

Joseph had to think for a minute before the conversation he'd had with Gage and Gia at her bar came to mind. "Yeah. I remember. What's the incentive?"

"Well, here's the deal, Joseph. You come in third place and I'll give you the best blowjob you've ever had in your life. I'll suck you so good and have you yelling so loud, the neighbors will think I'm killing you and call the cops."

Joseph had to grin at the cocky smile on Gage's mouth. But as the recipient of plenty of his blow jobs, he knew the man had reason to be so sure of his skills.

Bikes started up all around them, the revving and rumbling loud and echoing as the noise bounced off the metal overhang. Gage leaned in close to whisper in his ear. "If you come in second, I'll fuck you just the way you like. Hard and deep and fast. I won't even let you get all the way out of this suit. Just peel it down enough to bare that sweet ass. I'll have you up against the wall, your hair in my fist. You're such a slut about it, I could probably make you come just by pulling on it."

Joseph looked at Gage with his heart racing, his body practically vibrating with lust. He hoped it was possible to ride with a hard-on. Because he was about to. He let Gage take the helmet from his hands and carefully push it down onto his head. Joseph slid the visor up. Swallowing hard, he asked the question burning in his brain. "And what about…" He cleared his throat. "What if I win?"

"Oh, if you win?" Gage shoved his hands in his pockets. A slow smile curled his lips as he took a step back. "If you win, Joseph, I'll let *you* fuck *me* however you want for as long as you want."

CHAPTER 67

If you win Joseph, I'll let you fuck me, however you want, for as long as you want."

Gage's voice echoed in Joseph's head as he sat at the starting line. *Jesus Fucking Christ.* He didn't know why Gage had even bothered to give him his music to pump him up. That "incentive program" was enough to do it all on its own. Trust Gage to come up with yet another way to push him right to the edge.

Joseph got focused as the announcer called everyone's attention to the track. He zeroed in on the light, watching as it turned from red to yellow to green. The instant it changed, Joseph released the clutch and took off. He was tempted to go all out from the start, but knew he had to pace himself and his bike. This was the longest race he'd ever done, fourteen laps of 2.2 miles each, with a lot of nasty turns. He rode smart and he rode clean, staying at the front of the pack. Coming up on the third turn, Joseph leaned into the curve. His bike responded beautifully, his left knee so close to the ground he could feel the friction in the air over the asphalt. Joseph smiled inside his helmet. He loved these new tires, they had the perfect combination of slip and grip.

He took the next curve with the same confidence. But as he came out of it a rider cut in front of him, too close to be safe. Joseph's eyes widened and he got a good look at the black and blue suit of the rider. His heart in his throat, he felt the back tire of the powerful machine start to lose traction.

****

Gage watched from the pit as Joseph dominated the beginning of the race. He was holding his own, riding aggressively enough to stay in the front of the pack without blowing his load and taking off from it too early. He was impressed. And he might be biased because Joseph was his, but it looked to him like Joseph had the talent and mental strength to move past amateur racing and into the professional circuit. He hated to see him miss out on the opportunity. It wasn't the only reason Gage wanted him to focus solely on racing, but it was a big part of it. Danny, Fred and Tony came up to him.

"He's looking good out there," Fred said.

Gage nodded, about to respond. But he stopped, tensing up as he noticed a rider in blue cut Joseph off. What the fuck was that asshole doing? That was a dick move and could cause a pile up of several racers on the track. He watched, his fists clenched, hoping Joseph would handle the dangerous situation.

****

Joseph's jaw clenched tight, but he stayed calm. He didn't fight his bike. Keeping it loose, using only the tiniest adjustment to prevent himself from going into a slide. He had control of the bike again in an instant. Joseph increased his speed, ready to overtake the other rider. He was tempted to return the favor, but for all he knew it had been an accident. Ignoring the urge, Joseph kept his cool.

He'd fallen behind but he didn't let that throw him either. Regaining his position wasn't easy, but he managed it. He got his head firmly in the game, flying past the others on the straightaways and taking each turn with tight precision. Just like always, it was only him, his bike and the track.

As they approached the end of the race, Joseph was in front. He could see the podium with the checkered flag ready to be waved. He had his sight set on the thick yellow line painted across the asphalt. And out of the corner of his eye, he could see the bright blue of that other rider coming up fast on his right. Joseph's lip curled and he bent even further over his bike. No fucking way he was letting that rider take this victory from him.

****

Joseph was sweaty inside his bike suit. He unzipped it a little and took off his helmet to breathe in the cool air. People were cheering. A girl in the crowd raised her shirt, flashing her tits. And over the loudspeaker, Joseph heard: *"And stealing a hairsbreadth of a victory, newcomer, Joseph Naderi!"*

Grinning, Joseph raised his helmet over his head, waving it at the crowd. He'd done it. He'd won the race in spite of the asshole riding dirty on the track. Now, he had a prize to collect. But before he could ride off he was approached by the announcer, who had a microphone in his hand. Joseph went through an interview, happy to answer questions on the race, get in a few plugs for his sponsors and let these new fans get to know him. To his frustration, that wasn't the end of the celebration. The paddock girls, racing's version of cheerleaders, came over and draped a first place medal around his neck. Joseph posed for pictures with them and a few others.

Finally, everyone stepped back. Joseph put his helmet back on and started his bike. He sped off, popping a wheelie and riding it almost all the way to the pit. One last burst of applause broke out over the track at his winning salute.

Slowing his speed to a crawl, Joseph rode right up to Gage. He was standing there waiting, his arms crossed over his chest. Taking his helmet back off, he cut the key. "I won."

"Yes, you did," Gage answered with a smirk.

Joseph kept eye contact with his boyfriend as he swung a leg over the bike to dismount. He walked over to him, determined to find some place private and close so Gage could make good on his promise. Before he reached him however, Gage's eyes flicked away, over Joseph's shoulder.

"Looks like you got some people who want to congratulate you."

Joseph turned. Danny, Fred, and Tony were there of course, clapping as they walked towards him. And so were Max, Lila, Gia, Nate, Renee, Nico and several others. Joseph was glad to see his friends, even though he groaned inwardly. It looked like the celebration he was looking forward to was going to have to wait.

****

Gage pulled into the parking lot of Big G's Bar and Grill. The lot was packed, Joseph recognizing several cars and bikes that belonged to his friends. There were also cars he didn't recognize, but they had racing stickers on them. Joseph figured his announcement that he'd be at Big G's afterwards had brought the fans out. He was glad to see it, since bringing Gia some traffic was the whole reason she'd agreed to sponsor him. Danny, who'd ridden over with him and Gage, spoke up from the back seat.

"Hope you're not too hungry Joseph. It might be awhile before you get that celebratory steak with this crowd."

Joseph laughed as he got out of the truck with Danny and Gage, the three of them walking up to the door. Just before they reached it, Joseph grabbed Gage's wrist and held him back, letting Danny go in without them. Joseph pulled Gage around to the side of the building, Gage following without a word. He pushed Gage up against the wall. "I won," he said again.

Gage's lips curled in a slow smile. "I know. I was there."

"I want my prize." He leaned in and kissed the smile off Gage's mouth. Joseph kissed him hard, sucking at his tongue and nipping his bottom lip. Joseph pressed his body close against his boyfriend's, rubbing against him.

Gage raised his arm. Joseph thought he was going to put it around him. But Gage, unpredictable as always, raised it over his head, resting the back of his hand against the brick wall. He tucked the fingers of the other into the waistband of his jeans, tugging them down slightly. Gage thrust his hips up and Joseph felt the hardness of Gage's erection against his thigh.

"So Joseph gets to fuck me." He darted his tongue out, running it over his lip. "You sure you want to do this here and now, Pretty Boy? It won't be very comfortable." Gage looked to his right, at the dumpster down the alley. "And it stinks," he said, wrinkling his nose. "But we can if that's what you want. It'll still be good." He thrust his hips forward again. "Just thought you'd want to do this at home. In the bed. Or on the couch. Maybe the floor. Hell, you can fuck me in the front yard if that's what you want. It's all about you, Big Winner."

Joseph ran his eyes over his boyfriend. His jacket fell open, showing the t-shirt tight over his chest. The shirt rode up a little at the hem, revealing a sliver of hard torso. He raised his gaze back to Gage's, seeing the teasing gleam in his dark eyes. Joseph leaned in to kiss Gage once more, his growl of frustration rolling into his lover's mouth. Gage was right. He didn't want this to be rushed, up against a wall in a smelly alley. He took a step back but gripped the front of Gage's shirt in his fist. Gage's eyebrows shot up at his aggression.

"Don't order the chicken. It takes fucking forever to cook." He yanked Gage away from the wall. "Let's go eat."

CHAPTER 68

inally. They were finally at home after dinner and hanging at Gia's bar for a couple of hours. When the waiter had come by to take their order, Gage asked about the chicken. Joseph kicked him under the table and with an exaggerated sigh, Gage closed his menu and said, "Looks like I'll be getting the sausage tonight." Joseph had burst out laughing, refusing to tell the others at the table what was so funny.

Now they were home. Gage headed upstairs.

"Guess I'll take a shower."

Joseph followed behind him, watching as he shrugged out of his leather jacket on the way up. When they were in the bedroom, Joseph hooked a finger into the back of Gage's jeans, stopping him before he could go into the bathroom. Gage looked over his shoulder at him with an eyebrow raised.

"You can shower after," Joseph said.

Gage turned completely around. "You sure about that, Joseph? I'm kinda dirty."

Joseph shook his head and pulled Gage close. "You know I like you dirty. Sometimes I think you come home with extra grime on your clothes just to get me riled up."

Gage grinned. "Maybe."

Joseph gripped the back of Gage's neck, sliding his fingers up into the short strands of his hair. He pulled his lover in for a kiss. It was soft this time. Now that he had Gage here in their bedroom, knowing he'd be inside him soon, he wasn't as frantic. He didn't want to, but Joseph ended their kiss so he could pull Gage's shirt over his head. Once Gage's broad chest and thick arms were revealed, Joseph ran his palms over the warm, firm skin over his lover. He bent low enough to brush his lips everywhere he'd touched. Glancing up at Gage, who was watching him closely, Joseph sucked a nipple into his mouth, pulling hard, running his teeth over it as he sucked. Gage winced, a muscle flexing in his jaw. But when Joseph pulled back, Gage grabbed his head, guiding him to his other nipple. Joseph smiled just before he sucked that one into his mouth, this time biting down a little bit harder.

Gage's hips rocked forward and Joseph looked down, noting the hard bulge behind the denim of his jeans. He straightened and gripped Gage's hips. His thumbs teased over his waistband as he brought their bodies close, rubbing their shafts together. But with Gage still in his jeans and Joseph in his racing suit, the layers of material kept them from fully feeling each other.

Joseph walked backwards to the bed, his hand again behind Gage's head to keep their lips fused together in a kiss. Ignoring the fact that he still had his motorcycle boots on, Joseph eased back onto the bed to sit with his back against the headboard. With the grip Joseph had on him, Gage hadn't had any choice but to follow. Now Joseph pulled him in between his legs. "Suck me."

"You still have your bike suit on."

Joseph arched a brow. "I know. Maybe I'll fuck you while I'm wearing it."

"Fine with me," Gage said with a smile. He unzipped the suit, tugging it open just enough to get at Joseph's erect cock. When Gage took him into his mouth, Joseph groaned, pressing his head back against the headboard. He spread his legs wider and gripped Gage's head with both hands, pushing him up and down so that Gage was sucking him at the pace that he wanted.

Joseph watched Gage from heavy-lidded eyes. Gage's mouth was hot and wet on his cock, his tongue devilishly playful as he teased from the underside of the head, all the way down to his balls. The way Gage kneeled there as he sucked had his ass slightly in the air. The back of his jeans gaped and Joseph saw that he wasn't wearing any underwear. With another groan, Joseph pulled Gage up and rolled him to his back in one smooth motion.

"As much as I love the way you give head, I don't think I can handle too much of it tonight if I want to be inside you for long."

Gage laughed. "Guess we'll have to keep practicing till you can."

Joseph shuddered at the thought of not only having Gage tonight, but again as well. He slid on top of his boyfriend, kissing him deep and hungry. Joseph circled his hips, pressing down and grinding his erection against Gage's over and over. To his surprise, Gage's legs came up, squeezing him tight. His eyes closed, his head arched back into the pillows. Joseph pulled back to stare in wonder. He'd never seen Gage look so vulnerable during sex. He liked it. And he appreciated that a man as dominant as Gage didn't have a problem opening up to him like this. Leaning down again, he ran his tongue down Gage's throat, before sucking the skin into his mouth. He left a passion mark of his own, just as Gage so often did to him.

The kissing and grinding went on until Joseph was so hard, he thought he'd explode before he ever got inside his boyfriend. He eased off of Gage to quickly open his pants and flip him over onto his stomach. Gage exhaled in a startled rush, but it turned to a groan as Joseph pulled his jeans down and caressed his ass, slipping his hand around to grasp his cock. Joseph pumped him slowly, watching in surprised delight as Gage's hips rolled back into his touch. He took both hands and cupped Gage's ass, squeezing and cupping the firm curves. Joseph could have watched Gage writhing like that for him all night, but that wasn't all he wanted. He shrugged out of the top of his bike suit, pushing it down enough to completely free his stiff cock.

Leaning over to their nightstand, he got a bottle of lube. He slicked himself up first, then poured some between Gage's ass. After tossing the bottle on the floor,

Joseph eased a finger in. He watched Gage, waiting to see if there was any resistance. There wasn't. Gage was relaxed beneath him. Until Joseph brushed his finger over a smooth spot inside him. Then Gage tensed. His eyes opened wide, a sound that was a sultry mix of grunt and moan escaping his parted lips. Joseph smiled and continued to stimulate that spot, adding another slick finger. He leaned down and took Gage's earlobe between his teeth, sucking it into his mouth and whispering, "You like that?"

"Fuck yeah," Gage answered. "Bet I'd like it even more if that was your dick rubbing against me like that."

Joseph had to laugh. Taking his fingers away, he grasped his cock. He didn't push inside yet, just slid his shaft up and down between the tight curves of his lover's ass. It looked amazing and felt even better.

"This is how you want me?" Gage asked, his voice muffled slightly by the pillows beneath him.

"Yeah," Joseph said. He rubbed his face over the back of Gage's neck. "So I can smell the sweat on your skin and breathe in the scent of exhaust in your hair. I love the way you smell, Gage. My sexy, dirty bad boy." Joseph licked the bump between Gage's shoulders, then smoothed his hand down Gage's spine. "And I can run my hands over this beautiful dip in your back while I fuck you. That's what I want."

Gage laughed softly. "Nothing on me is beautiful."

Joseph frowned. "You're wrong about that. Everything on you is beautiful to me." He kissed Gage once then returned his attention to being inside him for the first time. Joseph didn't often top with his partners, but he wasn't a complete bottom. He was definitely looking forward to this.

Easing his way into Gage, Joseph felt how tight he was. He expected that, so he went slowly, making sure Gage was comfortable. The slide into him was the most exquisite torture Joseph had ever experienced. He was ready to blow as soon as he bottomed out in Gage's tight ass, his balls pressed against his lover's skin. Joseph bit his lip and moved. Pulling back, he eased forward, again slowly. His eyes nearly crossed at how hot and tight Gage was, His body trembled from the strain not to pound into him like a wild man. Gage's voice floated up to his ears, low and husky as ever.

"Is this how you want to fuck me, Joseph?" Gage raised his hips, pushing back against him.

Joseph groaned at the movement, his cock sliding deep. His head hung loose on his neck, his hair swinging in his face. "Trying to give you time … to adjust," he panted.

Gage's hand clamped around his wrist. "Fuck me how you want to, Joseph."

With a curse, Joseph stopped holding back. Bracing his fists against the mattress, Joseph let himself go, his hips pistoning back and forth as he pumped into Gage. His chest was tight, his skin heating and growing damp as he slammed into his lover again and again. Gage was groaning, still raising his hips to meet his thrusts. Joseph shook his hair out of his face so he could watch the muscles of Gage's ass flex and clench around his cock, watch his cock disappear into that ass as he greedily fucked him as hard as he could.

He leaned down, but before he could initiate a kiss, Gage reached for him and grabbed the back of his neck, roughly pulling him into a kiss that was deep, and messy, and wild. Joseph cursed into Gage's mouth. His climax was approaching, but he wasn't ready to come yet.

Joseph rose up onto his knees, pulling Gage up with him. He slid a hand into Gage's hair. Gripping it tight, Joseph held Gage's head back against his shoulder so they could continue their kiss. Their tongues twisted and thrust, getting scraped by teeth as they slipped between each other's lips. Beads of sweat trickled down Joseph's back into his suit as he worked to bring their bodies together fast and hard. Joseph slipped his hand down

Gage's torso, past his hair-roughened chest, his fingers skimming over the soft hair on his stomach, following the trail until he reached Gage's cock. Joseph wrapped his fingers around it, squeezing tight and pumping. Gage's hand came down on top of his. He gripped himself too, his fingers squeezing even harder, forcing them to pump his cock faster. Joseph wanted to laugh at this strange game of one-upmanship, but he couldn't. Because Gage's ass was clenching tight on his cock, making Joseph's balls draw up hard and his breath catch in his throat. Gage bit Joseph's lip, and whispered against his cheek.

"I'm coming, Joseph."

"*Fuck*," Joseph cursed again. "Come for me Gage. I need to feel *your* ass squeezing *my* cock this time."

His thighs tense, Joseph fucked into Gage harder, angling up to make sure he hit Gage's sweet spot. Gage's body jerked and he came with a wildly unreserved loud curse, his release spilling into Joseph's hand, getting both their fingers wet. Joseph let go of Gage's hair. He wrapped his arm around Gage's sweat-slick chest, holding on tight as his hips stuttered forward. That squeezing grip on his cock was so hot, so tight that Joseph couldn't hold back. He came in a burst of pleasure so strong his fingers tingled and his toes curled inside his boots. His vision blurred and Joseph threw back his head. A long, hoarse shout slipped from throat as his cock pulsed deep inside Gage again and again and again.

****

Joseph eased them down onto their sides, staying inside his lover as long as he was able. He kissed the side of Gage's neck, licking at a bead of sweat on his shoulder. Finally, he withdrew and Gage turned onto his back.

"That felt good. No wonder you like getting the D so much."

Joseph started to laugh until it clicked what Gage meant. "Wait. You've never uh…"

Gage arched a brow. "Played catcher? Nope."

Joseph slapped a hand onto his forehead with a groan. "You should have told me. I could have been more gentle or something."

"I wanted exactly what you gave me. And if I'm sore, well turnaround is fair play."

"Since when do you play fair?" Joseph teased with a grin. Gage didn't respond other than to shrug and grin himself. "So why now?" Joseph asked.

"It's you and me, Joseph. We give and take, yeah?"

Joseph smiled at his boyfriend. "Yeah."

CHAPTER 69

Things between Joseph and Gage were going well. He'd settled even more into living with Gage. They'd developed an easy routine in taking care of the house, going out with their friends, and spending time apart when they needed. And the sex between them was just as hot as their first time. It would have been perfect, except for one thing. Joseph was noticing Gage's odd reactions whenever he talked about starting his practice. He would either quickly change the subject or make a comment along the lines of him not needing to work so fast on it.

Joseph knew it wasn't that Gage didn't want him to do anything. He was always supportive of his racing, going to the track with him to practice and researching new parts and tires for his Diavel, so obviously it was something else. He wasn't sure what was going on, and he decided it was time to find out. Joseph planned to ask Gage about it when he got home from work in a few minutes.

When Gage came in, Joseph had a simple dinner of Sloppy Joes and fries, Gage's favorite, on the table. He smiled when he saw the meal and headed over to the sink to wash up.

"Hey, hey! Getting some gourmet cooking tonight. I knew there was a reason I liked you."

Joseph laughed, waiting for Gage to sit down before he started putting food on plates. "So my ass has been trumped by ground beef? Not sure how I feel about that."

"Trust me, Joseph, nothing could ever trump your ass," Gage said with a playful leer.

****

Once they were done eating Joseph brought up what he'd been working on. He'd used a bidding site to get a logo designed and had ordered flyers to mail to local customers. As he expected, Gage's face immediately stiffened and when Joseph was done talking, Gage asked if he wanted to go play pool that weekend. Joseph set his glass down. "Why do you keep doing that?"

"Doing what?"

"Avoiding the subject whenever I bring up starting my practice."

"I'm not avoiding the subject. You told me about it and I listened. Then I moved on to something else. Nothing wrong with that."

"There is something wrong with that. You've got a problem with it and I want to know why."

Gage leaned back in his chair. "Fine, maybe I do have a problem with it."

Joseph arched a brow. "And that is?"

"I don't see why you need to be a lawyer right now. You can do that when you're old. You've got talent out on that track and you're wasting it."

Joseph was taken aback. "How am I wasting it? I race don't I?"

"Yeah, you race," Gage scoffed. "When you feel like it, and on small amateur tracks instead of hitting the big leagues."

"You know I couldn't do any more than that, Gage. I didn't have the time or the resources to devote to racing enough so that I could move up."

"So what's your excuse now? You quit your job at that shitty firm and I got people to sponsor you. Yet, instead of getting out there, you spend all day playing on the computer."

Joseph's face flushed hot with anger. "I'm not *playing* on the computer. I'm researching how to start a business, you should know how that works."

Gage shrugged. "Nope, I don't. When I wanted to open up my shop, I went out there and did it. Didn't waste any time checking Google and taking notes like a good little schoolboy."

Joseph's fists clenched on the table top. "Well, maybe you *should* have done some research. Then you wouldn't be using Excel in your shop like an *amateur* instead of a program that makes sense like a *professional*."

Gage rolled his eyes. "If it ain't broke, don't fix it. I don't see a need to bring in any fancy computer shit when things are working just fine the way they are. You're the one that needs to change. Unless you're scared to be a little fish in a big pond instead of the big fish on the tiny track you are now."

Joseph got up from his chair. His nostrils flared as he breathed in deep, trying to control his anger. "I don't need you judging me on what career path I choose to take."

"Fine. Guess prancing around in your skinny little suits is more important than doing what you really want to do."

Joseph glared at Gage. At first glance, he appeared casual and at ease as he lounged in the chair. But Joseph could tell from the tilt of his head and the sharp glare in his eyes that he was pissed off too. He didn't know why Gage was needling him like this, but he knew he didn't have to sit there and take it. "You know what? Fuck you, Gage. There's nothing wrong with the way I dress *or* being a lawyer. And if you have a problem with either that's too damn bad." He turned away and swiped his keys off the counter.

"Where are you going?" Gage called out.

"For a ride on that bike you don't think I'm utilizing properly. You're pissing me off." Joseph saw Gage tense from his lazy pose, his expression changing, but he didn't stop. He just slammed out of the house and took off on his bike.

CHAPTER 70

Joseph sped out of Gage's neighborhood. He didn't understand why Gage had come at him like that. What did it matter if he raced full-time as a professional or part-time as an amateur? It was his choice! Gage didn't get to choose what he did for a living! And even if Gage did have a preference for one over the other, there was no need to mock his efforts at being on his own as a lawyer.

Joseph came up on a busy four-way stop intersection. As he inched forward waiting for his turn to go, he realized he shouldn't have left the way he had. Not only was it dangerous and irresponsible to ride like this, with his concentration barely on the road, but it finally clicked in his brain Gage's reaction to his leaving. He'd taken off on his bike, pissed after an argument. Just like Riley used to do. Joseph cursed at himself and shook his head. This whole situation was awful, and he'd made it worse by repeating Riley's actions. Gage was probably at home worried. Joseph took a deep breath, calming himself so he could get home safely. His turn came up so he proceeded through the intersection.

The road was clear. Until suddenly it wasn't. A small hatchback blew through the intersection without stopping at the driver's stop sign. Joseph cursed again. There was no way he was going to be able to avoid colliding with the car. His options flashed through his mind at the speed of light. If he tried to swerve in front of it, he might get hit head on. If he tried to speed up and beat the car, his bike would probably T-bone it and he'd be flipped over the hood. If he took a preemptive fall he might get by with minor injuries, while the Diavel took the brunt of the crash with the car. His heart pumping, his teeth clenched so hard it felt like his jaw was going to crack, Joseph started to lay the bike on its side…

****

Gage sat completely still at the kitchen table, listening to the roar of Joseph's motorcycle tearing off down the street. He couldn't believe that had just happened. No scratch that. He could believe, because he was a fucking idiot to go after Joseph like that. When would he fucking learn to have a rational discussion with people instead of attacking them to get what he wanted? And Joseph… Joseph was an asshole for leaving in the same fucking way Riley used to after spouting his preachy bullshit about riding without his head in the game!

He shot up out of his chair, every muscle in his body strung so tight he felt like he was about to snap. He stood there, heart pumping, eyes not blinking, until with a roar he sprang forward. Gage grabbed his plate and flung it at the wall. The thing smashed into pieces, a puff of dust lingering in the air after it. That did nothing to alleviate his fury and fear so he didn't stop. He picked up every fucking plate and glass and bowl on the table, throwing them everywhere in the kitchen in a pissed off frenzy. Glass exploded in the air, the shards littering the floor. Tomato sauce and dents in the drywall marred the walls. Gage didn't give a shit. He didn't give a shit about the damage to the kitchen and he didn't fucking give a shit if Joseph wrecked his fucking bike! It would be Joseph's fault if he died! With another roar, Gage picked up a chair and swung it at the door jamb. The thing disintegrated, chunks of wood falling to the floor. A sliver of wood flew out, catching him on the cheek.

Gage finally stopped. His armpits were cold with sweat and blood trickled down his face. He swiped the back of his fist across his cheek, smearing the blood under his eye. Gage took a look around the kitchen at the destruction he'd caused, staring at it for a moment. He shrugged. Gage went into the living room and dropped down on the couch. To wait.

****

"Oh my god, sir! I'm so sorry! My girlfriend was crying so I was texting her and I didn't even see that stop sign! Are you okay?"

Joseph stood with his weight braced on his right leg. His left was shredded up the thigh from the skid he'd taken on the street. His back and ribs were sore, his shoulder stinging. He looked at the young kid with his distraught face. "I would say this in a nice way, but my goddamn ribs hurt too bad to be diplomatic. Don't fucking text and drive!"

The kid's face crumpled even further and he started apologizing again. Joseph just closed his eyes in pain and irritation. He was about to instruct the kid to call the police when he heard the sound of a siren. A passerby must have called it in. Before the squad car pulled up, the kid's phone went off, probably with another text. When he reached for it, Joseph lost it.

"Put that fucking phone away! And get your insurance card and driver's license out." The kid practically squeaked and ran back to his car to get the information just as the police officer arrived.

Joseph watched as the officer got out of the car. It was a tall woman with long black hair pinned into a bun at the nape of her neck. She walked over slowly, assessing the scene from behind mirrored sunglasses. If his ribs didn't hurt so badly, Joseph would have laughed. He didn't think cops still wore those douchey CHiPs shades. She took the sunglasses off and Joseph saw that she had a pretty but hard face. The name on her badge read Officer Coleman.

"What happened here?"

The kid came running back over, still flustered, tripping over his own feet. "It was my fault! I was texting and ran the stop sign. I'm so sorry! Am I getting a ticket for this? My parents are going to kill me!"

The lawyer in Joseph wanted to tell the motor mouth to shut up and stop admitting fault. But since he'd been the one to be hurt as a result of the kid's inattention, he didn't say anything. The officer took notes from them both, collecting their names and information. Several tow trucks had driven up by the time they were finished. Joseph knew it wouldn't be safe to attempt to ride his bike, regardless of whether or not it would start. And the front right wheel on the hatchback was damaged. They were both going to need assistance leaving the scene. The trucks were parked in a row, further impeding the traffic from the wreck. Their flashing lights added swirling color to the swiftly darkening scene. Almost in unison the drivers got out and approached them. Surprisingly, the kid looked to Joseph.

"Which one should I use?"

Joseph grit his teeth. His skin was burning and his body ached. He didn't have time to babysit. He just wanted to get home. "Just pick the one closest so the others can clear out of the damn street. And call your parents so they can meet you here."

The kid nodded and obeyed him, while the officer looked at him with amusement. "Which one are you going to choose?"

"None of them. I have someone I can call."

Joseph took his phone out of his pocket. Thankfully it hadn't been on the side of him that had taken the fall, so it had survived the crash. He slowly opened up his phone, bringing up Gage's number. He wasn't looking forward to this call, imagining Gage's reaction when he heard he'd been in an accident. The phone had barely made the connection to ring when Gage's voice came through.

"Hello?"

"Gage. I need you to come get me."

****

Joseph rode along in Gage's truck. His bike was in the back. Gage had only spoken once since he'd come to pick him up. He'd raced up to the intersection, the Dodge coming to a rocking stop as Gage parked and jumped out of the truck. He'd rushed over, his face tense with obvious worry. Running his eyes over Joseph he'd asked one question: "Do you need to go to the hospital?" When Joseph shook his head no, Gage walked away to pick up the Diavel and wheel it over to his truck. He'd said nothing as Joseph and the kid helped him lift it into the back. Gage had given the kid the mother of all death glares, which made him squeak again and scuttle over to the sidewalk to wait for his parents. Gritting his teeth through the pain that had his whole body aching, Joseph had waited with him until his parents showed up. He'd suffered through the kid's confession of what caused the accident and then another round of apologies from the parents before he could leave.

Now they were home, Gage pulling into the driveway and exiting the truck, still without saying a word. Joseph slowly followed behind as Gage strode into the house, leaving the door open for Joseph to come in.

Gage finally spoke. "Take a shower to get the blood and dirt off of you and I'll bandage you up," he said as he went up the stairs.

Joseph started to follow him, but as he passed by the kitchen something laying on the floor caught his eye. Stopping, he saw it was a piece of wood. Joseph flicked on the kitchen light, his eyes going wide in surprise at what he saw. Glass was all over the floor. Sloppy Joe sauce and bits of ground beef was on the walls. A chair lay in pieces. Staring in disbelief, Joseph wondered if Gage had done this before or after his call. He realized it didn't matter. This was anger for sure. But it was also worry. Gage might barely be speaking to him, but he'd clearly been terrified. He wouldn't have reacted in such an extremely violent manner if he wasn't. Feeling even more terrible about the way he'd left and the accident he'd been in as a result, Joseph turned off the light and went upstairs to shower.

****

Gage looked at Joseph laying on his side on the bed. He was naked so that nothing touched his injuries. Fortunately, he'd been wearing his padded motorcycle jacket, and the armor had protected his upper body as much as possible. But there was still bruising popping up on his back and over his ribs. Unfortunately, he'd been in jeans, which had done nothing to protect his lower body. His left leg had a wide swath of skin from mid-thigh to hip that was scraped and scratched and gouged. More bruising mottled the skin up and down his leg. Gage wanted to scream at him that this was what happened when you took off half-cocked, and he was lucky that he wasn't dead. But Joseph was watching him with worry in his expressive eyes and his mouth was turned down in a frown of pain. So Gage said nothing. He silently cleaned the wounds, checking to be sure there weren't any pieces of clothing or gravel stuck in his skin. The sounds of paper wrappers tearing and a jar opening were loud in the otherwise silent bedroom as Gage bandaged the scratches and put arnica ointment on the bruises.

Wiping his hands on his jeans, Gage asked Joseph again if he needed to go to the hospital. Joseph shook his head no, so Gage went downstairs to get ice packs and a glass of water. He came back into the bedroom, loosely tied the ice packs to Joseph with Ace bandages wrapped around him, and handed him a couple of aspirin and the glass of water. He watched as Joseph swallowed it down, taking the glass from him when he was finished. Gage set it on the nightstand and went to leave the room. Joseph called out to him before he made it to the hallway.

"You're not staying with me?"

Gage turned back. Joseph lay there, his normally active body vulnerable in its forced stillness, his face drawn with pain. Gage knew he should stay, but he couldn't deal with him right now. Shaking his head in the negative, Gage continued on out of the room.

****

Gage drove up to Max's big house. When he parked and got out, he noticed a silver Audi in the driveway but he didn't pay it any attention. He rang the bell, waiting with his hands stuffed in his pockets. It took much longer for Max to answer the door than usual. When it finally swung open Max stood there shirtless, looking uncharacteristically flustered.

"Gage, what's up?"

Gage realized Max wasn't immediately stepping aside to let him in. It clicked that he probably wasn't alone. "Hey, man. Had a fight with Joseph. Was hoping to talk, but it looks like you're busy."

Max looked over his shoulder then back at Gage. "Yeah, I've got company. Sorry, man."

Gage shrugged. "It's no big. I'll talk to you later."

Gage turned and shuffled back to his truck. He drove around aimlessly for a while then headed to Jay's Liquor Shop. He walked in, grabbed the first thing he saw, paid and walked back out. This time when he was behind the wheel, he knew exactly where he was headed.

****

Black wrought iron fences gleamed in his headlights as he pulled up to Woodlawn Cemetery. Gage put the truck in park and killed the engine. At this hour the gates would be locked, so Gage didn't bother to get out. He just looked out across the manicured lawns to where he knew Riley's grave was. He sat there staring for a few moments as he remembered their last fight. Riley wanted to go on a week-long trip to Miami for a big sports bike festival. Gage didn't want to take off for seven days when he was just opening his shop. Looking back now, Gage knew they could have come to a compromise, Riley going down for the full week while Gage came for a few days only. But they hadn't. And Riley had taken off, only for Gage to get a call soon after. Gage remembered that call. How he'd stared at the phone before picking it up with a shaking hand, his stomach queasy as he said hello. He didn't understand how, but he'd known that something had happened to Riley. Tonight had been nothing but deja vu, although thankfully the phone call he received wasn't a devastating end to his world.

Doing his best to shove those memories away, Gage pushed the brown paper bag down enough to get at the bottle of liquor he'd bought. Cracking it open, he took a long drink. Gage immediately started coughing, his throat burning and eyes watering. Sliding the bag the rest of the way off, Gage looked at what he'd grabbed. Wild Turkey. He took another swig and coughed again, warmth spreading across his chest as the bourbon settled in. Gage took another drink, then another and another. Each time he coughed a little less. Eventually, his whole body was warm, his ears tingling with his buzz. Gage gripped the neck of the bottle. His vision was blurry now, but he still stared off into the distance. He'd almost lost Joseph tonight. Because he couldn't learn from his past mistakes and had been a dick to him, just like he had to Riley. He didn't deserve Joseph, not if he was going to keep breaking the promise he'd made to himself to be careful with him.

Gage knocked his head back against the seat, immediately regretting it as things started to spin. Not only had he been a dick, he'd also been full of bullshit. There was another reason Gage didn't want Joseph starting his own practice, one he didn't like admitting even to himself. That reason scared him and it was why he'd reacted the way he had. Gage sighed. Screwing the cap back on the bottle, he let it drop between his legs. The adrenaline and fear had finally siphoned off, leaving him exhausted. On top of that, his head was swimming from the bourbon. He wanted to talk to Joseph, to get this straightened out, but there was no way he was able to drive home. And trying to explain himself on the phone, while drunk, sounded insane even to his partially functioning brain. He'd have to talk to Joseph tomorrow. Gage checked to be sure the doors were locked, reclined the seat and passed out.

CHAPTER 71

ale morning sunlight filtered into the room. Joseph rolled over. The bed next to him was undisturbed. That was expected. He'd woken a dozen times during the night, he would have known if Gage had come to bed. Getting up, Joseph pulled on a loose pair of shorts and a t-shirt, doing his best not to disturb his bandaged leg. He limped downstairs, half hoping Gage was sleeping on the couch and he just hadn't heard him come in. But the living room was empty. Joseph sighed and went into the kitchen to clean up the mess from the night before.

As he swept up glass and wiped down walls, Joseph couldn't even imagine the rage that had gone through Gage in order to cause this. They needed to talk so it didn't happen again. When he was done, Gage still wasn't home. Trying not to worry, Joseph grabbed his phone and texted Gage. *Where are you?* Within seconds, he got a text back: *There in five.*

Joseph went to the front door, pulling it open to wait. A few minutes later, Gage drove up. When he got out, Joseph took in how rumpled he was. He'd obviously slept in his clothes. As Gage came inside, Joseph noted his bloodshot eyes, smelling the liquor on him as he passed into the living room.

"Where did you sleep last night?"

"I was alone if that's what you're asking."

Joseph didn't say anything to that. He had for the briefest of moments, wondered if Gage had handled his emotions the way he used to. But that thought had quickly left his brain. Joseph didn't believe Gage would wreck what they had in that way. Unfortunately, that wasn't what Gage took from his silence. Gage glared at him for a moment before barking a harsh laugh.

"So not only do you get on your bike and take off while pissed, *just like Riley used to*, and which scared *the fuck* out of me in case you were wondering. Now you think I slept with someone? Did you see the kitchen in there, Joseph?" He swung his arm out towards the kitchen. "That's how I expressed my feelings last night, instead of fucking them away like I used to. That could turn out to be an expensive habit. Next time serve us dinner on paper plates when you're setting me up like that."

He turned his back on Joseph and went to leave the room. Before he could get too far, Joseph caught up to him and grabbed his arm. "Wait, can we talk about-."

Gage turned, flinging Joseph's hand off of him. Joseph took a wary step back, watching as Gage's face turned red with anger. Joseph put his hands up, but for some reason that pissed Gage off more.

"Do you think I would hit you?" Gage asked in a hard voice as he stalked back over to him.

Joseph shook his head that he didn't. He tried to prove it by not flinching as Gage's hand flashed out, grabbing him by the back of the neck and pulling him close.

"Do you have any idea what you mean to me? I would *never* hit you." Gage pressed their foreheads together, his eyes tightly closed. "If you would have been killed last night, Joseph… I don't know what I would have done."

For once, Joseph didn't know what to do, or how to handle Gage. "I'm sorry."

Gage's voice was a dark, pained whisper. It didn't fit with the happy sunlight spilling into the room, warming them both. "Why are you sorry, Joseph? Are you about to leave me?"

"No. Of course not," Joseph answered in surprise. "I'm sorry for what I did last night. It was irresponsible and dangerous. I could have been hurt more than I was. But mostly I'm sorry for what I put you through. If I'd stopped to think for half a second, I would have realized the awful associations that would cause.

Gage pulled back, opening his eyes to look at him. "Don't ever do that again."

Joseph shook his head as he met Gage's eyes, worry clear in their dark depths. "I won't, I swear."

Gage stared at him for a moment before he finally released the hold on his neck. "I'm going to shower," he said.

But Joseph stopped him again. "You're right, Gage. I was setting you up. I wanted to know why you were so reluctant to discuss my plans."

Gage shrugged. "And now you know."

Joseph shook his head, watching Gage carefully. "No. Now I know half of it. There's no way you would have antagonized me like that just because you wanted me to focus on racing because of my talent. You wanted me mad, mad enough to be pushed into giving up law altogether. Why?"

Gage looked at Joseph standing there. He was hunched over slightly, his left arm tucked close against his side. His weight was braced on his right leg, his left one bent slightly and resting on his bare toes. Gage blew out a harsh breath. "Sit down before you fall down, Joseph."

Joseph gingerly lowered himself to the couch, wincing as his body made contact with the cushions. Gage paced in front of him. It was now or never. He wished it was never, but Gage knew he needed to say this.

"You're right. I was trying to goad you into saying fuck it with your business. And part of it is because I can see how amazing you are out there on your bike." Gage roughly shoved his hand through his hair. He couldn't believe he was about to say this. It made him sound like an insecure pussy. "The other part is because I can't help but think, that as long as you're a part of that corporate world, I might lose you."

Joseph's head snapped up. "What?"

Gage sighed, shoving his hands into his pockets. "I see how different we are, Joseph. Yeah, we joke about opposites attracting the pretty boy to the guy with grease under his fingernails. But is this just a phase for you? Your lawyer boyfriend said you needed to come back where you belong. Oil slick said you were just playing at being with a bad boy. How do I know those motherfuckers aren't right?" Gage rocked back on his heels, staring up at the ceiling. He didn't want to see Joseph's face during this admission. "I figured if I kept you down on my level, in my world, then I wouldn't have to worry about you leaving me for the classy folks you'd be mingling with as a lawyer." Gage stood there in embarrassed silence when he was done.

Joseph called his name. After a moment, Gage looked down at him. Once he did, Joseph held his hand out. Gage took it, allowing Joseph to pull him down until he was sitting next to him.

"You are not keeping me down. Your world is different, but it's on the same level as any man who wears a suit to work, instead of jeans like you. And I am not *playing at being with a bad boy*. I'm with you because I *want* to be with you. All of the things that make you different are *why* I want to be with you, Gage. I feel like I can really be myself with you. With Ashton, I felt stiff. He hated the fact that I raced, wanted me to cut my hair, and his idea of fun always involved being seen at important functions. And Montoya, he might approve of me racing, but I get the vibe off him that outside of that, things wouldn't be much different with him than they were with Ashton. Besides, I'm pretty sure he'd trot me out to show off to his friends like a trick pony." Joseph shook his head. "So no I don't want to be with guys like them."

"And the lawyer thing?"

Joseph was quiet for a moment before he answered. "It's something I worked hard for. And it's how I always planned to support myself. Even now if I chose to enter the professional race circuit it'd be awhile before I started making any money, if I do at all. I do love racing, but that wouldn't be very responsible."

Gage reached out, lacing his fingers through the ones on Joseph's uninjured arm. "Hear me out. You've got someone subletting your townhouse, so you don't have to worry about paying rent or utilities. You have enough sponsorship money to pay for your racing gear and entry fees for several months." He smiled. "And you have a boyfriend who'd be willing to fix your bike for the low, low price of another plate of Sloppy Joes. So maybe you put the lawyer thing on hold for a year. Give professional racing a serious try and see what comes of it. You could even play pool more if you'd like."

"I have other expenses than those Gage. And I can't live here with you without contributing anything. That wouldn't be fair."

"I'll worry about what's fair." Gage slid onto his knees, carefully pushing Joseph's legs apart so that he could move between them. He looked up at his lover, reading the indecision on his face. "Let me do this for you, Joseph. I want to. You can work in my shop in exchange if that will make you feel better. Or we can keep track and you can pay me back. We'll figure it out. Just let me do this."

Joseph looked at Gage kneeling in front of him. He was slightly uneasy at the thought of being dependent on his boyfriend. But maybe this was a necessary step to take in order to cement their relationship. And he did want to see where he could go with his racing, he'd just always felt it was best to have a steady, dependable career. He'd already taken one big risk in quitting a secure job. Did it really matter if he took another to see how racing might turn out? Clearly this was important to Gage. He wouldn't have humbled himself to admit what he had and ask for this if it wasn't.

"Alright, I'll try it, but on several conditions. First, I only want to race, not play competitive pool. I just want to do that for fun. I'd rather concentrate on racing rather than split my time between the two. Second, I'll do it for six months, not a year. And third, I'll keep helping Gia, since I already said I would."

Gage smiled, a look of triumph crossing his face. "All of that is okay with me. Six months is fine. I bet you'll see you want to stick with it before that window is up."

Joseph smiled too. "We'll see."

CHAPTER 72

Two weeks later, Joseph sat on a stool in Gage's shop, his laptop balanced on his knees. He was looking at the site for a race coming up in two weeks out past Beaumont, while Gage worked.

"Gage, I don't know if I should enter this one just yet. "It's big and long-."

"That's what she said," Gage interjected without looking up from what he was doing.

Joseph laughed once then continued expressing his misgivings. "Seriously. I don't think I'm ready for it."

Gage jumped to his feet and came over to him. "You'll find out if you're ready by trying it."

"Yeah, but I could also spend more time on smaller circuits, make sure I'm comfortable there and then move up."

"C'mon, Joseph. We talked about this. Balls out. You've got the talent and the skill. It's all a mental game from here on."

They *had* talked. Well, Gage had. He'd talked about his plans for Joseph on the professional circuit and how Joseph needed to get back on his bike as soon as he was healed and the bike was repaired. Joseph had mostly listened. Things felt rushed, but maybe that was just nerves, especially after his fall. Joseph looked down at the screen again. The turns on that track looked insanely tight. He ignored the twinge of pain that went through him as he remembered crashing to the ground not long ago. Joseph knew it was psychosomatic and he didn't want it to catch hold in his head. He could do this. He looked back up at Gage. "Nothing ventured, nothing gained, right?"

Gage gripped his chin and gave him a quick, hard kiss. "That's right."

****

Joseph sat with Gage out on the back patio. The night was fairly quiet, traffic was light and the bugs were driven into hibernation due to the cool weather. They were both enjoying hot drinks from the coffee shop down the road. Joseph suddenly set his cup on the table with a frustrated groan. "I'm a crappy son."

"Why?"

"Because I didn't let my mother know I was in an accident."

Gage brushed one index finger over the other in the symbol for shame. "You're horrible Joseph. You ought to be ashamed." He tapped Joseph's phone laying on the table between them. "Call her now."

Joseph picked up his phone, pushing the button so he could wake it up and check the time. "It's after nine o'clock. That's not too late, but my father will be home."

"And you don't want to talk to him?"

"I told you he doesn't want to talk to me. I don't want it to be uncomfortable if he picks up."

Gage quietly sipped at his drink before he answered. "They've got caller ID, right?"

Joseph nodded.

"Then if he gets to the phone first he'll know it's you. If he answers, I'd take that to mean he wouldn't mind hearing your voice. If he doesn't want to, he'll let it ring until your mom or little brother picks up."

Joseph looked down at the phone in his hand. He knew it was simple, and he couldn't be hurt through the phone, but it didn't stop the nervousness that went through him as he made the call. It rang twice, his tension growing with each ring. When the connection was made, the voice he both dreaded and longed to hear came through the phone.

"Hello?"

"Father. It's me." His throat went dry from nervousness and he had to clear his throat to finish. "Joseph."

"I know. I saw on the caller ID. How are you?"

Joseph was surprised that his father was actually talking to him. He started to give a real answer to his question, but realized the senior Mr. Naderi was just being polite. "I'm fine. Is mom home?" There was silence for a moment. Joseph could feel Gage staring at him, but he kept his gaze focused on the table in front of him. His father finally answered.

"Yes, she is. Hold on."

The line went quiet again. There was indistinct conversation before his mother came on the line.

"Yousef, how are you?"

Joseph laughed a little bit. "Actually, that's why I'm calling."

His mother's voice sharpened with worry. "Is everything okay?"

"I'm fine now, but I was in an accident on my bike a couple of weeks ago."

"What? Yousef! Why didn't you call me? Are you alright? Who took care of you?"

Gage sat there smirking at him. He could clearly hear the agitated shrieking of his mother. *Shame, shame, shame,* he mouthed. Joseph rolled his eyes at Gage's teasing. "I'm sorry, Mother. I didn't call because I didn't want you to worry. Other than some scrapes and bruises I'm fine. And Gage, the guy I told you about, he took care of me."

"Gage. Your boyfriend? Is he there now? Let me talk to him."

Joseph held out the phone. Now he was the one smirking while Gage looked faintly panicked. "She wants to talk to you."

Gage took the cell and spoke in the most polite tone Joseph had ever heard him use. "Hello, Mrs. Naderi."

His mother must have calmed down, because her voice no longer rang out loudly from the phone. Joseph followed along with the side of the conversation that he could hear.

"You're welcome." Gage paused, nodding. "Of course I will." There was an especially long pause while Gage frowned at whatever his mother was saying. "I think that needs to happen too." Gage smiled, the sound of it reflected in his voice. "If you need me to do anything, just let me know. Good night, Mrs. Naderi."

Gage passed the phone back and Joseph took it with a questioning frown. Gage just shrugged. He said goodbye to his mother and hung up.

"What was that about?"

"Don't worry about it." He changed the subject slightly. "So your dad answered."

Joseph shrugged. "Yeah."

"Guess he didn't mind hearing your voice. Why didn't you talk to him?"

"I did. You heard me."

"Oh, I heard alright."

Joseph was uncomfortable with this subject. Hearing his father's voice made him wish they still had a relationship, even though he knew that would never happen. "Gage don't, okay. He was just being polite. After the way he threw me out and cut me off, that's the most I can hope for out of him."

Gage reached for his hand, lacing their fingers together. "Time changes a lot of things, Joseph."

Joseph pulled his hand away. "Well, Cyrus Naderi isn't one of them so let it go."

"Fine." Gage took another sip of his drink. "I like your mom." He looked at Joseph with a teasing grin. "Yousef."

****

Another race day. Joseph's bike was put back together. His injuries were nearly completely healed. He had a new bike suit, this time in black and yellow. Patches representing his sponsors adorned the leather and mesh. He looked ready.

Joseph caught a glimpse of bright blue out of the corner of his eye. Turning, he saw a rider wearing a black and blue racing suit. His eyes narrowed in concentration as he tried to determine if it was the racer who'd nearly caused him to wipe out at the last race. But things had been happening so fast, and he'd been too focused on the race to take in any details other than the color of the suit. Afterwards, his mind had been on claiming his prize from Gage so he hadn't sought the guy out.

This rider had stylishly messy blonde hair. He didn't look the type to do anything underhanded, he was smiling and joking with everyone around him. As Joseph watched Montoya came up to him. He was surprised when Montoya smiled warmly at the blonde, resting a hand on his lower back. A frown on his forehead, Joseph got up and walked over to them. He smoothed his expression out before he reached the two.

"Rafael, good to see you." He held his hand out. Montoya looked down at it for a moment. He rubbed his palm up the blonde's back before he finally accepted Joseph's handshake.

"Joseph, hello. I'm not sure if it's good to see you. That boyfriend of yours isn't about to jump out at me, is he?" Montoya smiled, but the comment still stung.

"No, Gage is fine. And he's over there," he said as he pointed over at his bike.

"Oh, I see you got a little group together." He nodded at the patches on Joseph's race suit. "And some sponsors. Good for you. I'm sponsoring Hunter here."

The blonde held his hand out, a cocky smile on his face. "Hi, I'm Hunter. Nice to meet you, Joey."

Joseph glared. "I prefer Joseph."

Hunter cracked his gum. "My mistake."

Joseph looked down at the bike Hunter was straddling. For the first time, he noticed what it was. The MTT Turbine Streetfighter. It was one of the most expensive and most powerful racers out there. "Nice bike," he said to Hunter.

"Thanks." More aggressive gum chewing. "Having Mr. Montoya as a new sponsor certainly comes with its perks."

Montoya laughed. "The best bike and crew money can buy."

"It's a little much for racing at this level, isn't it?" Joseph asked.

Hunter smirked. "I didn't get the upgrades to make sure it was legal for this event. So you still might have a chance. Besides, this is my last ride on the amateur circuit before I move on to the pros. Figured I'd go out on top."

Joseph gave a tight smile and took a step back. He was about to excuse himself when he heard Gage's hard voice behind him.

"I thought I gave you very clear instructions on what you were to do when you saw Joseph at a race track."

Montoya held up his hands in a placating manner. "I assure you I am not poaching on your territory, Mason. Joseph stopped by to talk to me. I was merely being polite." He gestured at Hunter. As you can see, I have other things that concern me. But if you're so worried you'll lose Joseph, maybe you should keep him on an even tighter leash."

Joseph's face burned at Montoya's insinuation. He looked at Hunter. He was still cracking his gum, his eyes gleaming with amusement at what Joseph knew was his expense. Again, Joseph started to excuse himself, and again Gage prevented him from doing so.

Gage walked close to Hunter, looking up and down at his race suit. "You're the one who nearly caused Joseph to crash two weeks ago."

Hunter cracked his gum. He didn't deny Gage's charge. "Accidents happen," he said with a shrug.

Gage's eyes flicked between Hunter and Montoya. He'd clearly come to the conclusion that Joseph hadn't wanted to address. "Accidents my ass. You tried to run him off the track on purpose. And you," he pointed at Montoya. "Put him up to it."

Montoya laughed. "You are delusional and have seen too many biker movies. I did nothing to risk anyone's safety on the track."

Gage got up close in Montoya's face. "I'm delusional? You're delusional thinking I won't kick your ass again after pulling a stunt like that!" he shouted.

Joseph grabbed Gage's arm, tugging him away from Montoya. "Gage! Calm down. They'll kick you out of here if you start something!"

Joseph dragged Gage away from the two guys. As they left he heard Hunter give a long, low whistle and say, "Woah, what the hell was that?" and the beginning of Montoya's response. "Trash…"

Once Joseph had Gage back over to their set up he let him go. He was still wild, pacing back and forth.

"You better win this race, Joseph! You win it and show that slick motherfucker that money won't buy you a goddamn victory. You hear me?"

Joseph nodded. "I hear you, Gage. I'll try," he said quietly.

Gage faced him, his eyes wide and manic. "Don't try! Fucking win it!"

Joseph took the helmet Danny handed him without saying anything. He pushed it down on his head and mounted his bike. The announcer started calling for riders to take the track. Joseph wouldn't have time for his ritual, but it didn't matter. He didn't feel like anything could pump him up. He was nowhere near in the head space he needed to be as he wheeled his bike over to the start line. Behind him, he could hear Gage yelling, "Win it, Joseph!"

CHAPTER 73

Joseph didn't win it. He didn't even place. Well, technically seventh was a place, but it didn't get him a spot on the podium. All he got was claps on his back from his friends, assuring him he'd, *get 'em next time*. Not wanting to look like a sore loser, he'd gone to the official after party to hang with the loyal fans who supported him win or lose. Now after a long drive, he and Gage were home.

Joseph was exhausted and looking forward to a hot shower and then bed. Unfortunately, Gage didn't feel the same.

"I'm wired. Can't stop thinking about what we can do to get you a win on that track. And that fucking Montoya! Can't believe that piece of shit! I know he had something to do with you almost eating asphalt at the last race. There's no way it's a coincidence that one race that guy is nearly running you off the track and the next he's got a shiny new bike courtesy of his sugar daddy."

"Gage let it go. There's no way to prove whether it was an accident or not. Regardless, antagonizing Rafael won't make the situation any better."

Gage looked at him with his head cocked to the side. "Rafael, huh?"

"Gage, don't."

"Don't what?"

Joseph sighed. "Just let things with Montoya drop, alright?"

"You should have won that race. The only reason that piece of shit won is because of that bike."

"If that's the case then why did I come in seventh instead of second?" Joseph asked wearily.

"I don't know, why did you?"

"I told you I wasn't ready for that track." Gage started to say something, but Joseph cut him off. "I'm tired. I'm going to bed."

Gage smiled and came up to him. "That's fine with me. I still got adrenaline pumping through me. And I need you to take it away for me," he said as he rubbed Joseph's back.

"Not tonight."

"What do you mean, not tonight?" Gage smoothed a hand up his neck to grip his ponytail. "C'mon Joseph. Let me have you." He brushed a kiss over Joseph's lips. "You know I'll make you feel good. Then you'll sleep like a baby."

Joseph shook his head. "No. I'm tired and I don't feel like being your emotional scratching post tonight." Gage stiffened and pulled back. His grip on Joseph's ponytail tightened, his face hardening.

"What did you say?"

"You heard me."

"Oh, yeah. I heard you alright. I just don't know why those words fell out of your mouth. That was the deal you made when you took me on. You're there for me when I fucking need to *fuck*, remember, Joseph? Didn't think you'd welch on the deal and sulk like a spoiled brat when something didn't go your way."

Joseph narrowed his eyes at Gage. He was sick of this. "Maybe I am sulking. But I should be able to sulk all I want, without you manipulating me into coddling you with your emotionally stunted growth."

Gage's eyes widened in sarcastic mock surprise. "Coddling? Joseph is using his big words. That must mean you're really angry."

Joseph shook his head. "I'm not angry. I'm just tired."

Gage released him, stepping back with a sneer on his face. "Fine, then. Go to bed if you're so fucking tired."

He turned to walk away. Joseph stared after him for a moment. Is this what the next six months would be like? An endless cycle of anger, manipulation and forgiveness? The thought of it tired Joseph even more. His mouth was open and talking before his brain knew what was happening. "I need a break." Gage stopped for half a second before he continued on his way. He didn't even bother to turn around with his response.

"Whatever."

CHAPTER 74

Joseph left Gage. He couldn't go home because his house was being sublet. And he didn't want to drag any of his friends into his private business by asking to crash with them. That left him with no other option than to stay at a hotel. The one he'd chosen was nice, but still reasonably priced enough for him to be able to afford for a few weeks if it came down to that. He'd already been there for one.

He'd done lots of thinking in his solitude, realizing two things. One, he was in love with Gage. Two, he couldn't stay with Gage if he was going to continue blowing up and manipulating him in order to get things his way. Both things were important. But he was worried the second might outweigh the first. A knock came at the door, interrupting his thoughts.

Joseph got up, pulling on a t-shirt over his bare chest as he went to the door. The face he saw through the peephole surprised him. Joseph flipped back the latch lock and opened the door. "Father?"

"Yousef. May I come in?"

Joseph was so surprised, it took him a moment to react. When he did, he swung the door back so fast he whacked it against his toe. He winced. "Of course."

Cyrus Naderi came into the hotel room. He was as well dressed as always. His sharp analytical mind had lead him to a position as a bank executive and he looked the part. He also looked like a slightly older version of Joseph. Their coloring, build and faces were so similar, it was only the slight gray at his temples and the few lines around his green eyes that revealed they were father and son, instead of brothers.

"It's been a long time."

Joseph simply nodded. Six years was a long time to go without seeing someone. Especially if it was your son.

"I wasn't sure if you would see me."

"I'd never refuse to see you, Father. But how did you know I was here? And *why* are you here?"

Cyrus stepped over to the straight-backed chair in front of the desk. "May I sit?" At Joseph's nod, he pulled out the chair and sat. "I went by your townhome, but the guy living there told me you'd moved in with your boyfriend. I went to his house, but he told me you were living in this hotel." He paused for a moment, looking like he was holding back a disapproving frown. "I tried your firm before I came here, but they told me you no longer worked there. What's going on, Yousef?"

Joseph sighed and settled on the bed. "I'm sort of going through a rough patch in my life."

"That's not like you. You've always been firm on what you wanted. Even if it was something I didn't approve of you doing."

Joseph had to smile at that. "That's true. But you're not here to ask me about my life, right?"

Cyrus sighed himself. "I think it's time that we talked about what happened after your graduation."

Joseph struggled not to be angry as he thought back to that night. His father yelling at him to get out. His mother crying. His little brother confused. And he'd just been numb. "I don't know what else you want me to say. I can't stop being gay."

"I understand that, Yousef. That's not at all what I mean." He took a deep breath. "I'd like to apologize. For the way I spoke to you and for banishing you from our family. As your father, I am ashamed of my actions."

Joseph leaned back, completely surprised. "Wow, thank you so much for saying that."

Cyrus looked away for a moment, straightening the cuffs of his button down. "I admit I was shocked. I thought it was something that you'd fallen into while you were on campus. And of course our culture hasn't always been kind to the gay community. I had nothing but incorrect stereotypes in my head. I didn't want what I perceived as the debauched gay life for my son."

Joseph was glad his father had apologized, but that didn't take away six years of bitter hurt. "So you kicked me out and banished me."

"I did. I was ashamed then because I worried what our friends would say about having a gay son. I'm ashamed now because I let something so small minded keep me away from my eldest for so long."

"Then why did you?"

"Like I said, Yousef. I was shocked and angry. It took me awhile to come to grips with it. Your mother helped. She never let your sexuality bother her and she fought to bring you back into our lives."

"Is that why you're here now? Because of her?

"No. I'm here because I want to be here. I never really let you go. I kept tabs on you through law school and your internship. I even put in a word for you with a few firms to recruit you, but you were scouted by one of the best all on your own. And after your mother put her foot down and demanded to start seeing you again, I always encouraged her to take a check for you. All of which you refused."

"I didn't need your help."

"I know that. And I'm incredibly proud of all you managed to accomplish on your own. As I said, your mother helped me to understand your sexuality isn't a choice and it doesn't change who you are. Even Darius helped. He's always leaving GLBT pamphlets all over the house. But it was you that really opened my eyes. I've watched you as you've gone about your life. And I see that you are no different than if you'd been dating women all this time."

Joseph looked at his father. He looked sincere. Cyrus Naderi didn't say anything unless he meant it. That made him think of something his father had said to him six years ago. "You called me *bacheh mozalaf.*" Joseph had tried to joke about that ugly term when he'd told Gage, but it had hurt to hear his father use it. It still hurt now.

His father winced. "I'm disgusted that I used that phrase. Not just because you are my son, but because it is offensive. I want you to know I haven't used it since. I'm very sorry I said it. I don't know how to make it up to you. You're too old to take to the toy store. Maybe I'll buy you a new bike."

Joseph let himself smile a little. "I might take you up on that."

Cyrus smiled too. Then he cleared his throat. "To answer your original question of why I'm here. I'm here to apologize and to ask you to consider allowing me to be your father again. I know that we have a lot to discuss and the healing won't happen overnight. But right now I'm here to let you know that I am educating myself about the gay community, I love you as my son, and I want you to be part of the family again. I understand if you need to think-."

Joseph sprang up off the bed and cut his father off. "I don't need to think anything over. More than anything I want to be welcomed home again. I honestly thought it would never happen, so I'm not going to turn it down now that it is. We will have things to work through. But I just want to have my family back."

Cyrus stood as well. He came forward, extending his arms towards Joseph. And Joseph didn't hesitate. They embraced for the first time in years, a reaffirmation of their father-son bond. Cyrus's voice was thick with emotion as he spoke.

"I've missed you son. And I'm so sorry for cutting you out of my life. I have a lot to make up for."

Joseph's own eyes were stinging with tears as he responded. "I've missed you too, Dad. And I accept your apology. All of them."

After a moment, they returned to their respective seats. The tension in the room was gone, replaced with a familiar feeling of comfort. Like his father had said, the healing wouldn't happen overnight, but they'd taken the first steps. Joseph knew he truly had his father back at his next words, especially since they were voiced in his stern *Yousef is in trouble* voice.

"Tell me why you quit your job, Yousef."

Joseph sighed before he explained the way things had played out with Pruitt, leaving off the part about what he had Gage had down in the parking garage of course. He finished with, "I was planning to start my own firm, but that's up in the air right now."

"And why is that?"

"I talked it over with my boyfriend, Gage and he convinced me to give racing full time and professionally a try." Joseph cleared his throat, slightly uncomfortable. He'd always strived to please his father and make him proud, even when they'd been estranged. It was part of the reason he'd been hesitant to date Gage, even though he'd never admitted it to himself. He'd worried that has father wouldn't approve because he wasn't a doctor or a lawyer or in some other white-collar position. Telling him how he'd quit his job and changed his plans because of his boyfriend made him feel slightly ashamed.

"Is that what you wanted to do, Yousef?"

Joseph shrugged. "I honestly don't know. I chose law because I know it's a respectable profession and deep down I wanted to make you proud. And I love racing, but I don't know that I'm ready to be on the level Gage was pushing for."

Bracing his elbows on his knees, Cyrus leaned forward. "Yousef, this is your life, your career choice. Forget about Gage for a moment and forget about making me proud. After what I put you through I have no right to judge. What do *you* want to do?"

Joseph thought long and hard, picturing what he wanted his life to look like. "I want to race, professionally. It's fun. I love the thrill and the competition. Pitting myself against other riders, not knowing if I'm going to crash and burn gives me the most amazing rush. And I know that with time and training, I can be successful at it. As for practicing law, I enjoy the mental challenge and it's a good source of income. I need that security, but I don't want it to be my life." Joseph stopped, letting the decision he'd just made sink in.

"Well, there you go. It sounds to me like you know what you want to do."

"I think I did all along," Joseph said with a smile. "I was just too scared to go for it." He sobered a bit. "But I don't know what to do about Gage." He looked at his father. "I'm sorry, we don't have to talk about this part if it makes you uncomfortable."

Cyrus shook his head. "It doesn't. And even if it did, I wouldn't let it stop me. Joseph, you were raised by a smart mother and a sometimes smart father. You have a good head on your shoulders. I don't know Gage, but I imagine that if you chose him, he is a good man. From what I saw the few minutes I spoke with him, he cares for you and was upset that you were gone. With that in mind, I'm sure he will accept whatever choice you make."

"Maybe. We were having other problems as well."

"Every couple has problems. My deplorable treatment of you was a heavy strain on your mother and I's relationship. But we worked it out. That's what you and your Gage will have to do."

Joseph smiled at his dad. That's really all there was to it. If they wanted to be together, they were going to have to work things out. They could work on Gage's issues, but Joseph knew he wasn't completely without fault. He was going to have to stop giving in to Gage so easily. He had a backbone, it was time he used it. His father spoke up.

"If you don't have any plans for the evening, I would like to invite you to dinner. It'd be a pleasant surprise for your brother. Not that he needs any more good news. He's been on cloud nine ever since we agreed to let him go to school in Florida.

Joseph grinned at the thought of having dinner with his family again and hearing that Darius would be able to attend his dream school. "I'd love to come over for dinner."

CHAPTER 75

For the first time in six years, Joseph went home. He'd followed his father down streets that he still remembered after all this time. When they reached the Naderi home, they parked, Cyrus in the driveway, Joseph in the street. His father waited for him at the front door.

"I thought we'd ring the bell, give them both a surprise."

Joseph grinned. "If either of them faints, you'd better catch them." Joseph rang the bell and waited. He could tell by the running feet that it was his brother coming to the door. All that youthful energy.

"Who is it?"

Joseph looked at his father. Cyrus put his finger to his lips, signaling him to remain quiet.

"It's me, Darius. I lost my key."

The door opened. "How'd you lose your-." Darius stopped, his eyes widening. "Yousef! What-." He stopped again, his eyes flicking to their father. "Is this for real?" At Cyrus's nod, Darius gave a joyful shout and launched himself at Joseph. "Yousef! Welcome home, big brother!"

Joseph caught his little brother in a hug, stumbling back a few steps from the force of it. His father's hands came up to his shoulders, steadying him.

"Finally! I knew it would happen. I knew it!"

Joseph squeezed his brother tight, tears coming to his eyes. He was glad his brother had held on to his hope that their family would be reunited after all this time. Joseph knew it was that hope that helped lead to this moment.

"Darius? What's going on out there?"

Joseph heard his mother's voice from somewhere in the house. He looked up just as she entered the foyer. She abruptly halted, her hand coming up to her mouth when she saw him.

"Yousef?"

He nodded, trying to smile through his tears. He reached a hand out and his mother rushed forward. When their fingers met, Joseph pulled her into the embrace with Darius. All three of them were crying.

"Let's get inside everyone. I didn't bring Joseph home just for him to stand outside."

But no one moved. His mother just cried harder and Darius squeezed him tighter. Cyrus's arms went around them all, enveloping them in one big hug. Joseph couldn't believe it. He was finally back home with his family.

****

"That was really good, Mom. Thanks."

"If I'd known you were coming, I would have made your favorites."

She came around to collect his plate, waving him back to his seat when he tried to clear his place himself.

"Sit down, Yousef."

He missed being bossed around by his mother so much, that he immediately sat. Darius started talking about the admission process for the schools on his list, asking Joseph's advice about the essays. Joseph relaxed back in his chair. It was almost like the six-year estrangement had never happened.

His mother came back into the dining room with a plate of walnut brownies. She set the plate down in the middle of the table.

"I expect you to come home on a regular basis now, Yousef. And next time, bring Gage with you."

"I don't know if I can guarantee that." He reached for a brownie but his mother smacked his hand. "Ouch!" Joseph looked up at his mother in surprise.

His mother shook her finger at him. "Yousef Naderi! I know you two are having problems. But I expect Gage to be with you."

"What? How did you know that?"

"I called him at this shop," she replied with a nonchalant shrug. "We talked for a while. He misses you, Yousef. He knows he made mistakes. But you boys can't resolve the problem if you're not even speaking to each other."

Joseph sat there dumbfounded. He looked around the table. His father was nodding in agreement with his wife. Darius was grinning as he ate his brownie. If he'd needed confirmation that he was welcomed back into the fold, discussing his love life with his mother while his father calmly looked on was it. "I can't believe you called him."

"Of course I did. It's my right as your mother-."

"To get to know who your sons are dating," he finished for her. "Okay, I will talk to Gage, I promise. Can I have a brownie now?"

Amira Naderi smiled and pushed the plate towards him. "Help yourself."

CHAPTER 76

Gage stood up and cracked his back. He'd been bent over what felt like an endless number of bikes today. Sponsoring Joseph had brought him an influx of new customers. He was glad for it, but it was looking like he and Danny might not be able to handle the load without working themselves to death. But maybe that wouldn't be a bad thing. Gage took a drink of the soda he'd opened earlier. He grimaced as it hit his tongue. The soda was warm and flat after being left out for a couple of hours.

As long as he was working, the stereo in the shop blasting, he didn't think too much about Joseph. But when it was quiet and he was alone, he kept remembering how he'd stood in front of their bedroom window, watching Joseph sling his bags into the back of his Z and drive off. He much preferred being worked to death.

The phone started ringing even though it was after six. He and Danny looked at each other. "You're closest," Gage said with a shrug. At this point, he was so tired he was happy to let the machine pick up. But Danny went over to answer it. Gage watched as Danny nodded a few times before he turned to look at him. Danny held the phone out, his eyes wide.

"Gage, you'd better take this."

Gage went over, his heart pounding so hard he was light headed. "Joseph?"

Danny shook his head.

Relief that it wasn't about Joseph took the edge off, but he was still nervous about what was waiting for him. Gage took the phone. "Hello?"

A crisp voice came through the phone. "Is this Gage Mason?"

"Yeah, who is this?"

"This is Mindy with the County Medical Examiner's Office."

****

Back at the hotel, Joseph packed up his things. He was going home. Not to his childhood home, to the one he shared with Gage. Although it had been surreal to sit with his family, listening to his parents give him advice on his love life, he realized they were right. He and Gage needed to talk. He planned to do so tonight; he just wasn't sure how to go about it. Should he call first or just show up? He was thinking showing up, but with a hot meal, was the way to go when his phone rang. He pulled it out of his back jean's pocket to see Mason Bike Shop on the screen. Joseph slid the green arrow to accept the call, surprised yet expecting to hear Gage's voice. But it wasn't Gage.

"Joseph? It's Danny."

"Hey, Danny what's going on? Is Gage okay?"

"Gage is fine. But he just got a phone call from the M.E. Heather, his old girlfriend, is dead. She OD'd on heroin last night. Cleaning lady found her in some flea bag hotel when she went in to take care of the room."

Joseph stumbled back, plopping down on the bed behind him. "Holy shit," he breathed. "How is Gage taking it?"

"I don't know. After the call, he blew out of here. I know you guys are apart, but I figured you'd want to know what happened, and maybe go check on him."

Joseph cleared his throat. "Of course. I was on my way over anyway. I'll let you know if he's home safe."

"Thanks, Joseph."

They hung up. Joseph shook his head. If he was this thrown by hearing of a stranger's death, he could only imagine how Gage was taking it. Especially since he blamed himself for Heather's addiction. Joseph took a moment to get himself together. Then he grabbed his stuff and went to Gage.

****

Joseph had to park in the street when he got to the house. Gage was there, but his truck was parked in a haphazard diagonal, taking up the entire driveway. Joseph went in, finding the downstairs dark. Gage wasn't in any of the rooms down there so Joseph headed upstairs. As he did, he heard the sound of the shower running.

Walking into their bedroom, Joseph saw the trail of Gage's keys, clothes, and shoes on the floor. He sidestepped it all and knocked on the open bathroom door so he didn't scare Gage. "Gage," he called out. "It's me, Joseph."

No answer from the shower. But Joseph could see him behind the frosted glass door. He was standing there under the spray, his arms folded and braced on the shower wall in front of him, his head resting atop them. Joseph didn't think, didn't hesitate. He just undressed and got in the shower. Water splashed in his face as he approached Gage, cautiously resting a hand on his back. "I heard about Heather. I'm so sorry."

Gage didn't move, just continued to lean against the wall, his back muscles and biceps practically bulging he was so tense. His skin was red from the intense heat of the shower and the uncomfortably hot water burned Joseph as well. Turning the handle so it was a little cooler, he moved closer to Gage. He still didn't move. Didn't turn around, didn't acknowledge Joseph in any way. But Joseph eased his arms around him regardless, cradling his back up against his chest. "I'm sorry," he said again.

Gage spoke, his voice so low that even though they were pressed together, Joseph had to strain to hear him over the rush of the water. "The last time she came to see me, I told her to stay the fuck out of my life. That I was done. I refused to help her, because my debt was wiped clean." He laughed and started thumping his forehead against the shower wall. "My debt was wiped clean," he repeated.

Joseph took his arm from around Gage to put his hand between his forehead and the tile. "Gage stop!"

Gage stopped but whispered once more. "No more debt."

Joseph gently turned Gage around. "Gage, I know what you're thinking." Gage blinked at him, his dark eyes watery and spiked with red.

"That's because an idiot could figure it out. I'm thinking this is my fault, because it is. So a smart guy like you shouldn't have any problem coming to that conclusion."

Joseph felt bad for him, but he wouldn't let Gage take the blame for Heather's death on his shoulders. "You're just as smart, Gage, so you know *I'm* going to say this *isn't* your fault. But no matter what I say, it's not going to solidify in your head until you're ready to accept that."

Gage reached out, caressing his face. His hand moved to Joseph's hair, wrapping the wet strands around a finger. "Joseph, why are you here, naked, in the shower with me?"

"I'm here because you need me, Gage."

Gage smiled. "Just like always."

He leaned forward and kissed Joseph softly. Joseph returned the kiss for a moment. When he went to pull away, Gage's hand came up to grasp the back of his head, holding him in place as he deepened the kiss. Joseph allowed it, curling his tongue against Gage's, gasping when Gage bit at his lip. Gage's hand trailed down his back to cup his ass. A single finger slipped between his cheeks, sliding light and delicate against his entrance. At that touch, Joseph forced himself to pull away.

Joseph looked at Gage, his wet hair flat against his head, a muscle ticking in his jaw. Joseph felt that aura of intensity that always seemed to surround Gage drawing him in. He would have to resist it. Joseph swallowed hard and said, "Gage, now isn't the time for this."

"It is," Gage answered. "You know what I need from you. Please don't turn me away." He kissed his way down Joseph's throat, resting his lips over his pulse. "Please, Joseph. I need you."

Gage straightened again to look at him. Joseph stared back, his heart racing, his breath hitching in his throat. How could he turn Gage away at this moment? He'd just lost someone, and Joseph knew the guilt and grief were tearing Gage apart. Joseph couldn't do it. He couldn't turn him away. Perceptive as ever, Gage read the surrender in his face. Gage grasped his wrists, raising his arms over his head. Leaning into him, Gage pressed him back against the shower wall. And Joseph let him.

Gage kissed him again, soft yet passionate. Joseph moaned at the heat of it. Everything was hot. The air in the shower stall, the water cascading over them. Their breaths mingling together in their kiss. And Gage's hand that slipped down to grasp his cock. Hot. So hot. Joseph's eyes drifted closed as he moaned, his hips arching up, pushing his shaft through Gage's pumping fist. Gage groaned, pressing even closer against him, his erection hot, hard, and silky wet as it rubbed against Joseph's hip.

Gage whispered against Joseph's mouth. "I knew you would come home tonight. I knew you would help me, Joseph."

Joseph forced his eyes open to look at Gage. His eyes were open too, focused on him. But they were full of pain. And it was that look that finally gave him the strength to say what needed to be said. "Gage, stop."

Gage's hand fell still. He tilted his head to the side, a confused frown on his brow. "Stop? Why?"

Joseph took a deep breath. "Because I love you. And this isn't healthy. I'm not letting you do this to yourself anymore."

CHAPTER 77

J oseph shut off the water and stepped from the shower. He grabbed two dry towels and stood there on the mat waiting.

Gage didn't leave the stall. "What are you doing?"

"We're going to talk Gage. And I mean *talk*."

Gage stepped out of the shower, ignoring the towel Joseph held out for him. "I don't need to talk. You know what I need."

"No. I know what you're *used* to. But we're not doing that anymore."

Water dripped from Gage's hair into his eyes as he walked up to Joseph. He pushed his hair back, not caring enough to take the towel from Joseph and dry off. Emotion swirled through him, making him tremble. Was it anger? He didn't know. His hand shaking, he pointed at Joseph in accusation. "You said. You said, *whatever I needed*, you'd give it to me, Joseph." His voice shook too, but he couldn't make it stop. "Remember? In the garage, that's what you said."

"I remember but-."

Gage didn't let him finish. He brushed past him and went to sit on the bed. He was still wet. He didn't care. His head hurt. Heather was lying dead in the fucking city morgue because he'd turned her away. Now Joseph was turning him away. Is this what he deserved? He looked up at Joseph, who'd followed him out of the bathroom. He opened his mouth, but this time Joseph cut him off.

"Stop. Don't say whatever it is you're about to, because I know somehow it will be you convincing me to go along with what you want. I remember what I said, Gage. And I meant it. I'll give you whatever you need, but that doesn't mean giving in to you."

Joseph came forward. He was still naked too, water running down his body. He must not have cared either, because he dropped down and kneeled between Gage's legs, resting his warm palms on his thighs. The touch wasn't sexual. Gage accepted that it wouldn't be.

"You can't keep letting stuff build up and then using sex to help you forget. You're going to destroy yourself. It's not fair to always expect me to help you deal. And if we keep fighting the way we do, we won't last."

Gage looked at Joseph. Droplets of water slipped down the strands of his hair. His soft green eyes were wide with worry and hurt. Gage hated that he'd put that look there, but he wasn't surprised. He'd said it to himself, the morning after Joseph had first stayed the night with him, that he brought the people he tried to love nothing but pain and death. So no, he wasn't surprised that Joseph was hurting right now. He just didn't know how to fix it. He thought of Heather instead. That was easier to deal with. "She had me listed as her emergency contact. *Me*. After I fucking got her hooked on drugs. Do you think she tried to call me as she was dying? Or did she just lay there by herself, cursing my name?"

Joseph squeezed his leg. Sadness pulled at his mouth as he spoke. "I don't know, Gage. Don't torture yourself with that."

His thoughts shot back to Joseph. It was all too much. The pain in his head increased, making him feel sick. He reached out to his lover, sliding his fingers into his hair. "I don't know how to stop hurting you."

"I don't think either of us do. Maybe we should see someone to help you with it and to deal with Heather's passing. And I mean both of us, we'd be in it together."

Gage recoiled slightly. He didn't like the thought of sitting on a cheap couch, sharing his feelings with some shrink. "I tried that once and it didn't work."

"Yeah, you did, a long time ago. Maybe the person you saw just wasn't the right fit. We have to try something, Gage. I know this situation with Heather is weighing heavy on your mind. You look like you're hurting with it."

"I am. My goddamn head is pounding."

Joseph reached up to cup the side of his face. Gage turned into to the touch, grateful to feel Joseph's skin on his, even if it wasn't in the way he'd hoped for. He sighed and closed his eyes. When he shivered, Joseph took his hand away and rose. "Where are you going?"

"I'll be right back." Joseph wasn't gone long. He returned with Tylenol, a glass of water and a towel. After Gage swallowed the aspirin, Joseph dried him off, from his hair to his feet. Gage followed his quiet order to get under the covers while Joseph dried himself off. Joseph threw the towel into the bathroom, then got in on his side of the bed. They lay on their sides facing each other. Joseph wrapped an arm around Gage and pulled him close.

"I know this might not seem like the right time to be bringing all this up. But you're going to be on a razor's edge dealing with Heather's death. And you already think it's your fault. We'll both need help to get through this. I know you don't want to, but please see someone with me." Joseph lowered his lashes for a moment. When he looked back at Gage, his eyes were still filled with worry but there was determination as well. "I can't stay with you if things don't change Gage. So will you try therapy, or will you lose me?"

CHAPTER 78

You don't want to be here."

Gage laughed. He was currently slouched down in a chair, his arms crossed over his chest. Joseph was to his right, sitting up straight in his chair. They were in a therapist's office, a place Gage thought he'd never be again. Until Joseph had made it a condition of them getting back together. The night of Heather's death, Joseph had forced him to face the fact that using sex to dull his anger was personally destructive and not fair to him. Gage had been reluctant to try counseling as Joseph suggested, but he didn't want to lose him. And he knew if he continued with the same pattern, he would.

That night, he'd looked at Joseph lying next to him, his eyes full of concern, waiting for his answer. His words from the shower had bounced around Gage's head. *I love you*. Gage felt the same way… but he couldn't say it back. He'd remembered the promise he'd made to himself, the day they shared donuts in bed. To never hurt Joseph. Because of that and because he didn't want to keep making the same mistakes that he had with Riley, he'd agreed to try therapy. And now, here they were.

This was their first appointment. Joseph had found a therapist that so far Gage felt comfortable with. Dr. Perry was young, covered in tattoos and dressed in skinny jeans and a t-shirt. Since Gage had expected to walk in to see a plump middle-aged guy wearing a cardigan, he was happily surprised. Even the office was different than what he was expecting. Perry had a home office in a glass-walled sunroom attached to the back of his house. Blood red throw rugs covered the painted wooden floor and they all sat on comfortable chairs made up of heavy black iron frames with thick cushions.

Gage finally answered the therapist. "What was your first clue?"

"Your body language is a pretty big tell. But you *are* here. Why?"

"I'm here because my boyfriend asked me to do this."

"Coming here because your partner asked you to is a good first step. But you know that you won't get the best results from this unless you're here because you want to be."

Gage looked into the man's hazel eyes. He did know that. He did know that and he did want to change. But right now this was all for Joseph. The therapist moved his piercing gaze to Joseph.

"Joseph, you got the ball rolling on this. Why are you guys here?"

Joseph looked at Gage then over to the doctor. "We're here because my boyfriend has an unusual way of dealing with his emotions. Anger especially. He has sex to forget about things and I don't think it's healthy."

Perry leaned back in his chair, crossing his feet at the ankles. "That's not unusual at all. People use lots of addictions to avoid facing things they don't want to deal with. Abusing drugs and alcohol are probably the most common methods, but people can also dull themselves with food, shopping, or sex," he finished with a nod at Gage. "But you're right, Joseph, it *is* unhealthy." He looked back at Gage. "Do you feel screwing your way through life's problems is okay?"

Gage's eyes widened. He hadn't expected a doctor to use language like that. "I didn't used to have a problem with it. But now that I'm just with one person it's starting to click."

"That's good," Perry said. "Before we start digging, both of you tell me what you want out of these sessions. Joseph?"

"I'd like to see him get angry and then talk to me about it without using me or manipulating me into going along with what he wants."

"And Gage, what do you want from Joseph?"

"I know I can be an asshole. And I play mind games to get my way." He looked at Joseph once, then back at the therapist. "But I need Joseph to stop walking out on me when things aren't going right between us. I can't trust that we'll stay together if every time we have a fight, in the back of my mind I'm wondering if this is the time he'll take off for good."

It felt like it was quiet forever, even though Gage knew it couldn't have been more than a few seconds. He finally looked up at Joseph, who was watching him with surprise on his face.

"I'm sorry Gage, I didn't even think about that."

Gage shrugged. "It's okay."

Perry interjected. "It's not okay to have that worry in your head, Gage. And Joseph, it's not okay to feel as if Gage is working you to get what he wants." Perry tucked his thumb under his chin, bracing himself on his fist. "It sounds to me like you both want to learn how to handle your disagreements in a healthy manner."

Joseph spoke up. "Yes, we want to be together. But this cycle we're in…" He shook his head. "It's not working."

Gage didn't say anything, just nodded in agreement with Joseph. Perry nodded too.

"We can work on these issues. I'd like to see you both together and on your own while we do." Perry took a moment to scribble a few notes on the leather-bound journal in his lap. "And you probably won't like hearing this. Gage, I think it would be a good for the two of you to abstain until you're only having sex because it feels good and you want to connect with Joseph. Not because you're using it as a substitute for something else. Can you do that?"

Gage laughed and looked over at Joseph. His mouth had dropped open in surprise. "I can. But I sure as fuck don't want to."

CHAPTER 79

Three weeks later, Joseph was at home in their study. He'd taken over the room to use as his home office. Since he was only taking on enough clients for part-time work, he'd decided that he didn't need to rent office space. Working from home saved him money and the commute was pretty sweet. He worked on his practice Monday thru Wednesday. Thursdays, Fridays, and Saturdays were for racing.

Joseph planned to spend a few months racing weekly on amateur tracks, working his way up through difficulty levels. And when he was ready he would enter the professional circuit. Gage knew his plan and encouraged him. Together they studied gear and upgrades. Gage went with him to practice as he ran time trials. But he no longer pushed. Joseph was thankful for the change. He loved having Gage's support, without the stress of rushing into things before he was ready. And Joseph was getting better at handling his losses and poor practice runs. Gage teased him good-naturedly, offering up some of the anger management techniques their therapist gave him. They worked for Joseph. He wasn't surprised, because he'd seen the positive effect they were having on Gage.

Sundays were Joseph's favorite day of the week because he spent them with Gage. They went to play pool, hung out with friends, or just lazed in bed watching TV. It was nice, but of course, it wasn't all roses and sunshine. They still disagreed on things, but they were slowly learning how to talk through it without Gage blowing up or Joseph walking out. Going in for therapy, with their amazingly down to earth counselor, helped. They'd been to several sessions, seeing the doctor twice a week. Because, in Gage's words, "If I can't be inside you until I have shit in my head right, we're going as often as possible." Joseph had laughed. But he agreed. Lying in bed with Gage was great, but it was killing him not to be able to kiss and touch his lover the way he wanted.

The front door slammed. Joseph straightened, distracted from his thoughts.

"Yo, Yousef!" Gage called out.

Joseph rolled his eyes. Gage had taken to calling him that on occasion, ever since he'd talked to his mother. They hadn't met yet, Gage and Joseph agreeing to work things out between them before he met his family. But Mrs. Naderi still called Gage sometimes. Joseph didn't mind, and he knew Gage enjoyed their conversations. He went to the living room to see Gage standing there, a big grin on his face. "What's up?"

"I got so pissed off at work today."

Joseph frowned, confused as to why Gage was happy he got mad. "What happened?"

Gage's grin grew wider. "Nothing."

"Huh?"

"You know how it's been crazy busy, right? Well, this guy came in with an old Harley and wanted me to get started on a rush job restoring it. He was already pissed at having to wait in line while I helped the people in front of him, because according to him, I cost him his whole lunch break. When I told him a rush wasn't possible he lost his shit." Gage went and flopped onto the couch. "I listened to his concerns, then told the guy I needed to go and check on something. I went into my office, closed the door and counted to ten. I was still a little pissed so I did twenty quick pushups. After that, I went back out there, politely told the guy I couldn't work him in until next Tuesday, but had referrals for some other places if he needed a rush." Gage winked. "Of course, I told him their work wasn't as good. And he agreed to wait."

Joseph grinned nearly as wide as Gage. "I don't want to sound like a proud papa because that would open up a whole other reason for therapy, but I'm proud of you Gage."

Gage laughed. "Thanks. And I didn't even have to use my fingers to count to ten," he joked. "I know it's a small thing, but before I would have blown up at the guy. Or I'd have let it build up, piling insignificant bullshit on top of it until I had to screw my brains out to forget about it all. But not this time. It's already gone."

Joseph went and sat next to Gage on the couch. He was so glad that Gage was taking the counseling seriously and actually putting it to use. "I feel like I should I take you out for ice cream or something to celebrate."

"Nope," Gage said as he shook his head. "I'm taking *you* out to celebrate."

****

Joseph looked at the big red letters of the giant office supply warehouse they'd just pulled up to. "How are we going to celebrate in there?"

Gage put the truck in park. "You'll see."

Inside they headed over to the computer aisles. Gage walked up and down the rows, Joseph trailing behind, until he found what he was looking for.

"Here we go." He waved his hand at the boxes on the shelves. "Pick me out the best one."

Joseph looked from Gage to the shelves. In front of him were packages for business accounting suites like QuickBooks, Sage and Quicken. The warmth of Gage's hand settled on his back.

"You were right. I need to upgrade my system. I figured since you did all that research and were so smart about setting up your practice, you'd know the best program for me to use."

Joseph recognized the apology. And he appreciated it so much more than Gage simply saying the words, *I'm sorry*. As they stood in the middle of the store, Joseph looked at Gage, who was watching him with a smile. Barely able to believe how far they'd come, Joseph felt absolutely positive that they would be able to make things work between them. He had to clear his throat a couple of times before he could speak. "If you go with Quick Books…"

****

"You sure were determined to buy me some ice cream. I think that was an excuse because you wanted some."

Joseph laughed. "Maybe."

Joseph had coaxed Gage into swinging by the ice cream place after they'd made their purchase at the store. Now they were back home, on the couch in the living room. Gage was currently wolfing down a chocolate covered sundae while Joseph slowly ate a dipped cone. Gage ate the last spoonful then looked at Joseph.

"You gonna eat that ice cream or play with it?"

Joseph arched a brow at Gage. "I like to savor my desserts, thank you very much."

Gage set his empty bowl on the coffee table and leaned in close to Joseph. "You're making a mess," he said.

Joseph looked down and saw the vanilla ice cream dripping down his hand. "Damn. Hand me a napkin."

Gage shook his head. "I got it."

He leaned in even closer and grasped Joseph's wrist. Joseph watched as Gage's dark head bent, his tongue coming out to lick up the ice cream on his hand. Gage glanced up at him, a teasing light glowing in his eyes as he delicately ran his tongue over the sensitive inside of Joseph's wrist. Joseph bit his lip as Gage closed his eyes and brushed his lips up to the base of his thumb. He sucked that skin into his mouth, lightly flicking his tongue against it. Sparks of sensation tingled out from that spot, making Joseph's breath come a little faster. When Gage bit down, Joseph moaned, his fingers clenching on the ice cream cone still in his hand. Gage straightened and took the cone away from him. His tongue darted out again, lapping up some of the creamy vanilla treat.

"Do you want any more of this?"

Joseph shook his head and Gage put the rest of the ice cream in his empty bowl. When Gage turned back to him, Joseph met his eyes, running his tongue over his lip. Gage groaned and reached for him. He slid a hand into Joseph's hair, pulling him into a desperate kiss. Joseph parted his lips for Gage's seeking tongue, moaning at the taste of sugar and chocolate and *Gage*. Joseph shifted restlessly on the couch. He wanted to be closer to Gage. He was hard behind his tight jeans, and Gage's rough kisses and possessive grip on his hair had arousal sizzling through his veins. Gage whispered his name, his scruffy beard softly scratching him as he trailed kisses down his neck. Joseph moaned again as Gage nipped at the skin over his pulse.

He was ready to climb onto Gage's lap and grind against him when Gage pulled back. Joseph took him in. Gage's chest pumped up and down with his heaving breaths, his eyes were heavy-lidded and his mouth swollen from their kisses. It had been too long since Joseph saw that look on his lover. He reached for him, but Gage caught his hand and pressed it down to the couch.

"I'm going for a walk," Gage said.

Joseph blinked. He wanted to protest, to tell Gage that they had improved enough in their relationship to say the hell with abstaining any longer. But he didn't. Gage was letting Joseph move at his own pace with his racing, so he needed to do the same for Gage with this. He took a deep breath to rein in his arousal. "Okay. I'll be upstairs when you get back." Gage pressed a kiss to the top of Joseph's head and left.

****

An hour later, Gage was back home, in bed with Joseph watching TV. The walk in the crisp fall air had cooled him off, literally and figuratively. Sex with Joseph would have been the cherry on top of their celebration sundae. But he didn't want to taint his success in controlling his temper by having sex the same night. He wanted to be sure he was doing this on his own. So after a few minutes of hot and heavy kissing, he'd thought it best to walk away for a while. He was sure he'd made the right choice. When he'd made it back to the house, Joseph was already showered and in bed, watching TV. He'd smiled and asked if he had a good walk.

Gage knew he was lucky to have Joseph. And even luckier that his lover was so understanding of the changes he was trying to make. They weren't easy. One in particular had been tough. He'd called Montoya to apologize and ask him not to take his anger out on Joseph. He'd struggled to get the words out, but he'd done it for Joseph. For his safety. Montoya hadn't admitted anything, but he had accepted his apology. That was enough for him. He'd successfully tackled that problem, and he knew he would eventually find success with his other issues, including dealing with Heather's death, as well.

"Did you want to watch anything else?"

Gage looked to see Joseph holding the remote. "No. I'm done for the night."

Joseph turned off the TV and flicked off the bedside lamp. Leaning over, he gave Gage a quick kiss.

"Goodnight, Gage."

"Goodnight."

Gage watched as Joseph turned on his side to sleep. Moonlight spilled into the room, caressing Joseph's sleeping form as Gage longed to do. He reached out to Joseph, but pulled his hand back before he touched him. Gage wanted this to work. And he understood why the doctor had asked them to abstain. He wanted sex with

Joseph to just be about the two of them and how good they could make each other feel. It shouldn't be him using Joseph to make himself feel better emotionally, no matter how much physical pleasure he gave in return. So he didn't touch him. Instead, he lay there on his side, waiting.

Once Joseph's breathing deepened, Gage scooted closer. He wrapped an arm around Joseph tight, tangling their legs together. Pressing his face into Joseph's soft, curly hair, he breathed in the faint hint of coconut shampoo. Gage took a deep breath and closed his eyes to go to sleep.

CHAPTER 80

on't forget to come home on time tonight. Joseph sent off the text to Gage. Business was still booming at Gage's shop. It was going to pick up even more, because Luis had finally agreed to start doing paint jobs there. Joseph had helped Gage hire more help, but the girl, Olivia, didn't start until next week. As a result, Gage and Danny had been working overtime to stay on top of things. But tonight, Joseph needed to make sure that Gage was home on time because they had Max's thirtieth birthday party to go to. Just before Joseph went to get in the shower, his phone chimed with a response. *Leaving in ten.*

Twenty minutes later, Joseph was out of the shower and standing in front of the bathroom mirror. He hadn't dressed yet, and only had on a pair of the tight black briefs Gage had bought him while he blow dried and straightened his hair. As he'd grabbed them out of the drawer, he'd told himself it was because they were the first pair he saw, not because they were Gage's favorite. He heard the front door open and slam closed, followed by Gage's feet on the stairs. He made a final pass with the flat iron through his hair as Gage walked into the bathroom. Gage smiled when he saw him, coming over to stand close enough for Joseph to feel his body heat.

Gage leaned in and sniffed at Joseph's neck. "You smell nice."

"Thanks. It's Gucci Guilty."

"You're too good to be guilty," Gage said with a soft laugh. Gage brought his hand up, resting his fingertips on Joseph's hip. One finger slipped under the waistband of the briefs, softly rubbing back and forth across the sensitive skin of his pelvis. "I like your hair like this. What did you do to it?"

He met Gage's eyes in the mirror. "I flat ironed it." Gage gave him a confused look, so Joseph gestured at the flat iron on the counter.

"That thing looks like a torture device." He ran his other hand through Joseph's hair. It fell smoothly back from his face, the subtle blonde highlights picking up the light. "Hmmm… well it did its job. Very pretty." Gage stepped away, taking the wonderful warmth of his body heat with him. "You finished primping? Bout to shower and it'll fog the mirror up."

Joseph nodded. "Yeah, I'm finished. I'll go get dressed." Joseph cleared his mess off the counter. By the time he was done, Gage had removed all his clothes. Joseph ran his eyes over his lover, noting the muscular beauty of his body. And his very obvious erection. While Joseph watched, Gage stroked himself once, slowly. He glanced back up to see Gage watching him too. Joseph tensed, his body responding. He didn't speak, didn't move. He didn't know what Gage wanted, if he was hinting that he wanted their celibacy to end. He tried to think of something to say. Before he could, Gage smiled at him, then turned away to get in the shower.

****

There was a good crowd at Max's place by the time he and Gage pulled up. "Looks like lots of people want to help celebrate Max's thirtieth."

"He deserves it. His first twenty were shitty."

They walked up to the house, Joseph carrying the gift they'd gotten for Max. Once inside, they were greeted by the people that Joseph had come to think of as his friends, not just friends of Gage's. Gia, Danny and his girlfriend, Fred, Tony and several others. Nate was there too, but he was distracted, checking his phone again and again in clear frustration. The one person he didn't see was the birthday boy.

After a few minutes, the group started to move outside to build a bonfire. Joseph excused himself to go to the bathroom. The one off the hall was occupied. Joseph felt comfortable enough in Max's house that he went to the one in the master bedroom. He reached for the doorknob on the partially opened door and started to go inside. But movement in the low light of the room caught his eye. It was Max, arguing in a heated yet low voice with someone. Joseph couldn't see who that someone was, until arms went around Max, pulling him into an embrace. Joseph's eyes widened and he stepped back. *Was Max…?* Joseph let the thought trail away. It was none of his business. He went back down the hall, this time finding the guest restroom empty.

****

Outside the bonfire was going strong. Everyone had gathered around it, roasting hot dogs and marshmallows. The fire kept the coolness of the fall evening away, while the scent of the burning mesquite scented the air. A few minutes after Joseph joined the group, Max arrived outside as well. He was alone. Someone handed him a cup of hot cider, then immediately started telling a story of Max's days as a tattoo apprentice. Max smiled, shaking his head at all the stuff he'd had to do as the shop bitch.

Joseph finished his drink. Gage took their empty cups and stepped aside to throw them away. When he came back, he stood behind Joseph instead of next to him like before. Joseph turned to look at him with a quizzical smile. When Gage just shrugged, he turned back around.

Joseph jumped a bit as Gage's arm went around his waist. Gage didn't say anything, so Joseph stood there in his embrace, listening to more stories meant to teasingly embarrass Max. After a few minutes, Gage's thumb slid under his t-shirt, rubbing softly back and forth over his stomach. Joseph still stood there. Until the roughness of Gage's palm slid under his shirt as well, one finger dipping past his belt buckle to teasingly stroke low on his stomach. Goosebumps broke out on Joseph's skin. He didn't know how to react. Maybe Gage was just being affectionate and didn't mean to arouse with his touch? But then Gage pulled Joseph back against him and he felt the hardness of Gage's erection pressing against his ass. Gage rubbed his cheek against Joseph's hair, his voice a seductive whisper in his ear.

"I miss being inside you, Joseph."

Joseph shivered, unable to do anything more than make a small noise of agreement. Gage stepped back from him and Joseph looked over his shoulder, watching him walk away. When he reached the patio door, he held it open and crooked his fingers at Joseph. Then he turned and went into the house. Joseph followed.

Once inside, Gage held out his hand. Joseph took it, and let Gage lead him into the study. Compared to outside, it was quiet in the house. The snick of the door closing and Gage locking it behind them sounded unnaturally loud. Joseph turned to see Gage leaning back against the door. His head was tilted low, his hair falling into his eyes. For some reason, nervousness buzzed through Joseph. But he didn't resist when Gage pulled him into his arms. Gage brought their bodies together, claiming his mouth in a fierce kiss. Joseph kissed him back, leaning against him. Gage's hands slipped down to squeeze his ass and Joseph moaned, grinding his hips into Gage's. Gage licked at Joseph's neck, speaking in a rough whisper against his skin.

"I can feel how hard you are. If you're even half as hard as me, you feel like you're about to burst. Is that how you feel, Joseph?"

Joseph nodded with another moan, as Gage pushed a hand into his jeans, his calloused palm gripping the bare skin of his ass. He had a feeling they weren't going to stop like they had the other night on the couch. And he wanted to be sure they were on the same track. Joseph pulled back, breathing hard.

"Gage, why are you doing this?" he asked.

Gage brushed a thumb over Joseph's lips. "Because you're gorgeous. Because I love you. And because I'm fucking horny."

Joseph laughed. "Those sound like good -. Wait. What was that part in the middle?"

Gage smiled. "C'mon Joseph. You know I love you. There's no way I would have agreed to talk about my feelings with a shrink if I didn't." He shrugged. "With all the bullshit in my head, I couldn't say it before. But I do and I have for a while."

Joseph stared in amazement before he smiled. "I knew it. Ever since you sacrificed your sexy windswept hair to wear a helmet for me."

Gage gave an amused shake of his head. "Come here." He tugged Joseph close again with the grip he still had on his ass. "I want to see every single bit of you."

Gage slowly undressed him, pushing his jeans and briefs off after Joseph kicked off his shoes, sliding his blazer off his shoulders and raising his t-shirt over his head. Joseph stood there as Gage leaned back against the door and looked at him. He started to step closer to Gage, but his boyfriend stopped him with a shake of his head.

"I've always thought you were beautiful, Joseph. But I used to just admire your body for the way it would make me feel." He reached out and lightly ran his fingers over Joseph's stomach. "But now… now I can appreciate your hard muscles, and the dip in your hips and this soft dark trail of hair because it's you and I love you. Does that make sense?"

Joseph nodded slowly. "I get it. And I love you too."

Gage smiled and finally pulled Joseph back into his arms. He turned him around, reaching down to grasp his cock. Gage stroked Joseph with one hand, while with the other, he opened his jeans. Joseph heard the zipper going down and hissed as the heat of Gage's rock-hard cock slipped in between his ass. Gage kept stroking him, while he moved his hips, sliding his cock up and down, whispering in Joseph's ear how good he felt.

In no time at all, Joseph was moaning and writhing against Gage, pushing his ass back so that Gage's thick cock pressed even harder against his entrance. Gage took his hand away from Joseph and he moaned a protest.

Gage laughed softly. "Do you want me to keep doing this or do you want me inside you?"

His blood was racing in his veins, throbbing in his cock. Joseph sucked in a breath so he could answer. "Inside me."

"Then let me get us ready."

Joseph impatiently waited as Gage took out the small packet of lube that he'd apparently brought with him tonight. But he couldn't stop writhing against his lover, desperate to feel Gage inside him. His movements must have been too much for Gage to take, because he cursed, and with only the slightest bit of preparation, pushed his cock inside him. Both of them cried out loudly at that first thrust, forgetting that they needed to keep quiet so they weren't discovered.

Gage bit at the sensitive place where neck and shoulder met. "So impatient."

Joseph exhaled hard. "A month, Gage. It's been a month."

"I know."

Gage kissed the spot he'd just bitten and started thrusting into him with long, slow strokes. His hand returned to Joseph's cock, pumping him at the same speed. Joseph groaned, reaching up and back to tangle his fingers in Gage's hair. The pleasure was already flowing through his veins, making his spine tingle and his body feel heavy with desire. He moved in rhythm with his lover, digging his fingers into the muscles of Gage's thigh.

Gage wrapped an arm around him tight, as tight as he did when he was sleeping, making Joseph's heart pound. He'd woken several times over the past few weeks to Gage holding him in a close embrace, almost as though he were afraid he would lose him in the night. Joseph had no intention of leaving Gage, and he wanted to make sure he knew it.

He brought his other hand up to lace his fingers through Gage's, not caring when Gage gripped him so hard it almost hurt. "I love you Gage. All of it was worth it to have you." Gage squeezed him even tighter, resting his lips against the back of Joseph's neck. He stroked into Joseph slowly, his face buried in his hair. He could feel Gage's hot breaths on his skin through the strands as Gage told him again that he loved him. Joseph's body was tingling with pleasure, but he couldn't help but smile at the two sides to his boyfriend. The bad boy who snuck away to have sex in his friend's house. And the lover who did whatever was necessary to keep them together, and held him close in the middle of the night.

Joseph's smile faded, changing into a moan as Gage increased the speed with which he stroked into him. The thickness of his cock stretched him, making him feel wonderfully claimed by his lover as Gage brushed over that sensitive place inside him. Joseph pushed back against Gage even harder, his thighs trembling, his balls drawing up tight as his orgasm pulsed in his shaft. It was a struggle to keep his voice quiet, whispering to Gage that he was coming. It was even harder once Gage started stroking him swiftly, forcing him to the edge of his release until Joseph had no choice but to let go in a spine-tingling, shuddering climax that took his breath away. Gage groaned, pumping Joseph through his orgasm, his hips moving faster and faster until he too was shaking with pleasure. Gage squeezed his arm around Joseph impossibly tighter just as he felt the heat of his release deep inside him. Gage's voice was muffled against Joseph's neck, but he heard each of the four words he spoke:

"I love you, Joseph."

****

Joseph walked back out to the party with Gage, catching a glimpse of them in the hallway mirror. Their hair was a mess, their clothes rumpled. Beard burn and a small love bite marred his neck. And they both smelled like sex. One look was all it would take for anyone to figure out what they'd been up to. But Joseph didn't care. They had come together in a way that solidified the love and passionate attraction they had for one another and that was all that mattered to him.

Gia came around the corner, her eyebrows shooting up when she saw them. "Oooh, y'all. I don't even want to know." She held a hand up as if she were blocking them from talking and continued on past them without another word.

Joseph looked at Gage, biting his lip to hold back a smile. "I think she guessed our secret."

Gage snorted in dismissal. "When can we get out of here? It's been so long since we got physical, I'm not sure if I did that right." He slid a hand into Joseph's hair, tugging him close to whisper in his ear. "Need to get you home so I can practice."

Joseph laughed. "You did just fine and you know it." He paused. "But we can go as soon as Max cuts the cake."

"That's all we're waiting for? Hell, I'll cut it for him."

Joseph laughed. "You can't cut Max's cake. It's his birthday."

"Fine then. I'll just *strongly* hint he get to cutting." Gage let go of Joseph's hair to grab his hand. "And if that doesn't work, I'm cutting it myself. Let's go."

Joseph willingly followed Gage back outside to the bonfire. When he'd ridden into that garage and met the arrogant mechanic, he would never have suspected that they would engage in such a crazy, turbulent, passion-filled relationship. Or that they would fall in love. It hadn't been easy to get to this point, but he was glad that he'd given his bad boy a chance.

Titles by Christa Tomlinson
Martini Seduction
The Sergeant
A Second Chance for Three

And Coming November 2014
Bad Boys Need Love Too: *Nate*
Bad Boys Need Love Too: *Max*

Christa Tomlinson is an exciting up and coming author in erotic romance. Her first self-published novel, The Sergeant, was an Amazon Best Seller for Gay and Lesbian Erotica for seven weeks straight.

Although Christa graduated from The University of Missouri-St. Louis with a degree in History, she prefers to write contemporary romance. She loves to create stories that are emotional and lovely with sex that is integral to the characters' romantic arc. Her books include straight couples, curvy couples, gay, and multicultural couples. Love is love and everyone should have their story told.

Christa lives in Houston, Texas with her two dogs, and is a semi-retired member of Houston Roller Derby. She enjoys hearing from readers. You can follow her on Twitter at @christa_writes and on Facebook at Christa Tomlinson. For more on Christa's work, including deleted scenes, excerpts, and free reads, visit ChristaTomlinson.Blogspot.com

email: christa.tomlinson@yahoo.com
Twitter: @christa_writes
Facebook: Christa Tomlinson
Amazon: amazon.com/author/christatomlinson
Goodreads: Christa Tomlinson
Mail: PO Box 40841 - Houston, TX – 77040